STOCKTON-ON-TEES BOROUGH LIBRARIES

D0806376

leg drap~
in her hand. Nove.
teenage angst poetry ate up ..~s. ~. ..~. youth. .~~..
Annie splits her time between corralling her husband
into helping her with their cows, baking, reading, barrel
racing (not really!) and spending some very happy hours
at her computer, writing.

Marion Lennox has written over one hundred romance
novels, and is published in over one hundred countries
and thirty languages. Her international awards include
the prestigious RITA® award (twice!) and the *RT Book
Reviews* Career Achievement Award for 'a body of
work which makes us laugh and teaches us about love'.
Marion adores her family, her kayak, her dog, and lying
on the beach with a book someone else has written.
Heaven!

0060337443

Also by Annie O'Neil

Making Christmas Special Again
Risking Her Heart on the Single Dad

Dolphin Cove Vets collection

The Vet's Secret Son
Healing the Vet's Heart by Annie Claydon

Available now

Also by Marion Lennox

English Lord on Her Doorstep
The Baby They Longed For
Cinderella and the Billionaire
Second Chance with Her Island Doc
Rescued by the Single Dad Doc
Pregnant Midwife on His Doorstep

Discover more at millsandboon.co.uk.

CHRISTMAS UNDER THE NORTHERN LIGHTS

ANNIE O'NEIL

MISTLETOE KISS WITH THE HEART DOCTOR

MARION LENNOX

MILLS & BOON

All rights reserved including the right of reproduction
in whole or in part in any form. This edition is published
by arrangement with Harlequin Books S.A.

This is a work of fiction. Names, characters, places, locations
and incidents are purely fictional and bear no relationship to
any real life individuals, living or dead, or to any actual places,
business establishments, locations, events or incidents.
Any resemblance is entirely coincidental.

This book is sold subject to the condition that it shall not,
by way of trade or otherwise, be lent, resold, hired out
or otherwise circulated without the prior consent of the publisher
in any form of binding or cover other than that in which it is published
and without a similar condition including this condition
being imposed on the subsequent purchaser.

® and TM are trademarks owned and used by the trademark owner
and/or its licensee. Trademarks marked with ® are registered with the
United Kingdom Patent Office and/or the Office for Harmonisation
in the Internal Market and in other countries.

First Published in Great Britain 2020
by Mills & Boon, an imprint of HarperCollins*Publishers*
1 London Bridge Street, London, SE1 9GF

Christmas Under the Northern Lights © 2020 by Annie O'Neil

Mistletoe Kiss with the Heart Doctor © 2020 by Marion Lennox

ISBN: 978-0-263-27990-0

MIX
Paper from
responsible sources
FSC® C007454

This book is produced from independently certified FSC™ paper
to ensure responsible forest management.
For more information visit www.harpercollins.co.uk/green.

Printed and bound in Spain
by CPI, Barcelona

CHRISTMAS UNDER THE NORTHERN LIGHTS

ANNIE O'NEIL

MILLS & BOON

This book is dedicated to Scarlet Wilson, a fellow writer and a wonderfully dedicated district nurse, who worked throughout the Covid-19 pandemic with her usual flair and panache. You, and the countless other nurses like you, keep the world a better place. Thank you.

CHAPTER ONE

AUDREY LEANT AGAINST the ferry railing to peer into the cloudlike sea mist. If she spread her arms out wide she'd look just like the heroine in *Titanic*. Excepting, of course, the tiny little differences.

She was a short-haired brunette, not a ringleted redhead. She was wearing woolly tights and about nine other layers of clothes versus an opulent gown and a neckline dripping in jewels. Plus, she was nowhere near being able to afford a maid or first-class passage to Scotland, let alone America and, more to the point, she was completely alone. No Leo in sight.

Sigh.

Not that she wanted one. Too rakishly handsome. Too much potential for her to be snared and then, without so much as a moment's notice, dropped like a hot potato. At Christmas. Well. The lead-up to it, anyway.

Her thumb skidded along the smooth terrain of her ring finger. Yup. Still empty. That was what happened when you threw your diamond ring at your naked fiancé and his...whatever she was. Elf? Santa's little helper? Super-svelte Mrs Claus?

It had been hard to tell, seeing as the curvy blonde had grabbed all of her Christmas-coloured clothing and clutched it to her *entirely naked* body as Audrey had absorbed the fact that someone who wasn't her was having sex with the man she was meant to marry on Christmas Eve.

Time, it turned out, did stand still sometimes. And not really when you wanted it to. She'd always remember the look on Rafael's face: sorry, but…not sorry.

His lack of contrition had ripped open her deepest, darkest fears and laid them bare. He'd not really loved her at all. Hadn't meant a single one of the sweet nothings he'd whispered, nor a single, solitary promise that he'd made. She'd thought he'd been the answer to all her hopes and dreams, but it had all been a mirage. Seeing him look at her without a fraction of remorse… She'd never felt so small.

The only good thing to come out of the roiling mess of emotional debris was the vow she'd made. She would never, *ever*, let herself be led up the Swanee ever again. She was mistress of her own destiny from here on out. New job. New home. New life. For the next five weeks anyway. Even if it all felt absolutely terrifying.

Fighting the inevitable sting of the tears that had been lurking, un-spilt, these past three days, she spread her arms out wide, relishing the assault of wintry sea air.

'Eh, lassie! You'll not want to fall into those murky waters.'

Audrey lurched in surprise, nearly doing precisely that.

The man, a member of the ferry crew if his uniform was anything to go by, grabbed hold of her until she was steady again. She threw him a semi-grateful smile and then her eyes flicked up. *Ugh.* Perched atop his knitted blue cap was a headband bearing two multi-coloured, fairy-lit reindeer antlers.

She grimaced. Couldn't he see she was having a *moment*? A melodramatic moment, to be sure, but it was certainly a step in a better direction than drowning in a sea of her own tears—the more likely option if she'd stayed in London. Stupid London, with all its cheery Christmas lights and decorated windows and restaurants and bars bursting with yuletide cheer and mistletoe kisses. And, of course, her ex-fiancé. She was well shot of the place.

'Consider me duly warned,' she said, in a tone that sounded miles away from the Audrey she used to be.

What a difference seventy-two hours and a bit of awkwardly placed tinsel could make.

The sailor gave her a *your call* look and took a step back. 'Fair enough. Advance warning, though. When we hit the dock there'll be an almighty thud. You'd be best to come back away from the railings.'

As if actual bruises would be a problem. He should see her bruised heart. 'And how long will that be, then?'

He squinted into the murk, then gave a nod as if his X-ray vision had just clicked in. 'About ten minutes. Twelve, max.'

Plenty of time to get her Kate Winslet vibe back.

She gave him the side-eye, which proved sufficiently powerful to get him to back off.

Alone again, she closed her eyes and shook her head, willing the bracing North Sea wind to blow the dark memories away. When she opened them again everything looked just the same.

Miserable.

It was only two o'clock in the afternoon. It got dark *early* up here in Scotland. If she hadn't triple-checked the boat's destination a dozen times before and after boarding, Audrey might easily been convinced they were heading to a wintry Brigadoon rather than her new island posting: the Isle of Bourtree.

The town was called Bourtree Castle, which had sounded promising in the same way Windsor Castle did, but a quick internet search had made it pretty clear Bour-tree Castle was no place for royals. Tiny population. Ever diminishing. The 'castle' was actually a pile of rocks. And the only way to get to Bourtree was by the ferry. Which only ran three times a week.

Trust her to find the one locum position in a Scottish Bermuda Triangle. Perfect for the way things were going for her. Very, very badly.

She let go of the railings again.

'You're not the locum district nurse, are ye?'

Audrey whipped round. This guy had most certainly never seen *Titanic* and— Wait a minute... 'How did you know?'

The twenty-something redhead shrugged, his felt ant-lers bobbing in the wind. 'I know everyone else on the boat, and Coop said I should keep an eye out for you. So... *voilà*!' He spread his hands out wide. 'Job done. Welcome to Bourtree.'

He nodded out towards the foggy gloaming beyond the boat where, now, she could just see the odd twinkle of light.

'And Happy Christmas.'

Bah! Audrey scowled. *Christmas.*

She replayed everything he'd said. 'Hang on a minute. Who's Coop?' There'd been no mention of a Coop when she'd got her posting.

'Dr MacAskill.'

She was still none the wiser. 'And he is...?'

'House calls doctor. Well, he's a flash A&E doc from Glasgow, but he's come back to Bourtree to help out until they find a proper replacement for Old Doc Anstruther. He's retiring.'

'Ah.'

It was an awful lot of ancillary information. If memory

served, she was pretty sure Dr Anstruther was the one she was meant to contact regarding her accommodation. With her luck it'd be a leaky igloo.

'Folk want him to stay on, but no one's banking on it.'

'Who?'

The sailor shot her a *keep up* look. 'Coop.'

'Oh?'

'Yeah. He's island born and bred, but...' He stopped himself mid-flow, as if he were about to give away a state secret. 'Anyway, they're taking bets down the Puffin, if you want to lay down a fiver.'

'What's the Puffin?'

'Pub. It's where pretty much all social life begins and ends on the island. You'll find out all you need to know about Cooper and anyone else on the island if you sit there long enough. So mind you don't do anything too outrageous, because before you know it all of Bourtree will, too.'

Intriguing. And also annoying. If he was doing house calls that most likely meant they'd be teamed up when necessary. She really could've done with working on her own, using the downtime between patients to sort the rest of her life out. Then again, this 'Coop' character sounded a bit of an enigma. Focusing on someone else's dilemma would be better than thinking about her problems.

'Why wouldn't he stay? It's a nice place, right?'

Please, please, please say yes.

'Ach, it's nice enough. But Coop's not lived here for fifteen years. For what it's worth, I think he'll stay. It's not like back in the day when—' Another guilty look pulled him up short.

'Understood,' she said, not really understanding at all—but what did it matter? She was leaving in five weeks.

If this Coop character left tomorrow or stayed forever it wouldn't matter a hill of beans to her.

More importantly, it was growing increasingly tricky having this conversation with the sailor. His nose was bright red with the cold, and looking him in the eye was virtually impossible with the blinking antlers bobbing in and out of her eyeline.

She drudged a bit of civility from the caverns of 'The Audrey She Used To Be', gave him a polite smile and said, 'Happy Christmas to you…erm…'

'Scottie,' the man said, with a light touch to his knitted cap.

He turned and went, the sound of a whistled 'Silent Night' travelling in his wake.

Bleurgh.

Christmas.

Even so…just because she wasn't getting married in three weeks' time didn't mean *everything* was awful. She had a five-week locum post that would allow her to recapture the passion of her true calling: district nursing. And the accommodation that came with the job would keep her off the streets until she figured out what to do next. She had several hundred miles of cushioning between her and the wedding she'd no longer be having.

What a fool she'd been to pay for the celebration herself. She'd thought it would act as proof that she wasn't marrying Rafael for his money. Or his movie star good looks. Or his charm. A triumvirate of desirables that he clearly felt free to spread around.

Fat lot of good the wedding insurance had done her. They didn't pay up when you cancelled because your fiancé was a snake.

C'mon, Audrey. He's an out-of-the-picture snake now. It's your life. Your destiny.

As she plumbed her brain for another nugget of positivity, the cosy faux fur lining of her coat nestled against her neck. There! She was warm. She gave the puffy down ankle-length coat a grateful pat. It had been her final purchase before leaving London behind...perhaps for ever. Pristine white, able to withstand arctic cold and, as an added bonus, two deep, hand-warming pockets. A winter essential up here in the North Sea—even if it had reduced her bank account balance to zero.

But now that Christmas was off, she was newly homeless, and was going to have to start her whole entire life over again, thanks to her lying, cheating ratbag of an ex-fiancé, a little bit of comfort shopping had seemed necessary.

Her phone buzzed deep in her pocket.

She pulled it out. A message from a number she didn't recognise.

Dr MacAskill here. AKA Coop. Hope you're ready to hit the ground running. Several house calls to make when you land.

This, followed by a slew of Christmas emojis.

Oh, good grief. This locum posting was beginning to hit a rather unpleasant chord. An 'out of the frying pan into the fire' type of chord.

At least there was work to do. If she couldn't spread any cheer, the least she could do was help improve people's health. Seeing patients had a way of reminding her just how fragile the lives everyone led could be.

She'd learnt that particular life lesson the hard way. Her mum had passed away when she'd been a little girl and her father, after devoting himself to raising her, had suffered a fatal heart attack two years back.

At least he'd been doing what he loved. Fishing. Knowing he'd died with a smile on his face had taught her to cherish each and every moment life offered—the good moments, anyway. A proviso she hadn't really considered for the past six months whilst Prince Bloody Charming was wrapping her round his duplicitous little finger.

She harrumphed, then squinted into the pea-souper. Nope. Still couldn't see more than a metre or so. They should be getting closer now. There'd been some lights a minute ago— Oh! Wait a minute. Her heart soared, then plummeted. Was that a *Christmas tree* glittering through the fog?

A lighthouse? Acceptable.

A Christmas tree as a beacon of hope? Nope. No way. Not after what she'd seen under her own Christmas tree. Correction.

Her former Christmas tree. The one she'd decorated to Rafael's exacting standards. Standards she'd thought she'd be embracing as her own right up until she'd realised they were double standards.

An uneasy feeling swept through her. One that was becoming a bit too familiar. Had she been so dazzled by her surgeon fiancé's fancy lifestyle that she'd failed to notice his 'love' lacked emotional depth?

She fuzzed out a raspberry. He'd wooed her straight and simple. Even the hardest of hearts would've melted with his golden spotlight shining upon them. The elf he'd been wooing under their Christmas tree had certainly looked enamoured.

Whatever.

That was then—this was now. Christmas tree or not, Bourtree Castle was where she was going to have to reinvent herself. Make herself a harder, less vulnerable, more man-savvy Audrey than the one who had existed seventy-two hours ago.

She looked down at her immaculate white down coat and grinned. The Ice Queen of Bourtree Castle. Perfect. She was ready to let the past go and let her new life begin.

She grabbed on to the railing with her mittened hands. She wouldn't be caught out when the boat lurched into place against the dock. She wouldn't be caught out by anything ever again.

'Nice outfit, Coop!'

'Black Friday special,' he shouted back to the dock worker, who laughed and gave him a jaunty salute before heading towards the end of the dock where the ferry was due any minute.

He had to hand it to the islanders. It had been a week since his gran's funeral, and not one person had yet to grind in the guilt that had enveloped him since she'd passed. There'd been a fair few queries about a wake, but he'd get there. Eventually.

Perhaps the collective tactic was to jolly him into paying his penance in the form of taking up Doc Anstruther's post when he retired. Or maybe—and far more likely—they were letting him stew in the sludge of his own mistakes while they got on with their lives.

Whatever. He couldn't worry about that now. He had a district nurse to collect and patients to see and joy to spread. He'd get a smile from each and every one of his patients if it killed him.

He gave his feet a stamp and his leather-gloved hands a brisk rub. Island cold was definitely different from mainland cold. A childhood on Bourtree should've made him immune to it but, despite the layers, fifteen years away from the island meant that today's wind was digging straight through to his bones.

His gran's voice came through clear as a bell. *'There's*

no such thing as bad weather, Coop, only bad clothing choices. Every day's fine as the next so long as you're dressed right.'

His grandmother had had a truism for everything. Even him.

'Cooper, your problem is you're too busy looking to the future to notice the here and now. Stop and smell the roses, laddie. Otherwise the only thing you'll end up with is a life with no memories and no one to share it with.'

So here he was. Trying to make some good memories on Bourtree. Memories he wished like hell he could share with her.

He looked up the long cobbled lane that led to the enormous Bourtree Castle Christmas tree. The castle ruins and the glittering tribute to Christmas spearheaded the small town square some twenty-odd metres above the docks. He gave the tree a respectful nod. He'd chosen it as a visual reminder that the Christmas spirit started at home and, like it or not, Bourtree was home. For the foreseeable future anyway.

A big man—muscular, not fat—wearing rugby shorts and a short-sleeved shirt walked up alongside him and the small crowd of folk waiting for the ferry coming in from Glasgow.

Strewth. Shorts and a T-shirt in this weather? The man was either mad or Bourtree Castle through and through. Red hair, face covered in freckles, light blue eyes. Could be from any number of families on the island.

'Coop.' The guy gave him a nod and a smile.

'All right, mate?' Cooper replied, not at all sure what the man's name was.

He looked familiar. Had they been in the same class at school, or had Cooper seen him in one of his gran's stacks of local papers, fist in the air, cheering some sort of rugby triumph?

He still had a face full of acne… The cauliflower ear was new. As was the nose that looked to have been broken a few times and…yup…the scar cutting across his eyebrow. A scar mostly likely 'won' when the opposing team had crushed him at the bottom of a scrum pile.

It was a level of tough-as-nails that Cooper had never aspired to. Not that he shied away from sports. He went to the gym. Ran regularly. Did his weekly weights routine. But bulking up to get tangled in a pile of men who could throw a caber as easily as they could a toothpick? No, thanks. Fixing their compound fractures afterwards? Yeah. That was more his thing.

'Gone soft over there in Glasgow, have you?' the man asked, taking in Cooper's layered ensemble and foot-stamping.

'Hardly!' Cooper barked, despite the fact they both knew otherwise. 'Life on the mainland's like bootcamp in the arctic. Harder.'

The white lie dug the sharp knife he'd been carrying around in his ribs just that little bit deeper. Who the hell *was* this guy? He should know him. He squinted, stripped away the crinkles round the man's eyes, then tried to imagine him scrawny. That was it. He used to be scrawny.

'Robbie? Robbie Stuart?'

'Aye. Well done. Knew you'd get there in the end. Changed a bit, me, haven't I?' Robbie grinned, thumped his chest with one of his fists, then gave Cooper a proper thump on the back with the other. 'Good to have you back on the island, even if—well—we're all missing her. Your gran. Never met a woman with more spark in her. Or more sense of community spirit—specially this time of year. The Nativity'll never be the same. Like herding cats to pull that

thing off, and she always did it. A tough-as-old-boots islander through and through, Gertie was.'

'Aye, well…' He was trying to fill the Gertie void as best
he could, but growing up on Bourtree hadn't exactly been
a bed of roses for him. A change of topic might be in order.

'What sort of get-up do you call this?' He tipped his
head at Robbie's shorts and T-shirt ensemble.

'It's my work gear, isn't it? I just finished a PE session
down at the college, then got a call from my brother to
come and pick up my wee sister, as he's helping out Dad
down the shop.'

Hearing about family members helping family members as naturally as they breathed should've been a heart-
warmer. Especially this time of year. Instead it dug that
proverbial knife in deeper still.

'Do you remember Rachel?' Robbie asked. 'She's living over in Glasgow now. A librarian at a kiddies' school,
but comes home twice a month, rain or shine. Sometimes
it takes a bit of wrangling, what with her roster and her
boyfriend and all that, but she makes it work.'

Cooper, to his shame, neither remembered Rachel nor
knew her routine. To say he hadn't been a regular on the
Bourtree-Glasgow ferry would've been a massive under-
statement.

He'd spent most of his time on Bourtree plotting ways
to get off the island, not back on it. Staying away had been
a far easier way to avoid stories about his mum and dad. A
car accident had taken them in the end. Little wonder with
the way they'd regularly shirked the drink-driving laws.

Each time he had a patient suffering from liver failure,
he thought of his parents and how they'd got off easy. It
was a painful way to go.

'Speaking of get-ups…what's this for?' Robbie asked,
tweaking the fabric of Cooper's jacket between his mas-

sive fingers. 'You preparing to throw yourself down some chimneys?' He laughed at his own joke.

'Picking up the new district nurse,' Cooper corrected.

'Oh, aye? Getting your foot in the door with Dr Anstruther, are you?'

'Just helping out.'

He was testing the waters. Seeing if working here would do something—anything—to ease his guilt over not having been here for his gran. The 'uniform' was as much a buffer for him as it was for the patients who might not be so keen to have the island bad boy turn up at their door with a doctor's case in hand.

He should've told Doc Anstruther he'd take the job the day he arrived. Made the decision as quickly and cleanly as a surgeon made an incision. He knew they were taking bets down at the pub about whether or not he'd stay.

It was a simple bet— would he stay or go? —but really he knew it went deeper. The decision he made would cement the way folk thought about the MacAskill name. Was he a good islander like his grandmother? Or a bad seed like his father? His sister had made her own decision by moving to New Zealand years back. Cooper had kept folk guessing long enough.

He knew opinions about him swung to both ends of the spectrum. Some thought his grandmother's firm but fair hand in raising him and his sister once their parents had died had made all the difference. Others weren't so generous.

A fair call, when being here tapped into his darker side. Anyway... He hadn't made the call and he wouldn't yet. He'd learnt the hard way about making promises he couldn't keep. If he made this promise he'd have to know in his marrow he was going to keep it. The intention was there. All he had to do now was see if he had the follow-through to ensure the island still had a 'good' MacAskill on it.

'Good to have you back for a wee while, Coop. And as Mr Holly Jolly himself, no less.' Robbie gave him another thump on the back. 'Brilliant. Your gran would've loved this, she would.'

Despite himself, Coop's lips curved into a half-smile as they both examined his outfit. His grandmother *would've* loved it. Thick black boots with a solid tread. Dark red trousers. A huge but lightweight jacket that fitted like a dream over his thermal top, wind-resistant fleece and gilet. Some might argue that the floppy hat with ermine lining was a bit OTT, but if there was a beautiful woman teasing him about it he'd flirtatiously suggest that it brought out the blue in his eyes.

But he was with Robbie, and not feeling remotely flirty. He was feeling antsy and guilty and quite a few other things he was used to shoving in a box to worry about when hell froze over.

He glanced at his watch. The ferry was making a real production of pulling in half an hour later than scheduled.

Fog.

Surprise, surprise.

'This the new regulation uniform, then, Coop?'

'For house calls,' Cooper said, playing it straight.

'Aye, well… I dare say folk'll appreciate the effort.'

'Hope so.'

And he did. Truly, he did. He might not be able to fix the way his gran had gone—alone—but he was going to pour every ounce of energy he had into making sure no one else's loved ones felt sad, or lonely, or any worse than they had to over the Christmas holidays. He'd chop down a Christmas tree for each and every one of them if necessary.

He jogged in place for a minute.

'What's this, then, Coop?' Robbie gave him a jab in the ribs. 'It's a bit late to get fighting fit for the new district nurse, isn't it? Bit of a hottie, is she?'

'No idea.'

Romance was the last thing on his mind. Another of his periodic relationships had bit the dust a few months back, and he'd been too busy working to think about it since. Too busy working to be here for his gran during what had turned out to be her final days. The promise he should've made to her years ago—that he'd make her proud of the man he'd become—he'd had to make over her grave.

'Never met her. I just hope she's a good nurse. We've got to go straight out on some calls.' He nodded out towards the car park, where the medical four by four stood ready and waiting.

Robbie's eyes opened in surprise. 'I still can't get my head wrapped round the fact Cooper MacAskill is doing calls on Bourtree. I thought you'd be too much of a bigshot over there in Glasgow for the likes of us.'

Cooper only just managed to keep his expression neutral. 'Doc's busy in the surgery, so I said I'd do the house calls and take the nurse on her first few scts of rounds.'

Robbie nodded. 'Someone down at the Puffin said you were doing a few days to help out Doc Anstruther, but I said I wouldn't believe it till I saw it. Cooper MacAskill on Bourtree?' He laughed, as if the idea was ridiculous.

Cooper gave his best stab at a nonchalant shrug, gritting his teeth against having his face rubbed in the past. A better reaction than connecting his fist to Robbie's nose, anyway. An instinct from back in the day.

If he decided to stay, punching people wouldn't exactly be kicking things off on the right note, so he took a deep breath, smiled, and prayed for the ferry to dock. Immediately.

Ach, well. If he decided to become the island's doctor he'd better get used to having these sorts of conversations. He owed it to Bourtree. More importantly, he owed it to his gran. Not that doling out aspirins and wrapping up sprained ankles while the doctors over in Glasgow got properly stuck into the type of emergency medicine he was trained for was his idea of heaven, but the simple truth was nothing could change the fact he'd not been by his gran's side when she had passed away.

Just a cold.

He should've known better. It was pneumonia season and, no matter how hale and hearty she'd been, older folk were always more vulnerable to contracting it after a virus. Particularly when they insisted upon riding their bicycles and paying house calls to elderly friends on a wintry Scottish island constantly cloaked in a shroud of cloud.

He should've been here. Driven her around. Brought her hot toddies and tea when the first round of sniffles hit. Nodded and smiled as she and her friends nattered on about needlepoint or whatever it was they talked about, whilst he daydreamed about life back in the A&E in Glasgow. He should have put an oxygen mask on her when she got short of breath.

'It's taking a wee while to find the mooring, isn't it?' Robbie nodded at the ferry, which was crawling towards the docks at a snail's pace.

A pace Cooper would've railed against if it were an ambulance pulling into the bay at Glasgow Central.

'Island pace', his gran had called it.

Slow down, Coop. Nothing's going to change for the sake of an extra ten minutes.

That was what she hadn't understood. He'd been wired differently. Wired to respond to things in an instant. To a parent whose mood could turn on a dime. To an unkind child whose taunts might gain traction. A grandmother to please, a sister to protect, a reputation to—

Anyway… His ability to respond quickly meant A&E medicine suited him to a T. A seemingly innocuous situation could change to life-threatening in a matter of minutes. Seconds, even. A nicked artery. A septic wound.

A grandmother's cold shifting into pneumonia as her grandson made excuses, yet again, as to why he couldn't come back and have a wee look in on the woman who'd raised him when his own parents had fallen so short of the mark.

'So, when'll you be heading back to Glasgow?' Robbie asked as the ferry staff finally started securing the boat to the dock and a crowd of foot passengers began to gather out on deck to disembark.

'Good question,' Cooper said, eyes peeled for an unfamiliar face as the small crowd of regulars bowed their heads against the wind and headed for the car park or scanned the small group of folk he was standing amidst for a loved one. 'One I don't have an answer for.'

'What?' Robbie gave him a punch on the arm. 'I thought you would be high-tailing it back to the mainland as soon as Gertie's immediate affairs are settled. Even put money on it.'

Cooper felt the muscles in his jaw twitch. There had definitely been a time when he would've done that. But not after what he'd done. Not with the burden of guilt he now bore.

'Coop! MacAskill!'

Cooper looked up and saw one of the sailors pointing out a woman in an immaculate white ankle-length coat.

When his eyes landed on her face the wind was knocked out of him. And not because of the cold.

Dark brown almond-shaped eyes, the perfect shade of

chocolate, met his straight on. A smattering of freckles made her look younger than he suspected she was. Somewhere around his age? Younger, more likely. Thirty to his thirty-five?

Her hair colour was a bit lighter than her eyes—a chestnut colour styled into an exacting pixie cut. As if she were a woodland faerie with a rulebook as long as her arm. Her overall aesthetic wasn't one that would've landed her at a modelling agency, but there was something about her that appealed to him at a core level. The upward tilt of her chin. The dubiously arched eyebrow.

The huge down jacket made her look expensive, but when he caught a glimpse of her nails as she clutched the coat round her neck he saw practically trimmed, clean nails rather than talons. She was a bit taller than average. Easy enough to pick up and carry over a threshold if she were— Hmm… Best not go there.

Her lips, bright red—from the cold, no doubt—were tipping into a frown. Just as he supposed his own mouth was.

For some reason he'd been expecting a sturdy, no-nonsense, silver-haired, woman who bustled. Most likely because that was exactly what Noreen, the woman she was filling in for, looked like.

Audrey Walsh was decades away from being silver-haired. Nor did she have the look of a bustler. She seemed more hustle than bustle. And, from the way she was giving him the side-eye, no nonsense to the core. Which was a good thing. This was the busy season—and he wasn't talking about Christmas parties.

Speaking of which… She didn't look remotely impressed by his effort to spread Christmas cheer to their patients. Which was a bad thing.

'Ho-ho-ho,' he said. 'Welcome to Bourtree Castle.'

Her nose wrinkled as she pasted on a wary smile. 'I got

your text about needing to head straight out to some calls. I presume this…' she wiggled her fingers at his Santa outfit '…is going to come off before we get to work?'

A burst of fire flared hot in his chest. No way. This was for his gran. And a district nurse should know more than most that house calls were about far more than taking temperatures and heartrates.

'Nope. In fact…' He held up the clear bag in his left hand, waving his right hand as if he were presenting her with a free car rather than a fancy dress costume. 'I've got something here for you to put on before we head out.'

Audrey's expression turned icy. 'Not a chance.'

Perhaps the jacket she was wearing should've been a hint that she was more Snow Queen than one of Santa's cheery helpers. But the Snow Queen's heart had melted in the end, so…

He held up the costume again. 'Sure? It's thermal lined.'

CHAPTER TWO

'No,' AUDREY REPEATED. 'Absolutely not.'

This was not at all the escape from Christmas and heart-break that she'd been hoping for when she'd accepted this post.

Her mental checklist had been simple.

A place as far away from London as possible.

Tick.

No excessive Christmas decorations. Anywhere.

Fail.

A crusty old doctor.

Fail.

Epic fail, in fact.

Cooper MacAskill was jaw-droppingly gorgeous. Dark hair. Piercing blue eyes. Full, sensual lips. And he was dressed as Santa Claus. How could she hate all things Christmas when Sexy Santa was standing there offering her a chance to be his adorable elf? It was almost hilarious. And equally cruel.

Of all the tricks fate could've played on her, it had landed her on an island with a gorgeous, Christmas-loving doctor whose accent was already sending shivers of pleasure down her spine. This would absolutely *not* do.

'I'm not going to wear it. If you insist, I will turn around and get straight back on that ferry.'

And head back to…where, exactly? She had nowhere else to go to. And she'd signed a contract.

'What's wrong with it?'

Cooper looked genuinely perplexed. As if it hadn't even occurred to him she'd refuse or…and this was being generous…as if he cared what she thought. He gave her a scan that, once again, sent a stream of shivers down her spine.

'It looks like it'll fit.'

She hid her discomfort with a huff. 'I don't want to wear the elf costume, Mr Kringle.'

'That's *Dr* Kringle to you.'

Though there was a smile playing upon his lips, something flashed bright in his sapphire-blue eyes. A flare of will, daring her to contest him. Challenging her for trying to strip the joy from something he obviously held dear.

Why couldn't he hold something else dear? Like… erm…pre-guessing what someone's temperature was, or always having a medical run-bag that was immaculately kitted out. But, no. She got a hot doctor whose passion was doing house calls dressed as Santa Claus.

A bit weird for someone the islanders were taking bets on about leaving… He seemed to be embracing Bourtree Castle's Christmas cheer as if he was going to stay here for ever. No matter what the odds were. So why couldn't she do the same? Be happy in the here and now?

Because she was completely *miserable*, that was why! She'd just been dumped. The life she'd thought she was living had turned out to be a mirage. A tinsel-laced, fairy-lit, holly-decked mirage. With mistletoe. Far too much mistletoe.

Cooper jiggled the elf costume, its candy-striped arms waving as they caught the sea breeze.

A despairing wail formed deep within her. She wasn't

a killjoy. Honestly. She'd used to love Christmas as much as this guy seemed to. More, even! Just not this year.

Then she thought of the patients they'd be heading out to see as soon as this costume situation was settled. House-bound, mostly. Or very, very ill. Vulnerable. She could do it for them... She *should* do it for them. Wasn't helping people why she'd become a nurse in the first place?

Her resistance softened. Okay, fine. But only during business hours.

'I will wear the hat,' she acquiesced primly. 'But that's it.'

Cooper was adjusting his own hat and repositioning his big black belt round what had to be a pillow. It definitely wasn't his own belly. Not with that much movement.

When their eyes met again, she could've sworn he winked. Not a sexy wink. More like a complicit *thank you* wink. One that said he got it. He understood that her protest went beyond the realms of not wanting to look silly. It was strangely intimate. It made her feel vulnerable and safe all at the same time. As if she had, for the first time in her life, been properly seen.

'Right. Just a quick briefing,' he said, as if the moment hadn't happened. 'I'll be going out with you for the next week or so. Introducing you to folk, showing you how things work round here.'

'I can't imagine they're all that different from how they work anywhere else,' she griped.

She'd been hoping for some alone time. Precious min-utes in between patients to howl lovelorn songs in the car with tears pouring down her cheeks. Or feisty 'I Will Sur-vive'-type power ballads. Disliking this too-attractive-for-his-own-good doctor was becoming easier by the second. She glared at him. She bet he'd tune his radio to whatever channel played twenty-four-hour Christmas songs.

'Island folk don't take to change that easily,' he said, by way of an explanation.

'Well, nor do I, but sometimes you have to go with the flow, don't you?' Her thumb automatically moved to her bare ring finger. She caught Cooper's eyes snag on the movement. She scrambled to divert his attention. 'So…is this your year-round uniform?'

He cocked his chin to the side and smiled, one of his teeth catching on his full lower lip as he considered his response. When he finally answered, his voice was honest, straightforward, and annoyingly lovely to listen to.

'First time I've worn one. Nor am I a year-round resident.'

'Then why all the fuss? The costume, the introductions?'

Light glimmered then darkened in his eyes. Another shared moment she couldn't entirely put her finger on. It felt as if he was trying to tell her he was battling his own demons.

So…the space she was craving so much—he needed some, too.

'Here.' He deftly changed the topic, reached out and easily lifted one of her heavy duffel bags from the ground where she'd dropped them. 'I'll take this.'

He glanced at the bag. It was huge. Contained pretty much everything she owned.

'If I didn't know any better, I'd say you were running away from home.'

Their eyes met and meshed. Oh, *sugar*. He'd seen everything she'd been trying to hide. Caught a glimpse of the pain and grief she was trying to outrun. Something shifted in her chest. This locum posting was either going to be much harder than she'd anticipated or…because of whatever it was that had just passed between the pair of them…healing.

It was a powerful feeling. It made her want to reel back her lightning-fast assessment of 'Dr Kringle' and his love of Christmas costumes.

She rearranged her scarf, using the task to mask the fact she was actually checking him out as he did a quick flick through his phone's text messages. Not that she fancied him or anything. Obviously. Even so, she'd have to be blind not to notice he wasn't hard on the eye. If you liked tall, sparkly blue-eyed, ebony-haired men who dressed as Santa Claus. Which she didn't.

Because if she'd learned anything the hard way, it was that if something came wrapped up in a too-good-to-be-true package it *was* too good to be true.

Why did they have to be wrapped in Christmas cheer? Couldn't they just wear red scrubs, or their normal uniforms and spread joy the old-fashioned way? A smile, a thorough medical examination and a nice cup of tea?

Not that she'd done many house calls lately. Rafael had convinced her to start taking shifts at an elite paediatrics hospital. He'd said it gave the pair of them a 'better profile'. Silly her for thinking caring for people under any circumstances gave a good impression. What she did as a district nurse might not be showy, but it certainly improved the lives of those who received her visits.

'Eh, Coop!'

A huge man shouldering a neon pink duffel bag crossed to them and whacked Cooper on the back. Cooper held his ground. Blimey. He was made of stern stuff. Audrey would've gone hurtling to the floor with the amount of welly that had backed that friendly thwack.

'Who's this, then?'

Cooper shifted his stance, almost as if he was body-blocking the rugby player. Strangely protective for someone she'd just met and point-blank refused to play Holly Jolly Christmas with.

'Robbie Stuart,' he said, turning to her as he did so, 'meet our locum district nurse, Audrey...'

'Walsh,' she filled in. It would've been Audrey de Leon in twenty-three days and five hours' time, but...nope. 'Plain old Audrey Walsh.'

Cooper's eyes narrowed, as if he was clocking up another titbit of information about her. *Hates elf costumes. Running away from her life and thinks her name is boring.*

She popped on a smile. 'Shall we go and see some patients?'

'Good idea. Robbie...' Cooper gave him a goodbye nod.

'You should come down to the Puffin tonight,' Robbie called after them. 'A whole bunch of us'll be meeting up after the Nativity rehearsal for a wee drink. Folk'll be dying to meet you—see if they can rope you into helping now that— Sorry, Coop.'

Audrey threw a questioning look in Cooper's direction.

'The Nativity's an annual island tradition,' he explained. 'Don't go if Christmas isn't your thing. As for the "wee drink" part—the whole of Bourtree will most likely be there, especially once news has travelled that you've arrived. New arrivals are always big news here on Bourtree.'

'A bit like the bets on whether you're going to stay or not?'

The moment she said it, she knew she'd made a mistake. His blue eyes darkened and a barely disguised flinch whipped the smile from his lips.

Why had she stuck her foot in it right when they'd seemed to be developing the tiniest sliver of camaraderie?

'Sorry. I— It's none of my business.'

'No, no.' Cooper shook his head, gave Robbie a half-wave and began heading towards the car without so much as an attempt to meet her apologetic face. 'Everything's fair game on Bourtree. You'll learn that soon enough, too.'

'Sounds ominous.'

He gave a shrug that all but screamed, *That's life, kid. Get used to it*.

He did have a point. Though she'd already been through all her ex's faults with a fine-tooth comb, she was pretty certain *she* had some home truths that needed examining. Not to mention the warning signs in their relationship that she should've heeded. Like the whole 'no personal possessions around the flat' thing. As if they lived in a show home and making it appear remotely homely would weaken their stance as a power couple.

If this was only easing open the can of worms labelled *Warning Signs*…she was scared to pull the lid entirely open.

Cooper opened the back of a brightly marked medical four-by-four parked further up the dock, slung her bag on top of a gurney, then the smaller tote that she'd been carrying behind it. He closed the doors and turned to her, his eyes sparking. Maybe from some sort of unspent fury or… maybe it was the lights from the Christmas tree.

It was hard to tell. Same as her, she supposed. Two people treading the fine line between contentedness and fury that life hadn't turned out the way they'd planned. When he spoke, she knew straight away that what she'd seen had come from somewhere dark.

'Some people try to outrun their demons. Some run straight into their arms. I meet my challenges head-on. Now, let's go see some patients.'

'I'm sorry to be rushing out the door like this,' the young mum said. 'I've got to pick up the kiddies from school and get their tea on at home. I'll come back when Deacon's home from work and can look after the wee ones, but I'll have to shoot off again for the Nativity rehearsal.'

'Do you have a good role?' Audrey asked.

The first smile they'd seen from Mhairi since they'd arrived surfaced. 'Brilliant role. I'm Frigg.'

Audrey looked at Cooper. *Frigg?* Not one of the usual cast of characters she was used to in a Nativity.

He gave a little *I'll tell you later* shake of the head, then addressed Mhairi—'An auld Scots name pronounced Vah-ree,' Cooper had explained as they'd waited for her to answer the door.

He told her that they'd look after her father and would ring her with any updates.

Mhairi threw an anxious look back towards her father's bedroom, then tugged her hand through her thick batch of wayward curls. 'It's difficult taking you seriously, Coop.'

'Why? I'm still me beneath all this.'

He lifted his Santa hat off his head as if to prove it. A thick, wavy black head of hair that reached his collar was revealed. If anything, the 'reveal' seemed to make him a little bit less mortal and Audrey a bit more wary. Mhairi, too, from the dubious sound she was making.

'I suppose so. It's just that…well…we're so used to Dr Anstruther or Noreen coming out. I mean, they're just a bit more familiar with everything…so I don't worry so much when I have to go.'

Cooper nodded, trying to keep his expression neutral. He'd encountered this attitude more than once over the past week. Sure, everyone knew he was an A&E doctor over on the mainland, but no one had actually seen him in scrubs. Performing a tracheotomy. Calling for a crash cart when someone flat-lined, only to bring them back to life before it arrived.

No. They'd seen him hauled out of fights in the school yard. Racing a motorcycle he had been too young to ride. Playing truant. And because of that he'd have to earn their trust, centimetre by painful centimetre. It was a job that could take years. Years of patience he wasn't sure he had the reserves for. But today he had it. And that was what counted.

'Mhairi, I know you're worried, but we will look after your dad to the best of our abilities. I am still a doctor underneath all this Santa gear. And Audrey here is one of the finest nurses London has to offer. If the two of us can't figure out how to help him, we'll get Doc Anstruther out to have a look after surgery—all right?'

Despite the gravity of the situation, and Mhairi's obvious concern for her father, Audrey felt a little tug of pride that Cooper was already assuring one of the islanders that they could trust her. It wasn't as if he'd seen anything beyond her CV. Maybe all that prickly interaction down at the docks had been a case of miscommunication. A false start.

Mhairi tugged on the coat she'd taken off the back of a wooden chair. 'I'd stay if I could, but I'm already running late.' She made a frustrated sound. 'He's not at all his usual self,' she continued, scooping up a pair of car keys. 'I've never known him to not get out of bed. That's why I rang. I always come by for a cuppa and some shortbread before I pick up the little ones, and he's usually pottering about the place, fussing about with whatever project he's been working on, but he's still in bed. Said he's not been out since yesterday. Blinds drawn…everything.'

Cooper helped her pull her jacket into place. A gentlemanly gesture he performed as if it had been drilled into him from an early age.

'Bed might be the best place for him if he's feeling

poorly, Mhairi. If we think he needs to be in hospital we'll get him there.' He named a premier hospital in Glasgow and said he had some contacts there who would be sure to give him the best care if it was anything serious.

Mhairi froze, hands gripping her collar. 'But—that's over on the mainland.'

There was the aversion to change Cooper had mentioned, thought Audrey.

'Aye, but there'll be folk there to look after him round the clock. It'll take some of the pressure off you. It's a good hospital.'

'Is it the one where you work?' Mhairi asked.

'I know it well and can recommend it.'

Interesting, Audrey thought. That wasn't really an answer.

Mhairi shook her head and dropped her keys back onto the table. 'I don't like the idea of it. Especially over Christmas. The folk there won't know him. And he'd hate it, being away from us and the grandkids. We're all he has.'

The sentiment spoke to Audrey loud and clear. *Family.* It was something she'd always ached for—especially as a little girl, growing up in the shadow of her father's grief over their shared loss of her mother.

'You know what it's like to have to fend for yourself, Coop,' Mhairi said. 'It's not nice.'

Cooper gave his jaw a scrub and said nothing, but an electric tension Audrey couldn't put her finger on crackled between the two.

'Sorry, Cooper...' Mhairi put up her hands in apology, then dropped them. 'I didn't mean anything by that.'

'I know.'

An awkward silence hummed between them as he picked up her car keys and handed them to her, effectively ending the exchange.

Audrey jumped in, feeling a protective impulse to cover for Cooper's silence. Whatever was going on with him, he wasn't comfortable talking about it, and that was definitely something she could relate to.

'No one's going anywhere right now. Our job is to try and keep your father out of hospital. Why don't you let us get on with our examination and we'll let you know as soon as possible how things stand?'

'How long will you be here?' Mhairi's eyes darted between Cooper and Audrey.

'Five weeks,' Audrey said.

'No,' Cooper corrected with a soft smile. 'She means today.'

Ah. In that case...

Audrey gave Cooper a *This is your call* look. She knew they had other patients to see. Back in London she would've raced from patient to patient as best she could, willing there to be more hours in the day, but perhaps things worked differently here. The part of her that needed to know compassion still existed hoped that Cooper would say they'd stay as long as necessary—without, of course, compromising any other patient's health.

'Your father won't be left on his own if we have any critical concerns,' Cooper said solidly.

Another piece of Audrey's heart softened for him. A dangerously slippery slope if she didn't watch herself.

'Promise?'

Audrey didn't miss the look that passed between them when Cooper promised. It was as if he was staking his personal reputation on the commitment. No patient left unattended, no matter what. It was a big promise to make. Particularly when they had other patients to see.

'You'd better get on away down the road. School'll be over soon.'

Mhairi opened the kitchen door, took a step out, then turned back. 'You know, on second thought, I think I'll bring the little ones back here—unless you think he's got something infectious. They can have their tea in front of the telly as a special treat, and that way I can keep an eye on Dad.'

Cooper gave her a nod. 'Fair enough. We'll call you.'

The way he said it put an end to the matter, but in a kind way. Mhairi's father would get the care he needed. End of discussion.

When she'd left, he turned around and nodded towards the bedroom door. 'Right then, Audrey. Let's see what you're made of.'

A few minutes later, after running through the elderly gentleman's medical history and conducting a few preliminary checks, Cooper found his concerns were as high as his daughter's had been. Audrey's too, if her furrowed brow was anything to go by.

Glenn Davidson, their octogenarian patient, was not in a good way. He had a fever, was dehydrated, had low concentration and was very weak. They'd ruled out flu, as he didn't have any congestion or a sore throat. The fatigue and fever he was feeling was something he'd felt creeping up on him rather than something that had hit him in a blast, as flu symptoms often did. Besides, he'd assured them, he'd had a flu inoculation back in September.

'Had it right before your grandmother, I did,' Glenn had said weakly, rocking back and forth on the edge of the bed as if the movement was literally jogging his memory. 'We'd made the appointments together so we could swap magazines.'

Audrey's eyes shot to Cooper.

He looked away.

He'd not mentioned the glaring scarlet letter on his chest to her. A for abandonment. Perhaps he should have. But there was a part of him that was grateful that a new colleague meant a clean slate. She had no idea who he was and vice versa. Yet another chance to try and be the man he'd always hoped to be. Honourable. Loyal. Kind.

Moments like these were pointed reminders that he had quite a journey ahead of him before hitting any of those milestones. He'd known about Gran's flu shot, so hadn't been worried—but, like Mr Davidson here—his gran had been elderly, making her more vulnerable to chest infections.

Pneumonia didn't care whether or not you'd had a flu inoculation.

He should've been more like Mhairi, moving his world around to be there for her. His gran had been the woman who'd protected him all his life, and what had he done? Spread his wings, as she'd taught him, then flown too far from the nest to be of any use.

'Any history of Alzheimer's?' Audrey asked in a low voice.

Ah. A simple question, not an accusatory glance. He'd have to start checking his guilty conscience at the door if he was going to get through the day with his focus where it needed to be: on his patients.

Cooper shook his head in the negative, then busied himself with jotting down a few notes on Mr Davidson's chart. He would tell Audrey what had happened when they were done here. It would put all the little asides everyone was bound to make in context. Besides, there'd been something in Audrey's eyes that had given him reason to believe she had her own set of troubles. Who knew? Maybe she'd understand and he'd have an ally.

And maybe a kangaroo would bounce into the room and wish them all a happy Christmas.

'Is that too snug?' Audrey looked into Glenn's watery blue eyes as she adjusted the blood pressure cuff.

'No, it's fine,' Glenn said, not sounding entirely convinced—or focused, to be honest. His attention had dipped in and out ever since they'd entered his bedroom. Although in fairness, Cooper's had, too.

He'd suggested Audrey take the lead, so he could get a feel for how she worked, but she seemed a bit edgy. As if his decision was less a vote of confidence and more an opportunity for him to loom over her, judging her every move.

She popped her stethoscope ear-tips into place, gave the instrument's metal head a bit of a rub between her hands, so it wasn't cold, then gave the inflation bulb a quick pump to see whether or not Glenn's blood pressure was as low as they suspected.

As she put the stethoscope bell to his forearm he began to droop forward. Cooper was there in an instant, helping her right him. 'Easy there, Mr Davidson. I've got you.'

The poor man was finding it hard to sit upright, and started muttering something about finding the dog…the dog would help. So far as he knew, Glenn hadn't had a dog for some years. Maybe that Alzheimer's diagnosis should be reconsidered.

'Shall we rearrange your pillows there, Glenn? Let you lie back in bed? Is it dizziness you're feeling or fatigue?'

'Both. I don't understand what's happening,' Glenn said, for about the tenth time since they'd propped him up in his bed and begun the examination. 'Can't wrap my head round it.'

'Is this normal for him?' Audrey whispered to Cooper. That increasingly familiar blaze of defensiveness charged through him. He didn't know the ins and outs of every single human on Bourtree. No one did. Except, perhaps, his gran and Dr Anstruther, who'd been here over forty years. And Mhairi. And the neighbours. And, and, and…

But this wasn't about him. This was about Glenn.

He knelt down on one knee so that he could look directly into Mr Davidson's eyes. 'Glenn. We weren't able to have much of a talk with Mhairi when we arrived as she was late picking up the children. Are you able to explain exactly what's bothering you?'

'Hurts,' he said.

Cooper's eyes darted from the blood pressure cuff to Audrey, then back to Glenn.

'The cuff? Glenn, you've got to say if it pinches, all right? No prizes for bravery today.'

'No, it's more…' Glenn drew his knees up towards his chest.

'Glenn?' Audrey asked as she swiftly released the cuff from his arm. 'Are you eating at all?'

He shook his head. 'Nah. Not hungry.'

'Have you been sick?'

'Nah. Nah. I just want to sleep. Or die.' He fell back into the mound of pillows they'd built behind him and closed his eyes against whatever invisible pain he was enduring.

'Have you been drinking plenty of water?'

Glenn gave a soft moan and muttered something about a wee nip being all he could manage and it had only been to try and stop the pain.

Cooper winced. Alcohol wasn't a brilliant solution to anything. In fact, it wasn't a solution at all.

Cooper's heart went out to him as his brain whizzed through all the possibilities and prayed to whatever gods were out there that his grandmother had never felt this low. Doc Anstruther had said she'd gone in her sleep. It had been little comfort to him, but seeing Glenn like this, in agony, he was grateful for the small mercy she'd been shown.

Audrey's eyes locked on Cooper's and the wheels were obviously turning behind those brown eyes of hers. The expression on her face made it clear she knew very well that this was definitely not the psychological terrain you wanted any patient to be treading.

Audrey gave her forehead a little scratch, then asked, 'How often are you going to the toilet, Glenn?'

Glenn looked at her, his eyes lucid for the first time since they'd entered the room. 'All the time. I stopped drinking water yesterday, because it was getting to be too much, and I didn't want to wear…you know…nappies for men.'

Audrey gave his hand a gentle squeeze. Cooper appreciated the gesture. Getting an older man to talk about intimate things such as hygiene and incontinence was tough. Particularly when he was a Scottish Islander. He'd been told once that each male bairn born to the island received the same welcome upon their first cry. *'A good hearty voice you have, laddie, now that'll be enough of that.'*

Glenn's voice lowered to a whisper. 'I barely made it back to bed the last time, before I had to turn round and go back.'

As one, Cooper and Audrey figured it out. UTI.

He gave her a nod that said, *You go ahead.*

'I think you've got yourself a bad urinary tract infection, Glenn,' Audrey said, catching eyes again with Cooper.

He gave a little *Of course it is* thunk to his forehead, out of Glenn's line of vision. He should've added up the symptoms. Discomfort. Fever. Distractedness. Pain.

'What does that mean?' Glenn asked.

'It means we can get you feeling much more like yourself with some antibiotics,' Audrey said with a gentle smile.

Cooper nodded. That was a great way to deal with a patient. Let them know the prognosis was good first, then let them know how it would happen.

'Will it be instant?'

'No,' Cooper said when Audrey threw him a *Help, please* look. 'But if we get some fluids into you and ask your daughter to pick up the prescription on her way over, after picking up your grandkids, you should be feeling better by morning and better still in a few days' time.'

'Don't you need to take samples or anything?'

'Aye, we will, Glenn—if you're up to it. But, as Audrey pointed out, all your symptoms add up to a classic UTI. They can drive men mad. You should be proud you've made it this far without hallucinating.'

Glenn barked out a laugh. 'I thought I was when *you* walked through the door, Coop.'

'Eh?'

Glenn waved a trembling finger in his direction. 'This get-up you're wearing. I thought Santa had come to take me away to my maker.'

Audrey tried and failed to squelch a smile.

'Thought I'd spread some Christmas cheer a bit early this year. Looks like I brought some Christmas fear instead.'

Glenn's clear-eyed look softened. 'I'd like to make it to Christmas.'

'Eh, well.' He gave the man's thin shoulder a gentle pat. 'You'll make it well past Christmas and Hogmanay, if Audrey and I have anything to do with it.'

'But you'll not be here for any follow-up,' Glenn said, the lift in his mood instantly plummeting. 'If I make it through to the New Year, that is. And of course Dr Anstruther will be off in the tropics somewhere...'

Audrey looked up at Cooper. This was his question to answer. Her contract lasted through until New Year's Day. He didn't have a contract. Not yet.

'Noreen'll be back, Glenn. She'll keep her watchful eye on you. Don't you worry. You'll be skipping through the spring heather before you know it.'

'Aye...' Glenn cracked a smile, then closed his eyes. 'That'll be right.'

'Right, Glenn,' Audrey said, adroitly sensing the older man's need for some rest. 'Let me pull this lovely blanket up around you.'

As Audrey pulled a brightly coloured blanket up around him Cooper's heart skipped a beat. There was only one person on the whole of Bourtree who would've put together a blanket with that colour scheme. Gertie MacAskill. His gran.

Luckily, Audrey missed the hit of recognition as she was too busy tucking it into place.

'Why don't we get you some water to have by your bed, Glenn? Is there any particular glass you like?'

He muttered something indecipherable as she moved away from his bedside and she and Cooper left the room.

'Good call on the UTI,' Cooper said as he popped his medical bag on the kitchen table and put everything back in order. 'You got there before I did.'

'I'm sure that's not true,' Audrey said, then added, 'I used to see them all the time amongst my older patients and he has pretty classic symptoms.'

'Used to?'

Audrey looked away, busying herself with opening cupboards to find a glass. 'I took a job at a children's hospital a couple of months back. It was great, of course, but there's a different sort of job satisfaction from district nursing.'

There was something in that admission, he thought. Guilt? Loss? Hard to put his finger on it. Maybe something had happened on one of her calls that had made her switch to a hospital. Some people found the intimacy of being in a patient's home too much. He was one of them.

'I don't know. Diagnosing UTIs isn't as exciting as a bustling hospital.'

'All my patients receive the same treatment,' Audrey bit out as she filled the glass with water over a pile of unwashed dishes in the kitchen sink. 'Whether they're at home or anaesthetised and about to go into surgery.'

Okay. Cool your jets.

'I wasn't suggesting otherwise.'

She set the glass down on the counter, then pulled on a pair of washing up gloves that hung over the tap.

'What are you doing?'

'What does it look like I'm doing?' She put the tap on full and gave the dishes beneath a big squirt of washing up liquid.

'Doing dishes isn't the normal remit of a district nurse.'

She looked at him as if his heart was made of stone. 'Cooper, the poor man's unwell. His daughter sounds like she has less time than either of us do and—' she held up three coffee mugs, then dropped them back into the soapy water '—these might offer some insight as to why Glenn's suffering. It looks like he's had nothing but coffee, whisky and…from the looks of this plate…a curry ready-meal. None of which are any good for a UTI. Offering him advice on what is and isn't going to help him feel better is very *much* the remit of a district nurse.'

Well, that was him told. And fair enough, too.

Cooper scrubbed a hand over his stubbly chin, hoping the conciliatory sound he'd just made would make up for the fact that he was wrong and she was right.

The truth was, he was only a handful of days into this house doctor gig and he was still trying to find the job's heartbeat. When he'd come back to Bourtree, Dr Anstruther had met him at the docks to drive him up to his gran's. He'd ever so casually mentioned that he was retiring on Christmas Eve and that he had the budget for another doctor up until then. It was intended to go to the doctor who'd be replacing him, but as there weren't any takers so far...

He'd refused at first. Said this was a one-doctor island. But Doc Anstruther had said there were a few cases he might find interesting. So far they'd yet to surface. And if anything truly disastrous happened, an air ambulance and doctors from the mainland would be flown in. They'd flown in for his parents. Too late, as it happened, but they'd been part of the inspiration for Cooper to become a doctor. Helping when people needed help most. Commanding instant trust. Respect.

Two things he didn't know if he would ever earn here.

He gave the back of his head a rub. What was done was done. Enough introspective soul destruction for one day. Luckily he had a perfect distraction in the form of an anti-elf-suit, pixie-haired district nurse, who'd left the bright lights of London to come here to Bourtree. Maybe she could throw some light on what made this type of medical practice more desirable than working in a hospital.

He pulled the top over his run-bag and began to zip it shut. 'I'm curious,' he said. 'Why didn't you try another discipline after paediatric nursing rather than take a professional move backwards?'

Her eyes widened. 'Who says district nursing is going backwards?'

Oh, hell. Talk about open mouth and insert foot.

Cooper backtracked. 'Sorry. I'm not dissing it. Not at all. It's a valuable service. But c'mon... Now that you've had a taste of it, you have to admit that life in a hospital is...'

He was about to say *the ultimate buzz* but he stopped himself. Getting an adrenaline hit out of other people's misfortunes wasn't what he meant. An ideal emergency department would be an empty one, but being a busy doctor with a non-stop flow of anonymous patients demanded full focus. Consumed more hours of the week than any other job he could think of. Hours spent improving people's lives, not destroying them, as his parents used to tell him over and over.

'If it hadn't been for you and your sister...'

The lives they would've led...

He cleared his throat and chose a simpler, less emotionally toxic tack. 'I'm just curious as to why you took this locum post rather than one at a London hospital. They pay better. There must be scores of jobs over Christmas if that's the goal. And yet you chose to come here. Why?'

From the look on Audrey's face, Cooper had done an *out of the frying pan into the fire* manoeuvre. So much for trying to steer clear of emotional toxicity.

'Not everything's about money and status, Dr *Claus*.'

She gave him a proper glare that tugged at an impulse to pull her into his arms and comfort her. Then, as quickly as her temper had flared, her lips curved into a weak but apologetic smile.

'Sorry. Touchy subject.'

'Money or status?'

'Neither.'

'A boyfriend obsessed with one or both?' he parried.

She chewed on the inside of her cheek. Whether she was fighting tears or conjuring up an acidic response to a question that was none of his business was difficult to tell. When she released it, he realised her lips were shaped like a perfect bow. A crimson bow that, if he were looking for a pair of lips to kiss, would be very inviting indeed.

'Something like that,' she said finally.

His eyes were still glued to her lips as she asked, 'Should we wrap up here and get to the next patient?'

There was a challenge in her tone. A dare for him to try and press her for more information. Fair enough. Calling his own love-life chequered would be putting it nicely.

He dragged his eyes away from her lips and took the glass of water to give to Glenn, doing his best to ignore the spark of connection when their hands brushed. He took the glass through to Glenn, made sure he was tucked up in bed, and gave him a reminder that they or his daughter would be back within an hour or so with his prescription, but to call if he needed anything.

When he got back to the kitchen Audrey was already heading to the car.

Fair enough.

He didn't like being pushed for answers to uncomfortable questions either. Why didn't he have a girlfriend? Why wasn't he married? Why didn't he have a family of his own when so many of his peers were already looking forward to their second or third child?

Questions people on Bourtree had never bothered asking him because they already knew the answers.

CHAPTER THREE

FOUR HOURS, ONE huge serving of takeaway fish and chips and seven patients later, Audrey and Cooper finally wrapped up the last of the calls. It was almost eight o'clock and, despite her cosy winter coat—now stained with mud, a streak of spilt tea and some errant ketchup from a friendly toddler—she was feeling the cold. The car's heating system had packed up after their second visit.

She could do with getting to her accommodation and slipping into a nice hot bath. Bubbles, a milky cup of tea and a chance to think about her busy day. Bliss. Although sitting down meant she might also think about the fact that she'd just had her heart crushed, her bank account devastated and, in five weeks' time, would have nowhere to live and no job to go to.

Cooper pulled the car onto the island's main road— there was only the one main coastal route, with loads of little twisty lanes shooting off it—to head back to the surgery, where she'd caught a fleeting glimpse of Dr Anstruther earlier in the day. So that she'd be in a better head space when she met him, she kept her dark thoughts at bay by making mental notes on each of their patients, most of whom they would see again either tomorrow or the next day.

On top of a couple of paediatric calls for some utterly

adorable babies—one of whom had a questionable chest infection—there was another elderly patient, bed-bound courtesy of Parkinson's, a twenty-something chap with compound fractures in each of his femurs from a skiing mishap, a stubborn 'remote IT consultant', who was refusing to believe diabetes was the reason behind the circulatory problems in his feet, and a heartbreaking case of a young mum who was losing her battle with metastic bone cancer and whose only dream was to make it through to Christmas so that she didn't 'spoil it' for her children.

The selflessness of the comment had brought tears to her eyes and sent Cooper straight out through the door on what she was pretty sure had been a pretend errand for 'some paperwork'. Proof, at least, that the man had a heart.

No. That wasn't fair. He had proved himself to be an excellent doctor, slightly shifting his demeanour to suit each patient. She had no doubt he'd be brilliant in a busy A&E ward, every bit the professional, and now that she had spent some time with him she was no longer remotely attracted to him. Nope. Not one bit.

She hadn't even considered tucking an errant wave of his dark hair behind one of his ears. Or spent one idle moment wondering what it would be like to run her finger along his stubble to see if it was soft or rough to the touch. Nor had she even once considered what it would be like to touch his lips with her own. One hundred percent not at all.

Any emotional sparks that had flown had been likely due to her hypersensitivity about…well…*everything*.

If only wedding insurance paid out when the groom turned out to be a lying cheat. If only wedding insurance could erase your memory and let you start your adult life all over again—or at least from the point where she'd finally decided to sell the small house where she and her father had lived. That had been the moment when she'd begun to lose sight of herself, as if the house and all its memories, had anchored her to the woman she'd thought she was. The woman she'd wanted to become.

Rafael had actually laughed when she'd told him what it had sold for. It had been a lot to her, but her modest nurse's salary hadn't prevented it from falling into the 'fixer-upper' category. She'd put half of the money into a pension that she couldn't touch for years to come and then, like a complete and utter fool, she'd poured the rest of it into the wedding.

Rafael only liked the finest things in life, and for once she would be able to give him the very finest. What did it matter, she'd thought, if she spent all the money on their one special day? They'd be pooling resources after they were married and her splurge would make memories for a lifetime.

Nightmares, more like.

It was money she now desperately needed for a deposit on a flat somewhere—rented or otherwise—and to get on with her life. Without it she was right royally screwed. But keeping that shame to herself was critical if she wanted to leave here with her dignity intact. Not easy when she was busy biting Cooper's head off for his comments about money and status.

She owed him an apology on that front. He wasn't to know it had been Rafael who had encouraged her to leave her post as a district nurse. It shamed her now, how quickly she'd leapt at all his suggestions. Changing jobs. Moving in together. Planning a discreet but ultra-lush wedding away from prying eyes...

They'd decided on a tropical island in the end. Staying in one of those amazing houses on stilts above an azure sea. First-class airline tickets. Spa treatments. Champagne on arrival. The lot.

It physically pained her how eager she'd been to please him. She'd been the shy, mousey type her whole life, and Rafael was the polar opposite. Assured, socially confident, and completely aware that his place in the world was amongst the upper echelons.

Maybe that had been it…the reason he'd cheated. She'd been too lowly for him. He'd wanted to pull a Prince Charming on her when she'd been quite happy being Cinderella before the ball—minus the stepsisters, obviously.

'You've done well today,' Cooper said, apropos of nothing.

A warm hit of appreciation bloomed in her chest. A welcome heat, as it was bloody freezing in his car.

'It's nice getting to know people in their home environment,' she said. 'I know paramedics and A&E docs are often seen as the real frontline, but I always like to think house call doctors and district nurses are the true healthcare SAS.'

'How so?' Cooper asked, sounding genuinely interested.

She flushed a bit when he nodded at her to go ahead. It was something she could be a bit too passionate about…but what the heck? She'd be gone in five weeks, and it wasn't as if she was going to be falling into his arms any time soon—or ever—so… 'Being in a patient's house makes a big difference in helping diagnose certain health problems.'

'In what way?' he asked. 'I find the less I know the person, the easier it is to be clinical about a diagnosis.'

She made a thoughtful noise, but then shook her head. 'That just makes it easier to make the hard decisions.'

Cooper nodded. 'Go on.'

'I think knowing a person and the environment they live in gives you a much better grounding for understanding a patient. It's easier to sift through to the real problem.'

'How's that?'

'Well,' she said. 'Take Jimmy, for example.'

'Jimmy Tarbot?'

He was the diabetic patient they'd seen earlier. He was about her age and, despite the fact he was facing potential amputation of his toes, he refused to acknowledge the fact that what he ate really did make a difference—that his diabetes wasn't just a case of 'bad genes'.

'Yes. He's obviously in denial about how bad his diabetes is.'

'He lets us come in and give insulin shots on a daily basis.'

'Yes, but…' Audrey didn't want to step on any toes here. 'It's a guaranteed visit from the outside world, isn't it?'

Cooper gave her a quick look. 'Go on,' he said again.

'He says he wants us to do the jabs because he has a fear of needles, but did he seem remotely freaked out to you?'

Cooper took a beat before answering in the negative.

'So,' Audrey continued, 'he's obviously hungry for company, but he isn't making any visible changes to make sure his health changes and he won't need the injections. Which is a little weird for someone who has a fear of needles, don't you think?'

'He told me he was on fruit and veg. Lean meat. The whole nine yards.'

'Did you look in his bin?'

'No.'

'There were several bakery bags in there, as well as a pink box which looked suspiciously like a cake box to me. Talbot's Bakery and Café? That's on the High Street, isn't it?'

Cooper nodded. 'Aye. But he says he doesn't go out. That's why we make these calls rather than give him injections down at the clinic. Because he's housebound.'

'Oh, I believe he doesn't go out. But not necessarily because he can't.' Audrey began ticking things off her fingers. 'There's absolutely nothing around his car to indicate it's left the drive recently. The refrigerator only has a pint of milk and a loaf of white bread in it. When I asked him about it, he said he gets one of the lads from the market to drop his shopping by on his way home. I'm guessing that's a trip via the bakery. Plus,' she added with a playful smirk, 'he told me when I asked him. About the needles. That he fakes being afraid of them.'

'I should've bought you a detective's hat—not an elf's hat.' Cooper flashed her a smile. It was so warm and genuine, it caught her off guard. As if she'd been hit by an actual ray of sunshine. 'I have to say, Audrey—and this is no offence to Noreen—but I can see why he'd fake a fear of needles if a beautiful woman like you was calling in on him on a daily basis. Who knows what he tells Noreen?'

She flushed right up to her hairline. The last thing she'd felt over the past few days was beautiful. Having the comment come from Cooper felt special. He certainly didn't seem the type to dole out compliments like candies. Then again...the man was wearing a Santa suit.

Audrey tried shrugging it off. 'I'm leaving soon. Sometimes it's easier to tell a complete stranger the truth rather than have the people you care about knowing about your vulnerabilities.'

She'd run for the hills as soon as her life had fallen to pieces. Hadn't told a soul. Packed her bags and left. Here, within such a close-knit community, it would be awful to feel ashamed of how or who you were.

'Do you think there's anything else that's keeping him hidden away in his house?'

Cooper thought for a minute, then said. 'I remember Jimmy from school. Shy as a mouse, he was. Would barely meet your eye when you talked to him. Everyone called him Big Jimmy, and he never seemed to mind, but maybe…'

'What?'

'Well, I think he struggled to find his "crew". He was never one for team sports. Always playing computer games and coding. Although he was in with the drama students for a while. Working backstage and such. That sort of thing.'

'Perhaps he's too embarrassed to go out. Never developed a thick skin against the name calling. Can you imagine what it must feel like to go out, knowing everyone is judging your weight, and wanting nothing more than to buy cake?'

'No one likes to be judged.'

Cooper's dark change of tone was so abrupt Audrey felt a bit shocked. Was he speaking from experience?

He gave her a quick glance, then faced the road again. 'I still don't see what any of this has to do with a better diagnosis.'

Audrey huffed out a sigh. Wasn't it obvious? 'Now that we know he's not actually afraid of needles, we need to find ways to get him out of the house. Get him active.'

Cooper laughed. 'You like a challenge, don't you?'

'What do you mean?'

'You're going to try and change a man's habits? A man who's not left his house in years maybe? It's not easy to change a well-worn routine.'

'There are plenty of reasons why a person might change their routine,' she replied hotly, knowing her answer was fuelled by the fact that the night she'd found Rafael and his lover she'd been meant to be home late. She'd come home early from a regular girls' night out to surprise him, little knowing she'd be the one getting the surprise.

Cooper was drumming his fingers on the steering

wheel, then he gave it a thump. 'I can see where you're coming from, but I'd be willing to lay down money that you'll not convince him to change his ways.'

She yanked her seat belt away from her chest and whirled on him. 'What *is* it with you? One minute you're all nice and complimentary, and the next you're taking little jabs, trying to cut me down.'

'Hey! Whoa.' Cooper pulled the car over to the side of the road. 'I'm trying to get to know you. Figure out how you think.'

And making a right hash of it.

'Oh, I see, Santa. Is this for your naughty and nice list? Or is it some sort of special island greeting? Building a person up, then tearing them down for your own amusement.'

He stopped himself from answering that question in the nick of time.

She was right, to an extent. He'd had a sharp tongue as a boy, and it hadn't been entirely smoothed as an adult. It was the main reason he'd been deemed 'not suitable' management material. Which was fine. He was an 'in the trenches' type of doctor. Even so, saying *exactly* what he thought wasn't always the wisest course of action. But when you'd been raised in a house where your own parents had freely informed you that they wished you'd never been born...

It was no excuse to be unkind. He needed all the allies he could get right now. Audrey was a lovely, hard-working woman who clearly wanted to do the very best for their patients. It was inevitable that she saw things from a different angle. And he'd been nothing but bloody awkward all day.

The Santa costume was his way of putting a shield between himself and the islanders' judgmental gazes, not something to bring everyone closer together. No one had been blunt enough to say anything, and any condolences for his loss had been whispered out of earshot of Audrey, but he was sure he could sense their judgement in the air. Well-deserved judgement.

He made a mental note not to ask Audrey for a full psychological assessment unless he wanted a hard, very uncomfortable look in the mirror. He also reminded himself to try not to push her buttons with such regularity. There was obviously a lot more going on beneath the calm, professional surface Audrey had let their patients see. Something he instinctively felt he could relate to if they were to open up to one another. Which, all things considered, was unlikely.

'Please,' he said, putting out a hand. 'Accept my apology. I'm used to the rough and tumble of an inner-city emergency department. There's not much time for manners there. How about we rewind and work on things from… I don't know…? How about hello? Would that work? Give each other a clean slate and start over?'

'I've got a better idea,' Audrey sniped, instead of laughing and taking his hand as he'd hoped. 'Why don't we keep this professional relationship precisely that.'

'What? Professional?'

She pinned on a smile that definitely didn't hit her eyes. 'Top of the class, were you?'

'Not at charm school.'

The corners of her mouth twitched and then, even though he could see she was trying not to, she finally smiled. A hit of pride sent his heart banging against his ribcage. Teasing a genuine smile out of her made him feel like a medal winner. Maybe that was where he'd gone wrong. Too much time trying to keep his emotions at bay when in actual fact a bit of time in the emotional trenches made moments like this much more rewarding.

A few minutes later, with a more companionable air between them, they pulled up to the surgery.

'Let's get you to your accommodation, shall we?' he said.

Audrey got of the car and stretched. 'I could definitely do with a hot shower and a nice warm bed.'

'I'm afraid that won't be possible.'

They both turned at the sound of a male voice.

'Dr Anstruther?' Cooper squinted against the bright security light that popped on as a figure came down the alleyway alongside the high street surgery.

'Hello, there, Coop.' Dr Anstruther emerged onto the street. 'Audrey.'

Cooper was sorry to see the much-respected doctor looking very much his seventy-odd years this evening. 'What's going on? Is everything all right?' he asked, and beckoned to Audrey to join them.

The silver-haired doctor gave Cooper a clap on the shoulder, then put out a hand to shake Audrey's. 'Finlay Anstruther, dearie. I know we met earlier, but we were both so rushed it wasn't much of a greeting. And I'm afraid you'll not be getting much of one now.'

'Why?' Cooper asked when Audrey failed to.

'Erm, well…' His eyes travelled up to the flat above the surgery, where locum doctors and nurses stayed.

Cooper's stomach dropped. 'Has something happened?'

Finlay Anstruther winced. 'Aye. Boiler's gone. Water pipes burst after that freeze we had the other day, I'm guessing. I've not been up there for a few days, but when my Emily went in to give the place a wee clean a couple of hours back—disaster. I was trying to fix it myself, but then I saw the staining on the ceiling of my office down in the surgery—'

He made a despairing noise. One that didn't speak well for the safety of working in the surgery.

'Why didn't you call any of the lads?'

By 'lads', Cooper meant the men he'd been born and raised with, right here on this island. Men taught their trade by their fathers as they'd been taught by their fathers before them. Unlike Cooper who, if he'd followed his own father's path, would be leaving two orphaned children behind about now.

Finlay tugged a hand through his shock of white hair. 'Son, it's not good. Not good at all.'

'The flat or the surgery?' Cooper asked.

'Both.'

'Ah...' This was awkward. 'Anything we can do about it tonight?' He fastidiously avoided Audrey's pained expression while he waited for Finlay's inevitable answer.

'No, not really, son. Audrey, I'm ever so sorry. Everyone's up at the Nativity rehearsal, and it's not as if the flat'll be habitable any time today or...'

The fact he'd left the sentence unfinished spoke to just how bad the burst pipe problem actually was.

Audrey looked between the pair of them as if she were watching a game point rally at Wimbledon, and then, unexpectedly, she laughed. 'It looks like Baby Jesus and I share a similar housing problem. But surely there's a B&B I can stay in, or a hotel? There's no need to worry about me.'

Cooper and the veteran GP exchanged a charged look. 'Not this time of year, darlin',' Finlay offered, then repeated his apologies.

He promised to speak to all the relevant tradesmen tonight, to see what could be done, but in the meantime... He and his wife had put their house on the market, and had most of their things in storage in advance of his retirement, so there wasn't a room for her there...

Cooper had half tuned out as his brain was heading down a very narrow tunnel. He'd known Finlay was going to hang up his hat, but now that he was talking about actually having put things in storage and literally preparing to up stakes it was like a bucket of icy cold North Sea water on his face.

There was a job for life if he wanted it, here on Bourtree Castle. *Was* this what he wanted? To stay here for ever? To have the folk of Bourtree growing accustomed to him dressing as Santa as he did his rounds each Christmas? As the Easter bunny in spring?

Or, to really boil it down to its purest essence, did he want the people of Bourtree to think of him as a doctor they could rely on to stay?

When he tuned back in Finlay was rattling off the number of folk who had come back from the mainland to stay with family, drop presents off in case the ferries were grounded owing to bad weather, make Christmas cakes with grans, bird houses with grandads... The list seemed to go on for ever.

Cooper stopped the flow of excuses in the only way he knew how. 'She can stay with me, Finlay.'

It was a step closer towards 'getting to know you' than he would've preferred, but he was hardly going to leave Audrey here on the High Street with her fingers crossed that someone would offer her a room for the night.

'Um..."she" is right here,' Audrey said, about an octave higher than she normally spoke, air quotes hanging in the wintry air. 'And "she" will not be staying with you. Now, Finlay, are you sure there's—?'

'There's nowhere else, dearie,' Finlay said sorrowfully.

'Not this time of year. We're such a small population at the best of times, what with folk seeking their fortunes elsewhere.' His eyes flicked briefly to Cooper's, but there was no malice in his words, just acceptance. 'Cooper's offer is a good one. I'd take it. Now, if you two'll excuse me, Emily's going to have my head if I don't get down the church hall sharpish. Coop, shall we meet up at the usual time to discuss what to do about the surgery? The reception area's fine—it's my room that's the potential problem.'

'Fine. Put it out of your head for tonight. As you say, it'll be a problem solved tomorrow. Now...' Cooper turned his attention to Audrey as Finlay headed off towards the church. 'Don't look so worried. It's not a smelly bachelor pad. It's more...'

He saw her eyes narrow suspiciously as he sought the perfect word to describe his grandmother's house.

'More what?'

'You'll see,' he said, tossing in a smile to reassure her that it wasn't *bad*...it was just...well...she'd see.

'Gosh. It's...wow...um... Your grandmother's sense of style is... I've never seen anything like it.'

Cooper smiled at Audrey's understated response to his grandmother's house. He probably should've warned her. Or given her a pair of sunglasses before he flicked on the overhead lights.

Opening the front door each night was such a bittersweet experience it was strangely helpful, having Audrey here. Most of the girlfriends he'd had would've smirked and made snarky comments about the doilies and the abundance of crocheted bric-a-brac. It was partly why he'd never brought anyone to Bourtree. No chance he'd subject his gran to their sneers.

But Audrey was different. She seemed delighted by it.

Though she hadn't found the perfect words to describe it, he got the sense that she felt as though she'd been allowed to see something special. And, as nearly everything in here had been made by his grandmother, it was.

He took off his coat and made a show of shaking the down into submission as he watched Audrey absorb just how much his grandmother had loved using the woollen mill's bin-ends, whether or not they matched. Her ethos had been the brighter the better. Every day needed a bit of sunshine, according to her, and for nine months of the year in Bourtree? You weren't going to get it from the sky.

Audrey took a step into the lounge and ran her hand along the knitted—or crocheted?—blanket that was draped over the back of the tartan-patterned sofa. 'Did she make *all* of this?'

She sounded impressed.

'Sure did.' It was good to be able to feel a puff of pride about her, the woman who'd raised him when his mum and dad had proved utterly inept at parenting.

He scanned the room along with Audrey. His gran had made each and every blanket, cushion cover, tatted picture frame. To be honest, she'd taken her love of household needlework to an entirely different level. He'd was quite certain every bairn on the island had been swaddled in one of his gran's blankets at one juncture or another. And then, of course, there were the doilies. Dozens of the things. On every armrest…under every china figure. The figures were women, mostly in period dress, their china skirts caught in an invisible breeze as their bonnets dangled from their fingers.

'No Christmas tree?' asked Audrey.

'Nope,' Cooper said, a bit too briskly for someone wearing a Santa suit. 'Believe it or not, I'm not usually in the habit of decorating for Christmas.'

'But it isn't about you, is it? Shouldn't it be about what your grandmother's routine is—?'

'Was,' he quietly corrected, rawly aware of how wrong it felt to describe someone as full of life as his gran in the past tense.

Audrey turned and touched his arm. 'Oh, Cooper, I'm so sorry. I suppose I should've put two and two together, but we were so busy—'

'Bickering?' Cooper finished for her.

'No, not bickering.' Audrey looked around the small lounge again, as if hoping to find the right word. 'We were…figuring one another out. And please do accept my condolences about your grandmother. Was it recent?'

'Just over a week back,' he said, a harsh sting of emotion scraping his throat as he fought against admitting that he should've been here and hadn't been. He *could've* been here. He'd done ten days on the trot at the hospital and had been owed a few days off. Weeks, really. But had he taken them?

Of course not.

Winter was always busy in the A&E and, as usual, there had been no one for him to go home to, so he'd signed up for a double shift after a quick call to his gran, to remind her to make sure there was more lemon and honey than whisky in her hot toddy. As if she'd needed reminding. She knew what too much booze did to a person.

'It must be tough, being here with all these memories.' His eyes snapped to Audrey's. Was she telling him something?

'Is that what you're doing?' he asked. 'Dodging memories?'

Any warmth that had bloomed between them vanished. 'No,' she said crisply. 'I prefer to focus on making new ones.'

So that was a yes, then.

He thought of the way her thumb kept creeping towards her bare ring finger. Not that he'd been wondering about her availability. Much…

'If you don't mind, Cooper, I'd like to see my room. It's been a long day.'

'Of course. Sorry.'

He did the short tour from the centre of the house, pointing out where everything was. Lounge, kitchen, dining room… His room upstairs. His gran's at the far end of the corridor, leading out to the back garden, the dining room opposite it.

'This looks like it was her knitting room rather than her dining room,' Audrey commented.

Cooper resisted taking the statement as a barb. He and his gran hadn't sat down for a proper meal in the dining room in well over a decade. On the rare occasions when he'd come home he'd insisted on taking her out to the Puffin. A meagre thanks for all she'd sacrificed to keep him on the straight and narrow.

The money he would give now to have one more meal with her the way they'd used to…kitting out the table as if the Queen herself were coming for tea.

'Why not?' his gran had used to quip as she pulled out a crystal tumbler for his soft drink. *'You never know which moment will be your last, so best to make all of them special.'*

He'd used to think that comment had been about his parents. He supposed the difference was that theirs had been an accident waiting to happen with the way they drank. His gran's death had been preventable, and it was on him that it hadn't been prevented.

He showed Audrey into his sister's old room. It was kitted out in soft yellow and cream colours. Apart from a picture of the two of them, from when they were kids, it could easily have been a room in any B&B. His grandmother's room had the nicer view, but it was far too soon to turn it into anything other than a place to reflect on the ways he could improve himself.

'Oh, it's much more…um…neutral in here,' Audrey said.

Cooper shrugged. 'My sister always preferred to blend in.'

Audrey cocked her head to the side, interested. 'I didn't know you had a sister.'

Cooper shrugged. 'She's a few years older than me and she moved to New Zealand years back.' They'd both been 'surprises' to his parents. Unwelcome ones.

'Did she come back for the funeral?'

No. She hadn't. Like him, she'd found growing up as a child of the island's two lushes complicated. She had a family of her own now. A happy life. Kept herself to herself. As if he, too, was part of her complicated history. *Fight or flight.* They'd both chosen the latter. Unfortunately in different directions.

'Long trip.'

'I suppose it is,' she said, with a hit of compassion warming those dark eyes of hers.

He waited for the inevitable follow-up comment. Lord knew he'd received enough of them as he'd shaken everyone's hand at the end of Gertie's funeral. *'Not good enough for your sister, are we? Your gran gave you two bairns everything she had. The least Shona could've done was fly up to pay her respects.'*

Cooper had pointed out that the biggest floral tribute had been from his sister, but absence didn't make the heart grow fonder in the islanders' eyes. It chipped away at the loyalty they believed you owed them.

He pointed at the fireplace at the far end of the room.

'There is central heating, but it's not brilliant. If you like, you can light the fire.'

'Oh, I've never had a fire in my bedroom before.' Audrey's eyes glittered with excitement.

'Grand. If the weather drops, as it's meant to, we'll need all the wood fires going. But don't worry—you won't have to blast your way through the wood pile or anything.'

'Why?'

Because chopping wood had been about the only way he'd kept his sanity over the past fortnight. As if physically pounding out his sorrows would eventually bring him peace.

'That's my job.'

Audrey instantly stood up straighter, irritation replacing the glee of having her own wood fire. 'I suppose you think I can't chop wood because I'm a girl?'

'I wouldn't dare suggest such a thing,' Cooper said, the corners of his mouth twitching ever so slightly.

Oh, he wanted to annoy her, did he? *Job done, pal.* That showed her what softening her stiff resolve to dislike him would do. Catch her out at the first opportunity. Well, she wasn't having Cooper suffer from the delusion that she was a poor helpless girl unable to fend for herself for a moment longer.

'I bet you think I'd freeze to death by the end of the week if left to my own devices.' She balled her hands into fists, waiting for him to confirm her comment.

Rafael would certainly have said as much. What she'd initially seen as gentlemanly behaviour, she was now beginning to see for what it was: good old-fashioned sexism. She'd been in charge of the fluffier things in their relationship, like their wedding. Rafael had been in charge of everything else.

It had been more subtle than that, of course. But the fact she'd been so blind to the effortless shift her life had taken back to the nineteen-fifties made her want to show hindsight exactly how firm a grip she had on her future.

If Cooper wanted to wear the 'Me Man, You Woman' mantel he'd have a fight on his hands. Even if she didn't have the remotest clue how to chop wood... Surely she could take a stab at it? It wasn't brain surgery. In the same way that changing a patient's dressing required a deft touch, she suspected wood-chopping had its own art.

An art she might be terrible at. *Oh, crumbs.* Why had she started an argument she didn't know if she could win?

The hint of humour had disappeared from Cooper's features and been replaced by earnest entreaty. 'I'd never suggest you couldn't do something because you're a woman. And not just because my grandmother's ghost would give short shrift to that.'

Audrey tried to imagine a gran ghost appearing and chasing Cooper out of the house. She smiled.

'What?' he asked warily, as if he, too, could see the image.

'I don't have the slightest idea how to chop wood,' she admitted reluctantly.

'Oh?'

He looked surprised, but not shocked. Nor did he look disappointed. It struck her how conditioned she'd become to holding her breath whenever she'd admitted something to Rafael—something she didn't know how to do. Had she really wanted to be a part of such a marriage? A lifetime of feeling anxious about being herself?

Cooper leant against the doorframe. 'Want me to teach you?'

Wow. That fell into the realm of 'not remotely expected'. 'Yes!'

'Is that a real yes, or a yes just to prove a point?'

There wasn't any attitude accompanying his question. It was just a question—plain and simple.

'I think I'd like to learn how to chop wood,' Audrey said.

'We can do some next time we hit a bit of daylight, if you like,' he said, flicking his thumb towards what she imagined was the back garden.

'Sure. Sounds good.'

They shared a smile that lit a small flame of hope in her. Not just for herself, but for her working relationship with Cooper. He may have some far-out ideas about seasonal 'uniforms', and he ping-ponged from grumpy to genuinely caring at the drop of a hat, but maybe this interchange was a sign they wouldn't spend the next five weeks bickering after all.

A swirl of something she didn't want to acknowledge whirled round her belly, teasing at areas she'd thought would never show signs of life again.

Interesting.

And not a little bit scary.

Cooper put his hand out and gave hers a solid shake. 'I'm looking forward to you taking over that part of the household workload.'

There was a twinkle in his eye as he said it, and a shot of electricity running up her arm as his hand shifted away from hers just a little more slowly than in your average handshake. As if he'd felt the same spray of energy running between them.

He cleared his throat and abruptly pushed himself up and away from the doorframe, giving his hands a brisk rub. 'Right, then, lassie. I know it seems early, but I'm away off to my bed. Are you hungry or anything?'

She shook her head. 'Those fish and chips were amazing. And huge.'

'Best in Scotland,' he said, a charming hint of pride ribboning round the statement. His eyes met hers, then flicked away. 'Right, so... Can I get you a tea or a hot chocolate for a nightcap?'

She shook her head. She didn't want to put him to any more trouble than she already had. 'I'm fine. A hot shower and bed will do me just fine.'

'Right you are, then.' He tipped an invisible cap and bade her goodnight.

She sat down on the bed, enjoying a little bounce when she discovered it was covered in inviting layers of hand-stitched quilts. She wished she could've met Cooper's gran. She must never have had an idle moment. Or been short of a lesson to share.

Her own childhood had been lovely, but a little bit lonely. It had pretty much just been her and her dad. He'd done the best he could to keep her happy and engaged, but she'd always envied other children who came from huge extended families, and had genuinely been looking forward to starting a family of her own with Rafael.

Which did beg the question... Had it been the family she'd wanted rather than the man? Perhaps she'd forgiven him all his controlling quirks because she'd had her eyes on a different prize. Children to laugh and play with. A family life that she herself had never had.

Whatever... That had been then, and a family was so off her radar right now it wasn't worth the energy even to think about it. She was a blank slate, waiting to discover what her real goals and dreams were.

So she'd lost a lying, cheating fiancé? There were worse things in life. Like losing a dearly loved grandmother. Seeing how Cooper was struggling with his emotions in the wake of losing Gertie…it touched her.

She looked round the room again and smiled. If, beneath the gruff exterior and the Santa suit, Cooper was anything like his gran, she was pretty sure there was a heart of gold buried beneath that red jacket of his.

CHAPTER FOUR

'IT'S NOT LOOKING GOOD, is it?'

Audrey, Finlay and Cooper all looked up at the large hole in the surgery's main examination room ceiling while Cooper aimed his heavy-duty torch around the area.

'Looks like a nice kitchen,' Audrey said dryly.

'Oh, it is,' Finlay agreed, a bit more earnestly than he should have considering there was a metre-wide sinkhole in the centre of it. 'Very.'

'Shall we get everything you need out of here and into the spare room, Finlay?'

Audrey was almost grateful to have someone else's problems to worry about. Almost because this particular problem meant she'd be staying with Cooper for the fore-seeable future. If he'd have her.

She got the impression he was more the lone wolf type than a happy-to-have-a-housemate kind of guy. And also, she'd kind of accidentally imagined him getting undressed and climbing into bed last night, and that was an imaginary picture she hadn't been able to un-see. In a good way. A too good for words type of way. Which, of course, was strictly forbidden.

Cooper, who clearly hadn't thought about *her* getting undressed, was thinking far more practically. 'I think we should get everything we need and take it to another *building*.'

Audrey scanned the scene again. He was right. It looked as though a wrecking ball had dropped through the ceiling.

'C'mon, you lot.' Cooper abruptly flew into action. 'I'm pretty sure I saw some spare boxes back in the storeroom. I'll call the church. Finlay, can you ring whoever's on reception today and have them meet us there? We'll set up in the hall, like you did before when the blood drive folk came over.'

'You remember that?' Finlay asked.

'Aye,' Cooper said tightly, his features retracting in a micro-flinch.

He clearly remembered, but, Audrey amended, he didn't like being reminded that there was a lot he *hadn't* been around for.

Finlay gave Cooper's shoulder a pat. 'Nice thinking, son.'

Cooper's jaw relaxed, as if being called 'son' and treated as one of the island's own was a salve to whatever was troubling him.

She'd not yet had the courage to ask, but she was guessing things with his parents hadn't been that brilliant. Or maybe it was something with his grandmother...

'Are you happy to help with the packing up?' Cooper asked, when he noticed her staring at him a bit too intensely.

'Absolutely.' She held out her hand for a box, hoping he hadn't noticed her cheeks colouring.

Staring at Cooper, with all that tangled dark hair, those bright blue eyes, and much more than a hint of a five o'clock shadow, was a bit too easy. A bit too pleasurable.

Funny, considering she'd thought she'd never get lost in another man's beauty after— *Enough.* She needed to draw a line under that entire humiliating chapter. She lost three months of her life and a sizeable chunk of her dignity to that man, so onwards and upwards. It was the only way to move on.

As they began to pick up and dust off the essential things they needed, Audrey felt herself overcome with an unfamiliar sense of lightness. As if she'd been sprinkled with some sort of fairy dust.

Something about this disaster was striking her as... Well, not *funny*, exactly—because it was clearly an expensive problem, and the wrong time of year to have it, and it would definitely mean she'd be spending the rest of her stay at Cooper's gran's unless the Bourtree tradesmen were as efficient as Santa's elves—but she'd thought her entire life had fallen apart four days ago. Now she had been literally shown that all kinds of things could very easily go from bad to worse...and worse seemed survivable. Meaning she had more strength of character than she had given herself credit for.

She would survive this break-up. And the heartbreak, such as it was. And, more to the point, the shame.

She might not have shed her last tear, and would very likely never enjoy Christmas again, but that was something she was prepared to live with. Particularly when the clouds had cleared just enough for her to begin to appreciate the little things so much more than she had.

Like hot chocolate.

She grinned at the memory.

Last night, while she'd been in the shower, Cooper had made her a mug of hot chocolate despite the fact she'd said she didn't want to put him to the trouble. He'd slipped it onto her bedside table with a note and an alarm clock set for this morning.

It had been a kind gesture. One that had made her feel more welcome than she'd ever imagined feeling here. She'd gone on to sleep like a baby under all those dreamy quilts, and in the morning had woken up feeling cared for and protected in a way she hadn't felt since her father had died.

Family. That was what it had felt like. Being cared for by someone who understood the importance of being part of something bigger than yourself.

'You all right, Audrey?'

She looked up to see Cooper staring at her oddly. Somewhere amid his packing efforts he'd swirled a thick strand of silver tinsel round his neck. It gave him an air of carefree joy, whilst everything else about him was solid, focused male energy.

That increasingly familiar spray of heat blossomed in her belly as their eyes met and held. She wasn't about to tell him she was having an epiphany that a mug of hot chocolate could prove that there was still good in the world, so she gave him a neutral smile and carried on working, thinking that maybe—just maybe—she might have a tiny bit of room in her heart for Christmas after all.

An hour later they'd relocated to the pleasant church hall. It was a large, wood-floored, stone-walled room that could easily be divided into four smaller rooms with the portable partitions the church used for Sunday school and the like. There were also many boxes overflowing with animal costumes marked NATIVITY! DO NOT TOUCH!

By the time they'd set up, had a thorough run through the patient roster with Dr Anstruther and gone out to start their rounds, the sun still hadn't risen. But the Christmas lights twinkled away, strung as they were across the High Street and all the way up to the castle ruins, and, of course, so did the enormous Christmas tree. Quite a few lights were appearing in the High Street shops, too, indicating that the island of Bourtree was coming to life.

Cooper's phone started ringing just as they climbed into the big medical four-by-four. From what Audrey could glean, a hysterical mother had reached her wits' end with her teenager, who was refusing to go to school. Again.

Cooper spoke to her in his reassuringly steady brogue. 'Right, that's fine, Helen. We'll be over just as soon as we've made one other call on the way. No, no. It won't take long. You'll get to work on time, so stay where you are. Audrey and I— Audrey's the locum district nurse, remember? Noreen's off to Australia to see her grandbaby.'

There was a pause while Cooper listened.

'Yes. She's exactly the sort of person you'd want to talk with Cayley, okay? Listen. Put the kettle on. Make yourself a cuppa and we'll be there soon. Audrey and I will help you through, okay?'

Wow… Rafael had always made Audrey feel insecure about her choice to be a district nurse—to the point where she'd actually changed jobs. Cooper made her feel she was at the top of her game. It was an incredible feeling. Having someone who barely knew her honour the professional choice she'd always known deep in her heart was the right one for her.

'Thanks for that,' she said, before she could stop herself.

'What?'

'Speaking highly of me. Professionally, I mean.'

His brows arrowed towards his nose. 'Why wouldn't I? You're great at what you do.'

'It's just that—'

She stopped herself. Telling him that she'd allowed her fiancé to belittle her professionally was a bit too raw a confession right now.

'I jumped down your throat yesterday and…well, it's nice to know you noticed me. Because—I mean—you're really good at *your* job, and it means a lot to know that you think I'm good. I mean workwise… Obviously.' Heat began to creep into her cheeks. 'I think I'll just stop talking now.'

How embarrassing. She might as well have said, *I fancy you, but I don't want to, plus it means more than I can say that you think I'm good at my job.*

His look intensified for a moment, and then, as if he'd come to a conclusion, he looked away and turned the key in the ignition.

A few awkward moments later Audrey noticed something. 'No Santa outfit today?'

He flashed her one of those enigmatic smiles of his and gave the tinsel around his neck a flick. After he'd pulled the car out onto the main road, he dug in his pocket and pulled out the Santa hat. 'I thought I'd give Christmas more like just a nod today. Save my cool threads for the proper lead-up.'

Audrey swallowed back a comment about him changing his tune rather quickly, because the truth was that somewhere beneath that smile of his was a man grieving for his grandmother. A woman he clearly missed with all his heart. To be honest, Audrey was beginning to think the whole costume thing had been more to cheer him up than the patients they were seeing.

'I hope I didn't put you off,' Audrey said. 'I know I was pretty grumpy about the elf costume.'

She hadn't meant to be a party pooper... It was just that yesterday she'd been feeling emotionally bruised and vulnerable. Funny how fewer than twenty-four hours on this island had given her some much-needed space to breathe. Space, she was beginning to realise, Rafael had never given her.

'You weren't grumpy,' he said amiably, turning the car onto the coastal road that circumnavigated the island. Then, 'Maybe a little...'

'I'm sorry,' she said, more heartfelt than before. 'It really wasn't anything personal.' Not personal to him, anyway.

'No bother,' he said distractedly.

He pulled the car off onto a small, vaguely familiar lane and after a few minutes Audrey realised they were back at Jimmy Tarbot's.

They checked his insulin levels and gave him his injection, and Audrey was in the kitchen, making him a cup of tea before they left, when Cooper popped in, his medical gloves still on, and had a quick nosy in Jimmy's bin.

Rather than point out that it looked as if he was taking a page out of her book, she asked, 'What are you looking for?'

'Evidence,' he said, jiggling his eyebrows in a TV detective sort of way.

'Of what?'

'The tomato soup and salad he told me he had for his tea last night.' With a grim expression he lifted out an empty family-sized box of lasagne and an equally empty tub of double chocolate caramel ice cream. 'Not happy,' he said, peeling off his gloves and popping them into the disposal bag in his medical kit. 'He was also asking after my gran's biscuits.'

Audrey frowned. 'Is that a euphemism for something?'

Cooper cracked a smile and shook his head. 'No. My gran—Gertie—had this tradition of making endless amounts of biscuits around Christmas time. She'd bring them to folk, especially the ones who were housebound, so suffice it to say Jimmy's had a fair few through the years. She always made him a special batch—low sugar, or something like that.' He gave his jaw a scrub. 'She'd know what to do to get Jimmy out and about. Better than giving him a lecture and rooting about in his bin, anyway.'

Something squeezed tight in Audrey's chest. Cooper looked genuinely invested in Jimmy's welfare. As if he had to pick up where his grandmother had left off and pour kindness into a community that sometimes struggled to stay afloat.

Cooper abruptly clapped his hands together, then gave Audrey a cheeky grin. 'I might have an idea.'

Cooper headed back into the lounge, where Jimmy seemed to reside permanently on the sofa. The duvet stuffed behind it suggested he might even sleep there.

'Hey, Jim!'

Audrey didn't actively earwig, but she caught a few things. Something about getting his next injection down at the church. And if Jimmy needed someone to come here and help him to get up and out of the house that'd be fine.

She turned on the tap to wash her hands and missed the end.

Cooper came back in and shouldered the medical run-bag. 'All right?'

'Yes, indeed.' They left and went to the car. 'So,' she asked, 'are we picking up Jimmy later?'

Cooper nodded, his eyes on the rear-view mirror as he reversed the car out onto the road. 'Aye. I think he's becoming a bit too reclusive for his own good.'

'And you think a trip to the church hall would help?'

'I think knowing the islanders don't mean any harm by still calling him Big Jim would do him good.' He shot her a quick smile. 'And I've got an idea.'

'Plan to share?'

'No.' He shook his head, a mischievous twinkle lighting up his eyes as he said, 'Not just yet.'

Audrey laughed. 'Okay, mystery man. Who's next?'

Ten minutes later, as they stood in the hall of their next patient's home, the light mood they'd been enjoying in the car had evaporated. Cayley, Helen's thirteen-year-old daughter, was refusing for the third day in a row to go to school, and this time wasn't even bothering to make up a fake illness. That was the part that had her mother worried.

It wasn't the kind of call they'd normally make as part of rounds, but Audrey had seen, when Cooper had taken Helen's call that morning there had been something about it that had made him say yes instantly.

'I simply don't know what to do.' Helen twirled her hair into a swift French twist, though it was still wet from the shower. 'She won't get out of bed. Keeps crying and saying she won't go to school again. Ever. She's only thirteen! That's no way to spend a childhood.'

Cooper gave Audrey a look, then returned his focus to Helen. 'I'm happy to talk to her, but if it's a sensitive issue…you know…' He swallowed uncomfortably.

Audrey was pretty sure where he was going with this, and found it a little bit adorable that a hardened A&E doctor should have trouble alluding to feminine matters. Maybe it was the fact he'd gone to school with Helen that did it? Who knew? He was a hard one to read, Cooper.

'Maybe she wants to talk about female issues?' Audrey gently finished for him.

'Which would be a talk much better had with you, Audrey.'

Cooper gave her a quick nod that managed to speak volumes. He wasn't feeling uncomfortable about 'female issues'. He was simply being considerate of his patient, and he was letting her take the lead. This would, after all, be the kind of call she'd be doing on her own in a week's time, unless the situation warranted two people.

Which begged the question…what would Cooper be doing? Leaving for Glasgow? That wouldn't be… Well, she didn't know what she felt about that, so it was probably best to go back to the 'live in the here and now' remit she'd assigned herself.

She forced herself to tune back into what he was saying.

'Audrey'll most likely suss it, but if she finds she needs prescriptions, or anything, I'll be happy to step in.'

Again, Audrey experienced a warm hit of gratitude. Cooper's belief in her abilities gave her a morale boost she hadn't known she needed. Sure, the whole rest of her life was a calamity, but her nursing skill—the one thing she'd always honoured about herself—was being given respect.

Why had being a district nurse never been good enough for her ex…? *Pfft.* Another question for another time.

'Will I go in with you?' the worried mum asked.

'Absolutely,' Audrey said, but then, after a second, thought it best to ask, 'Or do you think there's anything she'd be nervous about saying in front of you?'

'Not at all,' Helen said. 'That's why I'm so worried. Cayley and I have always been close. We've never kept secrets from one another.'

'Then let's go and find out what this is about,' Audrey said, giving her a reassuring smile.

Helen put a hand on her arm before they headed up to the bedroom. 'You should probably know that her father and I are no longer together. Not for a few months now.'

'Okay.'

Helen's grip tightened on Audrey's arm and her eyes darted towards Cooper. 'Brian, my ex, was often away on the oil rigs, and suffice it to say he played away as well. I've tried to keep the gossip away from Cayley, but it's a small island, so…'

She didn't need to finish the sentence. Audrey had been working in a small hospital when her wedding plans had imploded, and the last thing she'd wanted to do was face

the other nurses when news had spread like wildfire that
the wedding was off.

'Right you are. Well, let's go in and have a chat, shall
we?'

Keeping the memories at bay was proving difficult, so
Cooper did what he imagined Audrey would do. Popped
the kettle on.

He stared out of Helen's kitchen window. She lived a
couple of streets back from Bourtree High Street in a small
but cosy terraced house. Two up, two down. A brightly
painted front door. A small garden where she could peg
out the laundry in the summer and keep a wood pile in
the winter.

For as long as he could remember, Bourtree Castle folk
had always liked to say they never needed nowt beyond a
home like this to have a nice life. His parents hadn't been
able to hold on even to that. Their bill down at the pub had
always kept the dream of a home of their own out of reach.
So they'd all crammed into his gran's house.

And when they'd hit that sharp bend down at the far
end of the island and forgotten to turn the car along with
it...well...

He turned as he heard Cayley's muted voice through
the ceiling, pitching and peaking as she presumably explained why she wouldn't leave her room. Whatever she
was going through, it was hitting her hard.

Cooper had three mugs of sweet tea ready to go by the
time the women came out. Audrey had her arm around
Helen's shoulders, and she gave her a proper, reassuring
hug before turning her around to accept the mug Cooper
held out for her.

'Everything okay?' he asked, when no one said anything.

Audrey and Helen exchanged a quick look. Then

through an unspoken agreement Audrey began to explain. 'The children at school have been picking on her.'

An acrid taste rose in Cooper's throat. Kids could be great, but they could also be bloody cruel. 'What about?'

'She has a crush on a lad in the class above her and he already has a girlfriend.'

Cooper looked between the pair of them. 'Kids get crushes on people who aren't available all the time. Why give Cayley a hard time about it?'

'The girlfriend—' Audrey began, then backtracked. 'Bear in mind we're talking about twelve and thirteen-year-olds here—raging hormones, first loves—'

'That early?' Cooper asked before he could stop himself.

He'd been so busy having fights behind the bike shed with the bullies who'd taunted him about his parents he'd not had time to worry about falling in love. To be honest, he wasn't entirely sure he'd ever made the time.

Yes, he'd had girlfriends. Here and in Glasgow. But he was pretty sure something all his exes would agree on if—God forbid—they ever got together and had a chinwag about him, was the fact that he'd never invested enough time in any of them. He'd cared about them—of course. But had he ever made a one hundred percent emotional investment? Nope. Getting too close to people meant disappointing them in the end. That or discovering they never wanted you in the first place.

Loving someone with all his heart only led to pain. His grandmother being the latest case in point.

'Whether or not it's true love isn't the point,' Audrey said, with a bit more bite than he would've expected.

'Okay. So, what *is* the point?'

'The bullying. They're saying she's been cheating with the boy when she hasn't. And they're saying she's—' Audrey threw an apologetic look in Helen's direction. 'They're saying she's her father's daughter.'

Ah. The penny dropped. 'They're bullying her about something she has no power over?'

Audrey nodded, her brow crinkling as their eyes met. His heart strained against his ribcage as he looked into her eyes. She wasn't looking *at* him. She was looking directly *into* him. Into everything that had made him the man he was today—including the young Coop emerging from behind the bike sheds, wiping away the blood before the teachers saw. And the boy rearranging his features to look as though he didn't have a care in the world when all he wanted was parents who had his corner. Who loved him.

'So, what are your thoughts?' he asked, his voice a bit rougher than usual.

Audrey lowered her voice after a quick look back towards the stairwell. 'I think she could probably do with a week or so off school. It's been going on for some time, and she's become very anxious. She's lost weight…isn't sleeping well. It'd be best to do something before she's properly unwell—'

Helen interjected. 'I know I should've kept a closer eye on her, but I've had to do double shifts to get some money in for Christmas, since we're not getting any from her father.'

'What?' Cooper only just managed to contain a blast of rage. 'Brian isn't paying his maintenance costs?'

Helen shook her head. 'We've not even got through the divorce proceedings yet. I'm so behind on everything, I—' Her face screwed up tight and the tears began to flow. 'I've been trying so hard not to have anything else in Cayley's life change, but with the mortgage and the bills and Christmas coming, I guess I've let it all get on top of me.'

'Brian should be sending you money whether or not a

judge has decreed it,' Cooper said. Unable to stop himself, he barrelled on. 'A man has a child—he needs to accept responsibility. Not leave someone else to sort out the pain at being rejected.'

The words were out before he could stop them. So much for keeping his cards close to his chest.

Both women fell into a thoughtful silence.

Damn.

It wasn't like him to put a knife to his own chest and bare all. He yanked the tinsel from around his neck and stuffed it in his pocket. 'Apologies, ladies. Topic's a bit too close to the bone.'

'I know, Coop,' Helen said gently, throwing a quick glance in Audrey's direction before continuing, 'And we're all so proud of you. The man you've become despite everything.'

Again he felt that flare of fury. And this time it was coupled with the heat of Audrey's inquisitive gaze.

Terrific. Now there was yet another person added to the list of people who would judge him because of his past. His parents' reputation as the island's drunks would always be a yoke round his neck. It was why he'd left. Why he'd found it hard to return despite how much he loved his gran.

That loyalty speech he'd given worked both ways. She'd sacrificed a lot for him. Raised two sets of children when she should've only had to raise one. It had been her turn to be looked after, but he'd found the memories too painful. Doubly so when he considered how badly trying to outrun them had panned out.

He shoved the thought into a dark corner.

'Are there any counselling services here on the island?' Audrey asked, tactfully turning things back to where their attention should be: on Cayley.

Cooper gave her a grateful nod. He could've done with

someone like Audrey to talk with back in the day. Or a counsellor. Anyone to take the burden off his gran.

Her method had been to set him to a task. An unchopped wood pile being the most frequent chore. Or a job down at the Puffin, scrubbing pots. Loading boxes at the woollen mill. Burning off his rage had worked for him. Mostly. Talking probably would've taken care of the rest, but of all the things he and his gran hadn't done it was talk. As if acknowledging just how badly things had gone with his parents would have shattered them both.

He quickly flicked through the list of resources he kept on his phone. 'There's someone at the school. I'll give her a ring and see if she can pop over here in her lunch hour and have a chat. There's also a specialist who comes over once a fortnight, so long as the weather's all right for the ferry.'

'That sounds great,' said Helen. 'I just—I want to help her. Take away the pain. But—I feel like this is partly my fault. That there's something I must've done to drive Brian away, you know?' Helen wiped away a fresh wash of tears with a tissue Audrey handed her.

Helen's admission drove a stake into Cooper's heart. It had never once occurred to him that his grandmother might've been carrying the burden of guilt all those years. That the reason she'd never pushed him to come back was the sorrow she'd felt that her son had treated his children so badly.

It doubled the love he felt for her in an instant. Love he wished like hell he'd shared with her. More proof, if he needed any, that he wasn't fit to love anyone properly. Not with his broken bag of emotional tools.

'Hey, shush…' Audrey gave Helen a hug. 'You're doing the best you can in a bad situation.'

Helen blew her nose again and did her best to put on a brave face. 'I'm really sorry, but I've got to get to work.

The counselling sounds good…but once a fortnight doesn't sound all that brilliant. Do you think that's enough?'

'It's early days yet,' Audrey soothed. 'It sounds like the local counsellor is a good resource. If you add a talk or two with the specialist to that, you could probably avoid putting her on medication,' Audrey said.

Helen's eyes widened. 'Do you think she'll need that?'

Cooper shook his head when Audrey sent him a questioning look. 'I've not seen her, obviously. But I trust Audrey's judgement. If she's up for a wee chat with me now, I can do a quick exam to officially sign her off school.'

Helen made a frustrated noise in her throat. 'I hate to think of her missing all her classwork. I know she's struggling with maths as it is.'

'I can help her,' Cooper said.

Helen gave him a suspicious look. 'Aye, that's nice, Coop, but I'd really rather have someone who's…you know…going to stick around for a while. She's had so much change already.'

Cooper wanted to protest. Say his plan was to stay for good this time. But something stopped him. Something that felt an awful lot like the truth.

He wanted to stay here. Wanted to make up for all those weeks and months—years, really—he'd stayed away when he should've been here with his gran, giving her that loving payback she'd so very much deserved.

An angry, orphaned teenager had probably been the last thing she'd wanted. His parents had died just as she'd retired, and he, more than anyone, knew how much she'd wanted to travel the world. But she hadn't. She'd stayed right here in Bourtree to look after him. And then he'd buggered off to Glasgow to seek his own fortune.

He might not be able to help his grandmother any more, but he could help Cayley.

'I'll do it, Helen.'

Audrey looked up from the paperwork she'd been filling out as if something in his voice had caught her attention. His desire to make good on a promise, no doubt.

From the smile appearing on her lips, it seemed she respected a man who made good on his word. But before he could get off track, wondering who or what had let Audrey down, his phone buzzed. It was Dr Anstruther, sending along the details for another house call to tack onto their list.

'Okay. So that's settled. Shall I have a word with Cayley to see how we stand?'

Audrey opened her mouth to say something, then clamped it shut, waving away his questioning look. 'You go on.'

A few minutes later he was drawing his talk with Cayley to a close. The poor girl was obviously stricken with an intense case of anxiety.

He'd seen far too many doctors write out prescriptions as a first response, but he hated to put children on medication, preferring to see if he could build a support system around them instead. Obviously in extreme cases he'd do whatever was necessary, but he could see little glimmers of hope for Cayley, and felt reassured that being around supportive people might help her.

His secondary role as maths tutor would be a handy way of ensuring she was getting on all right. And the fact she'd already opened up to Audrey was a good sign. Even if she hadn't said more than a few words, sometimes giving the body's nervous system a bit of a rest was the best way to make a change.

'So, you think you're up for talking to someone a couple of times a week?'

Cayley nodded shyly, her eyes not meeting his. 'Is Audrey free? Maybe she could talk with me instead of Miss MacIntyre or…?'

Cooper laughed. 'You mean instead of me?' Luckily, he didn't take this stuff personally.

Cayley nodded again, her brown eyes peeping up at him through her thick fringe. Bless. He didn't blame her. If he was having trouble the last person he'd want to talk to was—well…anyone, really. Saying that, he too could easily imagine sharing things he'd kept locked in his emotional black box with Audrey. Which was weird. Because if there was one thing he was not, it was a sharer. Maybe, just like Cayley, he needed someone in his life who would listen—and, more to the point, someone who wouldn't judge.

'Audrey's here for a few weeks, but I'm afraid she's going to be busy with her district nursing work.'

'And you?'

'I'll be around.' It was as close as he could come to a long-term commitment right now.

A silence fell between them.

Oh, hell.

'Look, Miss MacIntyre's free for a chat this afternoon if you like. And I'll be seeing you a couple times a week to go through your maths homework while you're off school. I'll also see about an appointment with the specialist counsellor who comes over from Glasgow. The main thing is we want you to know you've got a team of people around you. All here to listen.'

Cayley's mouth screwed up in the same tight moue her mother's had when she was about to cry.

'Hey, now, Cayley. Easy there, pet. I know things have been rough, but we're getting you help.'

The tears came. Desperation kicked in. He was used to lads straight in from bar brawls, not weeping tweens. Weeping tweens who were going through some remarkably familiar childhood trauma. He'd bashed through it with his fists and an axe. Cayley was too fragile to go that route. And, to be honest, it wasn't a route he'd recommend.

'Look. I'll have a word and see if Audrey'll pop in when she can, all right? She's just not a counsellor, that's all. I thought someone who's used to speaking to children who've been through what you have might be a bit more useful.'

'But Audrey *does* understand about broken hearts!' she cried. 'Her fiancé cheated on her just like Dad cheated on Mum.'

Wait a minute. What?

Oh, hell. The poor woman. While the knowledge gave him little solace, it certainly gave him added insight. And a strange feeling of camaraderie.

So it wasn't just him who hit the road when the going got tough. He'd bundled all his sorrow and rage into a machine-like focus to become the best A&E doctor he could. Helping people and then disappearing out of their lives. Audrey was only just figuring out how to process the pain. Poor lass. It definitely explained why a London girl had appeared out here in the middle of nowhere just a few weeks before Christmas. It might also explain her aversion to Santa. Not that there was an obvious way to connect the dots on that one, but…

Cayley wove her fingers together under her chin. 'I was hoping she might be able to help me. You know…teach me how to take control of my own destiny like she did after her engagement broke up.'

'I see,' Cooper said, trying to appear as if the news wasn't brand-spanking-new to him.

Audrey had been *engaged*? As mad as it seemed, he already hated the guy. And that was without knowing a thing about him. Once he did he was pretty sure he'd dislike him even more. Audrey was a woman to love. To cherish.

'I'll have a word with her. See if perhaps the two of you can have a hot chocolate or something.'

Cayley's eyes brightened. 'Seriously? You'd do that?'

'I'll ask her, sure. But no promises. Okay?'

'Okay.' Cayley solemnly nodded. 'Thank you.'

'You're very welcome, young lady. I'll ring your mum later on today, but in the meantime you rest up and take care of yourself—all right?'

She gave him a grateful smile and nestled back under her duvet, her eyes already half closed as the comfort of knowing help was at hand eased her into much-needed sleep.

As he wrapped things up with Cayley's mum, Cooper had more questions than answers occupying his mind—and most of them were about Audrey.

CHAPTER FIVE

AUDREY CLIMBED DOWN from the big four-by-four, stretched and shivered. The heating system in the car was still faulty and it had been a long day. Rewarding, but long. She knew that instead of the patient roster being 'a bunch of geriatrics needing their bedding changed'—as her ex had liked to describe her patients—there was a huge variety of reasons patients were unable to get to a doctor.

What had struck her most was the disappointment from the patients they'd also seen yesterday that Cooper wasn't dressed up as Santa again. Maybe she should've dialled back her grumpiness. It wasn't as if everyone else needed to be miserable because she was. And…to be honest…now that she was away from her life in London, she was beginning to see how blinkered she had become.

Wedding plans. Getting herself on high-profile surgical rosters so she could impress Rafael. Making sure she didn't embarrass Rafael at any of the seasonal soirées they'd been invited to…

There had been an awful lot of energy devoted to pleasing Rafael. Her father had often told her that loving someone meant celebrating the person you were, not changing who you were to fit someone else's plans. Why hadn't she remembered that when Rafael had opened that telltale blue box?

Cooper had been in an equally reflective mood in the car. Something told her his silence stemmed from what Helen had said about the islanders being proud of Cooper becoming the man he was 'despite everything'.

Despite what?

He definitely had issues with his father. That much was clear. He despised bullies—which spoke well of him as a man—and he honoured the responsibilities that came with being a parent. He hadn't really mentioned his mum. But he'd clearly adored his grandmother.

Audrey would've been better off falling in love with someone like him than Rafael.

Er... *What?*

Falling in love with *anyone* was strictly off-limits right now—especially Cooper. Work wasn't off-limits. She could think about that. And Cooper only professionally. *Obviously.*

Earlier in the afternoon Cooper had actually managed to convince Jimmy Tarbot to leave his house and come to the church hall for his insulin check and injection. There, more to her surprise, Jimmy had been cornered by an earnest-looking man with some questions about lighting for the Nativity.

She'd caught a glance of complicity passing between Cooper and the man as Jimmy had launched into a detailed explanation about the inner workings of the lighting system. A shared smile at a job well done. When Cooper had caught her questioning look he'd muttered something about Jimmy being on the stage management team at school.

In the car, he'd withdrawn into the brooding silence he sometimes cloaked himself in when they weren't with patients. Now they were about to get something to eat at the Puffin Inn. Maybe she should just ask him.

Yeah, right. And then maybe she should pour her heart

out to him about how she'd just been through the most confidence-crushing experience of her entire life. About as likely as her voluntarily jumping into the elf's costume still hanging in the back of the car.

'I've been thinking,' Cooper said as he came round to the front of the Jeep.

'Oh?' Audrey said warily. Hopefully mind-reading wasn't one of his skills.

'About Cayley.'

Ah. Good. She could talk about their patients all day if he wanted. She, too, had been worrying about the poor girl. 'Did you hear from the child psychologist over in Glasgow?'

He shook his head. 'Nah. It's crazy over there this time of year. I probably won't hear for a day or two unless I pull some strings.' He caught her gaze, then added, as if she was checking his professionalism, 'Which I might if she doesn't improve over the next couple of days. But I was thinking more along the lines of getting her out of the house while she's off school.'

Audrey rubbed her hands together and pointed towards the pub. Being somewhere warm to have this conversation was definitely going to help her brain work a bit better. 'I thought she had schoolwork to do?'

'She does,' Cooper said. 'But what kid do you know who can fill an entire day with schoolwork at home?'

Audrey threw him a smile. 'None.'

'Exactly.' He pulled open the door to the Puffin's entryway. The foyer was already filled with winter coats and a few pairs of work boots. 'I was thinking maybe we could get her down here.'

'What? The pub?'

He shook his head. 'No. Although having a job probably wouldn't be a bad idea either. It'd give her a sense of pride. Of accomplishment.'

Audrey nodded, adding yet another square to the Cooper quilt. It sounded as though he'd once done the same thing.

'I was thinking more of getting her down to the church hall.'

'Why? So Dr Anstruther can keep an eye on her?'

Cooper threw a wave in the direction of the evergreen-swagged bar, where a man and a woman were busy pulling pints for a row of men in ferry uniforms. He called out to them that they'd be eating dinner and would get drinks in a minute.

'I was thinking more of getting her a job on the Nativity. The fact that Dr Anstruther would be there is a bonus,' he admitted. 'And a helpful precautionary measure. He's known her since she was a baby. Either way, I'm sure they could do with an extra pair of hands, seeing as half the island are needing costumes.'

Audrey laughed. 'If I didn't know better, I would think you have some sort of vested interest in the Nativity.'

Something dark flashed through his eyes. *Ouch.* Looked as if she was back on touchy territory. Best to let him fill in the blanks.

As they silently worked their way across the thick wooden floor, worn with age, towards a table near the inglenook fireplace, Audrey noted the dip and then the rise of hushed murmurs as they passed the bar. A memory of the islanders taking bets on Cooper's staying power came back to her. Could that be what they were talking about? His lack of Santa suit could definitely sway things in the 'leave' direction.

Cooper strode on as if he'd heard and seen nothing.

The pub, clearly a good two or three hundred years

old, managed to have a solid, spacious feeling about it. It was just over half full, and conversation, now that it had returned to normal, was buzzing, but not overloud. The mismatched chairs had sheepskin throws or wool blankets on them, and if Audrey wasn't mistaken she was pretty certain that the ferry men sitting at the bar were in their stockinged feet.

It felt as warm and welcoming as the church hall did. Apart, of course, from the whispering.

Cooper held a chair out for her as if he'd been doing it for years. Ridiculous, she knew, but she blushed. When her ex had done it, it had felt showy. As if he wanted the whole world to know what a gentleman he was, rather than being simply content to do something kind for his fiancée.

For Cooper, being considerate seemed second nature. His grandmother? Or that heart of gold she suspected was lurking beneath the gruff exterior he was now sporting?

'We should have a word with the woman in charge of costumes,' Cooper said, pointing out the chalkboard menu on the wall as he did.

'What makes you think it's a woman?' Audrey teased, trying to lighten the atmosphere.

'It's always been a woman,' Cooper said, his eyes scanning the drinks menu he'd pulled out from between the salt and pepper shakers.

She bristled. How was she meant to know who was in charge of Nativity costumes on an island five hundred miles away from her home? Former home, anyway. Her indignation grew. Cooper was acting as if Audrey should know it was the natural order of things. Men on lights. Women on costumes.

Heart surgeons cheated. Nurses discovered their fiancés didn't really care if the wedding was on or off.

Unable to stop herself, she fuzzed her lips and rolled her eyes. 'Typical male.'

'Oh?' Cooper countered, a hint of a smile playing upon his lips. 'There's such a thing as a "typical male"? Who is this "typical" heterogametic, then?'

Audrey froze for a minute, then flopped back against the fluffy sheepskin on her chair. It was a good question, actually. One to which she didn't have an instant answer. A few days ago she'd wanted to believe they were all like her ex. It had made travelling the high road by herself a bit easier. But…even though Cooper was all sorts of shades of grey…she could tell he was more light than darkness.

'Fine. You got me. I'm trying to tar you all with the same brush.'

'It's a dangerous way to go through life.'

Though the smile remained in place, his voice was weighted with warning. He clearly felt he'd been tarred with too broad a brush at some juncture.

'Do you mean presuming everyone's the same?'

'Exactly.'

The light in his eyes could've been from the fire, but Audrey was pretty certain they were lit from within.

A woman wearing a Puffin Inn apron bustled up to their table. 'Can I get you two anything to drink? A lovely bottle of seasonal red to share between you—? Oh! Cooper. Hi, there. Sorry. I didn't…um… I'm ever so sorry about your gran. I was at the funeral, but I had to get back here after, and as there wasn't a wake—'

'No bother,' Cooper cut in, giving her a curt nod before looking at Audrey. 'Wine? Soft drink?'

'Hot chocolate,' she said.

'What? With your food?' The woman laughed, then gave Cooper a scolding look. 'Have you not got the heating system working in that Jeep yet? Dr Anstruther told me it was on the blink a few weeks back.'

Cooper shook his head, but offered no explanation.

'Bring it down to my Billy's place and he'll get it working for you in no time.'

Cooper glanced at her sharply.

'Cooper,' the woman said gently, 'he's not the same lad you knew back then. He's a father now. A husband. He's changed a lot.'

Cooper made an indecipherable noise, then said brightly, 'I'll have a Coke, if that's all right. Audrey? Do you know what you'd like to eat?'

'I can recommend the chicken and mushroom pie,' the woman said to Audrey. 'It's actually Cooper's gran's recipe. Absolutely brilliant. Isn't it, Coop? Gertie's chicken and mushroom pie. You must be half made of it, you ate it so much as a lad.'

Cooper kept his eyes fixed to the menu chalkboard and said nothing.

Audrey gave the woman a smile, then said, 'I'll have the pie. It sounds great.'

Cooper briskly asked for steak and chips, looked at Audrey, and then, clearly dissatisfied with his behaviour, reached out and touched the woman's arm before she left. 'Thanks, Fiona. I'll give Billy a ring tomorrow, okay?'

Fiona gave him a smile and a nod, then said their meals would be just a few minutes.

After she'd gone a silence fell over the table, until their drinks were brought over by a young man. 'Here ya are, Coop. Nice to see you back in the Puffin. Mum says to tell you the offer still stands.'

Cooper lifted his chin in acknowledgement, then raised his pint glass to the woman behind the bar. 'I'll let her know, son. Ta.'

'So?' Audrey said after she'd taken a sip of her hot chocolate. 'Are you going to tell me?'

'Tell you what?'

'About all these mysterious conversations.'

He opened his mouth, clearly about to shut her down, then took a swig of his drink and looked her in the eye. 'I've got what you might call a chequered past here on Bourtree.'

'In what way?'

'Just about every way you could imagine.'

'What? Were you the town ruffian?'

'Nope.' He shook his head and took another drink. 'Billy was.'

'What? Nice Billy who's married to our waitress?'

'He used to beat the proverbial hell out of me back in the day,' Cooper said.

You could see the admission was a big one. No man liked to admit they'd been at the wrong end of a fist.

'I'm so sorry, Coop.'

'Don't be.'

'But I don't understand why—'

He cut her off. 'My parents were the island drunks. When you were their kid no one let you forget about the footsteps you were going to follow in.'

'You don't have a drink problem.'

'No. It's the one thing I have to thank them for. I've known first-hand for a long time what alcohol dependency does to a person.' Cooper took another gulp of his soft drink, ran his fingers through his thick hair, then looked her straight in the eye. 'You want the whole story?'

'Only if you want to tell it.'

Her answer clearly caught him by surprise, and that surprise softened him. Took away a layer of the defensiveness he was cloaked in. Enough so that he began to talk.

'My parents should never have been parents...' he began.

He went on to tell her about their romance at school. Swift, fiery, culminating in a pregnancy—his sister Shona.

'They thought it sounded "fun" to have a baby or two, and then figured out it was more responsibility than fun, so they basically dumped us on my gran. She was my dad's mother, and she said she'd be damned if she'd see the bairns of her son be neglected.'

'What about your mum's parents?'

'They kicked her out when they found out she was pregnant. They'd never had much time for her anyway.'

'In what way?'

He lifted an imaginary bottle of wine and glugged it down.

'Oh.'

'Exactly. They moved to Glasgow years back. Before I was born. More pubs to choose from.'

'So, did you grow up living with your gran or your parents?'

'Both. Sort of. My parents never had enough money to have a place of their own so we all lived at my gran's. When they were around.'

'What do you mean?'

'There wasn't much work for them on the island—not with their reputations. They came back every now and again, when they got their hands on some cash.'

'So...where are they now?'

'Dead.'

The hot chocolate churned uncomfortably round Audrey's stomach. 'I'm sorry.'

'Don't be.' He sounded as if he meant it. 'They'd come back for my thirteenth birthday and left as soon as the candles went out on the cake Gran had made me. They got hammered, went for a drive around the island, forgot to turn on the bend where the island ends and—splash—they ended up in the sea.'

'Oh, Cooper.' Audrey covered her mouth with her hands.

'Honestly, Audrey…' Cooper waved his hand between them, as if he'd just told her he'd ripped his favourite shirt but had bought a new one, so it was fine. 'I've moved on. It's not the problem.'

Audrey stayed silent.

'I owe everything I am today to my grandmother.' His mouth quirked into a crooked smile. 'The good parts, anyway.'

'You must miss her.'

His expression darkened. 'I don't deserve to.'

'Why not? You obviously loved her very much.'

'I didn't show it.'

She and her father had never been hugely demonstrative. It had been more…built in. A given.

'Sometimes love is something you just know. It doesn't need big showy gestures.'

Big showy gestures like the ones Rafael had been prone to. Funny how she only now realised the huge bouquets of flowers and flashy outfits he had had delivered to her at work had always made her squirm rather than make her feel genuinely cherished.

'Audrey…' Cooper reached across and took both of her hands in his, as if he was imploring her to truly hear what he was saying. 'I wasn't here when Gran died. She told me she was sick. I told her she'd be fine, that she was tough as old boots, and then took another double shift. Then another. I told her I'd come on the weekend. Then I didn't. That's what I've done for the past fifteen years—constantly telling her I'd be there for her and not making good on my word. This time I well and truly failed her and there is nothing I can do to make up for it.'

Oh.

'I should've been on the next ferry out of Glasgow.'

'You weren't to know.'

'I knew her cold had turned into a cough. I knew she was eighty. I knew it was winter. I knew I had a hospital full of elderly folk suffering from "wee colds" that had turned into pneumonia—which, in some cases, would kill them.'

Cooper pulled his hands away from Audrey's. The warm comfort of them was more than he deserved. 'Nothing you say can absolve me. I left the one woman who properly cared for me to die alone.'

'Is that what happened?'

Shards of unbearable pain lanced through his chest. 'Yes.' It was the first time he'd admitted it out loud. 'Dr Anstruther had been checking in on her once a day. As had a couple of neighbours.'

'Had she rung them?'

'No, I had.'

'So you were looking after her the best you could. It sounds as though you were needed at the hospital.'

'Audrey. You're not getting it.' His voice thickened with emotion, but he ploughed on, punctuating each of his sentences with a sound rap on the table with his fist. 'I was needed here. My gran died by herself. There was no one holding her hand. No one making her breathing any easier. No one to tell her how much they appreciated the sacrifices she'd made. Telling her how very much she was lo—'

He cut himself off as a lorry's worth of emotion bashed him in the chest. Crying over his biggest mistake in life wasn't going to bring his grandmother back. Nothing would.

'She may have had a gruff demeanour, but she was the heart of this island. There are signs of her everywhere.'

As if on cue, a beautiful piece of chicken and mushroom pie arrived and was slid in front of Audrey. It was a generous portion, covered in golden pastry. Tiny mushroom-shaped pastry pieces floated in a glossy gravy that pooled around a fluffy mountain of mashed potato. Exactly the way she'd served it to him countless times as a boy. It had been his absolute favourite dish.

In contrast, Cooper's plate was simply what it said on the tin. A steak and some chips. His should've looked the better dish. A more expensive cut of meat. Golden, crunchy, perfectly made chips. A small piece of parsley on top. But somehow the meal he'd chosen didn't come close to matching the lashings of generosity and love he automatically endowed the chicken pie with.

'Want some?' Audrey asked, loading a mouthful of the gravy-rich pie onto her fork.

'No, don't worry.'

'Go on,' she urged, moving the fork towards his lips. 'I think you've earned it.'

He didn't know why, but deep in his heart he knew Audrey wasn't telling him he'd done a good day's work. She was saying that, despite his flaws, she admired him. That somehow, despite everything, his grandmother had understood he'd been running away from his demons, not from her.

Eyes connected to Audrey's, he accepted the pie. As he did so something pure and intense passed between them. Something vital that gave him the first kernel of belief that one day he might be able to forgive himself. Make some proper changes in his life. Starting with a show of gratitude for the woman who'd raised him.

As if reading his mind, Audrey asked, 'Did you plan on having a wake some day?'

'That's what Fiona was on about. The wake. They offered to let me have it here.'

'A wake is for the other people who loved her. It sounds as though there'd be quite a showing.'

'I don't know... I just wouldn't want it to turn morose. She would've hated people weeping and bemoaning her loss.' She would've set them all to work if that sort of carry-on began. The thought made him smile. Almost.

Audrey gave a half-shrug. 'My parents have both passed away and I found that their wakes were an amazing way to remember all the good things.'

He flinched. His parents' wake had been a disaster. Barely anyone had shown up. It had been him and his gran and a pile of sandwiches no one ate, plus a few neighbours who had popped in more for his gran than for him.

The fact they could've killed someone else as easily as they'd killed themselves had riled the islanders. If ever there was a group of people who looked after one another it was the people of Bourtree. Okay, but it wasn't as if everyone here was sainted. People were people. Some were kind, some less so, and—

He looked across the pub and saw Fiona greeting her husband Billy as he doled out waves and handshakes to the lads at the bar. He said something and they all laughed. Years back the same boys would've hunched over their pints and hoped he wouldn't notice them.

Cooper added 'ability to change' to the list of attributes a human could possess. Even him. But it had to come from inside. Not from a Santa suit.

'Want some more?' Audrey looked down at her plate, then coloured, realising she'd eaten the whole thing.

'Sorry.' She winced, her shoulders creeping up to her ears as she did so.

Cooper smiled, resisting the urge to run a finger along her jawline. There was something about her that got to him. In a good way. Sure, she'd come off the ferry all bristly and elf-resistant...but he could see how meeting a stubble-faced doctor in a Santa suit who dipped in and out of a good mood would've appeared pretty strange. Especially considering she was suffering her own piece of heartache.

He was tempted to ask her about it, but thought it would feel too much like trying to even out the 'bad luck story' playing field.

His phone buzzed in his pocket. 'Sorry.' He held up the phone. 'Work.'

Finlay Anstruther was on the line. The elderly doctor was busy attending an infant with a troubling cough, and he ran him through the facts of a potential emergency and asked if Cooper could attend it.

'Absolutely. We'll be there in two minutes.' He hung up the phone. 'Sorry, we've got to go. Suspected heart attack.'

Audrey was up and out of her seat straight away. They pulled on their jackets, and when Fiona rushed up to see if everything was okay she told them not to worry about the bill—they would sort it out later.

When they got outside, Cooper ran to the Jeep, grabbed the run-bag and the portable AED, shouldered them, then asked, 'Are you up for a wee run? Watch yourself—it's icy.'

Without waiting for a response, he held out his hand to Audrey and began to jog.

A couple of minutes later they arrived at a grey stone building down at the far end of the High Street. It had a bright green door and a colourful Christmas wreath hung around the polished brass knocker. Before they could knock, the door was opened by a distraught woman in her fifties.

'Oh, thank God, Cooper. James is in the lounge.'

Cooper entered, introducing Audrey as he did so. 'Is he still conscious?'

'Aye,' she said, leading them down the corridor. 'He's barely able to move, though. He's clutching his chest, complaining of a terrible pain.'

'Have you rung the emergency services, Karen?'

'Aye, but they say the helicopter's out at one of the other islands and taking him across on the ferry would be—'

Cooper silently finished the sentence. It would be too late.

They entered a large, comfortable-looking lounge at the centre of which was a huge Christmas tree that must've been almost three metres high. Lying on the floor next to it was a very pale middle-aged man with an impressive pot belly.

Cooper dropped to his knees and unshouldered the run-bag, aware that Audrey knelt on the opposite side of him, preparing the AED. The fact James was conscious was a sign this might be a false alarm.

'All right, there, James?'

'Been better, Coop. Sorry about your gran.'

'Aye, well…it's you we're worried about tonight.'

'Cooper?' Audrey had opened the run-bag and found some GTN spray as well as aspirin.

'Thanks, Audrey.' He took the medication, asked James's wife for a glass of water, then returned his focus to James. 'Can you tell me how you're feeling right now?'

'The pain's not so strong now. It was, though. Thought I was on my way to the pearly gates.'

'Hopefully that's some time away yet,' Cooper said, aware that you could never make promises of longevity.

He'd called too many times of death in the A&E to think otherwise. 'Shall we get some of these cushions under you to make you a bit more comfortable. Audrey…?'

Without being instructed she deftly put a sofa cushion underneath James's knees and a smaller one under his head.

'Are you taking anything for angina or your heart?'

'No, Coop.' His eyes flicked to the doorway, where his wife was just returning with the water. 'It felt like I was being kicked in the chest with a steel-toed boot. I was up there trying to put the star on the tree. I could barely breathe. Even my jaw felt pain. If Karen hadn't noticed me going white, we could've added concussion to the list.'

'So, you've been decorating your tree, have you?'

'Aye. Up and down the ladder I don't know how many times. Karen likes it just so, and you know the saying…'

Cooper shook his head, heartened that James was able to speak without pausing to get his breath.

'Happy wife…happy life.'

'That's a good saying, James. So…' He took a look at the huge tree. 'How often would you say you do this level of exercise? Going up and down a ladder like that.'

James huffed out a weak laugh. 'Once a year.'

'Have you experienced anything like this before?'

'Aye,' James conceded, and his wife let out a small gasp. 'Only every now and again, love. Usually when we're at a ceilidh or some such. Not the best time to cause a fuss, and it always passes.'

'Fair enough, but bear in mind that not saying anything could have some serious consequences.'

Still in the doorway, Karen asked, 'Is he having a heart attack? Don't you need to use the defibrillator or something?'

Cooper shook his head. 'I don't think so, Karen. We

only use the AED for two reasons. One is for folk suffering from ventricular fibrillation. If your James was enduring that, he'd not be conscious. The other is ventricular tachycardia. Basically, his heart would be beating too fast to get blood to all the right places.'

'I think he's saying I wouldn't be jabbering on like I am, love,' James said weakly.

Karen nodded. 'So…?'

Cooper looked at his watch. 'It's been about twenty minutes since you first experienced the chest pain, yes?'

James nodded.

'My educated guess is that you're having a pretty intense angina attack, brought about by physical exertion.'

Karen gasped. 'You mean this is *my* fault?'

'No one's saying that, but short, sharp bursts of exercise when you're not accustomed to it can highlight underlying heart trouble.'

'Like a disease?'

Cooper saw Audrey start to speak, then stop herself. He sat back on his heels and nodded for her to go ahead. She was one half of his team. There was no reason why she shouldn't explain it.

The smile he received in return hit him straight in the chest. She showed a level of gratitude for being 'given the floor' that didn't seem right. As if she was used to having her opinion doubted. Crazy, considering she was clearly very good at her job. More so when you took into account the fact she'd worked in one of London's premier paediatric hospitals.

He was lucky to have her. Doubly so, considering he'd all but poured out his entire life history to her. Something he hadn't done with a single one of his girlfriends back in Glasgow.

The word 'girlfriend' got stuck on a loop in his head.

He wondered what sort of girlfriend Audrey was. And, more to the point, what sort of boyfriend would've let her go. A fool, no doubt. Just as he'd be foolish even to think of going there. She was leaving. And he was— Well, he didn't know what he was doing, and the last person on earth a heartbroken nurse needed was him.

'Angina isn't a disease,' Audrey explained to the married couple. 'It can definitely feel like a heart attack, but the pain is actually a reaction to a lack of oxygen-rich blood to the heart.'

'Which he had because he was climbing up the ladder?' asked Karen.

Audrey nodded. 'If you're not used to it, yes. That sort of exertion can provoke an angina attack.'

'How do we stop it? Should he be on bed rest?'

Audrey shook her head and gave Cooper a quick glance. He nodded that she should carry on.

'It's best to get a proper diagnosis. We'll take full notes of what happened tonight and perhaps you should...um... Cooper? What's the protocol here?'

'You'll need to make an appointment at one of the hospitals in Glasgow.'

'Can't you do it?' Karen begged.

'We can do some of the tests. It's what they call a lifestyle assessment. Blood pressure, cholesterol levels, your BMI, your waist size...'

'Ach, Cooper, don't... I know I've eaten one or two extra pieces of pie over the years, but I've done all right.'

Karen sent them imploring looks. 'This is his favourite time of the year. Could he start a diet after Hogmanay, like everyone else?'

'Sounds like Cooper's saying I might be heading into the New Year in a coffin if I did that, love.'

'Whoa!' Cooper waved his hands between them.

'There's no need to head in that direction just yet. How about we go the hospital route? Get a series of checks? Maybe do a little Christmas shopping over in Glasgow?'

'What can they do that Dr Anstruther can't?' Karen asked suspiciously.

Cooper tried to hide a hit of frustration. Why were islanders so dubious about mainland hospitals? They did amazing work there. Saved thousands of lives. More.

Audrey jumped into the silence. 'An electrocardiogram. A coronary angiography...' She ticked off a couple more tests that would help them understand what had happened today. 'Those tests could help save your life.'

Karen burst into tears. 'Oh, James. Forgive me. I'll never ask you to decorate the tree again.'

Audrey hid a smile and Cooper tried his best to do the same. 'It's looking pretty good now,' he said.

They wrote down a few notes, then suggested a daily aspirin to create easier blood flow through the heart's arteries in case they were narrowed.

'Ring straight away if you experience any pain again,' Cooper told James.

After a few more assurances they left the house.

'Good work in there,' Cooper said.

'Just doing my job,' Audrey said, but he could see the compliment had hit its mark. She began to hum a little tune.

'Hey. Is that a Christmas carol you're humming?'

She stopped instantly. 'Oh, my gosh. It is.'

'That's not a bad thing, you know. As they say, 'tis the season.'

She pulled a face. 'For most people. Not so much for me.'

Cooper took a risk. 'Does this have anything to do with the heartbreak you told Cayley you were busy healing?'

Audrey winced. 'She told you that?'

'Sorry. Doctor-patient confidentiality doesn't seem to work the other way around. At least not when you need it to. Want to talk about it?'

Audrey waited until Cooper had opened up the back of the Jeep and swung the run-bag in to answer. 'Maybe…'

He gave her a nod. 'Zip up that warm coat of yours. I know the perfect place for a confidential talk. Jump in.'

CHAPTER SIX

'WHERE ARE YOU taking me?' Audrey wasn't nervous exactly, but... Okay, maybe a little.

'Here,' Cooper said, pulling off the coastal route to a viewing point at the north end of the island. He parked the vehicle so that it faced the sea.

'Dark out tonight,' Audrey said, looking for the moon and finding only the tiniest of slivers.

'Perfect.'

'For what?' She poked Cooper in the arm. 'What's with the aura of mystery?'

'You'll see.' Cooper smiled, undid his seatbelt and leant on the steering wheel to peer up at the sky. 'No light pollution up here. I imagine it's all Christmas lights and dazzle down in London.'

Audrey's nerve-endings crackled. 'Pretty much.'

'Ex-boyfriend in London, too?' Cooper asked.

His eyes were still on the sky which, now that she looked, Audrey could see was alight with stars. The incredible beauty of it took the edge off admitting, 'Ex-fiancé.'

'Ah.'

'I found him rocking an elf by the Christmas tree after a Christmas party hop.'

He gave her a rueful smile. 'That explains why you weren't keen to wear the elf costume.'

'Yup!'

She dug into her coat pockets and pulled out her gloves. As she worked each finger into place, she told him the rest. They'd been due to be married on Christmas Eve. She'd been stupid enough to insist upon paying for the wedding. Now she was jobless, and homeless—apart from this locum post and a room in his gran's house for the duration!

'You lived together?' he asked.

She nodded. 'I'd just sold my parents' house. Well…my house after my dad passed. Someone else's house now. I'd moved in with Rafael two weeks earlier.'

For the first time she felt a proper burst of anger.

'He didn't even let me unpack my personal knick-knacks. Said the flat was fine as it was. What kind of person does that? And what kind of idiot doesn't take it as a massive warning sign that things aren't going well? Maybe I knew all along. Maybe I wasn't unpacking things because there was a part of me that knew none of it was meant to be. Or maybe I'm reading too much into it. You haven't exactly changed your grandmother's place around…'

Cooper gave her a soft smile. 'I'm not changing my grandmother's place because I want to preserve what I can't have any more.'

Audrey's breath caught and constricted in her throat. 'Do you think that's what Rafael was doing? Preserving what he thought he couldn't have any more?'

Cooper shrugged. 'I wouldn't presume to guess, but the fact he cheated so quickly does suggest his heart wasn't in it.'

'But he's the one who proposed! We'd only been dating for three months!' Audrey yanked her voice down from screeching fury to simmering rage. 'He's the one who wined and dined me. The one who convinced me to leave my job and work in paediatrics. I couldn't really believe any of it was happening, to be perfectly honest. It felt…surreal.'

When what it should have felt like was a dream come true.

'So…' Cooper turned to face her, his expression not filled with pity, as she'd feared, more with empathy. 'Does that mean somewhere in your heart you knew it wasn't right?'

'No!' Audrey spat, and then, as if she was a newly filled balloon someone had forgotten to tie off, she deflated against the car seat. 'Yes. Maybe… I don't know. He was so different from the men I normally dated. Not that there were dozens of them or anything.'

'Different in what way?'

'Dashing. Rich. Famous.'

'A surgeon?'

'Yes.' She said his surname.

Cooper let out a low whistle.

'See? I told you.'

'Well…' Cooper looked back out to the stars. 'I don't know if this is going to make you feel any better, but the words you use to describe him aren't the words I would use.'

'Why? What would you use?'

'Arrogant. Opportunist. Lothario.' He took a breath and held it for a moment, as if debating whether or not to say the final part. 'In search of a British passport.'

Audrey's blood ran cold. 'What?'

'Look…' Cooper put up his hands. 'I don't know the guy from Adam, but I do know his reputation. We get patients who demand the best, and from what I hear your man there is an incredible heart surgeon. But he also *breaks* hearts.'

'Well, yeah. Obviously,' Audrey huffed.

'I'm talking about back in Argentina.'

'How do you know anything about Argentinian heart surgeons?'

He looked out to the sky again, grabbed a cloth from the car door pocket and rubbed the windscreen clear. 'Six degrees of separation, I guess.'

'What?' Now Audrey was getting properly confused.

'I went to a conference on emergency medicine a few months back.'

'So?'

'In Argentina.'

'Ah.'

'Your man—'

'He's not my man,' she snapped.

'Right you are. Apologies. Mr de Leon was there and, as such, so was the rumour mill. I didn't pay any attention to it at the time because, as you know, I know how harmful gossip can be.'

'What was it?'

'You're sure you want to know?'

'If it will help me understand why he did what he did, then go for it. Tell me everything.'

Cooper nodded. 'Over there he worked at the country's most exclusive hospital. His patients were politicians, film stars, Argentina's equivalent of royalty.'

'He's not up for malpractice, is he?'

'No,' Cooper said, and then quickly explained. 'He didn't only have access to his patients, according to those who worked with him. It seems he also had regular access to wives while their husbands were recovering in hospital. One of those wives turned out to be married to someone pretty high up in the government. A man who could make a medical licence disappear if he wanted to.'

Each of Cooper's words was like a little dagger in her heart. She had been conned.

She barely recognised her own voice as she asked, 'So he came to the UK to get citizenship in case his world crashed over there?'

'Looks like it. He definitely didn't lose his licence, because the UK is strict on that. But his reputation with women isn't nearly as golden as his surgical reputation. I know it's painful, but I hope it makes what he did seem less personal.'

It made her feel like a proper idiot—that was what it did. 'You must think I am the most naïve person to walk the earth.'

'Not at all,' Cooper said, with an intensity that made her look up and meet his eyes. 'You were conned by an expert.'

'It just feels so…' she sought the right word and could only come up with '…icky.'

'I know.'

'How?' Audrey barked a mirthless laugh. 'How on earth can you know?'

He pulled off his woollen hat and gave his head a scrub before tugging it back on. 'I suppose because I've been a bit of a conman myself.'

'How do you mean?'

'I told my grandmother that I'd be back to see her countless times. That I loved her.'

'Cooper. You obviously loved her. Anyone can see that.'

'But I didn't make good on my word. Having her die the way she did, alone, made me take a really hard look in the mirror.'

'And what you saw was Santa?'

They both stared at one another and then, unexpectedly, began to laugh. Proper belly laughs that carried on for ages—until all of a sudden Cooper looked out of the window and said, 'Quick! Get out.'

He leapt out of the car with such urgency Audrey followed suit.

'Here.' Cooper beckoned to her. 'Come and have a look.'

He held his arm out and, when she approached, put it around her shoulders then tugged her close to him, as if he'd been doing it for years. He pointed up to the skies and there, dancing in the heavens, were the most beautiful, celestial lights she'd ever seen. Greens, reds, golds. The colours of Christmas.

'It's the aurora borealis,' he explained, his arm still round her shoulders as if it belonged there.

It felt so nice she had to resist the urge to snuggle into him. Wrap her arms round his waist. Which was just plain wrong, considering she'd vowed not even to *think* about a man, let alone cuddle up to one until she got herself back to being the Audrey she respected.

A moment's weakness, she told herself. She'd just poured her heart out to him. And the fact he didn't think she was pathetic for falling for such a duplicitous conman had touched her. That and the fact she was drawn to him. To a man who understood what it felt like to love and lose and then wonder how on earth to get up again.

'The Vikings thought the northern lights were a reflection of the Valkyries' armour as they went into battle,' Cooper said, his blue eyes still trained on the heavens.

'Sounds scary.'

Cooper gave a little shrug. 'Apparently dying in battle was a great honour.'

Audrey snorted. 'I'd prefer to delay that honour for quite some time, thank you very much.'

'Now, that sounds like a woman who is taking charge of her own life,' he said.

A bloom of hope swirled round her heart. 'You think?'

'Absolutely.' Cooper looked down at her, his expression shifting. 'Do you want my honest opinion?'

Not it if involved kissing. His lips were so close…

She was staring at them as she said, 'I think I'm going to get it, whether or not I want it.'

He gave a good-natured laugh. 'Fair enough. I was thinking that for someone who's endured a broken engagement so recently…you seem more angry than heartbroken. Are you sure you were properly in love with the guy? Perhaps it was more—and don't take this the wrong way, because I'm not judging you—that you might've been in love with the *idea* of him?'

It was a good point.

She'd been so swept off her feet she'd barely had time to think these past few months. She'd had boyfriends before, but they'd never showered her with so many gifts and sweet nothings. With beautiful bouquets of flowers that had blinded her to the truth. Flowers wilted. Sweet nothings were exactly that. And that fancy flat he'd asked her to move into hadn't been a home.

Not like Cooper's gran's house was, anyway. Gertie's home gave an instant sense of comfort and healing.

Why had she fallen for such artifice? It wasn't like her. Not at all.

Had it been the promise of a family? An identity? Or the promise of being loved as much as her father had clearly loved her mother. The mother she'd never really known.

She thought back to those final days with her father. His insistence that Audrey must never settle for second best when it came to love. Never, ever compromise who she was, because true love didn't mean losing yourself. It meant becoming a better version of yourself than you'd ever believed possible.

She'd sure messed that up.

She looked up to the skies and thought of those ancient warriors heading off to battle. It was an interesting way to see the mesmeric whorls and flashes of colour. Proud and strong instead of fleeting and inaccessible.

Perhaps instead of writing her story as that of a wronged woman fleeing a humiliating situation, she owed herself a different version. Sure, she'd left with tears streaking her cheeks and remarkably little to her name, but she still had her name. Her nursing skills. Enough pride to get herself a job, a place to stay and to make a vow never to let herself be hurt that way again.

She'd already helped some of the people here on Bourtree Castle through the type of nursing she loved. And, although living with Cooper hadn't been part of the plan, in a way it was good to have someone else there. Surprise hot chocolate in bed was far better than sobbing herself to sleep at night.

Two wounded warriors seeking a new life…

A gust of arctic wind blew in from the sea. Audrey shivered. Cooper pulled her in a bit closer to him. She turned towards him, and as if by unspoken agreement he turned to her.

As their eyes met a heated pulse of electricity flashed between them and grew taut.

Cooper was very good-looking. More so than she'd initially given him credit for, given the whole Santa suit thing and…

Oh…wait a minute. Was he…?

Cooper was tipping his head towards hers. Audrey's heart began to pound. Was he going to kiss her?

The sound of blood rushing through her nervous system drowned out the sound of the waves as he reached out and tucked a stray tendril of her pixie cut behind her ear. Her skin felt as though it had been brushed by the same light that coloured the skies. Their bodies shifted slightly. They were aligning themselves so that...yes...their heads could ease into place for what surely had to be a kiss.

Did she want this? Her body seemed to. Did her heart?

Her brain made a loud, plaintive cry that travelled straight to her gut. What did her heart know? It had fallen for a complete idiot. A liar. A Christmas romance was not the wisest way to embark on her new life...whatever that might be. If this kiss happened, it would definitely be a rebound kiss.

She looked deep into Cooper's eyes for a sign. Something—anything—to say that whatever was happening between them was genuine. She didn't see promises, but she saw kindness and respect. Two things she now knew for certain hadn't existed in her last relationship.

He shifted so that one of his hands spread across the centre of her back and the second slid along her waist. They were standing closer than they ever had before. So close she could feel his warm breath upon her mouth. Feel the pounding of his heartrate as it matched her accelerated pulse. Her lips parted, her body all but making the decision for her.

At the last minute, just as her lips began to physically ache for his touch, for the completion of a kiss, he dropped his arms from around her and took hold of her hand. Together, silently, they leant back against the big Jeep, her heart still pounding.

It was the right decision. One Cooper had been strong enough to make for both of them. It was a strength she'd have to develop if she didn't want her life to come crashing down around her again. She wasn't staying here. Cooper might be. He might not be. He didn't know.

They watched the lights weave and wend their way

through the heavens with a new powerful energy coursing between the pair of them. As if the mesmeric lights had stamped an indelible mark on her and Cooper, uniting them for ever in this one magic moment. A moment of power. A moment of possibility.

'Right!' Cooper clapped his hands together and gave them a rub as they finished washing and putting away their supper dishes. 'How do you feel about gingerbread men?'

Audrey flopped down onto a cushioned kitchen chair with a grin. 'If you're offering to give me a plate of them with a huge mug of tea I'm all for 'em. I'm pooped.'

'Not surprised. It's been a busy couple of weeks.'

Audrey swept her fingers through her pixie cut, leaving a couple of locks of dark hair sticking out in adorably errant revolt. 'Is it always this busy on the island?'

Cooper gave a little shrug. 'To be honest, I'm not really sure. I know the islands struggle in general, but Dr Anstruther's been here for ever. As has Noreen, to be fair. The two of them are public health battle axes. Undeterrable. Who knows? Maybe now that we're around, more folk are calling in.'

Audrey made a hard to decipher noise. 'Difficult shoes to fill. Dr Anstruther's, anyway. I take it Noreen is coming back?'

'Oh, aye. Unless this whole grandmother thing pulls her to Australia permanently she'll be here for years yet. She's one of those women who claims she'll retire when she's dead.'

'It'll be a lot of work for her, with Doc A retiring.'

It would be a lot of work for a new doctor, too. But that wasn't the problem. The job of an island doctor wasn't just a full-time GP role. It was more... It was a calling. Community service. Above and beyond the regular oath of a doctor to do no harm. It was *being there* when people needed you most.

Not his forte.

But could it be? It wasn't as if anyone had pushed him behind the bike shed since his return. Taken a pop at him for having parents who didn't make the grade. Quite the opposite. He'd been welcomed with open arms. Arms he'd spent a lifetime telling himself he didn't deserve to be embraced by.

He slammed the door shut on those thoughts and did what he did best: focused on the here and now.

He gave Audrey a grin. 'All of which is precisely why we need a good biscuit fix.'

Audrey laughed and toed off her ankle boots. 'And where exactly is this magic plate of restorative biscuits going to appear from? Down the chimney?'

Cooper gave his eyebrows an impish jig. 'Me. And you. If you want to give me a hand?'

Audrey gave him a sidelong look.

A couple of weeks ago he would've caught a healthy dose of scepticism in those chocolatey brown eyes of hers. Today the look was more impish. Playful. Not as heated as that moment they'd shared beneath the aurora borealis, but he caught glimmers of that now and again—just as he was sure she saw glimmers of what was clearly a shared attraction in his own eyes.

Yes, things between the two of them had been...*interesting* since that night. And by 'interesting' he meant two weeks of loaded looks and his bloodstream lighting up like a Christmas tree every time their hands brushed—with or without gloves—and lots of weird throat-clearing when their eyes locked over some shared commonality only for them to remember they were in front of patients who needed their assistance.

'What are you actually talking about, Coop?'

He smiled.

That was another thing. Somehow over the past fort-night he'd become Coop, rather than Cooper. Dr Anstruther had become Dr A. And their regular patients, if they were happy with it, were also referred to by nicknames.

In short, Audrey had been accepted by the islanders with open arms. No more suspicious, 'Where's Noreen?' when she came in. It was smiles and hugs and promises to pass on information about how to make Helen's Scottish Tablet or Mr Gibbon's black pudding bonbons. The fact they'd even had to make supper tonight had been a change. Most of their patients were so busy plying them with sea-sonal nibbles they came home stuffed and ready for bed.

Another awkward time. They were always loitering at the bottom of the stairs, reminding each other of 'just one last thing' before yawns and fatigue finally forced them to their own rooms.

Cooper reached into a cabinet and pulled out a home-made scrap book. Inside were the recipes that had liter-ally made him the man he was today. He placed it on the table in front of Audrey.

He could tell Audrey was aware that the book was pre-cious to him. She wiped her hands on a tea towel, gave him a wide-eyed look and then, hands aloft over the thick coloured cardboard cover, asked, 'May I?'

'Please.' He nodded at the book, which had his grand-mother's script all over it except for the cover, where she'd used stencils: *Gertie's Good Eats*, it read. And they cer-tainly were.

He pulled out the chair next to Audrey and sat down.

'Are these all of your grandmother's recipes?'

'That they are.'

Audrey made a low *ooh* noise, then asked, 'The chicken pie is in here?'

Cooper nodded.

'Want to make it one night?'

He sucked in a sharp breath and Audrey instantly fell over herself apologising. 'Sorry. I shouldn't push. I know we've talked about her a bit…but it still must be hard. Living here. Seeing signs of her every day but not actually seeing *her*.'

Cooper nodded. 'It is. Sometimes I can't bear it. But I hate that I wasn't with her at the end even more.'

Audrey gave his hand a squeeze but said nothing. What could she say? He'd messed up one of those things you should get right. The only thing he could change now was himself.

He looked at Audrey as she began to flip through the pages. *She would be worth changing for.* He checked the thought. Change came from within and had to be composed of purity of intent. Otherwise… Well, you'd end up where Audrey was. Seeking solace from a romance that had been a mirage.

Was that what this was to him? A romance? *No*… Was it?

He definitely enjoyed their verbal sparring. And the way they'd worked together as a team pretty much from the start. She had the guts to stand up to him. The courage to press her patients for the truth. She was firm but fair. Like his gran. She was incredibly beautiful. And also very vulnerable. She deserved someone with a solid foundation. Someone who came from a good family with kind, warm hearts. Not a man who problem-solved by moving away from things that troubled him instead of facing them head-on. Owning his mistakes like a man.

Or was that what this was? Working here on Bourtree?

Owning his mistakes... Was this him working towards being the type of man a woman like Audrey could love?

Ach. Too intense. They were meant to be making biscuits.

He clapped his hands together. 'I thought we'd pick up one of Gran's traditions so that the islanders know that we—that I—well, that some of Gertie's traditions are still alive and well.'

'And you're talking about gingerbread men?'

'Aye. And snowballs and chocolate crinkle biscuits and jammy stars and—'

Audrey started laughing and waving her hands. 'Wait a minute. I don't know about you, but I'm not much of a baker. Wouldn't we be better off going down to the bakery and buying them?'

'Absolutely not. Homemade is the only way when you're a MacAskill.'

'Er... Cooper? I hate to point out the obvious, but... I'm not a MacAskill.'

Her tone was light, but when their eyes met their gazes held with a magnetic tension.

She could be. Of all the women he'd known, Audrey was the strongest contender. But he wasn't ready. Might never be.

For her sake he broke the eye contact. She deserved better.

'Ach,' he said, with a dramatic sweep of his hand. 'You're living here. Consider yourself an honorary MacAskill.'

Something lit up in her eyes that he couldn't quite identify, but it felt positive. As if being an honorary MacAskill worked for her. For now, anyway.

Cooper pushed his chair back onto its back legs and

gave her a faux shocked grin. 'So… Are you up for putting a bit of flour and butter together for the islanders?'

'And sugar and baking soda and who knows what else?' Audrey shot back, her voice bubbling with laughter.

'That's what Gertie's recipe book is for. To guide us along the way.'

She'd promised it to him years back. Said that when she was gone it would keep him well fed. On the straight and narrow.

'So…' Audrey shot him a cheeky grin. 'I suppose you're going to tell me you grew up making these biscuits every year and you're an expert?'

The smile dropped from his lips. No. He hadn't. It was one of an increasing bouquet of regrets jammed into his conscience.

His gran had used these biscuits to lure him out of his room after he'd been teased about his parents being pulled over by the police for being drunk and disorderly. To bribe him to come out in the car with her as she took plate after plate of Christmas treats to 'folk less fortunate' when his father had been fired from yet another job. She'd even made them out of season for the entire week between his parents' dying and the funeral.

A funeral, he had to remind himself, that had been for her son and her daughter-in-law. She must've been in deep mourning herself, and all the time she'd risen above her own sorrow to tend to his.

He'd never forget what she'd said as they lowered his father's casket into the ground. She'd taken Cooper's hand in hers, fixed him with a steely gaze and said, 'I'll get it right with you, son. I've made my mistakes. Now let's see if I can get it right.'

'Hey…' Audrey gave his leg a tap, her voice reflecting

his change in mood, and then picked up the book. 'Let's try. What's the worst that could happen?'

His becoming everything his grandmother had feared. Lonely, angry, furious at the world for being dealt a poor hand.

He looked down at the book, at his gran's scrawling penmanship, and saw nothing but love and dedication in each page. In each addendum to a measurement. Each little note scribbled on the margin.

Double vanilla if baking for Coop!

He'd change. He'd dig down to his very essence and become the man his grandmother had believed he could be.

Two hours later, Audrey and Cooper had discovered that they were both pretty terrible in the baking department. Regardless, making the biscuits together had lifted the gloomy atmosphere and elevated it to something bright and optimistic.

Now Audrey was lifting a deformed snowman—or was it a reindeer—?to her mouth as Cooper watched. 'You're brave.'

'We'll see just how brave in a minute.' She took a bite, chewed, and then smiled. 'Well, they look horrible, but they taste amazing.'

Cooper nodded and grinned. 'Maybe we should've chilled the dough overnight, as the recipe recommended.'

They both looked down at the handwritten note alongside the typewritten recipe that said, *Do not ignore!*

Audrey wiped her hands again, then began flipping through the pages. 'Maybe we can find an easier one.'

'One that suits the brain power of an A&E doc and a super-nurse?'

Audrey smiled up at him, the compliment clearly hitting its mark. He liked making her feel good. Bringing a smile to her lips. There was something…something inherently *honest* about who she was.

When he let himself think about how badly she'd been treated it made his blood boil. But, though they didn't talk about it too much, he got the sense that Audrey was well and truly prepared to leave the past where it was and do her best to move on. Perhaps he should take a page out of her book.

'This sounds good,' Audrey said, pointing to a recipe for Scottish Rarebit. 'What makes it Scottish?'

Cooper laughed. 'You know how Gran liked mustard more than just about anything?'

She crinkled her brow, then brightened. 'Oh, yes. You said it was in the chicken and mushroom pie, didn't you?'

'Yup. That's French mustard. The main difference between Welsh rarebit and Gran's is an extra wallop of the strong stuff.'

'Mustard?'

'Her own special homemade mustard.'

He tapped the side of his nose, then went to a cupboard, pulling out one of three jars that still remained. It'd be a tough day when he hit the last one.

Audrey read the label and laughed. 'This sounds like it'd put hairs on your chest.'

He cracked the lid open and took a spoon from the cutlery drawer. 'Care to find out?'

'What?' Audrey giggled. 'See if Gertie's Blow-Your-Socks-Off Whisky Mustard puts hairs on my chest? I don't know if I'm brave enough.'

The flirty atmosphere that had been dancing around them for the past couple of weeks ratcheted up a notch.

'You're brave enough,' Cooper said, meaning it. 'You shouldn't doubt yourself. Ever.'

A glint of pride lightened her dark eyes.

It felt good to know he'd put it there.

Not many women could leap from district nursing to a high-stakes paediatric hospital and then slip straight back into district nursing without so much as a blink of an eye.

If he'd met her at the hospital he would've asked her out. He also would've been guaranteed to mess up the relationship. Adding yet another woman to the list of girlfriends he'd disappointed. Perhaps that was why he'd met her now. When he was straddling the fault lines of the path he'd been walking. He could either let himself fall into the abyss or shore up his reserves and leap to solid ground.

'Do you really think so?' Audrey's gaze softened, but still held his.

The energy crackling between them intensified.

'It put hairs on *my* chest.' His voice dropped a notch and the space between them somehow closed. 'The mustard,' he added, for only one reason. To stop himself from kissing Audrey right this very moment.

'I think that's probably a good reason for me not to try it,' Audrey said, her voice barely a whisper.

Cooper put down the jar and cupped Audrey's beautiful face in his hands. He of all people should know that time was precious. 'I want to kiss you.'

Her breath caught in her throat. Cooper could feel her pulse accelerating beneath his touch.

She nodded.

'Is that all right?'

She nodded again.

When their lips met it was as if the rest of the world slipped away. Gravity, time, place…they all disappeared.

And in their place was touch, scent and an all-encompassing warmth.

Their light kiss deepened. Heat, energy, intention. Three elements of a kiss that all but melted them together. She tasted of cinnamon and cloves. Of the crisp island air. She smelt of nutmeg and oranges. For the rest of his life he knew those things would be evocative of Audrey.

As he pulled her closer to him, her hands slipped between them and took purchase on his chest. But she wasn't pushing him away. She was feeling the pounding of his heart as it bashed against his ribcage.

'Where do you see this going?' she asked, her lips moving against his.

'I—' He didn't know. 'My plan was to stay here. Take over from Dr Anstruther.'

'Was…?'

'Is.'

And at this exact moment it felt like the truth. He wanted it to be his truth. Would staying right the wrongs of his past? It would only work if it was well and truly what he wanted to do.

She blinked a few times. 'Have you told him that?'

'Not strictly speaking.'

She pulled back. 'Which means…no, you haven't told him?'

Cooper nodded. 'There hasn't been the right time.'

'He's retiring on Christmas Eve, Cooper. The island won't have a doctor.'

Fifteen years of defensiveness flew up to protect him. He fought against it. 'I know. There's an island a bit further down the coast that lost their doctor three years back and they've yet to replace him.'

'But you're not there. And stringing everyone along isn't exactly helping, is it?'

'I'm not stringing anyone along.'

'Well, why not call Dr Anstruther right now and tell him you want the job?'

And therein lay the problem. He would only make that call when he knew he could give the islanders one hundred per cent follow-through.

He missed the A&E. Missed the buzz of it. But already he knew he'd also miss practising medicine on the island. It was making him a better doctor. Having the time to talk and listen to his patients, properly made a real difference.

But there was a very real possibility the only reason he was loving it was because of Audrey. It was a moment in time—just like one of those snow globes you shook up and watched until the magic came to an end. Audrey had arrived when he'd needed some outside perspective, but she would be leaving. No-nonsense Noreen would be back in the new year. Dr Anstruther would leave. As would Audrey.

And then what? Was a life here without her what he wanted? Was a life *with* her—anywhere—what he wanted?

He brushed her hair back from her forehead and dropped a kiss on it. 'I know I don't want to hurt you. But as for the rest of my life… The honest answer is I don't know.'

'Me neither,' she said sadly. 'A rebound for me? A way to move beyond grief for you? Not exactly an ideal love-match.'

Their eyes met again, their arms tangling loosely round each other's waist… Each of them was no doubt thinking, *Is that what this is? A love-match?*

'Want a hot chocolate?' he asked, instead of probing deeper.

She nodded. 'And then I think we'd probably better pretend this didn't happen.'

'You sure?' It hurt to hear her take the practical tack…
but it also made sense.

'No… But it's not going anywhere, Coop. So what's
the point?'

'Temporary pleasure?' Even as he spoke, he knew it
was the wrong thing to say.

'I'll get my temporary pleasure from the hot chocolate,
thank you very much.'

'You're a wise woman.'

As she turned around he barely heard her, but just
caught the whispered words…

I hope so.

CHAPTER SEVEN

'So, YOU THINK that's something you might be interested in, dearie?'

Dr Anstruther's wife, Emily, glanced over Audrey's shoulder as if the pair of them were having a top-secret conversation and sharing MI6 information. For Bourtree, Audrey supposed it was.

Audrey was thrilled to bits they'd thought of her—but, hearing a certain Scottish brogue in her head talking about islanders not taking to change, she asked, 'You're absolutely sure it won't put anyone's nose out of joint?' And by 'anyone' she meant Cooper.

'Not at all. And the costume would fit you perfectly.'

Audrey looked at it again and had to agree. Not that anyone would know it was her, but... 'It would be my pleasure.'

She meant it, too. She'd only been here a few weeks, and already she felt more a member of this community than she had at her own home in London. Maybe she and her father had been too much of a self-contained unit after her mum's death. Too frightened to branch out and, in her father's case, love again in case they were blindsided by another devastating loss.

She hoped she wasn't doing that by being here. Teaching herself to close herself off to possibility. To love.

She thought of the kisses she and Cooper had shared, that she had stopped by demanding to know where he thought things were heading. How would he know? It was one kiss. How could she know? She wouldn't have a job in less than a fortnight. How could anyone know anything?

She smiled at the older woman next to her, about to sell her home of forty-seven years and move to Cornwall 'just to see what excitement lurks on the other tip of Great Britain'. She should take a page out of her book. Seize the day. Seize days that didn't include Argentinian fiancés with a penchant for fancy wine and slinky elf costumes.

Emily adjusted herself so that she was standing by Audrey's side. The two of them took in the hustle and bustle of the large church hall.

'Amazing to think all this chaos will be transformed into the Nativity in fewer than forty-eight hours.' Emily shook her head in disbelief, but the glint of pride in her eyes suggested she knew it would happen.

Audrey grinned. It was pandemonium. Hammers were clanging nails into place, groups of children were off in opposing corners of the hall singing entirely different songs. A man was trying to guide a donkey away from a table that held a dazzling display of Christmas biscuits…not hers and Cooper's, it had to be said.

'Is it normally this…um…?' Audrey tried to find a word for mayhem that sounded nice.

'Chaotic?' Emily filled in for her with a smile. 'Yes. Every year. Although there usually aren't so many people.'

'No?'

'Well, as Cooper may have told you, his grandmother Gertie was the driving force behind the Nativity. Those biscuits of hers had a lot to answer for.'

Audrey had gleaned as much—more from the patients than from Cooper, who only talked about his grandmother in stilted intervals. She got it. It had taken her ages to tell a story about her dad after he'd passed away without bursting into tears.

'You two make quite the team.' Emily gave Audrey's arm a pat.

Audrey's brow crinkled. Did she know about the kiss? Cautiously, she asked, 'In what way?'

Emily pointed across the hall to where Jimmy Tarbot was lugging a huge lantern towards the big doors that led to the church. 'We've not seen Jimmy out and about for years now, really.'

Audrey was about to say that all Cooper had done was suggest he come to the hall, but maybe it had been the magic combination of lone wolf Cooper making the suggestion, the GP's surgery being relocated to the church hall during Nativity season and…if she wasn't mistaken…the very pretty woman who was setting out a huge bowl of fruit at the end of the coffee and tea table.

'Who's she?'

'Angela. She works down the local bakery.'

'Ah…' Audrey smiled, connecting the dots.

'Anyway, young lassie…' Emily gave her arm a little pat. 'I'd best be off. You'll keep our little talk to yourself, won't you?'

Audrey made a *my lips are sealed* gesture, then threw away the imaginary key. Smiling, she sat back down to look at the costume she'd promised to 'attach some dazzle' to.

Twenty minutes later, she hadn't made much progress.

'Ouch!' Audrey pulled her finger away from the sparkly fabric. Yup… She'd just stabbed herself hard enough to draw blood.

She popped her finger in her mouth and stared at the hem

of the cape she was sewing. And by 'sewing' she meant *trying* to sew. Needlecraft was definitely not her speciality.

This whole thing of her and Coop keeping themselves busy so they could avoid the elephant in Gertie's house was beginning to fray at the edges. First it had been work—but they had proved such an efficient team that only the odd out-of-hours emergency required their presence. Then it had been cleaning out the surgery in advance of the builders getting in there—but the builders had decided it wasn't safe for them and that the whole project would have to wait until the New Year, so that the new GP could decide how he or she would like things.

That had thrown a spotlight on the fact that Cooper had yet to pin his name to the job. Which was annoying, because if he did she would know once and for all that she was leaving and he was staying and their paths would never cross again. Or, if he refused the job, she could possibly sound out Dr Anstruther about staying on to help Noreen until they got a new GP.

She tried to tackle the costume's hem again, succeeding only in having to pull the stitches out. 'Urgh!'

'Is that costume playing silly buggers with you?'

Cooper appeared from behind a large chunk of plywood cut into the shape of a camel. He saw her notice the shape, and pretended to be riding it. Goofball.

'It's a better effort than our Christmas biscuits, isn't it?'

She wanted to laugh. Of course she did. To laugh and pull him towards her, to kiss him and let the world fade into soft focus so she could tell him how much she cared for him. How she'd realised that her feelings were stronger than she'd thought ever since they'd kissed. Kissing that she'd stopped because suffering two broken hearts in a matter of weeks had seemed ridiculous.

Although this whole *not* kissing thing wasn't really

working for her either. She was all for a bit of denial, but something was telling her that despite her very best efforts she was falling for Cooper MacAskill.

'Need a plaster?' Cooper leant in, and the scent of island fir and spiced mince pies swirled in along with him. 'Or shall I get out my suture kit?'

'I think we were assigned the wrong jobs,' Audrey replied dryly, lifting the needle and cloth between them. 'How did I end up doing this and you on props? I thought doctors were the ones who were good at stitching?'

'I would love to show you my excellent stitching skills...' Cooper grinned, sending an unwanted trill of response round her tummy '...but I'm afraid Cayley has demanded I supply her with three camels immediately.'

'Cayley?' Audrey sat up straighter, letting the gold fabric fall onto her lap. 'I thought she was on costumes, like me.'

'Nope. She did it for a day or two, then spotted an open tin of paint and, according to Dr Anstruther, it was love at first sight.' Cooper nodded towards the far end of the church hall where Cayley was buttoning herself into a paint splattered coverall. 'She's been down here every day, apparently. When she's not doing her homework.'

He dropped Audrey a wink that made some butterflies flutter to life and take flight around her heart. His eyes dropped to her finger.

'So what's the situation? Are we counting you amongst the walking wounded?'

'Sitting wounded, more like.'

He knelt down beside her, leaned the camel up against the wall and took her hand in his.

Her instinct was to yank her hand away and snap *I'm fine, leave it*. Completely counterintuitive to the butterflies now tripping the light fantastic around her insides.

But Cooper had been nothing less than a gentleman since their kitchen kiss. Why would he suddenly opt for a public show of unwanted affection here, in the centre of the church hall?

Cooper pulled her hand up close to his face, presumably to look at it. The hum and whirr of activity round them blurred into a warm buzz, fuelling the growing intensity of the moment. His fingers traced the length of the one she'd pricked. A whoosh of tingles skittered up her arm and across her collarbones.

'Do you think I'll make it?' she asked, her voice little more than a whisper.

'There's one medicine I'd prescribe.' His eyes met hers and held tight.

'Oh?'

His lips lowered, and they were just about to reach her fingertip, her entire body buzzing with anticipation, when someone called out, 'It's snowing!'

A flash of something that looked like disappointment swept through Cooper's eyes before his smile returned. He pushed himself back up to stand and offered her his hand. 'Care to see a rare event out here on Bourtree?'

'What? It doesn't often snow here?'

'Not regularly. Looks like the Christmas faeries are intent on you having a magical Christmas whether you want it or not.'

She was about to protest, and then remembered how grumpy and anti-Christmas she'd been when she'd landed on Bourtree. Funny how hating Christmas had been replaced by so many other things. Positive things. Like caring for their patients. Learning who liked their tea which way and why. Making biscuits with Cooper. Seeing the aurora borealis with Cooper.

She forced herself to stop. The whole point of her 'exile'

to Bourtree had been to discover who she was. Not start another relationship.

Which made feeling Cooper's warm, supportive hand round hers that much more difficult.

When her hand had been in her ex's she'd felt helpless. As if she'd lost her own life skills and become reliant upon him to guide her through the maze of his world. A world that hadn't felt as warm as this one. In short, it hadn't been a love that had given her confidence. Far from it.

There was, of course, another way to explain why she and Cooper were drawn to each other. They were both broken. She by being hoodwinked and Cooper by having his eye on the wrong prize. But, as Cooper often told his patients, once they were healed they'd be stronger than ever.

Was that how it would work with her heart? As each day passed she thought less and less of Rafael and more about the life she wanted to live. A life that was honest and simple. A life filled with love and community. A life pretty close to the one she was living now.

Cooper dipped his head so he could look into her eyes. 'You snow-averse?'

'No, not at all,' she said. 'Let's go out there and see if there's enough for a snowball fight.'

He feigned shock. 'I thought you'd be more of a snow angel girl myself.'

The comment flooded her heart with warmth. 'Maybe a bit of both?'

'Well, let's find out.'

Out on the High Street, with the lights twinkling, the Christmas tree glowing up at the castle ruins, and the scent of mulled wine coming from The Puffin, Cooper couldn't help but feel as though he was part of something special. Particularly with Audrey by his side.

They'd been a proper team over the past few weeks. Not just as work colleagues but as something deeper, beyond the stolen kisses. He felt as if she saw him. The real Cooper. Flaws and all. And yet she still liked him, still stuck up for him whenever a patient began to shake their head about a prognosis or a recommended course of treatment.

Islanders could be stubborn, but so could Audrey when she believed in something. And he was hoping that something was him. He knew he had a way to go before he was perfect. Marriage material, even. But maybe she'd stay and see him through the transition.

'It's like being in a real-life snow globe, isn't it?' Audrey tipped her head up to the sky and stuck her tongue out to try and catch a snowflake.

He smiled. The last time he'd thought about a snow globe had been just after he'd kissed her. A moment's perfection he wondered if he'd ever catch again. Although it looked as if perfection could come in all shapes and forms.

'Want to get some mulled wine?'

Audrey's smooth forehead crinkled. 'Won't they need us back in the hall?'

Cooper pointed at the dozen or so people coming out of the church hall, clapping their hands and whooping at the snowfall. 'I don't think there'll be much going on there for the rest of the night.'

Her serious expression turned bright. 'In that case, I'd love some mulled wine.'

A few minutes later, warm cups of spicy red liquid in their hands, they strolled along the cobbled High Street up towards the castle ruins, where they could get a better view of everyone enjoying the midwinter evening.

Cooper pointed towards a wooden bench. 'Shall we?'

'Mmm…' Audrey said through a sip of her wine. 'Glad I wore my big winter coat today.'

They both looked at her not so immaculate white down coat.

Audrey started to giggle. 'This wasn't the most practical of choices, was it?'

'Did you buy it especially for coming up here?'

She tipped her head back and forth, as if letting the question find its own answer.

Her cheeks coloured and she stared down at the steam spiralling out of her thick paper cup. 'I know it sounds ridiculous, but after I discovered I was engaged to a cheater I wanted to feel pretty, you know? I know it's ridiculous, and that what matters most is more than skin-deep, but at the time it felt like knowing I was pretty, that it hadn't all been lies, would help. And when I put this on for just a moment I felt pretty. Caught a glimpse of the woman I thought I was beneath all the heartache. It didn't last, obviously, but…'

Cooper felt the pain in her voice pierce straight through to his own heart. He hated that she'd been made to feel so low. 'Are you still in love with him?'

She looked up, startled by the blunt question. Then, to his surprise, she snorted. 'Not even close.' She lifted the cup to her mouth again, her lips pushing forward to blow some ripples across the surface of her drink. 'I think you called it a few weeks back,' she said, staring at her drink again. 'I'm not sure I ever really was.'

He asked the obvious and most painful question. 'Why did you accept his proposal?'

Audrey sighed and looked up at the sky, awash with fat floaty snowflakes, now dappling her red knitted hat. 'I suppose I was a bit at sea… When my dad died a couple of years ago it was kind of— It was like the last link to my life as I'd known it was gone, you know? I trundled on…did my work, had my friends…but there wasn't that solid link any more. Nothing and no one to prove I'd made a mark on the world.'

She waved her mittened hand between them.

'I'm not trying to be all "woe is me" or anything. I know my nursing work helps people. But…they're not family. And in London community is a hard thing to find. Most of my friends were getting married or having babies, so their lives were extra-busy, and being the third wheel in someone else's life was never my thing. So when Rafael almost literally swept me off my feet I guess I thought I'd better jump at it. Make sure I didn't miss out on the chance to be a part of something. What I actually did was make myself blind to all the warning signs that it was the wrong man and the wrong life. Square peg. Round hole. Now I know finding the perfect fit is important. No matter how long it takes. Does any of that make sense?'

He nodded. It did make sense. What she was describing was exactly what it felt like when he'd heard Gertie had passed away. She'd been his anchor through any number of storms. The one family member he'd been able to rely on. When his parents had died he'd kept on waiting to feel like an orphan. He hadn't. But when Gertie had died, well past the age when he should've felt like an orphan… he'd felt like one.

Would slowing down, the way his gran had suggested, be the answer?

He held out his hand to Audrey and gave her mittened one a squeeze. He was enjoying getting to know Audrey. The real one. 'I understand.'

She turned to him, her eyes brimming with un-spilt tears. 'I know. That's why I told you.'

Cooper's heart began ricocheting round his ribcage like a pinball. 'Hey, don't cry.'

'Don't worry. They're happy tears.'

As she blinked, and the tears found purchase on her cheeks, he brushed them away with the backs of his fingers. She turned her cheek so that his hand was cupping her cheek, then turned it a bit more, pressing her lips to his palm. Still damp with tears, her lashes lifted and her eyes met his.

Audrey was telling him something beyond the obvious: She was over her ex because there hadn't really been anything to get over. It had taken a while, but she saw that now. She was also telling him that the feelings he'd hoped they shared were shared. And possibly worth exploring.

He did the only thing he could. He tipped his head towards hers and kissed her.

The short drive home was silent, but taut with expectation. Audrey couldn't stop running her fingertips over her lips, trying to recapture the heated magic of their spicy mulled-wine-and-snowflake-laced kiss. It had been slow and intense and, for the first time, it had made her feel complete in a way physical intimacy never had.

It wasn't like being absorbed into someone else's orbit... more like two planets gaining strength from being in a shared orbit. Scary, but exhilarating. And, more pertinently, the kiss had led to a shared look of silent complicity, and then a very brisk walk to the four-by-four to head home.

Just a few minutes from Gertie's house her heart began pounding with erratic skips and jumps. Every time she looked at Cooper—which was pretty much the entire drive home—bursts of fireworks pinged and exploded in her belly, in anticipation of more to come.

It put an entirely new spin on her feelings about Christmas and the magic of the season. It hadn't been ruined for ever, as she'd once thought. No. The magic of the season had been tiptoeing up to her in lovely Cooper-sized steps until she was ready to accept the fact that her life was her own and she was the one in charge of it.

And right now she wanted to know what it felt like to make love to Cooper MacAskill—with or without the promise of a long-term relationship.

Life was for living, right? Not for hiding away on remote Scottish islands waiting for life to find her. Which made her laugh. Life *had* found her. And much more quickly than she would've believed.

'What's so funny?'

'This,' she said. 'Us.'

'We're funny?' Cooper glanced over at her, but only quickly as the snowfall was thickening.

'Not ha-ha funny. It's more...' Audrey tapped her fingertips on her chin, trying to find the best word. 'It's more the situation.'

'How do you mean?' Cooper asked, a soft smile playing upon that generously delicious mouth of his. 'Two lost souls finding one another in the middle of nowhere?'

'Sounds like a country song.' She laughed. Her smile slipped away, but not the warmth in her heart. 'In a way I suppose our story is like a song. I wasn't the happiest of campers a few weeks back. You met me when I was smack-dab in the middle of a pity party.'

He gave her knee a light squeeze. 'I think you deserved a bit of a pity party. What you were going through was still pretty raw then, wasn't it? And it wasn't exactly as if I was a barrel of laughs.'

'You were amazing to your patients, so I was able to see through all your gruff and bluster.'

'Oh, yeah? And what was it you saw?'

'That you're a softie. That your heart is kind and true and, while you may not always get it right, you're man enough to face the things that scare you.'

'Wow.' Cooper gave his head a big shake. 'Remind me to call you the next time I need an ego boost.'

'I mean it, Coop. You're a good man. Take the compliment.'

He tipped an imaginary hat in her direction, sending another whirl of heat swirling round her bloodstream.

'The truth is…us being forced to stay together and everything…it's made me face a lot of things I don't think I would have otherwise,' she said. 'I don't think I've ever been very good at letting anyone really *know* me.'

'You're not alone. I tend to keep my demons to myself. Not that it's worked all that brilliantly, and I know I need to change.'

'No one's perfect, Cooper. Don't put so much pressure on yourself.'

'I could say the same to you. I've seen you at work and you're one of the best nurses I've ever had the privilege of working with. And that's not just because I fancy the pants off you.'

A hot whoosh of desire swept through her as she saw the heat return to his eyes. Cooper did seem to genuinely desire her. And it wasn't one of those hot flashes of attraction. It was one of those slow-burn attractions that had started as squabbling, turned into shared respect, and now… Now it was definitely mutual.

But she owed him some more honesty before they started ripping one another's clothes off.

'The truth is, I don't think I've entirely known who I was most of my life. Daughter. Nurse. Fiancée. I attached myself to roles and tried to find myself in amongst them as

I muddled along. Maybe it took having the world I thought I was living in ripped out from under me to understand what I really wanted from life.'

Cooper shot her another quick glance. 'And do you know what that is?'

It was a loaded question. One she'd set him up to ask. Dancing on the tip of her tongue was one word: *You*. But it was too soon for that. Too soon after having changed her entire life for one man to do exactly the same for another. Even if this time it felt completely different.

'I love nursing. *District* nursing. I definitely want to continue with that. I suppose I also want to prove to myself I can make it on my own, you know?'

'In what way?'

'Well, I have to find a job, for one.'

'You've got one. Everyone loves you here.'

She poked him in the arm. 'You know as well as I do there's a clock ticking on that.'

His thinned lips spoke volumes. He wanted her contract to end about as much as she did.

Unexpectedly, she saw his mouth curve into a chipper smile. 'There's always Glasgow.'

He'd mentioned that before. Was it his way of saying he wanted her close? Wanted to see if they could explore what was happening between them without a time pressure?

'What's so great about Glasgow?'

'About a million things I couldn't tell you.' He huffed a self-deprecating laugh.

'Why not?'

'Because I've always been too busy working to enjoy it.'

She saw something flash in his eyes. Something similar to what she'd begun to feel here on Bourtree. As if she'd come home.

'Is that something you'd like to do? Enjoy where you live?'

He gave the steering wheel a few taps as he considered his answer. 'It is,' he answered solidly, and then, more cheekily, as he pulled the car into the drive and turned off the ignition, he said, 'And right now I'd like to enjoy where I live with you.'

Audrey's body grew tingly as the charged sensual atmosphere that had hummed between them returned. Cooper leant across the car, cupped his hand along her jawline and gave her a deep, hungry kiss. One she returned with every fibre of her being.

'I'm falling for you, Audrey,' Cooper whispered against her lips when their languorous kisses came to an end. 'Every time I look at you I feel more alive than I have in years. Being with you, working with you, even making awful Christmas biscuits with you… It brings out the best in me, but I still worry that it isn't good enough.'

'For what?' She tipped her forehead against his.

'For offering you a future. You know…together.'

'Oh, Coop.' She took off her mittens, weaving her warm fingers through his cold ones. 'I don't think either of us knows what the future has in store for us.'

The way she said it implied that not knowing what the future held wasn't necessarily a deal-breaker.

'So…' He ran his thumb along the back of her hand. 'What are you saying, exactly?'

A saucy smile slipped onto her lips as the tip of her tongue swept the length of them. 'That maybe we should enjoy what we have right now. Who knows? Maybe we'll find out slow and steady is every bit as satisfying as fast and furious? Or maybe it'll turn out we're not a match, but we'll have had fun finding out.'

She leant in and gave him a slow, spicy, and decidedly

wicked kiss. One that promised much more than a snog in a vehicle that was quickly being covered in snow.

'Should we enjoy the slow and steady us in the warm?' He nodded towards the house.

Audrey laughed, and they climbed out of the car and bundled into the house.

The second the door was closed it was as if a switch had been flicked between the pair of them. Gone was the need to talk and explain. In its place was pure, undiluted, pent-up desire.

Cooper took hold of the zip at the top of Audrey's coat, locked eyes with her and said, 'I've been waiting a long time to do this.'

And he had. More than he'd realised. Yes, he'd felt a hit of attraction when he'd first laid eyes on her, but what he felt now was deeper. He began to ease the zip down centimetre by centimetre. By the time he got to what was underneath it he knew his blood flow would be at volcano-level heat.

'You're sure?' he asked as he teased the zip past the arc and dip of her breasts.

Her breath caught as she nodded, her body organically arching towards his. 'I'm sure.'

Suddenly the whole waiting game, the teasingly slow drop of the zip, became too much. He pulled it down to the bottom of her ankle-length coat in one swift move, then stood up, slipped it off her shoulders, picked her up and carried her up the stairs to his room.

Boots, jeans and her jumper were all discarded in a matter of seconds. And when Audrey stretched out on his cranberry-coloured sheets she looked like the type of Christmas present that left very little to the imagination, but was more than enough to send surges of desire arrowing straight below his belt buckle. She had on nothing more than a lacy wisp of a brassiere and some panties. Panties which, if he wasn't mistaken, had a pattern of snowflakes dappled along them.

She got up on her knees and reached out to where he was standing beside the bed. She tugged him closer and button by button undid his shirt. Her hand skidded across his nipples, instantly rendering them taut with the anticipation of her hot mouth upon them.

She wagged her index finger. *Uh-uh,* it said. *Not yet.*

Lifting her dark brown eyes to meet his, she began to undo his belt buckle. Flames licked southward each time her fingertips touched his bare skin. When she pulled the belt out of the loops in one long, unhurried movement, he could feel the pulse of his longing press against his jeans. As she began to undo the buttons on his trousers it was all he could do to contain a moan of desire.

When her hand brushed along the length of his arousal, he found his voice. 'Now it's your turn.'

He slipped his jeans off, tucked his arm around Audrey's waist and laid her out alongside him on the bed, so that he could feel the shared heat of their desire. She tangled her legs around his, pressing into him as she began to kiss him with a hunger he easily matched.

He pulled his fingers through her hair and gave her a deep kiss, tasting, exploring and loving—yes, loving— how being with her felt both brand-new and wonderfully familiar. As if they'd both known somewhere, deep within them, that this was the person they had always been waiting for.

Audrey's hands moved down his back to his hips, then dipped between his thighs, where the pulsing heat of his desire was building with every passing second. He took both her hands in one of his, then pulled them up and over her head.

'My turn.' He wanted to enjoy her body before he reached the point of no return. He slipped her fingers around the solid oak roundels that made up the headboard and dropped her a wink. 'No touching allowed.'

She whimpered in protest…and then again in pleasure.

Cooper could get used to this. Taking a leisurely tour of Audrey's body using his tongue and featherlight kisses to better acquaint himself. There were five freckles that formed a star at the base of her throat. They deserved some attention. And underneath the lacy strips of her bra her nipples were a beautiful dusky rose which…*mmm*… darkened when he swirled his tongue round them, teasing the soft discs to hard, erect nubs.

Her ribcage lifted and dropped in short, sharp inhalations of response and desire. They both knew she could let go of the bed railings at any time, but he was pleased to see she was enjoying the added level of eroticism as much as he was.

When he reached her hips he only had to hover above her skin, his breath barely skimming it, to produce a rippling of goosebumps. He dipped his fingers into the sweet honeyed folds between her legs, touching, teasing, taunting her until she let go of the bed, ran her nails raggedly down his back and begged him to be inside her.

The temptation proved too much for him. He wanted her, too. *Now*.

He pulled her into his arms so that their bare bodies pressed against one another. She held the length of his arousal between her legs, where the hot, wet sensation of the pleasure he'd already brought to her was almost all the invitation he needed.

He whispered something about protection.

'Please, Coop,' Audrey whispered after he'd swiftly sheathed himself. 'Now.'

He didn't need a second invitation.

In one slow, deliberate move he pressed his entire length into her. The heated, pulsing sensation of their bodies connecting was almost too much to bear.

He looked into Audrey's eyes to get a feel for what she wanted from him. He saw nothing but desire. Her hips arched up to meet his, instantly sending his body into a series of rhythmic thrusts. Her body matched the fluid moves of his, their most intimate nerve-endings set alight by the other, their movements building to a heated crescendo. Two bodies moving as one, thrusting and arching in complete synchronicity until climax came to them both.

Later, as he held her in his arms, he tried to think of a time when he'd ever felt so complete. He teased one of her pixie locks away from her eyes. 'You all right, there, darlin'?'

She smiled. 'That's the first time you've called me darling.'

'A milestone for both of us.' He dropped a kiss onto her forehead. 'Let it not be the last.'

CHAPTER EIGHT

'YOU TWO SEEM extra-chipper today.' Jimmy eyed them both warily.

Audrey hardly dared look at Cooper, because she knew her blush would be instantaneous.

Cooper carried on humming a jaunty Christmas carol.

'Is this jolly humming as you work thing because it's Christmas Eve?' Jimmy persisted. 'You're not going to show up in Christmas gear again tomorrow, are you? I claim no responsibility if you get stuck trying to make your way in down my chimney.'

Audrey laughed and shook her head in the negative. But, honestly, she'd wear a leprechaun outfit if that was all that was to hand, because she felt head to toe happy, happy, *happy*.

Making love to Cooper had opened up something in her she hadn't realised was closed. And she wasn't just talking about erogenous zones, although...*mamma mia*...those too.

Being with him had excavated a part of her heart she hadn't realised she'd been protecting so fiercely. The part that was desperately worried about pleasing other people. Towing the line. Not making a fuss. Aspiring to a love like her parents', when it was impossible to know where one of them started and the other began.

Perhaps that was why missing her mother after her death

had been so complicated. Her father and mother had been one unit to her, so growing up with a grief-stricken man had been like living with half a person. A man waiting, and failing, to be made whole again.

With Cooper she felt cared for, for being exactly who she was, mistakes and all. More to the point, she knew she was in charge of her own destiny. No one else. Being intimate with him had strengthened rather than diminished her desire to pursue the life she wanted.

It was a big lesson. Particularly when she'd always thought loving someone as intensely as her parents had loved one another only came in one shape and size. But love took different forms. Some couples were glued at the hip. Some people, like her ex, used loyalty as a façade to mask selfishness. In short, every couple was different.

She was, of course, far too nervous to admit to loving Cooper. Cautious hearts and all that... But somewhere beneath the scar tissue she knew something beautiful and strong was replacing the fear and sorrow her last relationship had left in its wake.

She hoped he was feeling the same way. Maybe the whistling was a sign that he was finally embracing the love he'd shared with his grandmother and moving beyond his grief.

As if to confirm it, he did a few play-boxing moves in front of Jimmy. 'Watch yourself, Jimmy, or we'll have you in a Santa suit *toute de suite*!'

'Ach, no.' Jimmy batted Cooper away. 'I'm a behind the scenes kind of guy, remember?'

'Aye, right you are, pal.' Cooper's expression changed. 'I hear the lights are going to be out of this world for the Nativity.'

'Better!' Jimmy grinned, pulling up the leg of his trousers to above his knee.

Audrey smiled at the pair of them.

She loved how Cooper's brogue became broader and more pronounced depending upon if he was speaking to her or one of the locals. It wasn't put on. It was organic. He wanted people to understand him. He was a man who had learned to live in two worlds, flicking between the two at the drop of a coin.

Which did beg the question… Would he make tonight—the night Dr Anstruther was officially retiring—the night he decided whether or not he would stay? He seemed so at home here…but she'd never seen him in A&E. He might be equally at ease there. Or more so.

The thought made her blood run cold. Colder still when she realised she had let Cooper's presence on Bourtree, and in a shared bed, no less, influence the choices she made about her future. Exactly what she'd promised herself she would never do again.

She'd heard from Noreen this morning, when Cooper had been in the shower. Noreen had news. She and her husband would, after a short trip home, return to Australia to be with her daughter and their grandchild for good. She'd asked Audrey if she would consider staying. She'd said yes, still basking in the glow of her night with Cooper.

That glow disappeared in an instant. She was going to have to look at everything afresh. Starting now.

She forced herself to focus in on the task at hand.

Cooper had primed the needle for Jimmy's injection, and after Audrey had given the area above his knee a little swab, he gave him the insulin. The visit didn't really need the two of them, but honestly it was better with two.

Her heart clenched.

If the job was better with two, had she been an idiot to accept it permanently? Would she spend the rest of her life like her father, feeling as if half of her had been stripped away?

Please, please let that not be the case.

Oblivious to her internal turmoil, Cooper let out a whoop. 'Jimmy? Is that you, hitting the fruit?' Cooper pointed at a bowl of apples and seasonal tangerines on the coffee table.

'Aye…' Jimmy said, the tiniest hint of colour pinking up his cheeks.

Audrey gave him a closer inspection. 'Jimmy? You've lost weight, haven't you?'

'Can you tell?' He gave his still very pronounced belly a pat. 'Down five kilos since you lot roped me into helping out with the Nativity. Cuts down on my night-time snacking,' he added with a toothy grin.

'It's clearly making you miserable, Jim,' Cooper said dryly.

'Aye, right.' There was a glint in Jimmy's eye as he continued. 'Sometimes leading a horse to water is a bit more helpful than the horse might think.'

'You mean stubborn mule, right?' Cooper gave Jimmy a play-jostle with his elbow, then packed up his kit.

Jimmy tugged on a pair of imaginary lapels. 'I'll have you know this stubborn mule's social calendar has become rather full since the good people of Bourtree realised my panache with stage lighting.'

'Oh?'

'Yes. I've been invited to have Boxing Day tea over at Angela's.'

Cooper shot Audrey a glance. If Jimmy hadn't been looking she was pretty sure there would've been a triumphant fist-punch as well.

'That's grand. Great news, Jimmy.'

Jimmy gave Cooper and Audrey a playful hooded look.

'Does this mean the two of you will stop rooting around in my rubbish bin now?'

'What?' Audrey feigned innocence while Cooper looked over his shoulder as if there might be someone else in the room who was guilty.

Jimmy waved off their feeble protests. 'I know I need to lose weight. It's for my health. And I owe you both a thank you for caring enough to mess around in my bin and get me out of the house. It's made a difference. The truth is…' His voice hitched for a minute as emotion got the better of him. 'The truth is I haven't been very honest with myself and it's high time I did just that.'

That makes two of us, thought Audrey.

'Glad to hear it, Jimmy,' Cooper said.

Audrey gave Jimmy a double thumbs-up. She'd be here to see his progress, but she'd let him know that later. Once she'd told Cooper. 'Keep up the effort. It's obviously paying dividends.'

'Right, my friend.' Cooper rubbed his hands together. 'I'm afraid we've got to make a move—but we're looking forward to seeing the show tonight in all its splendour.'

'So you're coming?' Jimmy looked shocked.

'Aye…' Cooper answered slowly. 'Why wouldn't I?'

'Ach, nothing.' Jimmy tugged his trouser leg back into place and feigned a sudden interest in peeling a tangerine.

'No, please…' Cooper perched on the armchair across from the sofa. 'Are folk saying I won't be coming?'

Jimmy looked at Audrey, then at Cooper.

A queasy feeling churned through Audrey's gut.

'Go on, Jim. You can say anything in front of Audrey that you'd say to me privately.'

'The stakes are up at the Puffin.'

'What?'

'You know…' Jimmy squirmed. 'The bets about whether

you'll stay or go. It's expanded to the Nativity. People thought you wouldn't go because of your gran, Coop,' Jimmy said awkwardly.

'And why would they think that?' Cooper asked tightly.

'You've not had a wake…you've not really talked about her to folk. And you've not said anything to Doc Anstruther. I mean, it's not down to you to make sure we have a doctor, but—'

Cooper finished the sentence for him. 'But folk are expecting it?'

'Aye, well.' Jimmy gave the back of his head a rub. 'They'd understand if you didn't want to stay, of course, but…'

'Oh, would they?' Cooper said, in a tone that suggested he was already mentally booking his journey back to Glasgow.

'Aye.' Jimmy nodded. 'Look, I'm only saying something because I want you to stay. And I've not put a bet down at the Puffin, if that's what you're thinking. What you've done for me has made a real difference. If you were to stay on…you know, as the island doc… I think people would be better off for it.'

Cooper just stared at him.

Audrey looked at her watch, desperate for this moment to end. Cooper would be leaving, and she would be staying. That was the new reality. One she'd have to come to terms with.

She waited until she knew her voice wouldn't shake when she spoke, then, 'Cooper, we've got to get on to Rhona's.'

'Aye,' he said, his eyes not moving from Jimmy's.

'Cooper, mate… I'm sorry if I stuck my foot in it.' Jimmy pushed himself up off the sofa to see them out. 'I just… You made me look in the mirror, you know?'

Cooper lifted his chin in acknowledgement. 'I know, pal.' He gave the man's shoulder a friendly thump. 'It's something we all need to do every now and again.'

They shook hands and agreed they'd see one another at the Nativity.

When she and Cooper got in the car, the atmosphere was more like the cold out of doors than the bubbly, effervescent mood they'd initially started the day with.

'You want to talk about it?' Audrey finally asked.

Cooper gave a hard-to-read shrug. 'Let's get through the day, all right? See how we go.'

The response whipped what was left of the warm fuzzies away from her heart. This wasn't the Cooper she'd grown to know and—and love? Was that really what it was she was feeling for him? Love?

She knew she loved waking up and knowing he'd be part of her day. Even more so when she'd woken up today in his arms. She loved how his doctor-patient care went beyond the obvious. How he listened to and took on board her perspective rather than dismissing it because she was 'just' a nurse. She loved how his mouth quirked on one side of his face and then the other before his smile became complete. She loved his touch, his laugh, his scent.

But this? This cloud that appeared from... Not from nowhere. It was a troubled-childhood-shaped cloud that had taken years to accumulate. The bullying, the fighting back, the parents who hadn't been interested in being parents. All those things and more had made a man who preferred to be an island unto himself rather than part of an island community...

Ten minutes later, Audrey bundled up her frustrations and put them away. Their patients deserved their full attention right now. Especially this one. She was pleased to see the 'back off' vibes Cooper had been sending out had faded. He was, at heart, a professional.

They were about to go into Rhona Gillies's house—she was the young mum nearing the end of her journey with bone cancer—and were all too aware it would be one of their last visits.

After he tripled-checked the cooler that had Rhona's blood transfusion supplies in it, he stopped, took a deep breath, and gave Audrey a pointed look. 'You sure you're up for this?'

It tugged at her heart that he cared. Would the new Bourtree doctor care? Would he or she even notice?

She quickly shelved the thoughts. It was Rhona who mattered now.

Audrey nodded. Making these sorts of calls was never easy, but they were part of the job and she felt honoured to be a part of them.

Charlie, Rhona's husband, opened the door before they reached it. Worry and fatigue were etched into his features. It was clear he knew how bad the situation was.

'How're you doing, Charlie?' Cooper asked.

'Rhona's pretty weak today.'

'Aye, that's to be expected,' Cooper said, in a way that managed to sound reassuring. 'It's why we thought the blood transfusion would be a good idea.'

'She's desperate to see the kiddies open their gifts tomorrow. I think if the grim reaper tried to come down the chimney before Santa she'd shoo him out and say he wasn't welcome until at least after lunch.' Charlie shook his head and tried for a laugh. 'You know Rhona... Stubborn as they come.'

'Aye, well, she's proved herself a proper warrior, hasn't she?'

Charlie coughed and cleared his throat, obviously unable to answer without letting emotion get the better of him.

'Charlie?' Cooper put down the cooler in the small porch area and indicated that he should close the front door. 'We're obviously here for Rhona. We'll get this transfusion in her, which will help with her anaemia and hopefully see her through Christmas, but when I asked how you were doing I was asking after *you*.'

Audrey's heart softened. Cooper had it in him to stay if he wanted. That heart of his wasn't as hard as he thought. But he was the one who had to believe in its strength. Not her.

Charlie tugged his hand through his hair, which looked as though it hadn't seen the working end of a comb in a few days. 'I'm muddling through. Work's been ever so generous. I've had the whole month off to be here with Rhona and the kids, so I can't really complain, can I—?'

He stopped, gave his face a scrub, then dug into his pocket for a handkerchief and gave up halfway through, letting the tears fall.

'I keep talking my way through that poem—you know the one about it being better to have loved and lost?'

Cooper nodded. '"'Tis better to have loved and lost, than never to have loved at all."'

'That's the one. I used to think it was about break-ups and moving on, but I get it now. It's about loving someone—really loving someone—and having that be enough, you know? Knowing you've felt real, genuine love even though you have to say goodbye far sooner than you imagined.'

Audrey watched Cooper closely for his reaction. If he were able to do that—concentrate on the love and the times he and his grandmother had spent together that were positive, rather than negatives—it would go a long way towards lifting the burden of guilt he felt.

Growing and learning from the mistakes they'd made

was the only way to move on, she was realising. Which did make her wonder… Could she do the same with Cooper? Love him, as she knew she did, and carry on here on Bourtree without him knowing that her life was richer for having known him?

Again, she stuffed the thoughts to the back of her mind, forcing herself back to the here and now.

'Wise counsel,' Cooper said, and his voice carried a weight of emotion that went beyond what was happening in the here and now. As though Charlie's words had hit their mark.

'I don't want to say goodbye,' Charlie whispered, then threw a guilty look over his shoulder towards the lounge, where his wife was in lying in her bed.

'I know, mate. And I wish there was something I could say to make it easier for you. But I suppose you've got to keep thinking of that poem, eh? All that you've had, rather than what you haven't.'

Cooper put his hand on Charlie's shoulder and the two of them stood there for a moment in silence. The only sounds surfacing around them were Charlie and Rhona's children, laughing as they built a snowman in the back garden.

Audrey waited until the two men, similar in age, had shared the equivalent of a life-affirming bear hug. A couple of thumps on the back and more throat-clearing. As difficult as this must be for Cooper—a man who claimed to prefer to keep his patients' personal lives at arm's length—it would be a much harder moment for Charlie. It warmed her to the marrow that Cooper wasn't backing away during the poor man's time of need.

'Right, then.' Cooper finally broke the silence. 'What do you say we get this transfusion underway?'

'Sounds good, Coop.'

They gave one another a couple more claps on the back and then, with a quick look back to Audrey, Cooper got to work.

Cooper tried to hide the conflicting emotions battling it out in his chest.

Rhona looked so thin and tired. Giving her this blood transfusion would almost certainly help with her anaemia—but was prolonging this battle she'd been waging with her cancer really the best thing for her?

'I feel better already,' Rhona said, happily contradicting his silent thoughts.

Her husband let out a huge sigh of relief.

'That's brilliant news, love. That was fast!'

Charlie beamed from the end of the bed, clearly pleased to see even the tiniest peak in his wife's energy.

'How could it not be? I've got more island blood in me now.'

Audrey deftly withdrew the needle from Rhona's thin forearm and applied a cotton pressure roll and sterilised dressing atop it. 'Island blood?'

Charlie answered for her, the pride in his voice almost palpable. 'A few weeks back—late November time—Gertie organised a blood drive. It actually happened the day she passed—' He stopped mid-flow, a stricken look seizing him as he connected eyes with Cooper.

'It's okay.' Cooper nodded a few times, settling the information into place. 'Sounds just like Gran.'

'It was. It was her to a T, Coop. On the phone from her sickbed, rallying the islanders to help my Rhona… Dozens of folk came. Of course everyone wasn't able to donate, for one reason or another, and there were all different types of blood, not all of them a match. But all we really wanted was for there to be enough for Christmas—didn't we, love?'

'It's worked out perfectly,' Rhona agreed.

Charlie gave his wife's leg a loving pat.

Cooper realised it was moments like these that he'd been hiding from by working in A&E. Moments that tested the power of his own tear ducts to obey his commands. Sure, some cases in A&E had got to him. But he hadn't gone to school with any of the people he'd treated. Hadn't watched them fall in love. Hadn't shared their wedding cake with them and watched them have children, only to realise that everything they'd built would soon be shadowed in contrast to the future they would actually lead.

Did knowing all this make him a better doctor?

Cooper flicked a quick look in Audrey's direction as she tidied away the transfusion kit. She would've noticed all the things Charlie was likely doing his best to ignore. Rhona's breathing was slower and noisier than it had been over the past few weeks. Her lips were dry. Her skin was cool, despite the room being so warm that both he and Audrey had stripped down to the red and green mismatched scrubs they'd agreed to wear today.

They'd sealed the idea with a kiss, back when they'd been giggling and touching and laughing over their pancake breakfast.

Waking up holding Audrey in his arms that morning, he'd never felt more alive. But the thought felt almost traitorous, standing here, as he was, next to a woman who had, at best, only a handful of days left to live. Doubly so when, back at Jimmy's, he'd mentally packed his bags and headed back to Glasgow, where distance anaesthetised the pain of loving and losing someone.

Being here, in the thick of precisely that type of love and loss, was throwing a spanner into the works of his tried and tested escape plan. Leaving felt as though it would be the coward's route. Staying had to be the right thing. But at this precise moment he wasn't sure he could separate right from wrong.

'Cooper, are you all right?' Rhona asked, her head sinking a bit further back into her pillow.

''Course, Rhona. Just making sure we've got you as comfortable as you can be.'

'I'm fine.' Rhona feigned a dizzy look. 'The morphine's keeping everything under control.'

They both watched as Audrey and Charlie left the room under the premise of preparing some hot chocolate for the children when they came in from playing in the snow.

'Are you sure you're okay?' Rhona pressed.

He wanted to say no, but he wouldn't.

He was being an arse to Audrey—dropping a sheet of ice between them so he could sort himself out just when he should've been more open, more honest.

He'd never let himself fall in love before, and—though it scared the absolute living daylights out of him—he was pretty sure that was what was happening now. A true Christmas miracle.

'Hey...' Rhona gave Cooper's arm a weak pat. 'Chin up. Christmas is coming.'

He smiled and, as had become his habit, looked across to Audrey, who'd just come back into the room. His eyes met hers, and the look they shared was so bittersweet it was all he could do not to pull her into her arms and tell her he knew he was being an idiot.

He could feel the past yanking him in the wrong direction when he should be looking to the future—a future with her. But until he separated himself from the ghosts of his parents, telling him the only thing he brought to the world was unhappiness, he wasn't sure the feelings he had for Audrey could ever reach their full potential. Which meant he'd have to let her go.

It was a thought so painful it felt as if the ghosts of the past were reaching into his chest and literally tearing his heart out.

His ultimate decision would have to be an honest one. She deserved nothing less. Her brown eyes spoke volumes. She cared for him. Deeply. But something had shifted between the pair of them at Jimmy's, and the blame firmly fell on his shoulders.

'Coop...?' Rhona tapped his arm again.

'Yes, Rhona—sorry. I was away with the faeries there.'

Her eyes swept between the pair of them. 'Aye, right you are, Coop.'

He pulled up a chair so he could be eye to eye with Rhona. 'What can we do for you, Rhona? Just name it and we'll do it.'

She was well aware they were into the palliative stage of her care, so if there was any step she wanted to make, he would help her do it.

'I want to go to the Nativity.'

'What? At the church tonight?'

'I want to see my family up there, doing what they do best. They won't go if I don't, and the Nativity isn't the Nativity if the whole of Bourtree isn't crowding up the church.'

He didn't hesitate. 'We'll make that happen.'

And a few hours later Cooper felt the satisfaction of a man who'd done all he could to make someone's final wish come true.

Rhona, nestled amongst a pile of his gran's quilts in a wheelchair, was front and centre in the church. Audrey had tucked hot water bottles around her to keep her cosy throughout the Nativity, and when they'd arrived Robbie's rugby team had been ready to lift the chair up and over the cobbled street, through the church's large wooden doors.

It had been an incredible moment of a community coming together for one shared purpose. To ensure a dying woman's last wishes were respected and carried out with as much love and compassion as they could muster. This, he thought, was Christmas magic. This was love. Being there when it mattered most, no matter how painful it was.

'Where's Audrey, Coop?' Robbie appeared at his side. 'Thought she'd be with you.'

Not with the way he'd been acting. Distant. Cool.

'She said she had an errand to run.'

Most likely she was checking the ferry schedule. Seeing how soon she could get off the island. He didn't blame her. He'd put the blinkers on after they'd left Rhona's. Poured all of the energy he should've been dedicating to Audrey into fulfilling Rhona's wishes when he knew damn straight he should've done both.

What the hell was stopping him from telling Audrey how he felt?

Robbie nudged him. 'Too bad the island can't have two nurses, eh? You two seem a good match.'

'Who says I'm staying?'

Robbie pulled back and stared at him. 'Seriously? You'd go back to Glasgow after all you've done here? The changes you've made in folks' lives?' Robbie shook his head. 'The island needs you, Coop.'

'The island needs a doctor,' Cooper corrected him.

A look of disappointment shadowed Robbie's features. 'You know as well as I do that Bourtree needs more than that.' And then he walked away.

Well, that told him.

Cooper found a perch at the edge of the apse, close enough to Rhona so that if she needed any help he'd be close to hand, but far enough away that she didn't feel as though he was hovering, waiting for the worst.

The vicar quietened down the excited murmurings of the congregation and gave thanks in advance for all those who had helped make the evening come together. Then he invited the island's children to come to the front of the church—regardless of age or faith—to sing carols and, of course, their favourite Viking battle song.

That got his attention. Back when he'd lived here, the Nativity had erred on the side of Christian tradition— Mary, Joseph, Baby Jesus and a donkey being the key players, the Wise Men, a few sheep and some Viking warriors playing a close second. His grandmother had felt the Vikings deserved a nod, seeing as many of the traditions—the Twelve days of Christmas, the Yule Log, and the seasonal ham—were theirs. He'd always enjoyed taking a role as a Viking guard back in the day. It had been his favourite because his gran had always been by his side in her own Viking costume.

Which did make him think...

'Bloody brilliant, isn't it?' Robbie materialised beside him and propped himself against the church wall as Cooper had.

The children were belting out a rendition of 'Jingle Bells' as delighted parents and grandparents clapped along. Cooper glanced at Robbie to agree, but realised he wasn't looking at the stage. He was looking at Rhona, her eyes glistening with pride, as her children went through their choreographed gestures, shaking their wrists, heavy with jingling bells on red ribbons, Charlie was by her side, his face wreathed in smiles as he looked between his wife and his children.

'It is that,' Cooper agreed, and he felt the warm spirit of Christmas slipping into his blood flow like oxygen. This was the flipside of knowing your patients well. It wasn't just the lows you experienced together—it was also the heartrendingly beautiful highs.

He let his eyes travel over the congregation, trying to see if he could find Audrey amongst them. Just a few weeks together and already he could spot her in a crowd in an instant. But her dark pixie head wasn't anywhere to be seen amongst the crowd. It wasn't the entire island's population, but it was certainly a healthy portion of it—apart, of course, from Noreen, who was still in Australia with her grandbaby.

Would she come back, he wondered, if her daughter's community was doing something similar? And if she stayed in Oz, would Audrey stay? Would the lure of Audrey on Bourtree be enough for him to finally move on from the past and make a future for himself here?

He continued to scan the crowd.

Dr Anstruther was here with his wife. Jimmy was at the lighting console, Angela by his side, the pair of them were singing along with the children. Glenn Davidson was holding up a phone, filming two children who kept waving at him—presumably his grandchildren. All of their patients, even the poor lad who'd broken both of his legs skiing, were present and accounted for.

Where was Audrey? He was physically feeling her absence and he didn't like it.

Perhaps she'd already taken the step back that all his girlfriends inevitably did. His sour mood had driven her away exactly when she'd needed him to be strong.

Daggers of pain slashed through him as he thought of what she'd been through with her fiancé. And he'd practically done the same. He hadn't cheated. He'd never do that to any woman, let alone Audrey. But he'd turned his back on her at precisely the moment she'd made herself vulnerable to him.

The re-enactment of the Nativity began. Mary entered the centre aisle of the church on the back of a donkey with Joseph, leading her past some Vikings towards the 'stable'.

Cooper only just managed to laugh along with the rest of the congregation as they asked everyone they passed if there was any room at their inn. All of the pews were stuffed, so, no. There was no room.

He could relate. His entire life he'd convinced himself that the islanders had wanted to squeeze him out. He'd done it for them. Left with a silent vow never to return. And for what? A barely furnished flat he never saw and a sad excuse for a social life?

He could be part of something here. Part of a community.

At the altar, where the children were dressed as sheep and chickens and one alpaca, Mary, Joseph and their newborn babe were granted shelter.

Just as he'd been cared for by his gran.

A swell of music came from the church organ, eliciting a series of oohs and ahs. Two wise men and one wise woman appeared from a far door. They were flanked by Vikings—one of whom was Audrey.

A complex mix of emotions washed through him as their eyes met, an electric heat searing straight through his chest. They'd asked Audrey to be in the Nativity, but not him. Had he jumped to the wrong conclusion about the islanders wanting him to stay?

Too late he realised he'd not even bothered to disguise his dismay. Audrey looked away.

A hush came over the congregation as the plain white church ceiling suddenly began to glow and shimmer with...the aurora borealis.

Jimmy had outdone himself. Celestial colours arced and curved across the ceiling, occasionally making contact with the handful of stained-glass windows, while the congregation as a whole began to sing 'Joy to the World'.

The beauty of it pierced Cooper to the core. He'd missed over a decade's worth of moments like these. Would moving back make him the man his grandmother had always believed him to be? A man who had the strength to endure whatever emotional storms he encountered? Or would it be a constant reminder of the fact his parents had never wanted him?

He stripped his past away from the equation and asked himself the most important question. Was making a future with Audrey or coming to terms with his past on Bourtree more important?

He looked across to Rhona. Charlie was kneeling beside her, as were her two children. Her eyes were closed, but there was a soft smile on her lips. A family's best and worst moment all wrapped up into one.

He made up his mind. He knew what he had to do.

CHAPTER NINE

'Here.' Cooper handed the mug brimming with hot chocolate to Audrey. 'You'll need this after making all those snow angels.'

'I blame the children.' She pinned on a smile she knew wasn't making it all the way to her eyes. Hot chocolate before she broke things off for good with Cooper was little salve to such a deep wound. But she was determined to press on.

'I don't seem to remember it was the children kicking things off,' Cooper said, his lips trying and failing to quirk into a smile.

He'd been edgy ever since they'd met up after the Nativity. In fairness, she had, too. It could've been the journey they'd just had, taking Rhona back to her family home. She'd been understandably worn out by the outing. How much time the transfusion they'd given her would give her now was anyone's guess. Christmas Eve and Christmas Day with her children had been her wish.

Sharing a life with Cooper here on the Bourtree had been hers.

She'd felt like a genuine part of the community when they'd asked her to participate in the Nativity…right up until her eyes had connected with Cooper's. And then all that joy had been stripped away. He hadn't told her what his plans were. But what she'd seen in his eyes tonight had told her everything she needed to know.

He didn't want her to stay. His island. His complicated emotions. His guillotine cutting her out of his life.

What an absolute idiot. She'd fallen into exactly the same trap she had with Rafael. And now, yet again, a man she'd thought she loved was calling the shots.

The only thing was…she really did love this man. And the fact that he didn't share the same feelings made this Christmas Eve far worse than the one she'd imagined having back when she'd arrived on this twinkly island all lit by Christmas magic, with Cooper in the centre of it all.

After weeks of unearthing the kind, generous, community-spirited man underneath the Santa suit…the man she'd fallen in love with despite trying to keep her emotions in check… Audrey knew it had all been a horrible, over-hopeful mistake. Audrey the Optimist had been blindsided yet again.

So what to do? Grit her teeth and force herself through the next few days without saying anything until one of them boarded the ferry? Or rip off the plaster and find out what was happening beneath that stoic, manly exterior of his.

'I thought you should know I said I'd take Noreen's post, but I'm going to tell her I've changed my mind.'

Cooper's eyebrows drew together and his eyes arrowed straight to hers. 'What?'

'I probably should've spoken with you first, but…' *But what?* 'I need to start making decisions for myself, you know?'

It felt wrong. Cooper's confused expression. The churning in her gut. The weird energy pinging between them. She loved Bourtree. She loved the patients, the work, the snow angels. *Cooper.* She loved him with all her being…

But she couldn't live her life at the end of someone else's yo-yo, and if ever she'd seen a man who had yet to decide where or how he wanted to live his life it was Cooper Mac-Askill. As such, she needed to take herself out of this picture and put herself in a new one. One of her own making.

'Audrey? What are you talking about?'

She put her drink down and sat down heavily at the small kitchen table where, only hours earlier, they'd been feeding one another fluffy bites of pancake, laughing and sharing syrupy kisses.

'Noreen rang this morning while you were in the shower. She's planning to stay in Australia and asked if I wanted first dibs on her job. I said yes. Too quickly, as it turns out. It's clear that things between us— Well, I think I'd be better off somewhere else. I'll ring Noreen and let her know. I'll stay until they can find a replacement, so as not to have any gaps in care, but I think it's best if I leave as soon as possible.'

Cooper opened his mouth to say something. If he was going to offer some kind of placation, she didn't have it in her to hear it. Tears were percolating so close to the surface she needed to finish her piece, go to bed, wake up, and then try and get on with her life. Just as she'd planned when she'd first taken this post.

She waved her hands between them. 'Rhona and Charlie have said I can stay with them. Not as a lodger. I'll be keeping an eye on Rhona, so Charlie can get some rest.'

Cooper gave his jaw a scrub, lifted his mug, then set it down again without taking a drink. It was impossible to read his expression.

'Is that what you really want?' he asked.

No. It wasn't at all what she wanted. But she had promised herself she'd never feel as if someone else was in charge of her life again, and when she'd seen that look in his eyes back at the church…his look of shock that she'd been invited to participate in the Nativity rather than him, a 'proper' islander…it had cut her to the quick.

It had also thrown a harsh spotlight on the fact that her feelings for Cooper might easily eclipse her power to steer her own life path. The fact she'd been able to sing had been little short of a miracle. But she'd trained her eyes on Rhona, desperately trying to channel an iota of the strength that incredible woman had shown—insisting upon coming to the church, ensuring her family's life carried on as normal, because one day soon, as heartbreaking as it was, her family would have to carry on their lives without her.

'Right, then. If that's what you want, I respect it,' Cooper said. He abruptly rose from the table, poured his drink down the sink and washed his mug. 'I'd best be off to bed. It's been a long day. You sure you're all right for morning rounds?'

'Of course,' she answered quietly.

'And you're comfortable staying here tonight, with me in the house?'

Her heart squeezed tight. She hadn't meant for Cooper to think she was frightened of him, or that she hated him. Quite the opposite. She was in love with him and she was protecting her heart against the fact that it was a love he clearly didn't share.

Being part of the Nativity, a part of island life, with her rounds and even seeing the northern lights, had made her feel safer and more cared for than she had in years. Making love with Cooper had been more than the icing on the cake. It had been the whole cake. Which was why, when he'd looked at her with such shock, such…dismay, she had known she wouldn't be able to bear having it all ripped away from her.

'I'm fine, Coop. Cooper,' she corrected herself. 'Look…

Don't take this personally, please. I'd stay here until the end of my contract if Rhona and Charlie didn't need me. It just seemed an easy way to…you know…wrap things up.'

'Sure.' He gave her a quick nod, with a flash of something darkening his eyes, and then, as she'd seen when they were at Jimmy's, that barrier fell into place and the distance between them widened even further still.

As heartbreaking as it was, she'd made the right decision.

'Night, then,' he said, as if they'd just decided to have porridge in the morning instead of toast. 'See you in the morning.'

And with that he turned and went to bed.

'Merry Christmas,' she whispered to the empty kitchen. 'And a Happy New Year…'

To say Cooper had slept badly was putting it mildly.

At five a.m. he put a night of tossing and turning to an end by throwing back the heavy quilt and heading to the kitchen to put on the kettle.

Why had he told Doc Anstruther he'd take the island GP job before speaking with Audrey?

Because he'd wanted it to be a surprise, that was why. Wanted to offer a future with him as his Christmas present to her.

An epically bad idea when the girl in question didn't want him as a present…or a future.

When he got downstairs Audrey was already there. Dressed in another pair of mismatched red and green scrubs, with a long-sleeved white shirt underneath, she was also wearing the elf hat from the costume he had failed to convince her to wear on the first day.

An olive branch?

'Happy Christmas…'

Her features were anxious, wary. Two things he'd never hoped to see when she was looking at him.

'Happy Christmas,' he replied, without much fanfare.

She made a tiny almost invisible wave, then let her hands fall to her sides.

A surge of frustration rose in him. Why was he acting like an arse? If he really loved her he should want her to be happy. And if not being with him and moving somewhere else made her happy then, yeah, like Charlie had said, it was better to have loved and lost, than never to have loved at all.

And, unlike Charlie, he would get the solace of knowing Audrey had chosen the life she wanted on *her* terms. He knew more than most how important that was. His grandmother had had a choice. She could've put him in care, followed her dream of travelling, but she'd stuck by him—even though he'd been a right royal pain in the posterior. She'd loved him. Through thick and thin.

Being dumped by the woman he loved on Christmas Eve definitely qualified as thin, but Cooper knew the only way he could live with himself was to take his grandmother's lead.

'How about we make ourselves a special breakfast before we head out?' he said.

Her expression softened. There. That was better. This whole heartbreak thing didn't have to include anger and bitterness.

They made a proper hearty breakfast. Cooper even unearthed one of the cookie cutters and shaped the toast into Santa and Christmas tree shapes, which made her laugh.

It was all a bit awkward…but it was *kind* awkward. A damn sight better than anything else.

She took a big gulp of her coffee, then asked, 'What

did you and your grandmother used to do for Christmas? Was your sister here too?'

Cooper shook his head. 'After my parents died, she left pretty sharpish. She found herself in New Zealand and hasn't come back since.'

'Have you been out there?'

He nodded. 'Once—back when I was doing my medical training. I did a six-month stint in one of the emergency departments in Auckland, so I could meet her husband and kids.'

'Oh, that sounds good. Have you thought about going back?'

'No. Don't get me wrong, it was nice, but...' He shifted a few baked beans round his plate. 'They didn't really feel like family. My sister hated all the questions people kept asking about our past, and in the end I felt more of a hindrance than a help, so I left.'

'And that was it?'

'We sent the odd Christmas card, but the lines of communication drifted until...' He made a *pfft* noise and drew his fingers apart. That was it. They'd not properly been in touch for a few years now. Apart, of course, from his telling her about Gertie. Maybe he should reach out to her again. Ring her, even.

An idea began to form.

'Do you fancy going to the pub later today?' he asked.

Audrey gave him a sidelong look. 'Is it even open?'

'Absolutely. It's a Bourtree tradition. It opens up in the late afternoon, after most folks have had their Christmas dinner.'

'Do they serve food?'

'They do. Some folk—the elderly and a handful of singletons—can always be counted on to eat there. We're invited to Doc Anstruther's. I was going to tell you last night, but—'

She held up a hand. 'I kind of kyboshed things last night. I'm sorry for springing that on you. I just thought if I didn't tell you straight away I might change my mind.'

A tiny spark of hope hit the flint in his heart. 'Would you?'

'Change my mind?' Her expression clouded.

Cooper could've kicked himself. *Let the woman make her own choices, man!*

He rose and collected their breakfast dishes. 'Anyway, I was thinking if we went down to the pub it might be a nice time for everyone to raise a glass to my gran. You know, with everyone together and all.'

'Sort of a mini-wake?'

'Exactly.'

'That sounds nice.' Audrey met his eyes, the connection growing taut as she said, 'I'd like that. And then I can head over to Charlie and Rhona's.'

He tried his best not to stiffen. This was her choice. Her call. Something about loving someone and setting them free flitted through his brain.

'Right you are. Well, then… How about we head out and get these rounds sorted?'

By the time they got to the pub Cooper was finding it difficult to keep up his jolly demeanour.

'You all right?' Audrey asked.

'Aye, sure.'

He wasn't, and Audrey knew it. Light banter and chit-chat had proved more difficult as the day had worn on. In the end, most of the car journeys between patients had occurred in silence. Thank goodness for Christmas radio.

'Shall I get you a…red wine, was it?' Audrey offered

as he helped her to take her coat off and hang it in the pub's entryway.

'No, you go on and take a seat. There's a table there by the fire.'

'Oh, you mean our table!'

Audrey pinked up a bit when he gave her a *What are you talking about?* look.

'It's the one where we sat the first time we came here.'

She fluttered her fingers, as if the gesture would erase the moment, and then began to weave her way through the already busy pub towards the table.

Our table?

Could Audrey be as unhappy about her decision as he was?

He didn't bother pushing his way through to the front of the bar. He needed the time to regroup. Stack his facts in the right order. Thank goodness for island time. Sometimes it was genuinely useful.

He turned and looked over towards Audrey, who was already chatting away with someone at one of the adjacent tables. They were pulling out a phone and showing her something or other. Audrey blinked, and then laughed as if she'd just seen something absolutely wonderful.

Gone was the bristly woman who'd arrived on Bourtree and made it very clear she was the type of woman who liked to keep herself to herself. In her place was a woman glowing with approbation and from being part of a community who not only cared for her, but respected her. Exactly what she had said she wanted from life.

She was needed here on Bourtree. People loved her and she loved them. She'd left London seeking solace for a broken heart and had found herself embraced by an entire community.

His heart bashed against his ribcage as a lightbulb went on in his head.

She'd taken Noreen's job because she'd wanted to stay. Right up until she'd thought he didn't want her to. This was the worst possible Gift of the Magi. They were giving each other the 'gift' of ending things before they could even start.

Madness.

Especially when he knew that loving Audrey was the most important thing that had ever happened to him.

He needed to lay to rest that scared, angry little boy whose parents had been so screwed up they hadn't known what they were saying half the time. Today was the day he would become the man his grandmother had believed in. Today was the day he would embrace the future she'd hoped for for him.

One that was honest and open and courageous.

One that—Lord willing—included loving Audrey right here on Bourtree.

Today's rounds should've been enough to convince her to stay if it was just the job she wanted. They'd been given Christmas chocolates, cards, and more mince pies than any pair could handle.

Cayley had given them both enormous bear hugs and said she owed all her confidence and her future career as a costume designer to them.

Jimmy had been concocting an enormous 'healthy' trifle to take over to Angela's before heading to the pub to raise a glass to the pair of them in thanks for finally getting him 'oop and oot the hoose'.

One family had even gave them an entire Christmas pudding, with warnings to mind their teeth as they'd been sure to hide a lucky silver coin in the centre of it.

There had been some tough visits, too. Elderly couples

struggling to make a cup of tea, let alone Christmas dinner. A woman with Parkinson's whom they'd found in tears because she'd stained her favourite Christmas dress after trying and failing to put some cranberry sauce in the crystal bowl her grandmother had always used.

Audrey had brightened each of their days with her smile and her warm cups of tea and, in one case, her tactical redistribution of their Christmas chocolates.

The toughest visit, of course, had been Rhona and Charlie. The couple had said they were getting on as best they could, and had tearily pointed out the small guest room where Audrey could put her things when she came over later that night. Because, yes, they had to admit, caring for Rhona was becoming harder for Charlie to do on his own.

Rhona had definitely looked less rosy-cheeked than she had the night before. But Cooper had been happy to see that once the short squall of tears had passed Rhona had had an aura of tranquillity about her. Acceptance. As if she'd come to terms with her future and made peace with her past, so that all she needed to do from here on was enjoy each and every moment she had with her family.

She knew she was loved.

That was it, wasn't it?

The one thing he hadn't told Audrey.

That she was loved. He loved her. With all his heart.

He'd let his grandmother slip from this world to the next without her knowing how very loved she was. He was damned if he was going to do it again.

'All right there, Coop?' the barman asked when he found himself, buzzing with adrenaline, at the head of the queue. 'Or should I say Doc, now that you're the one literally taking the pulse of the island?'

Cooper obliged him with a laugh, not even bothering

to ask how he'd heard the news…because that was Bour-tree Castle.

He was on the brink of ordering two glasses of red wine, then changed his mind. 'A bottle of champagne, please.'

'Celebrating, are we?'

'Something like that.'

'One new job or two?' the barman asked.

'Depends on how this goes,' he said, accepting the champagne bottle, nestled deep in an ice bucket.

The barman tapped the side of his nose. 'I'll lay my bets on two.'

Cooper reached out and shook the man's hand. 'Thanks, mate. I appreciate it.'

'Aye.'

Cooper nodded, his smile broadening. The plan was to toast new beginnings. Whatever they may be. With any luck he'd be buying everyone in the pub a round by the end of the night.

'Champagne?' Audrey couldn't hide her surprise. 'I thought we were going for red wine?'

'We were, but…' Cooper took his seat across from her. 'It's Christmas Day and we've both been working hard. I might not see much of you over the next few days, so I thought a wee glass of bubbly might be in order—'

'Oh, Coop,' Audrey interjected. 'About that—'

'No—please. I have something I want to say.'

He took her hands in his and, despite her vow to keep her wits about her, her brain started short-circuiting and fizzing the way it did whenever they touched, so listening was probably a good idea until she could put her own thoughts in order.

'I took the job here on Bourtree.' Cooper's voice was

heavy with meaning. 'Doc Anstruther's job. Yesterday morning. Before we got to Jimmy's.'

Her heart lurched against her ribcage. 'I see.'

'I'd like to stay—but not if it makes you unhappy.'

Her skin was all prickly. Had she completely misinterpreted what had happened at Jimmy's? The look they'd shared during the Nativity? 'Go on.'

'I took the job hoping I could find a way for you to stay, but it seems you're intent on leaving. To be honest, without you here, I don't really want to stay either.'

Her heart lurched up into her throat. 'Oh, Coop...' Committing to the job here on Bourtree had been a huge act of faith on his part. Especially if he'd done so not knowing whether or not she'd stay.

His serious expression lightened. He gave her a crooked grin. 'And now I want to try and stop both of us from leaving.'

'What?'

'I love you, Audrey. It's taken me a while to strip everything down, but I've realised there's one important thing in my life and that's you. Loving you has made me whole, and I couldn't bear to see you walk away without you knowing that.'

The butterflies that had all but taken up residency in Audrey's belly took flight again.

He gave the backs of her hands a soft rub with his thumbs. 'I should've told you earlier, but I was so busy being weighed down by what I presumed people were thinking about my past I forgot to focus on what was important.'

'Which is...?' she asked in a whisper.

'The future. A future with you, if you'll have me.'

'Oh, Coop, I—'

'Please. Sorry...' He pressed on. 'I just want to be very

clear. If you want to stay on Bourtree without me we can sort something out. I'll go. I'll stay. Whatever you want. I know you had choices taken away from you in your last relationship, and there is no chance I would ever do that. Your happiness is paramount to me.'

'Cooper, I—'

She tried to interject as he began to fill their champagne glasses, his words getting tangled with hers. He was pouring his heart out to her. It was adorable, and heart-rending, and not at all what she'd expected after his silence last night and his polite but distant behaviour today.

She was surprised she wasn't floating out of her chair. Her heart was so busy swelling with disbelief and relief and the type of joy she'd never imagined possible.

'Audrey Walsh…' Cooper held up his glass.

'Yes, Cooper MacAskill?' She was feeling a bit giggly now—and that was *before* she'd had so much as a sip of champagne. She wondered what would happen when she finally did have a sip.

Although…wait a minute…he wasn't going to—? Her heart froze in place.

'I want to propose a toast to the woman I love.'

Her heart gave a flip and then went all gooey. The man she loved, loved her. He was everything she'd dreamt of and more. Kind, generous, and more than those things— more than his beautiful eyes, his wayward hair, the stubbly chin she always wanted to run her fingers along.

He loved her as much as she loved him. Cooper MacAskill loved her. And it felt more real than anything she'd ever experienced.

'So…here it is. I propose a toast to you, the woman who was strong enough, courageous enough and smart enough to make me take a long, hard look at myself. I know now that I need to change. I got too blinkered. Too afraid of

what people thought of me to see the people who were actually there for me. Supporting me. Including you.'

'You know I love you too, Cooper.'

He closed his eyes and smiled. When he opened them
again, they glowed. 'Music to my ears, my love.' He
brought her palm to his lips and kissed it. 'It took hearing
you say you'd leave Bourtree to knock some proper sense
into me. I know you love it here. And I do, too, all things
considered. So...'

He raised his glass again.

'I'd be honoured if you would consider exploring what
we have together, Audrey. The last thing I want to do is
dictate how you live your life, or where, but...' He pressed
his hand to his heart. 'I've finally realised mine would
be unbelievably happy with you...here...if it'd make *you*
happy.'

Audrey laughed and clinked her glass to Cooper's. 'Of
course it would.'

Cooper whooped and punched the air. 'Are you telling
me you want to stay?'

She nodded. 'After I told you I was leaving it felt so
wrong.'

'Why didn't you say anything?'

She shook her head and scrunched her nose. 'I was
doubting myself. When I announced I was leaving you
didn't fight for me. But I hadn't fought for *you*. I chose
to run away before I knew the whole story. Again. It felt
like I was giving up on something that hadn't yet had a
chance to begin.'

She pressed her hand to her heart, as he had.

'Knowing and loving you has made me realise I'm so
much stronger than I thought I was. Seeing myself through
your eyes has been amazing. So when I thought you didn't

want me here…' She faltered, not wanting to relive that dark moment when she'd thought he wanted her to leave.

Cooper's expression softened into a loving gaze as he cupped her cheek in her hand. 'What do you see in my eyes?'

'Love,' she answered solidly.

'And what do you see now?' He rearranged his features, adding a decidedly higher level of heat.

'Lust!' She giggled.

'What do you get when you combine the two?' he asked.

'The perfect combination?'

'May I propose the toast I really want to make?'

'Yes, please.' She lifted her glass to meet his again.

'To us,' he said.

'To us,' she echoed, taking a sip. 'May I propose one, too?'

'Of course.'

'To Bourtree Castle's Christmas, for reminding us what really matters.'

'Hear, hear!' Cooper drank, then grinned. 'This is now, officially, my favourite time of year.'

'Me too,' Audrey agreed. 'And I think we'll both agree that is most definitely a Christmas miracle.'

Cooper leant in for a kiss, and she was more than happy to return it.

A few moments later she realised how much the whole world had melted away when she began to hear applause and cheers, and then, pulling back, she blushed when she saw that they were for her and Cooper.

Soon enough everyone was on their feet, raising and clinking glasses, sharing in the good news that Bourtree's newest couple had sealed their love with a very public, very satisfying Christmas kiss.

Two Christmases later

'And you're sure you're happy wearing it?'

'I wouldn't want to wear anything else.' Audrey grinned, giving her costume a proud pat.

'You make an amazing Valkyrie.'

'Valkyrie bride,' Audrey reminded him primly, then gave him a little twirl. 'Cayley did a brilliant job on it, don't you think?'

'My love, you could wear a potato sack and look fabulous.' Cooper dropped a kiss onto his brand-new wife's nose and then, unable to resist, pulled her in close for a proper kiss.

'Mmm…tickly.' Audrey ran a finger along Cooper's large white beard. 'Do you think one day our children will catch Mommy kissing Santa Claus?'

'I would put money on it.' Cooper grinned, pulling his beard down under his chin to give Audrey another quick smooch before her big moment.

'Sounds as if it's quite a crowd out there,' she said.

'There always is.'

'I'm so glad your sister made it.'

'Her children are loving Bourtree. I just heard them begging Shona to let them come back every year.'

'That'd be wonderful.' Audrey clapped her hands in a happy round of applause. 'Did she seem to like the idea?'

'She did. I think, like me, she'd built up such a fear about people treating her like they did back in the day, she'd forgotten about all the good things.'

Cooper was grateful he'd followed his gut and eventually, with Audrey by his side every time he made a video call, won his sister's heart back into his life.

'You're an amazing woman, Audrey MacAskill. I

couldn't have asked for a lovelier bride on a more mean-ingful night.'

Her smile turned into a sunbeam. 'If I didn't know bet-ter, Cooper MacAskill, I'd say you're more sentimental than I am!'

'I'm glad you didn't say cheap!' He laughed.

'Why would I say that?' Audrey gave him a weird look. 'Just because we wanted to have our wedding on Christ-mas Eve, and the only time was just before the Nativity... that's not a cost-saving measure. That's clever!'

He ran his knuckle along her jawline. 'That's my girl. Always looking on the bright side.'

Her expression grew serious. 'I wouldn't have married you if I didn't think we could see both sides of the coin together.'

'I know, darlin'. It was amazing, having just about the whole of Bourtree stuffed into the church to be with us as we exchanged vows. I can't believe Doc Anstruther came back from Spain!'

'I know! Another Christmas miracle,' she agreed with a grin. 'I loved having everyone being part of our day. It made it extra-special. Now!' She clapped her hands and pointed towards the doorway leading to the church. 'Go on out there. We've got to sing some joy into the world!'

He pulled her to him for a fierce, tight hug. 'You know I will always do everything in my power to make sure you're happy and safe.'

'I know, my love. That's the other reason I married you.' She popped on her Viking helmet and gave him a happy grin. 'Now, get on out there—otherwise we're both going to miss my grand entrance.'

He gave her a jaunty salute. 'Aye-aye, Cap'n. I'm look-ing forward to cheering the new Mrs MacAskill on her grand entrance.'

'And I'm looking forward to a long, happy future as Mrs MacAskill.'

Cooper pulled her in for another kiss, and Audrey was late for her cue. But no one cared because it was a happy day for more reasons than one.

And when they all raised their voices in unison Cooper's and Audrey's eyes met and locked, joy permeating every note and smile as they belted out the lyrics of 'Joy to the World'.

It really did feel as if heaven and nature were singing just for them on this, their special day, and for evermore.

* * * * *

MISTLETOE KISS WITH THE HEART DOCTOR

MARION LENNOX

MILLS & BOON

CHAPTER ONE

HE'D MISS HIS plane if he didn't hurry.

Dr Marcus Pierce was on Gannet Island under pressure. Three weeks before she'd died, his mother had gripped his hand and pleaded, 'Marc, please scatter my ashes from Lightning Peak. It's the most beautiful place in the world, the place where I found comfort when I knew I had to leave your father. You were at boarding school, so I knew you were old enough to cope, but it was hard on me. That first Christmas I hiked up there to watch the sunset and I knew I'd done the right thing. Can I die knowing I'll be resting back there this Christmas?'

Despite the strains on their relationship—sometimes he'd even thought, *What relationship?* because surely he'd learned independence when he was a child—there was no way he could refuse such a plea. But his mother might have found an easier peak, Marc decided as he fought his way along the little used bush path. There were plenty of scenic spots near Sydney. Spots that didn't involve a long flight in a small plane, a rugged hike up an overgrown path he wasn't too sure of, and then another rush to catch the plane home again.

But as he watched his mother's ashes settle in the bushland around him, as he soaked in the salt-filled sea breeze and gazed down at the tiny town beneath him and the ocean beyond, he had to acknowledge this place was breathtakingly lovely.

Lightning Peak was almost at the top of the mountain. Moisture was slipping from above, forming a waterfall dropping to a pool of crystal-clear water. The only sound was the splash of water as it hit the pool and then found its way into some unknown underground stream.

He was sitting on a rock looking out at seemingly the whole world. Behind him was a haven for animals, a waterhole in this most unexpected of places.

Gannet was the largest of a group of six gorgeous, semitropical islands—the Birding Isles—set far out in the Pacific Ocean. This island in particular had been a healing place for his mountain climbing mother. Louise had been a doctor, an academic researcher. She was highly intelligent but, apart from her disastrous attempt at marriage and motherhood, she was intensely solitary. He could see why Louise had loved it.

There was, however, little time for reflection. His return flight to Sydney left in three hours. Today was Tuesday, and on Thursday he was due to fly to Switzerland. He needed to tie up loose ends at the hospital tomorrow, and pay a couple of cursory Christmas visits to elderly aunts. He needed to get down this mountain now.

He turned—but then he hesitated.

There were three paths leading from the rock platform where he stood.

Actually, they weren't proper paths—they looked more like desire lines for the animals that drank from this rock pool. He hadn't come up the main mountain path, but a side track his mother knew.

'The main lookout's gorgeous but my favourite place is where the water is, on the other side of the mountain,' his mother had told him. 'The path's overgrown—hardly anyone knows about it—but I'll draw you a map. You can't miss it.'

He'd taken care, following her shaky instructions and hand-drawn map to the letter.

When you reach the massive lightning-hit split rock, walk around it and you'll find the path continues. Then there's a Norfolk pine half a kilometre along where the path diverges. Keep left...

He'd reached the rocky platform he was now standing on with a feeling of relief. Turning now though... Which trace of a path had he used when he'd arrived? He'd been so relieved to make it he hadn't noticed.

He glanced again at Louise's map. Close though she'd been to death, her mind had still been sharp, and her instructions to climb to the peak were brilliant.

Her instructions to descend...not so much. She'd have expected him to notice.

He should have noticed. The omission annoyed him. Dr Marcus Pierce was a cardiac surgeon at the top of his field, and his normal setting was one of intelligence, incisiveness and surety.

He wasn't sure now—and he didn't have time to miss his plane.

So think. All the paths had to go down, he reasoned. If he chose the middle one then surely it'd join with the main track somewhere below.

He checked his phone, and even though he was now officially on leave he saw he'd been contacted. He and his friends had booked to fly to Switzerland on Thursday night. The plan was to arrive on Christmas Eve—Saturday—for two weeks of skiing at St Moritz. He was therefore off-duty but, no matter where he was, the medical calls didn't stop.

In honour of his mother he'd switched his phone to silent, so now he had scores of queued messages. The sight was normal, grounding. It reminded him that he was a surgeon who didn't have time for indecision.

But still he stood with his phone in his hand, fighting unusual qualms. He had an urge to ring Kayla. Kayla was a radiologist, a colleague, part of his friendship group about to head to Switzerland. For the last few months they'd been intermittently dating.

But their relationship was fun more than deep, and Kayla was practical. She'd have thought he was overly sentimental if he'd told her what he was doing. Maybe she was right. His isolated childhood had taught him emotion only got in the way of calm good sense, and there was no use phoning her now when calm good sense was all that was needed.

He was wasting time. The middle path seemed more used than the other two.

Go.

Lightning Peak was Dr Elsa McCrae's happy place. Her place of peace. Her place where she could say to patients, *'Sorry, I'm up on Lightning Peak, you'll have to contact Grandpa.'*

She couldn't say it too often these days. At seventy-eight, her grandpa was slowing down. Robert McCrae was unable to cope with the demands of being a doctor on his own, and she tried to spare him as much as she could, but every so often a woman just needed 'me' time.

For once her afternoon clinic had finished early. It was Wednesday, only four days until Christmas. From now on her life would be packed, with patients thinking every last niggle had to be sorted before Christmas Day itself. Then there was Boxing Day, with the usual influx of patients with injuries from new toys, or islanders who'd eaten far too much the day before. She had a queue of things she should be doing right now—there were always things—but her need to get away had been overwhelming. This would be her only chance to regroup before the rush.

She reached the peak after a solitary two-hour climb, checked her phone to make sure there were no catastrophes back in town, then sat on the massive rock platform, looking out to sea. And let her mind drift.

The other five islands that formed the Birding Isles were dots in the distance. Five hundred kilometres away—well out of sight—lay Australia, Sydney, where the evac team came from, where her patients went when she couldn't help them here. There were no doctors on the other islands. Fishing boats took patients back and forth at need—or took Elsa to them—but, apart from her grandfather, Sydney was her closest medical backup.

Last week a visiting tourist had had a major heart attack. She'd somehow hauled him back from cardiac arrest, but he'd arrested again and died before the medevac team had arrived. If he'd been closer to a major cardiac unit... If she'd had colleagues to help...

'Stop it,' she told herself. If she wasn't here there'd be no one at all. Grandpa was failing, and there were no bright young doctors hammering on the door to take up such a remote and scattered practice. What was needed was some sort of integrated medical facility, with means to transfer patients easily between the islands, but the cost of that would be prohibitive. Money was a huge problem.

An hour's boat ride across to an outer island, a couple of hours treating a patient and organising evacuation, an hour's boat ride back—how could she charge islanders anywhere near what that was worth? She couldn't. Her medical practice was therefore perpetually starved for funds, with no financial incentive for any other doctor to join her.

She loved this island. She loved its people and there'd never been a time she'd thought of leaving. It'd break her grandpa's heart and it'd break her heart, but sometimes—like now—she wouldn't mind time away. Christmas shopping in the big department stores. Crowds of shoppers where no one knew her. Bustle, chaos, fun.

A boyfriend who wasn't Tony?

Tony definitely wasn't the one. After just one date he'd explained the very sensible reasons why they should marry, and he'd been proprietary ever since. He made no secret of his intentions and the islanders had jokingly egged him on. Of course she'd said no, and she'd keep saying no, but the pool of eligible guys on the island was depressingly small.

Sometimes she even found herself thinking she could—should?—end up with Tony. Or someone like Tony.

'You have to be kidding. No one I've dated in the whole time I've been here makes my toes curl,' she told the view, and her dopey beagle, Sherlock, came sniffing back to make sure she was okay.

'I'm fine,' she told the little dog, but she lifted him up and hugged him, because for some reason she really needed a hug. Last week's death had shattered her, maybe even more so because she knew her grandfather had heart problems. Plus he had renal problems. She was just…alone.

'But I'm not alone,' she told Sherlock fiercely, releasing him again to head into his sniffy places in the undergrowth. 'I have Grandpa. I have you. Even if I'm not going to marry Tony, I have the whole of the Birding Isles.'

'Who all depend on me,' she added.

'Yeah, so why are you here staring into space when they

need you back in town?' she demanded of herself. 'What dramas am I missing now?'

She rose reluctantly and took a last long look at the view, soaking in the silence, the serenity, the peace. And then she turned to leave.

'Sherlock?' she called and got a sudden frenzied barking in return.

He was well into the bushes, investigating one of the myriad animal tracks that led from this point. He'd have some poor animal cornered, she thought—a wombat, a goanna. A snake?

She wasn't too fussed. Sherlock might be dumb, but he knew enough to stay out of darting distance from a snake, and he never hurt anything he'd cornered. Her dog was all nose and no follow through, but once he'd found the source of a scent he wouldn't leave it. Sighing, she reached into her pocket for his lead and headed into the bush after him.

But she went carefully. This was cave country. The water from the falls had undercut the limestone, and crevices and underground river routes made a trap for the unwary. Her grandpa had taught her the safe routes as a kid, and Sherlock's barking was well off the path she usually followed.

But by the sound of his frenzied barking he wasn't too far, and she knew the risks. She trod carefully, stepping on large rocks rather than loose undergrowth, testing the ground carefully before she put her weight on it.

Sherlock's yapping was reaching a crescendo—whatever he'd found had to be unusual. Not a 'roo then, or a wombat or koala. She wondered what it could be.

'Sherlock?' she yelled again in a useless attempt to divert him.

But the response left her stunned. It was a deep male voice, muffled, desperate.

'Help. Please help.'

He was stuck. Uselessly stuck. Hurting. Helpless.

He'd broken his leg and dislocated his shoulder. The pain was searing, but his predicament almost overrode the pain.

He was maybe fifteen feet down from the chink of light that showed the entrance to the underground chamber into which he'd fallen. The hole must have been covered with twigs and leaf litter, enough to cover it, enough for small animals to cross. Enough to think he was following a proper path.

He'd been moving fast. There'd been a sickening lurch as his boot had stepped through the fragile cover, and an unbelievable sensation as the entire ground seemed to give way. Then the freefall. The agony of his leg buckling underneath him. A searing pain in his shoulder.

And then fear.

He was on rock and dirt, on an almost level floor. He could see little except the light from the hole he'd made above him. The rest of the cave was gloomy, fading to blackness where the light from the hole above cut out.

He'd dropped his phone. He'd had it in his hand, but had let it go to clutch for a hold as he'd fallen. Maybe it was down here but he couldn't find it, and whenever he moved the pain in his leg and shoulder almost made him pass out. He could contact no one.

No phone. No light. Just pain.

According to his watch he'd been underground for twenty-seven hours. He'd dozed fretfully during the night but the pain was always with him. Today had stretched endlessly as he'd fought pain, exhaustion, panic.

He was unbelievably thirsty.

He was finding it hard to stay awake.

He was going nuts.

He'd been calling but he did it intermittently, knowing the chances of being heard in such a place were remote. The effort of calling was making him feel dizzy and sick. He knew he had to harness his resources, but what resources? He had nothing left.

And when could he expect help?

First rule of bushwalking—advise friends of dates and routes. He'd told Kayla he had family business to sort from his mother's death and he was turning his phone off for twenty-four hours. He hadn't told anyone he was flying all the way to Gannet Island.

Panic was so close…

And then, through the mist of pain and exhaustion, he heard a dog. The dog must have sensed he was down here—it was going crazy above him.

And then, even more unbelievably, he heard a woman calling, 'Sherlock!'

Don't go to her.

It was a silent plea to the dog, said over and over in his head as he yelled with every ounce of strength he possessed and tried to drag himself closer to the hole.

'Help… Don't come close—the ground's unsafe—but please get help.'

Elsa froze.

She knew at once what must have happened. Someone had fallen into one of the underground caverns.

Instinct would have had her shoving her way through the undergrowth to reach whoever it was, but triage had been drilled into her almost from the first day in med school.

First ensure your own safety.

Sherlock was barking in a place that was inherently unsafe. Her little beagle was light on his feet, used to following animal tracks. Elsa, not so much. She'd be dumb to charge off the path to investigate.

She stood still and called, as loud as she could, 'Hey! I'm here. Where are you?'

Sherlock stopped barking at that, seeming to sense the import of her words, and here came the voice again.

'I've fallen underground. Be careful. It looks…it looks like a path but it's not. The ground's unstable.'

'I'm careful,' she called, making her words prosaic and reassuring as possible. 'I'm a local. A doctor. Are you hurt?'

'Yes.' She could hear pain and exhaustion in his tone, and his words were cracking with strain. 'Broken leg and… I think…dislocated shoulder. I fell…through yesterday.'

Yesterday. To lie wounded in the dark for so long…this was the stuff of nightmares.

Next step? Reassurance.

'Okay, we're on it. I'll call for backup and we'll get you out of there,' she called back. 'It might take a while but help's coming.'

'Thank…thank you.'

But his words faded badly, and she wondered how much effort it had cost him to call out.

'Is your breathing okay?' she shouted. 'Are you bleeding? Do you have water?'

No answer.

'Hello?'

Silence.

Had he drifted into unconsciousness? Collapsed? Was he dying while she stood helplessly above?

Triage, she told herself fiercely. She was no use to anyone if she panicked.

She flipped open her satellite phone, dependable wherever she went, either here or on the outer islands. Her call went straight through to Macka, Gannet Island's only policeman.

'Elsa. What's up?' Macka was in his sixties, big, solid, dependable. He'd been a cop here for as long as Elsa could remember, and the sound of his voice grounded her.

'I'm up on Lightning Peak, following the back path around to the east, almost to the top,' she told him. 'Sherlock's just found someone who's fallen into an underground cavern.'

There was a moment's pause. Macka would know straight away the gravity of the situation.

'Alive?'

'I heard him call but he's been stuck since yesterday.'

'You're safe yourself?'

'Yeah, but I need to go down. He's stopped answering and his breathing sounded laboured. I have basic stuff in my backpack.'

'Elsa...'

'It's okay. I have a decent rope and it was you who taught me to rappel.'

'Wait for us.'

'I can't. It'll take you a couple of hours to reach us. The light'll fail before you get here and I don't know how bad he is. Macka, I'll turn on location sharing on my phone. Can you take a screenshot now so you know exactly where I am? I'm not sure if this phone will work underground.'

'It should, but Elsa...'

'I can't see that I have any other choice,' Elsa said, hearing his deep concern. 'But I'll stay safe, you know I will. And Sherlock will be up top—he'll bark when he hears you.'

'Elsa, please wait for us.'

'But it sounds like he's lost consciousness,' she said, almost gently. Macka's first concern was always to protect her—there was still a part of him that thought of her as the kid who'd landed on the island as a neglected seven-year-old. But she was all grown up now, and triage told her what she was doing was sensible. 'I need to go down and see what's going on, but I'll take every care. Can you let Grandpa know what's happening? Tell him it's under control, though. Don't scare him.'

'I wouldn't dare,' Macka said, and she heard the hint of a rueful smile. 'Anything you say, Elsa.'

'Hey, I'm not that bossy.'

'Reckon you are,' he said, and she heard another smile. Then, in a different tone, 'Reckon you've had to be. But be careful.'

'Same to you,' she told him. 'Don't come up here alone; bring a couple of the guys from the fire station.'

She heard the trace of a chuckle at that. 'Hey, you know Tony's a volunteer. He'll want to come.'

'Yeah, like that'll help,' she said wryly, thinking of staid, solid Tony who'd been acting more and more possessive without any encouragement. 'Macka, do me a favour and don't tell him.'

'This is Gannet, love. This news'll be all over the island before you even disconnect.'

'Fine,' she said wearily. 'Bring the cavalry then. Only Macka, be careful yourselves. This place is dangerous.'

'Don't I know it,' he said grimly. 'Okay, love, let's make sure I have this screenshot with co-ordinates so I know exactly where you are, and get this rescue underway.'

CHAPTER TWO

ELSA HAD BEEN back on the island, working as a doctor, for five years now, and in that time she'd learned to be self-sufficient. The Birding Isles were a speck of six islands in the middle of the Pacific Ocean. They formed a tourist paradise, and tourists sometimes did stupid things. The permanent population of Gannet was seven hundred, but the numbers swelled dramatically over the summer months, and both tourists and locals quickly learned who Elsa was.

She was Doc, and she was fair game. Always. Her latest heart sink had happened only this morning in the general store, in a tiny sliver of time she'd managed between seeing patients. She'd been choosing rolls of Christmas wrapping paper when one of the local fishermen had approached her, hauled off his boot, stood on one leg and held up a grubby foot.

'Reckon me toe's rotten, Doc,' he'd told her, swaying on one leg as the other shoppers had backed away in disgust. 'Pus's been coming out for two days now.'

It was indeed infected. She'd told him to replace his boot and meet her at the surgery. Thankfully, Mae, the owner of the shop, had yelled after her, 'How many of these rolls do you want, Doc?' and a dozen rolls of garish crimson paper had landed on her desk an hour later.

The locals were great, but this type of interruption happened to her all the time. She'd try to go for a swim and someone would yell, 'Doc, the lady over here's got a fish hook stuck in her arm...' Or, 'Doc, a kid's just done a header into a sandbank. Hurt his neck...'

The nurses at the tiny Gannet hospital and on the outer islands were skilled and professional. Her grandfather still did what he could, but she was always first on call.

Like now. She'd slipped away for a last break before the Christmas rush, and she had to rescue someone down a hole.

But she was always prepared. The advantage of being accustomed to urgent calls wherever she went was that she always carried a basic backpack. Small things but vital. A satellite phone. A water bottle. Bandages, antiseptic, adrenaline, antihistamine, glucagon, morphine. She'd almost forgotten what it felt like to walk around without her gear, and she blessed it now.

If she got down the hole, she had supplies that might help.

And she had rope too. This island was a climber's paradise. Most climbers knew their stuff, but it was also a fabulous place for a family holiday. She'd had emergency calls before. 'Doc, there's a kid stuck on a ledge ten feet down with a split knee...'

During her island childhood she'd learned to climb well, and it was often safer and faster to climb to whatever drama was playing out rather than wait for Macka's team.

So she had what she needed, a light, strong rope that looped permanently around the sides of her backpack.

She formed an arrow of stones on the path, backup to show rescuers where she was. Then she headed into the bush, towards the sound of Sherlock's barking, moving from rock to rock, testing each one before she shifted her weight. When the rocks ran out, ten feet before the spot where Sherlock was peering down, she looped the cord around a solid eucalypt. Then she inched further, testing and retesting, until she reached the break in the ground.

It was easy enough to see what had happened. This looked like part of an animal path. Trodden leaf litter lay on either side of a gaping hole where someone had obviously slipped, clutched in vain, then fallen. The surface of leaf litter had obviously held up for light-footed native animals. For a man, not so much.

As she neared the hole she lay on her stomach and inched forward, testing all the way. Using her phone's torch she peered down into the darkness, but she could see nothing. She had another stronger torch, attached to her belt with a carabiner. She fumbled it free and peered again.

She could make out the floor of the cave, maybe fifteen feet down. She couldn't see the man who'd called out.

'Hello?'

Nothing.

Sherlock was on his stomach as well, quivering with excitement, trying to lick her face as she peered down.

'You found him. Well done, boy,' she told him, 'but you're going to have to stay up top and wait for the cavalry.'

She'd have to rappel. Rappelling without a harness was not her favourite thing—for a start the cord would hurt like hell as she'd need to form a makeshift 'seat'. It'd cut into her waist and groin, but there was no avoiding it. With luck, the guys up top would provide her with a decent harness to haul her back up again.

But that was for later. For now she headed back to the tree, fastening her cord as she needed, taking both ends, tying them around her waist, then looping the cord between her legs to form a system where she could safely control her descent.

To Sherlock's disgust she attached him to the same tree. 'Stay,' she told him, and he looked at her with disbelief.

What? I found him and you won't let me come?

One swift pat and she left him, returning to the hole, moving backwards, then leaning back, testing the strength of her rope, testing her control.

Sherlock was staring after her in concern.

'Needs must,' she told him, with a forced attempt at cheer. 'You do dumb things because you're a dog. Me, I'm a doctor, and that means I get to do things that are even dumber.'

And on that note she backed carefully over the lip of the hole and started her descent.

Rappelling on thick flax rope was relatively easy. Rappelling on thin cord was entirely different. The cord did indeed dig into her pelvis and her waist, and her hands struggled to keep their grip. But she managed.

She'd checked out all sides of the hole and figured the side she was on looked the most stable—the last thing she wanted was for the hole to suddenly enlarge, throwing dirt and rock onto the man below. She moved with infinite care, inching her way. It would have been less painful to move faster, but losing control could mean disaster.

She edged into the hole, catching a last glimpse of a concerned Sherlock before she was in the darkness of the cavern.

She had no hands free to hold her phone, and she'd had to reattach her mini torch to her belt. The light from the torch swung in all the wrong directions. What she needed was a headlamp. Her legs sought for a foothold and found none.

Five feet. Ten.

And at fifteen she finally felt solid rock.

Still she kept the strain on her rope rather than putting her weight on the ground.

She hung in her makeshift harness, fighting back pain as she grabbed her torch again.

There was a mound of leaf litter under her—that must have fallen from above—but the cave stretched out into darkness. The floor was strewn with rocks, dusty grey. At least it seemed solid.

And there he was. The man lay slumped, seemingly lifeless, slightly to the side of where she hung. Her heart hit her boots as she saw him, but as the torchlight hit his face he stirred, winced, then raised his hand to hide his eyes from the beam.

He was a big guy, tall, lean, muscled, built like many of the rock climbers who loved this place.

He didn't look like a rock climber, though. He was wearing fawn chinos and a short-sleeved shirt that wouldn't be out of place in an informal business meeting. His face was framed with short dark hair, dust and an impressive after-five shadow. A trickle of dried blood ran across his forehead and down to his cheek. Still she had the impression of inherent strength.

As he lowered his hand and looked at her, the impression of strength deepened. His piercing eyes surveyed her, as if she was the patient rather than him.

But he *was* the patient and he'd obviously just surfaced from unconsciousness.

She'd done a fast assessment of the cave now. The ground seemed safe enough. She undid her makeshift harness, looped it, tied it to her belt—the last thing she wanted was to lose it, leaving her stuck here—and stooped to examine her patient.

He opened his mouth to speak, failed the first time

and then tried again. 'You can't be real,' he managed. 'An…angel?'

'You guessed it. I'm an angel in scruffy jeans and a torn windcheater, with a daft dog barking his head off up top. An angel? Give me a minute while I figure where I put my wings.'

He managed a smile. Almost.

'Hey, I'm not a vision,' she told him, aware that, despite the piercing gaze, what this guy most needed was reassurance. 'I'm Elsa McCrae—Dr McCrae.' She reached for his wrist and was relieved to feel a steady heartbeat. Fast but not scary fast. 'And you?'

'Marcus Pierce,' he told her, struggling to get the words out. 'M… Marc.' His throat sounded thick, clogged. 'Also… I'm also a doctor.'

'Hey, how about that? A colleague?' Fat lot of good that'd be doing you down here, though, she thought. 'Does your neck hurt? Your back?'

'No. Just…my leg. And my shoulder.'

She'd already seen his leg. It lay twisted under him. And his shoulder? It was at the wrong angle. Dislocated? Ouch.

'Your head?' She was looking at the blood on his face.

'I hit it on the way down.' He winced. 'It's nothing. Didn't knock me out.'

'You fainted just now.'

'I never…faint.'

She fixed him with a look. If he was indeed a colleague, he'd know that was nonsense. 'You're lying. Everyone faints, given the right circumstances,' she told him. 'You certainly seem to have lost consciousness after you talked to me earlier.'

'I tried to drag myself under the hole so you'd see me,' he managed grimly. 'Stupid.'

'Yes, because if you'd succeeded I could have landed on

you when I climbed down.' She was making her voice deliberately cheerful, deliberately matter-of-fact. 'So passing out was a good thing. It seems your body is more sensible than your head. So lie still now while I see what's what.'

He closed his eyes. Just how much pain are you in? she wondered.

But first things first. Carefully she checked his neck, his movement, his vision. She tested his hands. 'Squeeze please.' She checked his good leg. 'Wriggle your toes?' His good arm. 'Squeeze my fingers.'

He squeezed and held for longer than he needed. She got that. He must have been lying here terrified.

But what she was finding was reassuring. No obvious head injury. No spinal damage as far as she could see. Just the leg and shoulder. And the fact that he was trapped underground.

Next?

She took her water bottle from her backpack and gently raised his head. His eyes flew open.

'Water,' she said, and got a flash of gratitude so great it almost overwhelmed her.

She held the bottle to his mouth. Half the bottle went down before he paused, wiping his mouth, sinking back with a grunt of thanks.

'If you knew how good that tasted…'

'I guess I do. You fell down yesterday? You've had nothing to drink since then?'

'I had a bottle in my bag,' he told her. 'I think…my bag fell with me but I can't see where it is. I tried to search…'

He didn't have to explain further. To drag himself around this rock-filled cavern in the dark with a broken leg… His face was etched with pain; his voice didn't disguise it.

'If it's down here then I'll find it,' she told him, still with that careful cheerfulness. 'But let's get you something for the pain first. Any allergies? If you're a doctor you'll know the drill. Anything I should know about?'

'You don't have morphine?' he asked, incredulous, and she gave him a modest smile, which was probably wasted given that she was working only with the beam of her torch and she was shining the torch on him. To him she must merely be a shadow.

But that was her job, to be a professional, reassuring shadow. 'I'm a Girl Scout from way back,' she told him. 'I was raised to Be Prepared. Brown Owl would be proud of me.'

'I'm proud of you,' he murmured, sinking back on the hard ground. 'No allergies. Feel free to give me as much as you have.'

She didn't. She'd been stuck before, on a ledge where she'd abseiled down, waiting for a helicopter to take an injured kid off. There'd been a five-hour wait and the kid had needed a top-up. She'd needed to keep some in reserve then, and she might need to do the same now. They might well be stuck here for hours. Or longer.

Her mind was racing now but, wherever it raced, she couldn't see a safe way out of here until morning. They'd need a stretcher and they'd need secure fastenings up top. The closest stable land was thirty feet from the hole. They'd increase the risk of ground collapsing if they weren't working in daylight. She'd definitely need her reserves of morphine.

She didn't say any of that, though. She swabbed his thigh, injected the drug, then carefully sliced away the torn leg of his jeans so she could see what she was dealing with.

That the leg was broken was obvious. She'd seen the rough stones under the entrance hole and thought he must have landed on those. The impact and falling awkwardly would have been enough to snap the bones.

But it wasn't all bad. She touched his ankle and was relieved to feel warmth, plus a pulse. 'Great news, your foot's still breathing,' she told him, taking him at his word that he was a doctor. It didn't take much medical training to know that a break could cut blood supply, and twenty-four hours without would mean dire consequences. 'But the leg does look broken.'

'Of course it's broken,' he growled. 'I couldn't have this degree of pain without a break. How badly?'

'I'm not sure,' she confessed. 'It doesn't look too bad from where I'm standing. When the morphine kicks in I'll check your toes.'

'Check 'em now.'

'No.' She wasn't having him passing out again. 'If you can bear it, just lie back and see if you can relax until that pain relief kicks in. Then I'll cut off your boot and check your shoulder. It looks dislocated—maybe fractured...'

'I think dislocated,' he told her.

'You might be right, but let's not investigate until the morphine's had time to work. Meanwhile I need to summon the troops. Lie back and think of England while I organise me a posse.'

There was silence at that, and she could almost see his mind sifting her words.

'A posse?' he said at last, sounding cautious. 'You mean...you're on your own?'

'I have my dog. Me and Sherlock.'

'But you've climbed down here without backup.'

'I'm not an idiot,' she told him, hearing alarm. He'd gone straight to the scenario of two people stuck down here rather than one. 'First, I've used a secure rappelling loop, so I can get out again whenever I want. Carrying you with me, not so much, but I've covered that too, because secondly I've already let people know where I am and what I'm doing. Which I'm guessing you haven't?'

'No,' he said ruefully. 'I know, it was incredibly stupid of me, but it's too late to do anything about it now.'

'Don't worry about it,' she told him, thinking though that he was right to feel dumb. Didn't he realise just how close to total disaster he'd been? But she guessed he already knew that. He'd had more than twenty-four hours to think about it. 'Our lovely Sergeant of Police and his troops will probably already be on their way,' she told him, keeping her voice brisk and cheerful. 'I just need to update them on what's needed.'

'So...' He looked as if he was struggling to get his head around what was happening. 'You're not part of a search party already looking for me?'

'Afraid not. Will anyone be wondering where you are?'

'No.' Blunt. Harsh.

'Then that's what you get for not letting anyone know you're here. Downside—no one knows you're here.'

'You think I'm an idiot.'

'Mine's not to judge,' she said primly. Talking was a good way to distract him from pain. 'I just deal with stuff as I find it.'

'And I'm...stuff.'

'I'm sure you're very nice stuff,' she reassured him.

'But idiotic stuff.'

She smiled, hearing the mortification behind his words, but she didn't say anything. It certainly wasn't her place to judge, but he needed to accept that his actions had indeed been foolish.

'So...' he said at last. 'You and your dog were just scouring the mountains looking for any injured...stuff?'

'Sherlock and I found an orphaned wallaby last week,'

she told him. 'So yeah, I guess that's us. Like St Bernards in the snow.' She wrinkled her nose. 'And that needs an apology. I forgot to attach the brandy keg around Sherlock's neck. The wallaby didn't need it, but here... Total fail. We'll be crossed off the Worldwide Beagle Rescue Association forthwith.'

He was looking dazed, struggling to follow the flippancy she was using to distract him until the morphine kicked in. 'So Sherlock's...a beagle?'

'Yes he is, and he found you. You owe him a month's supply of dog treats.'

'Who the hell are you?' It was almost a snap.

'Ooh, that's supposed to be my question.' She thought she wasn't doing such a bad job of distracting him. 'Drat, I have a whole questionnaire for new patients back at the surgery. Where's my form when I need it? But I already told you I'm a doctor. Elsa McCrae. FRACGP. General Practitioner. And you?'

'Marcus Pierce,' he responded. 'FRACS. FRACP. Cardiologist.'

FRACS—College of Surgeons. FRACP—College of Physicians. 'A heart surgeon,' she said, imbuing her voice with deferential awe. Thinking, though, that it was so often the intelligent ones that got themselves into dire trouble on the island. Smart didn't always equate to sensible, but she kept her voice neutral. 'That's great,' she told him. 'As soon as the morphine kicks in I'll get you to keep track of your pulse while I check your shoulder and take your boot off. Marcus, will anyone be out looking for you?'

'No.' A flat veto.

'You don't have friends on the island?'

'I came here to scatter my mother's ashes,' he said tightly. 'Privately.'

'I'm sorry,' she said, more gently. 'Did your mother live here?'

'She visited frequently. She loved this peak.'

She sat back on her heels, frowning. Thinking of his name. Pierce. Making associations.

Remembering a little lady with a fierce determination to climb every peak on the island. A lady who'd had to come to see her the last time she was on the island because she couldn't stop coughing. 'I know what's wrong with me, girl,' she'd said when Elsa had listened to her chest. 'I'm a doctor myself. There's nothing you can do to cure me. I just want something to alleviate the symptoms so I can climb Lightning Peak one last time.'

'Louise Pierce?' she said now, even more gentle. 'Was Louise your mum?'

'I…yes.'

'I knew her. She spent a lot of time here, at the Misses Harnett's guesthouse, and we were so sorry when we heard she'd died.' She sighed. 'I know it's easy to be wise after the event, but Rhonda and Marg Harnett were your mother's friends. They would have come up here with you in a heartbeat.'

'I didn't want complications,' he growled. 'I came on yesterday morning's plane and I was intending to be out on the evening plane.'

'And now you have more complications than you could have imagined.' She sighed again. 'I'm so sorry. But I need you to shush now while I try my phone and see if I can get reception from down here.'

She phoned and the satellite did her proud. The line crackled and broke but Macka heard her. 'It's up to you,' she told him. 'But I can't think it'll be safe to bring him up until dawn. Can you bring us a decent lamp, pillows, rugs and maybe a couple of air mattresses? I have a rappelling loop set up so we can lower stuff. Oh, and can you bring some dog food for Sherlock?' Her dog had ceased barking but she knew he'd be waiting patiently above ground and wanting his dinner.

She disconnected and turned to find Marcus looking mortified. 'Morning?'

'Sorry, but I don't think it's safe to bring you up until we have decent light.'

'Hell,' he said. And then, 'There's no need for you to stay down here too.'

'You know there is,' she said matter-of-factly. 'You've done the medical training. You know the rules.'

'I won't have blood clots. I won't pass out again.'

'Yeah, but I didn't bring the indemnity forms,' she told him. 'And it's no problem. Because of the remoteness of this island I did extra training as an emergency doctor. Rappelling into caves and being stuck underground will add enormous credit to my CV.'

She was swinging her torch beam around the floor as she talked. She found his phone first. Smashed in the fall. Thank God for Sherlock's hunting instincts, she thought. Without his phone he could have lain here until…

No. It didn't bear thinking about.

She also found a good-looking leather slouch bag, which held a wallet and, wonderfully, another bottle of water. On the strength of it she offered Marcus more.

He drank with gratitude. Despite the greyness of his face as she'd shown him his smashed phone—he must realise what he'd been facing even more acutely than she did—he was looking less rigid. The morphine must be taking effect.

'Right,' she said briskly as he settled again—or settled as much as anyone could on dirt and rocks— 'let's get you to work. Cardiac surgeon? I don't need the surgeon part so much, but can you keep track of your pulse while I get this boot off?'

He even managed a chuckle at that, a deep, nice chuckle, another great sign that the morphine was working.

Leg first. The shoulder needed attention but blood supply to the foot had to be her first concern.

She headed for his boot, blessing the sharp little everything tool she always carried. Yes, his ankle had a pulse, but she wanted to see pink toes. His foot was swollen—she'd expect nothing else with the damage to his leg—and the boot alone could now be constricting supply.

'So, your job...' he said, and she could hear the strain in his voice as she took her time to slice the thick, good quality leather. 'You're on permanent patrol up here? Is that how you make a living? Donations from the grateful lost? How many hikers do you find?'

'More than you might think,' she told him, remembering previous island walks interrupted as she'd come across lacerations, sprained ankles, insect bites—and, more recently and more dreadfully, the full-blown cardiac arrest.

She could have used a cardiac surgeon then, she thought bleakly. She'd never felt so alone, so helpless. Specialist help could have saved a life, but it was an ocean away.

'And the rest of the time?' he asked.

'I have a surgery down near the jetty,' she managed, hauling herself from just one of the memories of failure that haunted her. 'We have a hospital too. It serves all the islands. It's mostly used for our elderly—six of our ten beds are classified nursing home. The rest are simple problems—minor infections, patients waiting for evacuation to Sydney or continuing their recovery after being transported home. It's a very basic medical service but it's all we can manage.' She had his sock off now and was examining toes. 'Marcus, this is looking good. There can be no blood supply constriction at all.'

'Just the matter of a broken leg and twisted shoulder.'

'There is that,' she said, looking again at the damage. Thinking of possible movement. Possible consequences. 'Marcus...'

'My friends call me Marc.'

'You might not want to call me a friend when I tell you what I want to do,' she told him. 'That leg's definitely broken and I need to splint it to make sure circulation stays secure. You have lacerations and bruising where it must have struck rock, but nothing's piercing the skin. If I up the morphine and you manage to grit your teeth, I reckon it'll be safer to straighten it a little and brace it. It'll need to be braced before we move you tomorrow anyway, so I might as well do it now. Plus I might as well see if I can get that shoulder into a more comfortable position.' She tried to smile. 'It'll save you lying awake all night worrying about surgery in the morning.'

'You're all heart.' She saw him close his eyes, accept the inevitable. 'How are you at fixing dislocated shoulders?'

'Without an X-ray? I'd normally not even go there.'

'But in an emergency situation? Given the low risk? I've felt it. There's no suspicion of fracture.'

'You can't know that.'

'I felt it as I fell. It twisted hard but not hard enough to break. I'm sure this is a simple dislocation. Elsa, it's agony and I'm done with agony. I tried to put it back myself.'

'Yeah?' Like that was easy to do. 'With what results?'

'I did actually faint,' he admitted. 'So then I stopped.'

'Very wise.'

'But you could do it.'

'I might not be able to.'

'You could try. You're sensible enough to stop if it doesn't click into place fast.'

She sat back and considered. 'You'd accept the risk?'

'Yes, I would.'

There was a level of trust. He'd accepted her as competent enough to do no harm.

'I guess,' she said doubtfully. 'With the morphine on board… I could give you a muscle relaxant too.'

'Bless you,' he said simply and then moved on, almost colleague to colleague. 'The leg. What'll you brace it with?'

'That's the good side about you falling,' she told him, making her voice brisk, as professional as she could. 'We have a selection of bush litter around us. I can see at least three sticks I can whittle with my neat little knife to make a nice smooth brace. You'd have to agree with me though, Marc. You'd have to accept that I'll hurt you.'

He closed his eyes for a moment and then opened them, and his face had become resolute.

'Help me to sit up,' he asked her. 'I need to see my leg for myself first.'

'No.' She put her hands on his chest, firmly pressing him back. 'I know you've been trying to move but Marc, you must know there's the possibility of spinal damage. You fell hard. You know the rules. Let's get you safely X-rayed before you start shifting. We'll get you up on a stretcher and check you before you start doing fancy stuff like sitting up.'

'But…'

'No buts. You know what's sensible.'

He closed his eyes, looking grim. 'I'm supposed to be flying to St Moritz tomorrow, to be there over Christmas,' he muttered. 'For a couple of weeks' skiing.'

She raised her brows at that. 'Really?' She paused to

consider. 'I guess it could still happen. How are you at skiing on one leg?'

No answer.

She hadn't really expected one. She thought, tangentially, how amazing to live a life where you could pop over to St Moritz to ski when you felt like it.

He'd be a good skier, she thought. Okay, she didn't know for sure, but she could sense it. His body was solid, muscled, ripped in all the right places.

She was still holding him. She'd moved to stop him shifting and her arm had gone around his good shoulder as she'd tugged him back to a prone position and encouraged him to relax. She'd left her arm there for a moment. He was cold and she was warm. He needed contact.

Comfort?

But the comfort seemed to be working both ways. This underground dungeon was creepy. It was almost dark above them.

She had a phone light and a torch. She had a spare battery for her phone in her backpack. Help was on its way. There was no need for her to want comfort.

But still, as she held him and felt his inherent strength, she took it where she found it. She'd learned to do that. She had her grandpa's help when she needed it medically, but Grandpa was growing increasingly frail. She had Sherlock, but...

But there were still lots of times in Dr Elsa McCrae's medical life when she felt totally alone, and for just one brief moment now she let herself accept the feel of this man beside her. She let herself imagine that maybe she could depend on him.

Which was ridiculous. His mind was clearly focused on the next thing. Bracing his leg. Thinking about his shoulder.

'Okay,' he said briefly. 'Let's get it over with.'

She hesitated. She could—maybe she should—wait for more light. But it'd still be a couple of hours before help arrived. Macka was a great policeman but he wasn't the fittest bloke on the island. He'd have called on a couple of the fire brigade guys to help. They were fitter, faster than Macka but they didn't know the route.

Two hours. She released him and looked again at that leg and thought it did need to be fixed fast. If it was a compound fracture… She had no way of knowing for sure, and she had to work on the worst-case scenario.

'We do it now,' Marcus said, and she heard her own thoughts reflected in the tone of his voice. He'd know the risks as well as she did. 'And the shoulder if you can. Let's go.'

So she did.

CHAPTER THREE

SHE WAS NO orthopaedic surgeon and she wanted to be one.
She had no X-ray equipment and she needed it. She had
no help and she wanted that, too.

All she had were her instincts.

Do no harm. First rule in every situation. She had a leg
that still had circulation. She could leave it exactly how
it was. His shoulder needed to be X-rayed to make sure it
wasn't broken. She should leave that in place too.

But a dislocated shoulder was too excruciatingly painful for him to sleep, even with the morphine, and in the
morning he had to be moved regardless. The long night
lay ahead of them and the shoulder would be agony. And
if he moved during the night, if the leg twisted as they
tried to get him up, if his circulation blocked... It didn't
bear thinking about.

No X-ray machine would miraculously appear down
here. No orthopaedic surgeon was on his way with Macka.
She was on her own.

So what was new? She'd coped before, and she'd cope
again.

She could have waited until Macka arrived with better light but what she was doing depended mainly on feel.
Plus the cooperation of her patient. If she'd been back at
the hospital she'd use general anaesthetic. She couldn't use

it here but, blessedly, Marc's medical training would have him understanding the absolute imperative of keeping still.

Leg first. The shoulder was more painful, but the risk of blocked circulation to the foot meant it was triaged first.

She prepared one of the pieces of wood that had been shoved down the hole with the force of Marc's fall. She showed it to Marc, who made a crack about her whittling skills before falling silent again as she worked.

He was mentally preparing himself for what lay ahead, she thought. Morphine could only do so much.

Then, moving more slowly than she'd ever worked before, she inched the wood under his leg. With her hands feeling his leg, feeling for bone, she slowly, slowly straightened his knee, then straightened his leg, manoeuvring it onto her makeshift splint.

She cleaned and disinfected and bandaged and then fixed the leg as tightly as she dared to her whittled wood. Marc said nothing the entire time she worked, and she blessed him for it.

Finally she sat back and took a breath. It was cool and damp underground, but she found she was sweating.

'Well done,' Marc growled softly, and she caught herself. What was she doing sweating, when it was Marc who'd managed to hold himself rigid?

'Well…well done yourself,' she told him. 'I…' She caught herself, giving herself space to find the right words. To find a prosaic normalcy. 'The pulse in your lower leg is stronger. If I keep the morphine for during the night you should be able to sleep without worrying about shifting.'

'So now the shoulder.'

That was harder. She knew it'd mean more pain for him and she was less sure of herself. Heaven, she wanted an X-ray.

The simplest and safest technique for shoulder reduction was the Stimson technique, where the patient hung his or her arm down and weights were attached at the wrist. This was normally her go-to method but here there was no bed, no raised surface. Scapular manipulation also had to be ruled out. Given the possibility of back injury, there was no way she was rolling him into the position required.

Which left external rotation as the next best option. That could at least be done with the patient lying on his back. She talked to Marc as she thought it through. 'You reckon?' she asked him. He was, after all, a colleague—and it was his shoulder.

'Go for it,' he urged.

So she did. With his arm tucked in as close to his body as possible, gently, slowly she rotated, letting gravity—and pain—limit the amount of movement. She watched his face every inch of the way, watching the greyness, the tight set of his mouth, the fierce determination to get this done. As his pain level increased his arm automatically tensed. She backed off, waited, then inched again.

And then, miraculously, wonderfully, came the moment when it slid back into place. She saw his face go slack with relief and knew her own face must reflect it.

'Thank you,' he said, his eyes closed, his whole body seeming to sag. 'Oh, my God, thank you.'

'Think nothing of it,' she managed, and to her disgust heard a tremor in her own voice. 'I'll strap it now. It needs to stay strapped until I get you to where we can check for rotator cuff injury. You must know the drill. Hopefully now though you'll be comfortable enough to get some sleep.'

'Sleep...' He grimaced. 'Look, now we have everything braced, surely I can be pulled up to the surface.'

'Not on my watch.' She had herself back under control now. 'You heard what I said to Macka. He'll bring stuff to make us more comfortable, but I'm not risking bringing you up until we have decent light.'

'But if my leg's braced...'

'I'm not thinking about you,' she told him, only partly truthfully. 'I'm thinking about the unstable ground and a team up there who aren't trained cavers. I'm thinking about that ground collapsing. I'm thinking about half the Gannet Island fire department landing on our heads.'

'Oh,' he said doubtfully.

'And I've used the last of my bandages,' she told him. 'If a team of burly firefighters fall down here, my emergency kit's going to look pretty darned empty. No. We wait until morning when Macka—he's our island cop and he's good—can do a thorough recce of the ground.'

'Right,' he said, clearly not liking it but reaching acceptance. 'But you could go up. There's no need for both of us to stay down here.'

'Yeah,' she told him, thinking of clots, thinking of delayed concussion, thinking of kinked blood vessels that still might block.

'I can do my own obs.'

That brought a wry smile. 'Really? A specialist cardiologist doing obs? When was the last time you did such a thing? Don't cardiologists have nursing staff for that?'

'You're not a nurse.'

'No, I'm a family doctor in a remote community, and as such I've even done hourly obs on a pregnant turtle. Mind, it was a special turtle and I had her in a sand tank on my veranda but there you go, needs must.'

'Did you have a good outcome?' he asked, distracted as she'd hoped he would be.

'An excellent outcome. Seventy-three babies that we hope went on to become seventy-three of Gannet Island's finest. Never doubt my skill, Dr Pierce. I can do your obs, no problem. There's no need to be scared at all.'

'Believe it or not, I'm not in the least scared,' he told her. 'Not from the moment you slid down your rope.'

'Then I've done my job until now,' she said cheerfully. 'And I'll keep doing it if you don't mind. So you settle down and see if you can sleep and I'll check the whereabouts of the team up top.'

'Elsa…'

'Yep?'

'If any of the team up top fall and break a leg…or if there's an emergency in town tonight…another turtle?'

'Then Grandpa will cope,' she told him, making her voice more sure than she felt.

'Grandpa?'

'He's our other doctor on the island. He's good.'

'How old is he?'

'Seventy-eight.'

'Then…'

'If you're going to be ageist I'll need to report you to the med board for discrimination. Grandpa can cope.'

'But apart from Grandpa…'

'His name's Robert.'

'Apart from Robert, you're the only doctor on the island?'

'I am,' she told him soundly. 'Plus vet and sometimes nurse and sometimes cook and sometimes janitor. General dogsbody, that's me. Grandpa and me and my beagle, Sherlock, together we practically run this island. Now, could you please shush because I need to ring Macka again.'

'Elsa…'

'Shush,' she told him severely. 'You get on with being a patient, Marcus Pierce, and let me get on with being Doctor in Charge.'

* * *

Macka's team arrived half an hour later. Sherlock announced their arrival with shrill excited barks—as well he might. These guys were friends and it was way past his dinnertime.

'Is that our rescue team?' Marc had been dozing under the effects of the morphine but the barking and yells above them had him opening his eyes.

'Doc?' Macka called down, strongly authoritative. 'Shut up, Sherlock.'

Amazingly, he did. Macka's word was law on this island.

'We are,' she called up. 'But stay back. The ground's unstable. Can you see where I've tethered my rope? Don't come any closer than that. I want Marc out of here, but not at the cost of another accident. Who's there?'

'Denise and Graham. We can call on more if we need them. How are things down there?'

'Stable,' she told him. 'No need for rush. Don't come any closer, guys. This ground is a trap for the unwary.'

'But you're safe?'

'We're both safe. Marc has a broken leg and an injured shoulder, but we can hold out until it's safe to pull us both up. Marc's going to need a stretcher.'

'We have the rescue stretcher.'

'That's great,' she told him, thinking thankfully of their newly acquired piece of kit, a collapsible stretcher with straps that could hold a patient completely immobile while being shifted. Or, in this case, lifted.

There was still the possibility of damage to Marc's back. First rule of medicine—do no harm. Shifting him before she could take an X-ray was the stuff of nightmares.

'Can you hold out until first light?' Macka called.

'I think we must.' She wanted a steady ascent, everything in their favour, and if it meant waiting then they had no choice. She was looking at Marc, meeting his gaze, calm and steady. He'd know the options.

'Then we'll hold off,' Macka said, sounding relieved. 'Tell us what's happened?'

She told him. There was silence as he thought things through.

'Right, then. We'll get the gear down to you and set up here. Your guy… Marc? Is there anyone we need to contact on his behalf?'

Marc shook his head, looking grim. 'No one will miss me until tomorrow.'

She frowned at that but Macka was waiting for a reply. 'He says not.'

'Fair enough,' Macka said.

'You want us to ring your grandpa? How about Tony?'

'I'll ring Grandpa,' she called back. 'And don't you dare ring Tony.'

There was a chuckle and then things turned businesslike.

'Okay, we'll use your rope as a pulley and lower enough gear to make you comfortable for the night,' Macka told her. 'We brought the medical supplies you need, plus a couple of air mattresses and blankets. You can set the air mattress below the stretcher so it won't need another shift in the morning. We'll stay up here in case the situation changes but, unless it does, at first light we'll organise a line across to keep us stable, get a stretcher down there and winch you both up.'

'Can you contact the mainland to stand by for an evac flight?' She wanted an orthopaedic surgeon to take over care of this leg, the sooner the better. 'We ought to be able to get him to the airport by late morning.'

'That might be harder,' Macka called back. 'There's

bushfires on the mainland and the smoke's affecting all the major airports. Evac flights are detoured up north, but only if they're life or death—they have to come from Brisbane and the fires are keeping them flat-out. Normal commuter flights are already called off for tomorrow. Mae's going nuts because she has an order for forty Christmas turkeys. The way this is looking, they'll be lucky to arrive Boxing Day.'

'No! Five of those turkeys are for us.' She kept her voice deliberately light because the grim look on Marc's face had intensified. Had he still been hoping to make St Moritz?

It was sad about that, but it was tough for her, too. She'd have to take X-rays and set the leg herself. Grandpa would help, but doing such a procedure on someone who wasn't an islander and therefore couldn't be expected to accept the medical limits caused by their remoteness...

She'd worry about that tomorrow, she told herself.

There was a call from above them. A tightly wrapped bundle was descending, tied on her looped rappel rope. First delivery.

She caught it before it reached the ground. A lantern was attached to the side. She flicked it on and for the first time saw the extent of their cavern.

Or, rather, the enormity of it. It stretched downward on all sides. Marc had been so lucky that he'd landed on a site that was almost stable.

She didn't say anything though, just unfastened the bundle.

Two self-filling air mattresses.

'Hey, look at this,' she told him, holding the first up as it inflated. 'Who needs to go to St Moritz for luxury?' She shivered. 'Speaking of which, who needs to go to St Moritz for cold? Did you guys bring blankets?' she called.

'Coming down,' Macka told her, and ten minutes later

they had everything they needed to keep themselves if not exactly comfortable, then not too cold and not too uncomfortable.

It took time and skill to move Marc onto the combined mattress and stretcher but at last he was where he needed to be.

'Done,' she called back up. 'All secure.'

'Then dinner,' Macka called and an insulated bag came down. 'Deirdre's chicken soup and bread rolls. It went in hot so it should still be warm. She figured your guy might be feeling a bit off, so chicken soup might be the ticket.'

'Wow, thank you,' she called back and guided the bag down and nestled it beside the now almost comfortable Marc.

Who was looking at her in disbelief.

'Hot food as well.'

'Gannet Island's all about service,' she told him, smiling. 'Do you think you can drink some? Let me help you. No, don't try and sit up. Just let me support your shoulders while you drink.'

'I can...'

'I'm very sure you can sit up,' she told him severely. 'But you know as well as I do that you risk your leg moving and I'm still worrying about your back. If there's spinal injury... And if that leg loses circulation...' She paused while they both thought of the consequences.

'So you're telling me to lie back, shut up and do what I'm told,' he said, still grim.

'That, Dr Pierce, is exactly what I'm doing, and if you knew how much I, as a family doctor, have longed to say that to a specialist then you'll know that this night is not all bad.'

'For who?'

'For me,' she told him and grinned. 'Now shut up and let's get this soup into you.'

CHAPTER FOUR

MARC LET HER support his shoulders while he drank the soup—for which he was pathetically grateful. For the last twenty-seven hours he'd been in agonising pain. Thirst had broken through, so practically all he'd thought of was fear, water and the pain in his leg and shoulder.

This magical woman had fixed the fear, given him water and made his leg and shoulder little more than dull aches. Now she was pretty much hand-feeding him the most delicious soup he'd ever tasted.

She'd wedged her body under his, sitting on the ground at his head, using her body to prop the pillow of his air mattress higher. There was canvas between them, but it felt as if there was nothing at all. His head seemed to be pillowed on a cushion of warmth and relief and gratitude.

She helped him hold the mug to his lips and he felt the warmth of her hand and he thought he'd never met someone so wonderful in all his life.

'Marry me,' he murmured as he finished the last of his soup and she chuckled.

'That's not even original. There's Tony, who asks me that once a week, plus I get proposals from whoever else is grateful right now. I was propositioned only yesterday when I lanced old Roger Havelock's abscess. He'd been putting up with it for a week so the relief from pressure was nothing less than sensational. I could have asked for half his kingdom. Not that that's saying anything,' she added reflectively. She shifted back, lowering his pillowed head gently, and he was aware of a sharp stab of loss as she shifted away. 'Roger owns fifteen sows, two boars and a handful of scraggy chickens. Are you offering anything better?'

'Anything better than Tony?'

'I'm not into comparisons.'

'Yet you counted sows as an alternative proposal. Surely that means you're available?'

'I'm always available,' she said, and he heard irony in the tone. 'How about you? I'm assuming your offer of marriage was something you make to every doctor who climbs down a hole to save your life, but seriously… Are you sure you don't have anyone who'll be out of their mind with worry right now?'

'I'm positive,' he said brusquely. 'I don't have any close family and I'm supposed to be on vacation. I'm due to fly to Switzerland tomorrow night with a group of fellow medics. That includes Kayla, a colleague. She'll worry if I don't turn up to the airport without letting her know, but a phone call tomorrow will fix that. Our relationship's only casual. She won't miss me until then, and she'll have a good time without me.'

'I suppose that's a good thing,' she said doubtfully. 'You want to sleep?'

'I guess. You must need to, too.'

'I do, and apart from checking you I might even get a whole night without interruptions.' She hauled her mattress to lie beside his and spread out blankets. 'Maybe I should try this more often—jumping down a hole to get a good night's sleep.'

'Is it so hard to get?'

'Yes, it is,' she said, tucking her blankets around her with care. 'You try being the only full-time doctor for a group of islands where every tourist seems intent on putting themselves in harm's way.'

'Like me.'

'You said it.' She checked out his blankets, twitched another over him and nodded. 'There. Tucked in and settled. Pain level?'

'About two.'

'That'll have to do.'

'It'll do me. Thank you, Elsa.'

'All my pleasure,' she told him. 'Wake me if it gets above three. There are no medals for being a martyr.'

'Are there any medals for being a lone doctor and a heroine to boot?'

'I'm not completely alone,' she said indignantly. 'There's Grandpa. He'd be full-time if I let him but there's the little matter of renal problems and a dicky heart.'

'Renal problems?'

'Diabetes. Not so bad.' Mostly.

'And a dicky heart?'

'That's the diagnosis,' she said lightly. 'I told you I'm a family doctor. Nothing fancy.'

'Surely he's been off the island to find out exactly what's wrong?'

'He has,' she said and lay down and tugged the blankets up to her chin. 'But he hates being off the island. That's the biggest reason I'm here, but I'm not about to discuss Grandpa's health in detail with another patient.'

'I'm a cardiologist.'

'Says you. For now you're my patient. You're suffering a broken leg and sore shoulder, plus a severe case of being stuck down a cave. I suggest you try and sleep, Dr Pierce, before that morphine wears off. Like I intend to.'

'You're going to sleep before my morphine wears off?'

'Exactly. I'm not stupid. If I wait any longer you'll start whinging and I need my beauty sleep.'

He dozed and then he woke and sleep wouldn't return.

He lay and thought of the complications one broken leg entailed. He thought about his friends heading to St Moritz. He thought of Kayla. He'd told Elsa she'd go to St Moritz without him and of course she would. Their relationship was purely fun and casual. There was no need for her to stay and hold his hand.

This Christmas skiing vacation was an institution between a group of colleagues, something he'd done for six years now. Kayla was simply one of the group, and they'd started dating only recently. Their enjoyment of St Moritz had little to do with each other. They both enjoyed the hard physical challenge, the beauty of the slopes, the crowded bars, the excellent restaurants.

The avoidance of Christmas.

Though it wasn't totally avoided. The resort their small group stayed in took elegance to a whole new level, with sumptuous furnishings, exotic food, magnificent decorations and designer gifts for each guest. They'd arrive on Christmas Eve and the festivities would be in full swing. The setting was picture-perfect, a magical white Christmas full of people enjoying themselves.

As opposed to the Christmases he'd spent during his childhood, with his parents trying unsuccessfully to disguise mutual grievances. Stilted cheer in their harbourfront mansion. Gifts—something aspirational and educational and expensive from his father, something ecologically sound and expensive from his mother.

A part of him had almost been relieved the Christmas his mother had finally left. At ten he'd been old enough to realise that at least it had eased the sham of pretending not to hear the bitter fighting. Afterwards he could take his certificate from his mother saying he'd just donated a school to a village in Africa—surely what every kid wanted for Christmas—and thank her as if he meant it. He could accept his mind-bending educational challenge from his father and not have to figure how to negotiate the minefield of which gift he liked best.

Christmas when his parents were together had been a formal, rigid nightmare. Christmas as a teen when they'd been apart had been something he could almost get through.

Christmas in St Moritz?

Fun. Friendly. Busy.

Impersonal. Which was the way he liked his life.

The group congregating at the airport tomorrow would miss him, but only briefly. He was honest enough to suspect the short-term relationship he'd had with Kayla was pretty much already over. Kayla might even be secretly pleased she'd have a spare seat beside her on the long plane flight.

But then his tired mind drifted sideways. To the woman beside him.

Would a woman like this stay because her man had broken his leg?

She didn't have to tell him she was here on this island because of her commitment to the islanders and her grandfather—it was implied in almost every word she spoke. As for not talking about what was wrong with her grandfather... Patient confidentiality? Not so much. He was another doctor, a specialist, and the chance to talk to another professional about a worrying case would be grabbed by almost every colleague he knew.

Not by Elsa though. In that quick rejoinder about patient confidentiality he'd heard pain. Something grim in the background. Something she didn't need advice about.

Something she already knew? That staying here was putting her grandfather's life at risk?

She'd saved his life. Maybe he could help her in return. He needed to figure this out.

'You need more pain relief?' It was a sleepy murmur from beside him. She'd placed their air mattresses so close they were touching. He knew the reason for that too. He'd had a fall. She had no guarantee that it wasn't only his leg and shoulder that were damaged. If he was in hospital he'd be under constant observation for at least twenty-four hours.

'You know, this is the second night I've been stuck down here,' he told her. 'If I was going to die of internal bleeding I probably would have done it before this. There's no need for you to stay awake.'

'Which is why I'm sleeping.'

'You're awake.'

'So I'm dozing. You're a doctor. You know we can exist on dozes. So how's your pain?'

'Still okay.'

'Bladder?'

Hell, he was a surgeon at the top of his field. The physical dependencies this situation called for were humiliating.

'I'm fine,' he told her dourly and he heard her smile.

'Then drink more. Don't you dare stop drinking because you have too much pride to let me help you. You're a patient, remember.'

'I don't have to like it.'

'What's that quote about being given the serenity to accept things you can't change? I can't remember it exactly, but it's something like "*Grant me the serenity to accept the things I cannot change, courage to change the things I can and wisdom to know the difference.*" My grandpa has it on his wall and it's wise. So if you need the bottle, accept it with serenity.'

'Right,' he said wryly. 'But I don't need it.'

'And I'll accept that you're pig stubborn and we'll leave it at that,' she told him.

They lay in silence for a few moments. He thought she might have dozed off again but then her voice sounded cautiously into the dark.

'Tell me about St Moritz.'

'You've never been?'

'Hey, I've been to Sydney,' she said cheerfully. 'Is there a world past that?'

'Only Sydney?'

'No money to go further,' she told him, still upbeat. 'It took all Grandpa's resources to help me through med school. During vacations I came home and worked for my keep in the hospital. Actually,' she admitted, 'I've worked in the hospital since I was seven. One of my earliest memories is helping shell what seemed like a mountain of peas, but my official job was cheering patients up. Me and Loopy the Basset, then me and Peanut the Fox Terrier and finally me and Sherlock the Beagle—had to go in and find stuff to talk about. It was the best training for family medicine ever.'

'So what about your mum and dad?'

'Mum was your original hippie,' she said, almost curtly. 'My grandmother died when Mum was thirteen and Mum took it hard. She blamed Grandpa—"You're a doctor, why couldn't you save her?" Then she took up with the surf crowd who come here every summer. She ran away when she was seventeen, following her heart, only the guy her heart had chosen turned out to be a scumbag. Coming back here was never an option for her, though, and she died of an overdose when I was seven. Who knows where my Dad is now?—I certainly don't. After Mum died, Grandpa brought me to the island and, apart from the years in Sydney at med school, I've been here ever since. So I say again…tell me about St Moritz.'

He was silent for a moment, letting himself sink into the story behind the story. He was imagining a neglected child with a drug-addicted mother, a despairing grandfather, grief.

Hell, and he'd thought his childhood was hard.

'St Moritz,' she said again, and he gave himself a mental shake and tried to think of what she'd like to know.

'You've seen all those soppy Christmas cards with snow scenes and twinkling lights and carollers and reindeer…'

'Don't tell me there are reindeer!'

'I believe there are. Not on the ski slopes though, and that's where I mostly spend my time.'

'It's really white? Not just slush?'

'It can get slushy, but at this time of the year, especially when the snow's just fallen, it's beautiful.'

'I'd so love to see it. They say every snowflake is different. To stand in the snow…to taste snow on my tongue…'

'Would you let me give you a trip there—as payment for saving my life?'

It was the wrong thing to say. He knew it as soon as the words came out of his mouth. She was lying beside him, her arm just touching his. He wasn't close enough to really feel it, but he could sense the sudden rigidity in her. The withdrawal.

'Hey, you're just a patient and I don't need gifts from patients,' she told him, and her words were cool and stiff.

'Tourists have accidents on the island all the time, and it's my job to patch them up. You'll get a bill for services rendered.'

'What, standard consultation with medical procedure attached?'

'More than that,' she said with asperity. 'House call out of hours. Extended consultation. Minor surgery. You'll be slugged heaps.'

'Do you charge more than the government rebate?' he asked, knowing already what her answer would be.

'Even if I did it wouldn't equal a holiday in St Moritz,' she told him. 'Go to sleep.'

'I don't think I can.'

'Try,' she told him curtly and rolled over to face away from him.

And that was that.

Insensitive toe-rag.

A holiday in St Moritz! Grateful patients often gave her chocolates or wine, or nice handwritten cards. She never expected them, but when they came she appreciated them and shared them around with the receptionists and nursing staff. It seemed a thank you to all of them.

A holiday in St Moritz. As if.

But she lay in the dark, and for a little while she let herself imagine what it could be like. A plane ride to Sydney and then an overseas flight to Switzerland. A long flight. She wouldn't be the least surprised—given the insouciance of this guy's offer—if it'd be in business class, too. Then maybe a limo drive to the ski slopes.

Her receptionist had a passion for glossy lifestyle magazines, and they ended up in her waiting room. Occasionally, in the tiny spaces between patients, she let herself browse and dream.

There'd be a chalet—she'd seen the pictures. Luxurious resort suites. Views to die for. Maybe a sauna and a spa. Ski lessons with some gorgeous young Swiss, herself skimming down the ski slopes, then afterwards roaring fires, food and drink at expensive restaurants, laughter among friends...

And that was where the picture cut out. Friends.

She was so damned lonely.

Oh, for heaven's sake, what was she doing thinking she was lonely? She could count on almost every islander as her friend.

How many of them called her Elsa, though? From the time she'd returned to the island she'd been the doctor's kid. The islanders had taken her into their hearts, loved her, cared for her so her grandpa could keep up with his medicine. But mostly Grandpa had cared for her himself. She'd been his shadow and the locals had called her Little Doc. 'Here comes Doc and Little Doc,' they'd say, and if things got tricky then whoever was closest would spirit Little Doc away until she could resume her role as his helper.

So she'd been Little Doc until she'd come back from university, and then she'd been simply, proudly Doc. For Grandpa had never been into money-making, and so the islanders had chipped in to help fund her studies, too.

Grandpa called her Matey. She was Grandpa's mate. Everyone else called her Doc.

Except recently Tony. Tony called her Elsa.

Dating Tony had been a disaster. She should never have agreed to that first date. He'd almost instantly become possessive, and his use of her first name was a claim all by itself.

He'd caught her at a weak moment.

Because she was lonely!

The guy beside her stirred, and she thought she should

probably say something to cheer him up. She couldn't think of a single thing.

Instead she lay in the dark and for some unfathomable reason her future lay on her like a thick, heavy blanket.

St Moritz.

Why had one crazy offer disturbed her so much?

Or the way this guy had smiled at her?

He was just another patient. A tourist. He'd be out of here as soon as the smoke cleared enough for flights to resume.

More to distract herself than anything else, she let herself think of the situation on the mainland. What had seemed a series of small fires two days ago had merged into a much bigger front. If she'd been working on the mainland she'd be so busy—part of a team coping with burns, smoke inhalation, shock. Part of a team...

Oh, for heaven's sake, she was thinking longingly of a bushfire situation?

'What's the latest on the fires on the mainland?' Marc's deep growl cut through her thoughts, made her blink. Were his thoughts following hers?

He'd be worried about getting out of here, she thought. Nothing more.

'Latest report says there's light rain,' she told him briefly. 'I guess that's why the smoke's so intense. Slow moisture on burning bushland. No lives lost, though.' She thought about it for a moment. 'If it was worse... Do cardiologists cope with fire trauma?'

'Everyone copes when it's major,' he said simply. 'But if it's settling now I won't be missed. Plus I'm now officially on vacation.'

'Lucky you.'

'You think I'd prefer to be on vacation rather than helping out?'

'Everyone needs a break sometimes,' she said flatly. 'Lucky you if you can get one. Go to sleep, Marc, or at least let me. I'm not on vacation and I need sleep even if you don't.'

CHAPTER FIVE

THE EVACUATION BEGAN the next morning and it nearly killed him that he had to play the victim. The idiot who'd got into such trouble.

He *was* the victim. He *was* the idiot.

So he lay strapped onto his stretcher while they worked around him.

The inflatable stretcher was amazing. The night before Elsa had simply—or not so simply—manoeuvred it so it was lying on top of the air mattress. At dawn, as the team above prepared the gear to lift him, she used its pump to inflate the sides. The air-filled bumpers would protect him as it was hauled to the surface.

It had head, neck and spine support. It had full body, pressure-point-free immobilisation. It had cross fix restraints and ten carry handles.

'It's also X-ray-transparent and it'll carry anyone up to two hundred and fifty kilograms,' Elsa told him proudly, as she adjusted the straps that held him fixed. 'Though if you'd weighed that much we might have had to raise a small army to haul you up.'

He didn't smile. He was now totally immobilised and he'd never felt so helpless.

Above ground the team was fixing cabling from one side of the unsafe ground to the other. What that meant was that team members could safely fix anchors above the hole, then abseil down if needed, or have someone stay safely above ground to guide him up.

Elsa was explaining things as she worked. She was upping his drug dose as well.

'It's a great stretcher and we're a good team,' she told him. 'But we can't stop it being bumpy while we carry you down the mountain. I'm sorry, Marc, but there'll need to be a bit of biting the bullet on your part.'

'You guys are saving me. I won't be whinging.'

That brought a wry smile.

'What, you don't believe me?'

'We'll see,' she said enigmatically. 'We hauled a tourist up a cliff face a few weeks back. He'd been trying to take a selfie, climbed the safety rail to get a better angle and leaned out a little too far over a fifty-foot drop to the sea below. He was super lucky to be caught on a ledge fifteen feet down, with only a fractured arm and bruises. It took our guys hours to pull him up, but do you think he was grateful? The first thing he did was abuse us because we hadn't brought up his camera. He shouted at us practically the whole time before we managed to get him airlifted out of here. The fact that his camera had fallen the whole way down and the team would have been risking their own lives to get it simply didn't register.'

'People do stupid things,' he managed, chagrined that he was in the same category.

'They do, and you did, but at least you've been grateful,' she told him, smiling down at him. 'Speaking of which, I've been thinking of that St Moritz offer. I should say no and leave it at that, but if you're serious…'

'I am.'

'Then could we swap St Moritz for a reclining lift chair for our nursing home patients?' she asked tentatively. 'Or maybe even two if you're feeling super generous. We have a couple of oldies who can't get out of chairs without help, and it makes them feel so dependent.'

'I know how that feels,' he said grimly, feeling the straps holding him immobile.

'Then it's a great time to ask,' she said, and grinned again. 'Damn, I didn't bring a pen and paper or I'd have you sign a promissory note—before we bring you to the surface and you get all St Moritzy again.'

'I won't get... St Moritzy. I've said goodbye to that fantasy.'

'You'll be back there next year,' she told him. 'While we enjoy two great lift chairs.'

'You won't enjoy two lift chairs.'

'You want to bet? Seeing Marigold Peterson get up from her chair and walk out to the veranda without having to wait for a nurse to help her... You take your St Moritz, Dr Pierce. I'll take Marigold's pleasure any day.'

He looked at her curiously, this competent, brisk young woman. With the dawn had come natural light, filtering down and angled so he could see her. The night before she'd been a shadow behind the lantern, or maybe he'd been too hazy, drug affected to see her clearly. Now he had a proper look.

She looked competent. Determined. Her jeans and windcheater were filthy, her hair dust-caked, but he could see more than just a general impression. She was only little, a package of efficiency about five feet two or three. Slight. Wiry? He'd have to say that—there was no trace of an idle life or an indulged lifestyle about her. Her hair seemed almost flame-red beneath the dust. It looked as if it could be amazing but right now her curls were tied back in a practical, businesslike ponytail.

Watching her as she adjusted his straps, he had a sudden irrational urge to reach out and release the ponytail. He wanted to see what those curls looked like floating free.

Yeah, like that was a good idea. Patient hitting on doctor? She was leaving the lower part of his good arm free—so he could scratch his nose if he wanted—but looking at that determined chin, feeling the brisk competence she was exuding, he thought she'd have his arms tied down in an instant if he tried it on.

He had the very strong impression that Dr Elsa McCrae was not a woman to mess with.

And she had principles. She'd just knocked back what to her, he suspected, might be the holiday of a lifetime, in order to barter for two chairs for her oldies. He'd seen the flash of amazement in her eyes as he'd made his offer. He'd also seen regret slam home. Common sense had taken over. With this woman, it probably always would.

'You like family medicine?' he asked curiously, watching her face as she worked.

'I like making people feel better.'

'Then you've made me feel better,' he said—and to his astonishment he saw a hint of a blush.

But she brushed it away, got efficient again fast. 'Then I've done my job,' she said lightly. 'Now…you want to say goodbye to your nice cosy bedroom before we hoist you up?'

'I thought I was going to die in this nice cosy bedroom. I hate this nice cosy bedroom.'

'Then let's get you out of here,' she said and glanced up. 'Righto, people, haul him up.'

She'd say this for him, the guy was stoic.

The trip down the mountain was tough on the carriers,

but it'd be a whole lot tougher for the man on the stretcher. The path was rough, criss-crossed by tree roots. They were forced to detour round boulders the path makers had been unable to shift. With the dawn, five more of the islanders had come up to help, so there were two shifts of four to carry him down, but Marc had to endure the journey as best he could.

Elsa followed behind. She wasn't permitted to be a stretcher bearer.

'You slip and who do you think'll patch you up?' Macka had growled.

'Grandpa?'

'Yeah, and then he'd have this fella in one bed and you in another, and all the Christmas tourist influx to cope with on his own. You were a damned fool to go down that hole by yourself, Doc. We won't have you taking any more risks now.'

So she walked behind, watching her step, chatting to the guys on the alternate bearer shift, watching the man on the stretcher.

He was hurting—she could see that, but there was little she could do about it. She had his leg and arm firmly fixed but there was no way to stop the stretcher being jolted.

He'd said he wouldn't complain, and he didn't, but she could see the tension on his face.

And the mortification.

He was a cardiologist, a city surgeon. These guys were top of the tree in the medical profession. He'd offered her a holiday in St Moritz without blinking, and she'd heard in his voice that he was serious. He'd be earning big money. Huge.

He looked—what? Mid-thirties? He was lean, dark-haired, tanned beneath the dust. Even now, strapped to the stretcher and in pain, she could see an air of authority about him.

He was a guy who was used to being in charge of his world.

He wasn't in charge now. He was totally at the mercy of the people carrying his stretcher. Macka, a burly sixty-something policeman. Denise, the island mechanic, also in her sixties. Little, round, always grease-stained, she was the best square dancer on the island, tough as old boots. Graham, the local accountant, fiftyish, who wore prim three-piece suits for five days a week but as soon as he was out of the office he donned tartan lumberjack gear. Mike, a still pimply kid who'd just finished his schooling and would be off to university in the autumn, but who spent all his spare time climbing and abseiling.

The alternate shift consisted of just as motley a collection of characters, but every one of them was competent. They knew this island. They knew what they were doing.

Marc was forced to lie on his stretcher and trust them.

Elsa had once asked if she could have a go at being carried on the stretcher, just to see what it felt like. They'd strapped her down and taken her over a rough path and she'd felt almost claustrophobic, totally at the mercy of a team who could drop her at any minute. They wouldn't. She knew them and trusted them inherently, but Marc would have no such trust.

She watched his face and saw the strain and knew instinctively that this guy's life was all about control.

'Pain level?' she asked, coming alongside the stretcher. 'You want a top-up?'

'I'm fuzzy as it is,' he told her. 'I want my wits about me.'

'So if we drop you, you might be able to save yourself? It won't happen,' she told him. 'This team has never dropped a punter yet.'

He grunted and went back to staring straight upward. She fell back again and continued to watch him closely.

His control looked as if it was stretched to the limit. He didn't complain though. Not a whinge.

'He's a doctor, you say,' Macka said to her at the next change of shift.

'Yep.'

'You reckon we could organise a plane strike or something so we can set his leg and put him behind your grandpa's clinic desk for a week or six? Give your grandpa—and you—a bit of a break?'

'As if,' she said and then looked curiously up at Macka. 'Why do you say that?'

'It's only…well, I dropped in to pick up supplies before we came up to find you,' he told her. 'And I thought old Doc was looking a bit grey around the edges.'

'He's probably just worried about me.'

'Aye, that'd be it,' Macka said, but he sounded doubtful and Elsa winced and thought, *No, please, Grandpa, don't get sick.*

He had renal problems. He had heart problems.

He'd promised her he'd live for ever, and as a kid she'd depended on that promise. Now…not so much and the thought made her feel ill.

Her attention distracted, she stumbled on a tree root and Macka caught her arm and steadied her.

'Thanks,' she muttered to Macka, and then to herself she said, *Cut it out, focus on now.*

Finally they were down. Macka's police-van-cum-ambulance was parked near the start of the walking track. Elsa left them loading their patient on board and took her own car—and Sherlock—back to the hospital. Grandpa came out to greet her, and she had the opportunity to check him out as he bent to pat the exuberant Sherlock.

He did look tired, she conceded. Grey? Maybe. Robert McCrae had been the island's doctor for fifty years and he hated slowing down, but she was going to have to insist.

Though where did that leave her? When Robert had started here, the population of the island had been three hundred with practically no outsiders. Now it was a tourist mecca, its population of seven hundred exploding over the mainland holiday breaks. The outer islands had tourists flooding them too, and she and Robert were still the only doctors.

It wouldn't matter so much if tourists didn't insist on doing such risky things. Like Marcus Pierce, trekking up an unknown mountain trail by himself and letting no one know where he was going. If Sherlock hadn't found him… She closed her eyes, unable to bear thinking of the consequences.

But he'd be thinking of the consequences, she thought. He'd have spent over twenty-four hours thinking the absolute worst. He'd probably need trauma counselling if he wasn't to cop PTSD. She needed a trauma counsellor on staff.

The trauma counsellor would have to be her.

But for now she was late for morning clinic and Grandpa looked as if he needed a good lie-down—he'd also have spent a wakeful night worrying about her. And then there was Christmas! Without turkeys? Even as she got out of the car she saw the hospital cook flapping in the background, waiting to talk to her. Waiting for Elsa to solve the turkey problem.

First things first. A shower. She felt disgusting and she guessed she smelled disgusting too. She had to move on, and she needed help. 'Grandpa, you know the situation?'

she asked him. 'This guy needs fluids, intravenous antibiotics—he has a couple of decent lacerations—a bed bath to get most of the grime off before we can touch him. What's the situation with evacuation to the mainland?'

'Not possible,' Robert told her. 'There's still smoke haze drifting our way. Unless it's life or death we're on our own.'

'Then we ultrasound his shoulder and X-ray his leg and hope it's fixable here.' She grimaced. 'You know he's a doctor?'

'The worst kind of patient.'

'You'd know,' she said and managed a smile. 'Like me giving you orders to get eight hours' sleep no matter what? I'm betting you didn't sleep much last night.'

'I can sleep when I'm dead,' Robert said simply. 'Not when there's work to do. Go on and get yourself clean, girl, and worry about them who need it.'

The woman who appeared at his bedside an hour later stunned him.

In the gloom of the cave, layered in dust, wearing hiking gear, he'd thought she was good-looking.

Now though...she pushed back the curtain of the examination cubicle and he had to blink.

She was dressed in sky-blue trousers and a soft white shirt, both almost concealed by a white coat. Her shoes were sensible flats, but they were bright pink and she'd tied her hair back in a matching pink ribbon. The pink should clash with her hair, but it certainly didn't. She wore little if any make-up, but she didn't need it. She didn't need anything. With her flaming curls, her sparkling green eyes, the flash of colour in her clothing...she was enough to make a man feel better all on her own.

And he'd been feeling better anyway, soaking in the luxury of a decent mattress, pillows, warmth, no more bumping stretcher and enough painkiller to make him dozy.

'I think I've died and gone to heaven,' he managed. She smiled—and that made things even more confusing. It was a killer of a smile. A smile that made a man...

Get a grip. He needed to. It must be the drugs that were making him feel...woozy?

'Feeling better, then?' she asked.

'You'd better believe it. Did you ask for only two lift chairs? Try asking for a hundred. Half my kingdom if you like.'

'I'll believe it when I see it,' she said with a smile that robbed her words of offence. 'You have no idea of how many rescued tourists who've left the island promising largesse, never to be heard of again.'

'I keep my promises,' he told her, and her smile slipped. She looked at him for a long moment and then gave a determined little nod.

'I believe you will,' she said. 'Thank you. But mind, we won't hold you to it. Do nothing until you're well, and then think about it. I had no business to ask.'

'As I had no business to expect you to save my life.'

'It's what we do,' she told him. 'Our whole team, including Sherlock. Do you need to let your people know what's happening?'

'One of the nurses lent me a phone.'

'And you got through? Great. I guess no one will be able to rush to your side before the mainland smoke clears, but I hope you stopped them being anxious. Tell them they can ring me if they want reassurance.'

He thought of Kayla's reaction to his call. Admittedly, he hadn't told her about being trapped—he'd just said he'd fallen while scattering his mother's ashes—but even so she'd been less than sympathetic. She'd asked incisive questions about his injuries but once she was reassured about their severity she'd moved on.

She'd go to St Moritz anyway, she'd decided. She'd let their friends know their party would be one person short, but she was busy. She had to pack. There'd been brief words of commiseration before she disconnected, and that was that.

'No one wants reassurance,' he said brusquely, and Elsa gave him a searching look and then flicked the overhead screen to blank, so it showed only white light.

'Okay, then. You want to see your X-rays? They're re-assuring at least.'

'They're only reassuring if they show no break at all.'

'You still dreaming of St Moritz? Move on,' she told him and put up the X-ray.

It showed a clean break of both tibia and fibula. Slight dislocation but no splintering. It could have been much, much worse.

'I can set this,' she told him. 'Grandpa and I concur. We'd rather send you to the mainland to a decent orthopod, but you know the restrictions on flights at the moment. I did specific training for remote medicine, including ortho-paedics, before I came here, and so did Grandpa. We've both set breaks like this, and so far we haven't managed to put a single foot on backwards. Grandpa's competent with anaesthetics and I'll do the setting. The alternative is to leave it as it is until evacuation, but even with strong splint-ing we both know movement's possible. Which means cir-culation could be blocked. So I'm asking you to trust us.'

'I trust you.'

She gave another of her brisk nods, a gesture he was starting to know. And like.

'The good news is that your ultrasound shows little damage to your shoulder. No tears. It'll be sore for a while and you'll have to protect it, but you seem to have done no long-term damage.'

'Your grandfather told me that.'

'Right, then,' she said. 'You've had nothing to eat since your muesli bars before we started the trek. We'll wait another couple of hours to make sure they're well down, and then we'll set your leg. Meanwhile, I have a clinic queue a mile long so you won't see me until Theatre. The nurses will look after you.'

'They already have.' He looked into her face and behind the smile, behind the briskness, he saw strain. She would have slept badly last night, if at all. He knew enough of this woman to accept that her first responsibility would have been to check on him, probably hourly, so she wouldn't have let herself fall into a deep sleep.

'You've had quite a night yourself. Your grandpa can't run clinic while you have a rest?'

'I wish,' she said wryly. She was up-to-date with the clinic news now. 'Grandpa was up during the night himself, with a fisherman who decided at midnight that his finger was infected. He hurt it last week. It was only when his wife thought sweating in bed was a problem that they decided to call for help. So it's Grandpa who needs the rest, not that he'll take it.'

'I wish I could help.'

'You can, by being sensible and compliant and not throwing out a single complication,' she told him. 'Focus, Dr Pierce. I want an exemplary patient.'

'I'll do my best.'

'And I'll do mine,' she told him. 'Now, you rest for all of us. See you in Theatre.'

And she was gone, her white coat a blur as she closed the door behind her.

He was left with the impression of capability and practicality. And more. An indefinable something.

He'd made a lot more work for this woman. She should be angry with him. She was just resigned, he thought. And capable and practical.

And that indefinable…something.

CHAPTER SIX

IN THE END Marc's surgery was straightforward. Her grandfather gave the general anaesthetic—this was the way they normally worked, and it worked well now. The leg was relatively easy to stabilise. She cleaned and debrided lacerations, put in stitches to the deepest and put a back slab on his leg. It'd eventually be a full cast, but not until the stitches were out and the swelling had gone down.

Despite the reassurance of the ultrasound, she still wanted to test shoulder rotation without the pain caused by the bruising. She found nothing to disturb her.

He'd got off lightly, Elsa thought as she left him in the care of the theatre staff.

Next.

Somehow she convinced Robert to take a nap—which was a worry all on its own. Yes, he'd had to work during the night but both of them were accustomed to doing that. Her grandfather hated conceding weakness, and his agreement to have an afternoon sleep surprised her. Now, not only did she have a queue a mile long at her clinic, she had the niggling fear that he wasn't telling all.

'Maybe I'm coming down with a cold,' he muttered when she pressed him. 'Or maybe it's just worrying about you, girl. Tell you what, you stop worrying about me and

I'll stop worrying about you. Which means quitting with the diving down unknown caves.'

She grinned and asked no more questions, but as she sat in clinic and saw patient after patient, her sense of unease deepened.

And clinic was made worse by the fact that every patient wanted to discuss her night's adventures.

'They say he's a doctor. Louise Pierce's boy.' Marc's mother had been a member of the local climbing group, sometimes spending so much time here the islanders considered her almost one of them. 'Why didn't he take one of us up to the peak with him? Damned idiot, he could have killed you too.'

'No fear of that,' she told them. 'I had Sherlock and he has a nose for holes. He does the hunting. I stick to paths.'

'Except when you're rescuing tourists. What does he think he's doing, putting *our* doc at risk?'

And there was the nub, Elsa thought wearily as the day wore on. She was *their* doctor. She knew the islanders were fond of her, but they also depended on her.

She fielded a call from Tony, who put it more than bluntly. 'You had no right to put yourself at risk, Elsa. Don't you know what's at stake?'

'The whole island needs me. Yes, I know.'

'I need you.'

'No more than any other islander,' she said, trying to keep irritation out of her voice. One unwise date and he practically had her wedded, bedded and mother to half a dozen little Tonys. 'Tony, leave it. You know I had no choice.'

'If he's fool enough to have fallen…'

'I should have left him there, cold and hurting? I don't think so. Sorry, Tony, I need to run.'

'I want to see you. How about dinner?'

'No chance,' she said and cut him short. It was getting to the stage where hints weren't enough. 'Tony, stop it with the idea that we're a couple. We're not.'

And she did need to run. It was already Thursday. Christmas Day was Sunday and how on earth was she going to get everything done by then? Dinner was a sandwich grabbed from the kitchen fridge, eaten while she typed up patient notes for the day with her spare hand—who knew that a five-fingered typist could be so efficient? Finally she headed over to the wards to check all was well before she could—hopefully—get some sleep.

She found Marc propped up on pillows, his leg in traction, scowling at a laptop. Actually...not a laptop. She recognised it as a generic tablet usually kept in the kids' ward.

'What, is Dorothy Dinosaur not co-operating?' she asked, smiling at the sight of one gorgeous guy, sparsely dressed in a white hospital gown, holding a pink, sparkly, dinosaur-decorated tablet.

He didn't smile back.

'One of your nurses kindly unlocked it from kid-safe mode,' he muttered, still glowering. 'So I managed to download my files from the ether and I'm trying to get some work done. But every time I try to save anything, it defaults back to Dorothy and locks me down. And the nurse won't give me the password. She comes in when she has time and unlocks it again like she's doing me a huge favour.'

She grinned at that. 'Maggie's old school,' she told him. 'She likes discipline in her hospital, and to her everyone under the age of forty is a kid.' She tugged up a chair, sat and took the tablet from him and typed in the password. 'There you go.'

'You're not going to give me the password either?'

'I'm with Maggie. We have two small boys in the kids'

ward right now who'd barter their mother for the password. Who's to say you won't sell it on? Plus Maggie's knitting patterns are on this tablet.' She relented. 'You know you should be sleeping. Your body will demand sleep, even if your mind hasn't caught up yet. But I can lend you my spare laptop if you want. The med stuff is locked but I'll trust you not to try and break in.'

'Gee, thanks.'

'You're welcome.' She looked curiously at him. 'So you really came all this way without so much as a change of socks?'

'It was supposed to be a back and forth in a day trip,' he said, sighing and setting the tablet aside. 'Before she died, Mum told me it'd take three hours max to climb to the peak. The plane arrived at nine and was leaving at six, so getting here and back in a day seemed easy. I had a research paper to assess on the flight—a printout that's still sitting in a locker at the airport—so I didn't need my laptop. I can do urgent stuff on my phone, but that's now smashed.'

'So you're screenless.' She shook her head. 'That's truly horrible. But moving on...apart from your lack of screen, tell me what hurts?'

'Just about everything,' he admitted. 'But mostly my pride.' He pushed himself further up in the bed, grimacing with pain. He looked ruffled, she thought, and also... strangely defenceless? He was a big man, tall, lean, muscular. The dirt he'd been covered with was gone and he'd shaved, but his dark, wavy hair was ruffled as if he'd been raking it in frustration. Despite his immobilised leg, his arm in a sling and his loose hospital gown, his strongly boned face and what she could see of his ripped body combined to give the impression of barely contained strength. He looked powerful but confined, edgy to be gone.

His pride was hurting? Yeah, she could see it. For such a man to be in this position…

'I can't do much about your pride,' she told him, 'but I can do something about the aches and pain.'

'I'll make do with paracetamol.'

She grinned and motioned back to the tablet, where Dorothy and her dinosaurs were circling the perimeter of Marc's word document. 'I guess if you want to do battle with Dorothy you need to keep your wits about you, and the stronger painkillers might indeed make you feel a bit fuzzy,' she admitted. 'But there's no prizes for heroics, Dr Pierce. Your leg's a mass of bruises and lacerations, to say nothing of the break. Your shoulder must be giving you heaps. Plus your back… You can't see, but it's spectacularly black and blue.' Her voice grew serious. 'You were incredibly lucky not to break your spine.'

'I was incredibly lucky in more ways than one,' he said, and almost involuntarily he reached out with his good arm and took her hand in his. And held it tightly, as if reassuring himself she was real. 'I was lucky because of one Dr Elsa McCrae,' he said softly. 'Elsa, I'll never forget it.'

She stilled, looked down at their linked hands. It had been a casual gesture, an impulse, but their hands stayed locked.

She'd spent a long, scary night with this man. He must have been terrified when she'd found him, but he hadn't let on. He'd been matter-of-fact, uncomplaining, holding it together.

He was grateful. It was the only reason he was holding her hand.

Or maybe it was more than that. Maybe the terrors were still with him. Maybe he needed the contact.

She told herself that as she let her hand stay where it was. She'd had a hard night too. The work was piling up around her, but for just a moment she let herself be held. She felt the strength and comfort of his grip. She even let herself believe she wasn't alone.

But she was alone, and there was work a mile high to be waded through. She needed to get on.

She should tug her hand away.

But still she didn't. For his sake, she told herself. Not for hers.

'It'll be a darn sight easier to forget gratitude—forget anything else that's bothering you—if you let me give you some decent painkillers,' she managed, and was annoyed to find that her voice was unsteady. 'Have some now and I'll write you up more for the night. Just ask Maggie, she's on all night.'

'Maggie's scary,' he said, and she grinned.

'Better men than you are scared of Maggie. Wielding a bedpan, she's a force to be reckoned with, but she's a fine nurse.' Finally, reluctantly, she tugged back her hand and rose. Was it her imagination or had there been reluctance on his part to let her go? It was understandable, she told herself. He'd need human contact after feeling such fear.

And her reaction?

This was ridiculous. Moving on...

'Is...is there anything else you need?'

'A set of clean clothes?' he ventured, back to being practical. 'You cut off my pants. At least I didn't lose my wallet so I hope I can purchase something to wear.'

'I'd like to keep you in for a couple of days,' she warned him. 'I'm still worried about clots.'

'That's two of us,' he said grimly. 'I know the risks. So clothes can wait but I'd kill for decent pyjamas. Even more for a phone.'

'I can help there as well. Didn't you already use our ward phone? It has overseas capability—we cope with a lot of tourists and you'd be astonished at how many of them lose their phones. I'll tell Maggie to drop it in again.'

'I'd like my own,' he growled. Without his phone he felt stranded. Or even more stranded than he already was. 'Is there anyone on the island who could organise me one?'

'Jason,' she told him. 'He's a cray fisherman but he does a nice little sideline in technology. His boat's due in tonight so I'll ask him to come and see you tomorrow. Anything's possible if you're prepared to pay. In the meantime, Maggie will bring you my laptop. We'll even unlock the passwords for you.'

'Thank you,' he said stiffly, and she thought this was a guy who hated being out of control. Not having his phone, not having the internet would be killing him. But his next question surprised her. 'What about you? Are you going to bed now?'

'Soon,' she lied.

'Soon, as in after you've seen what…another ten patients?'

'Only one,' she admitted and then decided maybe she needed to talk to this guy as a colleague. For some reason he had her unsettled and she couldn't figure it out. 'Mathew Hobson rang fifteen minutes ago and thinks he might have been bitten by a redback spider,' she told him. 'He's on his way in. He'll be fine, though. He met one once and never got over it—now every time he feels a prick from an ant or mosquito he thinks the worst.' She glanced at her watch. 'He should be arriving any minute.'

'And then you'll get to bed?'

'In time. I have the thirty-odd Christmas gifts to wrap over the next couple of days, and I'm already way behind.'

'Thirty!'

She smiled and shrugged. She should leave—she didn't have time to stay and gossip with patients—but those dark eyes of his were watching her with a hint of warmth, of humour, of understanding. He *was* a colleague, she thought. A real medical colleague who understood the pressure she was under.

Like a friend.

Whatever, the need to tell him was suddenly overwhelming.

'I do a thing,' she told him. 'On Christmas Day.'

'A thing?'

'Well, it's not all me,' she told him. 'But the gifts are me. I'm not sure what you know about this island.'

'Not much.'

'Yeah, well, it's been a quiet little backwater for years. We don't have decent educational facilities here—the kids have to go away for school if they want to do more than fish or farm. We now have a big tourist network, but local kids don't see that as an opportunity. Most of our local kids leave when they're old enough. Some come back but most don't. That means we're left with an ageing population and at Christmas a lot of lonely oldies.'

'Which is where you come in?'

'A lot of us come in,' she told him. 'The year I came back to the island I copped literally scores of calls on Christmas Day from oldies who really did feel ill. There's nothing like loneliness to make a slight niggle seem like something frightening. Then the next year Jonas Cruikshank, a local farmer, committed suicide on Christmas Day. His wife had died six months earlier, neither of his kids could make it back to the island and it must have been all too much for him.' She shrugged awkwardly. 'The local church ladies had put on a welfare-type dinner, but he hadn't put his name down for it. Why would he? Come and admit that he was one of the lonely? He had far too much pride. His death hit us all dreadfully, so after that we decided to change things up a bit. Make Christmas fun.'

'You mean *you* decided to make it fun.'

'I did,' she said a trifle defensively.

'How?'

What was she doing, sitting talking when she had so much to do? This guy was a patient. She'd written him up for the drugs he'd need for the night—if he'd take them. Her work here was done.

But this was Christmas.

Jonas Cruikshank had been a friend more than a patient. His wife had babysat her as a little girl. Jonas had given her her first dog, the predecessor of a long line leading to Sherlock. His death had cast a pall over the whole island, and the next year she'd overridden all objections and done it her way.

And this guy had asked. He should be sleeping but he seemed wide awake and she wouldn't mind…just talking for a little while.

She shut her eyes for a moment, closing her mind to the to-do list still waiting for her. She tugged her chair back up to the bed and sat. And talked.

'For a start, I moved our communal Christmas dinner out of the church hall,' she told him.

'You're not religious?'

'I didn't say that. The churches on this island do a fabulous job, but the only one with a hall big enough to take us has walls covered in Easter images. They're beautiful but they're sad. I want fun at my Christmas celebration, Dr Pierce, not suffering. So I moved the whole thing to the footy ground training room. It's huge.'

'So let me guess,' he said, bemused. 'You now have portraits of sweaty, post grand final football teams, and rolls of past players?'

'They take 'em down for us,' she said smugly. 'They didn't want to, but three years back the whole team came down with norovirus two days before playing the grand final with one of the neighbouring islands. You have no idea how hard Grandpa and I worked to rehydrate those guys, and in the end we got them all match fit and they won. So the coach's speech included a public declaration that the footy club stood in our debt. Same as you. You're donating lift chairs, or I hope you are. They've donated a testosterone-free training room every Christmas, they take down their pictures and honour rolls and they even throw in a decorated tree for good measure.'

Marc chuckled. She met his eyes and saw a twinkle lurking in their depths. She chuckled too, and all at once she felt better. As if the weariness had lifted a little.

She should go now, she told herself.

She didn't.

'So you have a hall,' he prompted, sounding fascinated. 'What else?'

'I pull in favours wherever I can find 'em,' she told him. 'I also now have Douglas McCurdie's puddings, and that's really something.'

'Puddings?'

'Douglas is a local poultry farmer. His wife used to make a Christmas pudding which was a legend among her family, and when she died he found the recipe and started making them to sell. They're awesome but he's canny— he sells them for a ridiculous amount through a trendy Sydney outlet. But he was friends with Jonas, and when I twisted his arm he agreed to provide them—as long as he's on the guest list. He's lonely and it's a pride saver for him, too. And so it's spiralled. We have some of the best island cooks competing to have their food accepted. Grandpa and I have people we decree need to be invited, but the rest of the places are up for ballot, and that list's a mile long. But if you volunteer to help you become part of it. It's fabulous.'

'And the gifts?' he said cautiously, sounding entranced.

'They're just for the specials. If I did gifts for everyone I'd go nuts. But the islanders who don't have anyone waiting at home, or those too ill or elderly to have a decent Christmas themselves—they get a gift, and those gifts are personal. No handkerchiefs and socks from me.'

'Like what?'

'Little things,' she told him. 'You've already figured money on this island is tight so they can't be big. But I have spies in the welfare shop, with the fishermen, with the local tradies, with whoever I can think of to help, and I have a plan that lasts all year.'

He'd forgotten the pain in his leg. The pain all over his body. She had him fascinated.

'So tell me about your plan.'

'Well…like geraniums for Sandra Carter,' she told him. 'Sandra's been alone since her husband and her son drowned in a boating accident six years back. But she adores geraniums—she reckons she has every variety known to man. Six months ago we had an evacuation flight arrive without its usual doctor. They'd expected a routine problem, but it turned nasty so I had to go with them to Sydney. I needed to stay overnight and took a dusk walk and saw the most amazing geranium—I swear it was almost black. I knocked on the door and the lady gave me a cutting and it's actually grown. I reckon Sandra will be beside herself when she sees it. Not all my things hit the sweet spot, but I do my best. I have a "Beware, Vicious Dog" sign for May Trent with her ancient chihuahua. I have a perfect nautilus shell for Louise Addington whose grandson broke hers when he was here last holiday. I have a second-hand book on making artificial flies for Ron Nesbit—he spends his life fly-fishing. Oh, and I had another triumph—I found an ancient pottery wheel for Gay Ryan, who's always wanted to try throwing pots, and it goes with a promise of lessons from Chris Baker, who's an excellent local potter. That took me taking Chris's kid's appendix out to wheedle. So many things—and they all have to be wrapped.'

'Including the pottery wheel?' he said faintly.

'I'll use a long piece of string for that,' she told him. 'It'll lead to the janitor's room, where the wheel will be set up. I'll wrap a box with the end of the string in it to give to Gay. The trick is to make every gift look ordinary. It's become a bit of a thing—the islanders love it. I have people suggesting stuff now, but no one knows until Christmas Day what the gifts are. Actually, that's not true. Grandpa knows because he helps—he loves it too.' She paused and bit her lip. 'Or mostly he does. He's not even asking about it this year.'

And that was enough to haul her out of her story, to make her remember reality. 'Sorry,' she said contritely. 'That's far too much information about my hobby horse. You need to rest.'

'So do you.'

'I don't have a black and blue body. I'll send Maggie in with something.'

'You're worried about your grandpa?'

'Doesn't everyone worry about their grandpa? He should be...' She paused and managed a smile and shrugged. 'No. I was going to say he should be retired, but sitting in a rocker watching the world go by isn't his scene. He'll die in the traces. Except I don't want it to be...well, not for a very long time yet.'

This was personal. What was she doing, talking personal with a patient? Marc was watching her face—reading her astutely? The thought was unsettling.

If he was unsettling her then all the more reason for her to leave, but she didn't, and it was Marc who spoke up next.

'How sick is he?'

She sighed and spread her hands. Why not? She'd come this far. 'His renal problems aren't bad enough for dialysis or transplant yet, but they're worrying,' she told him. 'Plus there's his heart. He had a minor attack last year. We had to fly him to Sydney, where they put in a stent and gave him orders to slow down. Which he refuses to do. He should have gone back last month for a check-up but of course he won't. And don't you dare tell him I told you.'

'I won't. But you know I'm a cardiologist. Maybe I...'

'Could examine him before you leave? I'd like to see you try—I can only imagine what he'd say if he thought I was worrying a patient on his behalf.'

'I'm a colleague.'

'Says the man with his leg in plaster, an arm in a sling and bruises all over him.' She forced a smile back onto her face and decided she really did need to go now. The fact that this man was looking at her with empathy, with understanding, with concern...

She didn't need any of it. She didn't!

'Let me help you wrap your parcels,' he said, and she blinked.

'What, you?'

'That's hardly a gracious response.' He was sitting up in bed, smiling at her, and she thought he was bruised and battered, he was wearing a generic hospital gown and the man had no business to look as sexy as he did. Or have a smile that twisted something inside her that had no business being twisted.

'My arm's sore,' he told her, watching her with eyes that

seemed to see far too much. 'But it's not terrible. My leg will stop me hiking for a while but neither of them preclude me from being useful. My friends have gone to St Moritz without me, and I'm at a loose end. So how about loading me up with lists, gifts, wrapping paper and sticky tape? My wrapping might be a bit off, but I can cover things.'

'I can't...'

'Ask me? You weren't forward in asking for lift chairs.'

'That's different. That's for the hospital.'

'And this is personal? I don't think so.'

'But it is,' she said seriously. 'If you knew the pleasure those gifts give me...'

'Because they're for other people,' he said gently. 'Who gives you a gift, Dr McCrae?'

'If you saw the selection of chocolates out at Reception...'

'I'm not talking of chocolates.'

'They're more appropriate than an offer to fly me to St Moritz,' she flung at him and then flushed. 'No. Sorry, I'm very grateful.'

'You shouldn't feel grateful.'

'I don't, because I have all the gifts I need.' He'd been watching her, their gazes almost locked, but now she deliberately lowered her eyes, staring blindly towards the chart at the end of the bed. 'I...if you really do mean it... about the wrapping...'

'I really do mean it.'

'Then I may well take you up on it,' she told him, still not looking at him. 'You might still be running on adrenalin now, but I suspect you'll find you need to sleep tomorrow. Even if you don't think it, your injuries will take their toll. But if you're still here on Saturday... Maybe I could put a quarantine sign on your door and tell the nurses you're desperate for rest. A couple of them will be suspicious, but it'll give you privacy.'

'I'd barricade the door with my bed tray,' he told her solemnly. 'Secrets R Us. Speaking of which…'

'Marc, I really do need to go.' She did, too. This guy was making her feel more and more unsettled.

'Yeah, but I have a favour to ask,' he told her. 'My clothes are torn, filthy and bloodstained. And this gown…'

'It's a very nice gown,' she said and managed to smile. His gaze had met hers again and the twinkle in those dark eyes…

She had to get out of here!

'It's a great gown as far as gowns go,' he told her, the twinkle intensifying. 'But as far as secrets go… Every time I get out of bed I need to clutch my modesty around me and hope.'

'There's nothing under there the nurses haven't seen a hundred times before.'

'Dr McCrae…'

'Yes… Dr Pierce?'

'Could you please, please, please, see if you can find me some clothes. Some decent pyjamas.'

'I'm already on it,' she told him. 'Kylie—she's the lass who delivers your meals—has a sister who works in the charity store. I've sent her home with a list.'

'The welfare store!'

'There's not a great range on the island,' she told him. 'Mostly we buy online. It takes about a month to get here, but if you're prepared to wait…'

'So it's the welfare store or nothing.' He sounded revolted and she chuckled.

'You never know. I saw Brenda Larsen drop off her husband's purple pyjamas only last week. Linus has gone up a size, from enormous to eye-popping. They're a bit stretched across the tummy but otherwise in perfect condition. If you're lucky they might still be there.'

'Elsa…'

She chuckled and threw up her hands. 'I know, every sense is offended. I'll send Maggie in with laptop, phone and drugs but you do need to sleep. I'm going.'

'Before I toss a pillow at you.'

'I'm gone,' she said, and was out of there, tugging the door firmly closed behind her.

He lay and stared at the closed door for a long time.

Maggie didn't bring the laptop or the phone or the drugs. She would soon, he thought. He'd shown her he'd been irritated, and she'd be making her point. Nurses were a bad breed to get offside. He knew that. As a cardiovascular surgeon he couldn't get by without the help of his extraordinary team, and he made a point of ensuring they weren't stressed.

Maggie had been busy, and he'd pushed her too hard to try and get the tablet password reset.

Was the password so important? Elsa had said there were two little boys in the kids' ward. Did he know what was wrong with them? Did he know how busy the nursing staff were?

He was getting the feeling he knew how busy Elsa was. Too damned busy. Plus she was tired.

Because she'd climbed down into unchartered territory to save him. She'd spent what must have been an almost sleepless night. She'd accompanied him back down the mountain this morning and then operated on his leg.

She had a grandpa with a bad heart, and a community dependent on her as its only full-time doctor.

And he'd been making a fuss about a password.

Because his work was so much more important?

He thought suddenly back to medical school, to the first of the numerous sessions where specialists outlined their roles, where students were expected to think seriously about which path they'd take.

The cardiovascular surgeon had been impressive. He remembered the talk clearly. 'We're at the cutting edge of technology, saving lives which even ten years ago would have been lost. We demand the highest level of intellectual and physical skill. I believe it's the peak of medical expertise—exciting, challenging and, yes, immensely lucrative. Only the best of you need think of applying and only the best of the best will make the grade.'

That was for him, he'd thought. Studying was a breeze. Cutting edge surgery excited him. As for lucrative...who didn't want lucrative? With the wealth he'd inherited from his parents he hardly needed it, but still...

But Elsa...

He thought back to that same lecture, the small, greying man who'd represented family doctors.

'We're not cutting edge,' he'd said quietly. 'In most cases I confess we're not all that lucrative, although most of us make a respectable living. But we do save lives. Not as dramatically as my compatriots on this panel, no life-saving heart or brain surgery for us. But we find and refer, and along the way we pick up the pieces of people's lives and we do our best to patch them together. We try to stop the dramas before they start. Most of us have a community we care for deeply, and we'll do anything for them. A mum with postnatal depression...a coal miner with a cough he thinks is nothing...that's who we're here for and it gives us just as much satisfaction as our more esteemed peers.'

Marc had hardly listened.

His father had been a neurologist. His mother had

been a brilliant medical researcher. He was expected to be bright, and bright young doctors followed bright young professions.

They never saw mums with postnatal depression. They never saw a guy with a cold and pushed him to have a chest X-ray.

They never sat up late on the nights before Christmas and wrapped twenty or thirty parcels for needy locals.

He thought of his mother, who'd said she'd loved this island. Maybe she had, but she'd only come here to climb. She'd never have wrapped thirty gifts for people she hardly knew.

She'd been as selfish as he was.

Selfish? The thought made him wince. Was he? Dammit, he worked hard. He made a difference. Not everyone could be a hero.

Like Elsa.

There was a knock on the door and Maggie bustled in, her arms full of gear for him, her face set in prim disapproval.

'Dr McCrae's sent you the telephone and the laptop. You can use our phone tonight but she's organising Jason to see you tomorrow. There's also medication, but she says you don't want it. I dare say you'll try and sleep and then be asking me for it in a couple of hours when I'm busy with something else.'

'Are you busy?' he asked, but a sharp look was all he got for his pains.

'It's looking to be a big night.' She sniffed.

'Problems?'

'Nothing that need concern you.'

'I'm a doctor,' he said gently, probing to get past antagonism. 'If absolutely necessary I could get up and help.'

That produced a snort.

'I mean it.'

'You might well,' she snapped as she set her gear down on his tray. 'But a lot of help you'd be. One of our pregnant mums has just come in threatening to deliver, and she's only thirty-two weeks. The smoke on the mainland means she can't be evacuated, so Elsa has her hands full trying to keep that baby aboard. What use is a cardiologist with a broken leg?'

'No help at all,' he said humbly. 'Maggie…'

'Yes.' She tugged up the blood pressure machine and started taking his obs.

'Could you please give me the painkillers Elsa's written up?'

'She says you don't want them until later.'

'I didn't think I did,' he admitted. 'But it's true I'm hurting now, and if I take them then I'll go to sleep and won't need to disturb you later.'

She fixed him with a look of distrust. 'Why the change of heart?'

'Because I'm starting to realise that I need to lie here and be no trouble to you at all.'

'If you need us, we'll come,' she said shortly. 'Ignoring pain, ignoring any other worrying symptom might lead to more drama.'

'Then I won't ignore pain or any other worrying symptom,' he promised. 'But if it's humanly possible, for all our sakes I will cause no more drama.'

CHAPTER SEVEN

ON FRIDAY HE SLEPT. Which infuriated him. Every time he woke he found another two or three hours had drifted by. He'd stir when the nurses came to do his obs, or when his meals turned up. He was extraordinarily hungry, but meals simply seemed to make him sleepier. Jason arrived and set up his new phone and he managed to stay awake for that. Once he was back online he checked his hospital messages, but none of them seemed worth the effort of replying. He thought about opening his files on the borrowed laptop and doing some work, but that was as far as he got. Someone dropped in pyjamas. Getting rid of his hospital gown seemed important. He donned the boxer shorts but the T-shirt was too much trouble.

He slept.

Mid-afternoon he woke and found Elsa at the end of his bed, checking his chart. She smiled as she saw him stir.

'Excellent,' she told him. 'Your body's had a tough time. It needs sleep to recover and it's taking it. Told you so.'

'You don't need to sound so smug about it.'

'I'm enjoying the sensation of telling a specialist what's what,' she said, grinning. 'Allow me my small satisfaction, Dr Pierce. But all's good here. You can go back to sleep.' And she was gone.

Confused, disconcerted, still half asleep, there seemed

little choice but to obey, but adding to his confusion was the way Elsa's smile stayed with him while he slept.

Some time in the long distant past, when he was little more than a toddler, he'd had a nanny he'd loved. He had fuzzy memories of being ill and his nanny bustling in and out of the room, sitting on his bed, reading to him, cuddling him.

For some strange reason, Elsa was providing the same comfort. For over twenty-four hours he'd been truly terrified, and the echoes of that terror were still with him. So he slept, but the vision of Elsa stayed with him—Elsa somewhere in the hospital, Elsa checking his obs, Elsa just...here.

It made him feel needy, and he was not needy.

But maybe he was.

He remembered the day that same nanny had left, how useless his tears had been. He'd long got over the idea of needing anyone, but at the moment he seemed to have no choice. He seemed to need to take comfort from her presence. He'd go back to being solitary—of course he would; nothing else made sense—but Elsa's smile stayed with him as he slept.

It helped.

Friday might have passed in a sleepy haze for Marc, but for Elsa it was far different. Her pregnant patient seemed to have settled for now, but she was still uneasy about her. She checked and checked, and worried and worried. She wanted her evacuated, but smoke haze was still a problem. Meanwhile she had so much work it seemed to be coming out of her ears.

Late at night she did a final round and found Marc awake, but she was too rushed to stay for more than a few moments.

'You're looking good,' she told him. 'Great. Sorry, Marc, but I need to go.'

'It's nine at night. Aren't you done yet?'

'I have a mum bringing in a kid with an ear infection. Why she waited until nine at night to call me... Okay, I know, she was hoping it'd clear by itself because she's so busy. I get it.'

'I wish I could help.'

'Just don't throw out a fever. Go back to sleep.'

'What about your Christmas gifts,' he demanded as she backed out of the door. 'Wrapping? Have you done them yet?'

No. She hadn't. She had to find time. Somehow.

'Bring them to me,' he ordered.

'Really?' She was astonished he'd even remembered.

'Please,' he told her. 'I've slept all day. By tomorrow I'll be bored to snores.'

'You're recuperating.'

'So I need therapy. Bring me what I need.'

She stared at him for a long moment. He was propped up in bed, rumpled with sleep. His arm was in a sling but he'd abandoned the hospital nightwear—he was now wearing decent boxers, but his chest was bare. He was wearing a five o'clock shadow. His dark eyes were smiling and he looked...

Like she had to back out of here now.

'Gifts,' he said, his voice becoming gentle, and she wondered if he knew what highly inappropriate thoughts had just slammed into her head.

'G...gifts,' she managed to echo. 'I'll bring them in the morning.'

She fled.

Saturday morning—Christmas Eve—she was up at five. By nine she felt as if she'd done a whole day's work, but there was more than a day's work still ahead of her.

Mid-morning she checked on Marc, to find him propped up in bed waiting for her and demanding his 'therapy'.

'Okay, you asked for it,' she managed and half an hour later his room was crowded with gifts, scissors, paper, cards, list and tape. She put the Do Not Disturb sign outside his door and left him staring in some bemusement at what he'd let himself in for.

At midday she snagged his lunch from the kitchen, plus sandwiches for herself, and went to see how he was getting on.

She found him surrounded by a sea of wrapping paper, with a pile of oddly wrapped gifts beside the bed.

He had a geranium on the bed beside him and he was glowering at it.

'Wow,' she said, surveying the chaos from the door. 'This is fantastic. How many have you done?'

'Twenty-six,' he said darkly. 'And *done* is a very loose word. Wrapping doesn't seem to be my forte.'

She grinned. 'So I'm guessing you always get your nurses to do your dressings?'

'Always.'

'No matter.' She perched on the foot of his bed and picked up his chart. 'I'm an appalling wrapper too, so the islanders won't notice any difference.' She took a moment while she read the chart, and then she beamed. 'Good boy, no surprises here.'

'Tell me about your pregnant patient?' he asked, and she screwed up her nose.

'The smoke's cleared so finally we can evacuate her,' she told him. 'Things look like they're settling but I still don't like it and I don't want a thirty-two-weeker delivered here. I've had it happen before when the family wouldn't accept advice.' She hesitated and he saw trauma, tightly held. Then she gave one of her characteristic nods and moved on. 'Well, my advice is stronger now, or maybe it's not even advice. Erica's out of here. The plane's due at three. That's what I needed to tell you. They'll take you too, if you want to go.'

And that took him aback. He could leave. He'd be back in Sydney tonight.

To what?

His mates were in St Moritz, or scattered for the Christmas holidays—either that or they'd be on duty, working their butts off. If he was evacuated he could be admitted into the hospital where he worked. There he'd suffer teasing by the staff, plus—heaven forbid—jovial visits by the elderly consultant who always played Santa. Or he could sit at home with his leg immobile and feel sorry for himself.

Oh, for heaven's sake, what was he thinking? He was involved in an immense international research project. There was always work to do.

But he still might feel sorry for himself, he conceded, and he glanced up and saw Elsa watching him with what looked like understanding.

'Conflicted, eh?' she asked. 'If you go home you'll realise how much you're missing St Moritz, and you still need bed rest. You know you're welcome to stay here. We can keep you as an inpatient for a couple more days and then you can take the regular flight home. Oh, and you needn't worry about being bored. If you finish these I have a hundred paper napkins I need folding into the shape of little bells. Origami at its finest.'

'Bells...' he said faintly.

'It's only fair to warn you,' she told him cheerfully, 'before you make a decision. So your choice is a nice quiet flight back to Sydney, with well-trained medics to keep you safe, or a hundred paper bells followed by total chaos on Christmas Day. Maybe I didn't mention that as a hospital patient you get to be first on the guest list at our Christmas dinner. We can organise you a wheelchair if you'd like to go.'

'A wheelchair?' he said, revolted.

'A wheelchair it is until that swelling goes down and we can replace that back slab,' she said, in a voice that brooked no argument. 'So, Dr Pierce, what shall it be? You want to share our island Christmas, or do you want to make a run for it? Make up your mind because the evac team needs to know.'

She was smiling down at him, her head cocked slightly to one side like an impertinent sparrow. He found himself smiling back.

Christmas here—or Christmas in Sydney.

Christmas alone—or Christmas with Elsa.

It wouldn't be Christmas with Elsa, he told himself. He was simply one of her many patients.

Still…

'I will help you with the napkin bells if you decide to stay,' she told him generously and he thought of her sitting beside him, that glorious head of fiery curls bent over origami bells. He thought of her smile.

The decision seemed to be made for him.

Christmas with Elsa it would be.

What was he thinking? He was shocked at the direction his errant thoughts were taking. Was this some type of Stockholm Syndrome, where the captive fell for the captor?

Um, that might possibly be overplaying a broken leg and a hospital bed, he conceded, and actually Elsa had freed him, not captured him.

So was it gratitude he was feeling?

Of course it was gratitude, he told himself with a certain amount of relief. It had nothing to do with the way Elsa was smiling at him now, with that inquisitive, intelligent sparrow look. The look that said whatever he decided would be okay by her.

The look that said that, regardless, if he got on that plane she'd fold all hundred napkins herself, and then see patients and take care of her grandpa and get up on Christmas morning and do a ward round and lug these crazily wrapped gifts across to the footy hall and have fun.

Fun. There was the hub of the matter. He looked down at his pile of weird gifts and thought he wanted to be there when they were all opened.

'So what's your decision?' she asked gently, as if she guessed he was torn.

'I'll stay.'

'Wow, that's good of you.'

He grinned ruefully. 'Sorry. If it's okay with you, if you don't need my bed for someone else, if it's okay for me to join in your Christmas festivities…'

'Then you're very welcome. Now, about this geranium…'

'It's too…'

'Too big.' She smiled, a lovely, uncomplicated smile that said all was right with her world. 'The lady gave me a three-inch cutting and I had to carry it home in wet tissue and hope. And here it is, knee high and covered with flowers. When it started growing I had visions of it taking over the whole island—I had to check with our quarantine officer that it was okay to keep it. If we join two sheets together…you plonk it on the wrapping paper and hold it steady and I'll gather the paper together with a big ribbon at the top. What colour do you reckon? Red? Gold? How about rainbow?'

'Rainbow,' he said, slightly shocked as she hauled gaudy bows out of a box and laid them on his bed for his consideration. Memories stirred of elegant gifts in the past, mostly wrapped by the expensive stores they were pur-chased from. He didn't think he'd ever had a gift that looked so...so...

'How about that for Christmassy?' Elsa demanded as she finished attaching her bow and stood back to inspect their handwork. Scarlet Santa paper and a vast rainbow bow. The whole thing looked more like a scrunched ball of waste paper than elegant gift wrapping. 'Haven't we done well?'

'Very well,' he agreed faintly, and she grinned and touched his shoulder—a fleeting touch—doctor reassur-ing patient?

'You're doing good, Dr Pierce,' she told him. 'Grandpa will help me sneak these out later. Meanwhile you need to take a nap and gather strength for the bells.'

'Did you say a hundred?'

'Yep,' she said cheerfully, and then added, 'Nope, make that a hundred and one because we just added you to the guest list.'

CHAPTER EIGHT

Christmas Day

SHE REMEMBERED CHRISTMAS as a kid. There had been those first appalling ones with her dysfunctional mother—thankfully mostly a blur now. She did remember the last of those, waking to find her mother surfacing after yet another binge, with nothing planned, nothing to eat, nothing at all.

Her mother had simply forgotten it was Christmas—or hadn't thought of it in the first place.

And then somehow her mother had disappeared, and when her grandfather had swooped in to claim her Christmas had suddenly been magical. Yes, Grandpa had often been called out, but if she wasn't called on to 'help' in the hospital kitchen—she'd been chief taster—or if she didn't need to ride her brand-new scooter or play with her brand-new science kit, she'd go with him. And it seemed every single islander would be celebrating, welcoming her with hugs and mince pies and more sweets than one small kid could possibly consume.

Her island. Her people.

She did love this place, she conceded. Yes, sometimes she resented its demands, but she still remembered that first Christmas on the island, the feeling of being loved unconditionally, of being protected. Of belonging.

And today…

For a few indulgent moments after she woke she let herself stay where she was and just wallowed in the surge of excitement that was Christmas. The restlessness that had been with her for months seemed to have receded. Life was okay. It was Christmas and she was with the people she loved.

And Marc was here.

'But that has nothing to do with it,' she told herself out loud—or if it did it had no business doing so. This was Christmas excitement only. Marc would be gone tomorrow or the day after and she'd be left with…

Tony?

No, not Tony. She'd cleared that up—she hoped. One unwise date…

And that was the problem. The whole island seemed to be watching her, waiting for her to date. Plus all the rest. The islanders would like her to be even more wedded to the island than she was now. When eligible tourists rocked in—the male, single variety—she could almost see their collective nervousness. No one was to take away their Dr McCrae.

Which was fine with her, she conceded, because she had no intention of leaving. She owed the island too much. She loved the island too much.

However…

However, the pool of available islanders as life partners was limited, to say the least. Most of the young ones departed as soon as they could. There were maybe ten unmarried guys around her age on the whole island, and compared to most of them Tony looked good.

Wow, where were her thoughts going? There was a despondent thought to wake up to on Christmas morning. Did she need a reason to get up?

Of course she didn't. She struggled to retain the surge of excitement she'd woken with. She had a good life. A great life. She was the island doc. She didn't need to be anything more.

Except here was this gorgeous guy called Marcus, who'd fallen down a hole, who'd helped her wrap gifts and who'd smiled at her.

Get a grip, she told herself. She was indulging in a teenage fantasy, and she had no time for fantasies today. Grandpa would be heating panforte in the fire stove oven, waiting with a gift for her. Sherlock would be demanding a fast walk before she started work for the day. She needed to do a ward round. She needed to make sure of the final touches to the Christmas dinner.

And her fantasy?

'Marc's as real as Santa Claus,' she said out loud. 'Okay, he's flesh and blood and he'll be staying longer than a quick flit down the chimney, but not much longer. Put your sensible boots on, Dr McCrae, and get to work.'

Marc was accustomed to the extravagant Christmas décor of St Moritz at its glitziest, but the simple Gannet Island hall was a sight to take a man's breath away.

A giant gumtree stood behind the building, laced right to its tip with the island's delicate mistletoe. Who needed bought decorations with such crimson beauty at hand? Massive swathes of the brilliant clusters had been brought inside, creating an effect much more gorgeous than any commercial effort. The hall looked lovely and over a hundred people were set to enjoy themselves.

It seemed that what had begun years before as a Christmas party for hospital patients and for islanders who had no one to share with had grown. Elsa had told him that most island families organised their own Christmas dinner, but still almost all put their names in the ballot to attend this one. The ballot was for entire families, and if the family succeeded in the ballot then this party seemed to be the preferred option.

It meant the party wasn't just for the ill and the lonely. It was a true celebration.

The footy ground was right by the hospital. A couple of beefy footballers were in charge of patient transport, for anyone well enough to enjoy the day. Despite Marc's protests, they'd brought him in a wheelchair—'If you think I'm letting you use crutches before your shoulder's settled you can think again,' Elsa had told him sternly, so now he was seated at one of six vast trestle tables surrounded by…fun.

As everyone walked in they were presented with a hat. These weren't your typical novelty Christmas hats bought in bulk from a cheap supplier. These were knitted or crocheted beanies. Crazy beanies.

'They're an island project,' the guy sitting beside Marc told him. 'We no sooner finish one year's lot than we start another. It's called the Crazy Cap Club. We meet at the school hall every Thursday night and egg each other on to see who can crochet the craziest one.'

'You do it too?' Marc asked, fascinated. The guy he was talking to was an ex-fisherman who'd introduced himself as Wally, in a wheelchair that matched Marc's, in his eighties, a hospital patient with oxygen-dependent emphysema. Weathered from a life at sea, gruff, matter-of-fact, the thought of him with a crochet hook had Marc hornswoggled.

'Doc bullied me into it,' he told Marc. 'I was that tired of sitting on me bum all day, so she gave me a challenge.

Do one with a fish on it,' she told me. 'So I did. First one was a bit wobbly but Martin Crosby got it and still wears it out on his boat. That was three years back. This year my one's over on Hazel Mitchell's head. See…the octopus with the tentacles made into braids that hang down her back looking like hair.'

Marc looked and looked again. He'd met Hazel—she was the prim hospital administrator who'd helped him fill in admission forms. She was wearing a very proper skirt and matching jacket—in prim pink. Sensible court shoes and stockings.

And an octopus hat with braids.

And then Elsa came swooping over to their table. He'd been watching her—of course he had. She seemed to be everywhere, hauling people into conversations, rearranging seating. He'd seen her take one old lady who was shrinking at the end of a noisy table and almost literally sweep her up and deposit her in the midst of another table, which seemed just as noisy but the people there seemed to know her. They shoved along to accommodate her and were currently in the midst of swapping hats to figure which hat best suited who. She was giggling and sipping champagne and Elsa had moved on.

'I think your hat's the best,' she told Wally now, stooping to give him a hug, careful, Marc noted, not to bump the oxygen tube that obviously kept the old man alive. 'An octopus with dreadlocks…where will you go from there?'

'I'm thinking of a fisherman with fishhooks and fish dangling,' Wally told her, grinning. 'I got the pattern just about worked out. It'll take me all year to make but it's worth it. You know Muriel Cuthbert got last year's mermaid and she's using it as a tea cosy. Pride of place on the kitchen table, she tells me, and everyone admires it.'

'And why wouldn't they?' Elsa demanded, looking at

the hats on both their heads. Wally was wearing a Santa with seven elves stitched into the side. Marc was wearing a particularly mean-looking barracuda. 'Very fetching,' she said, grinning.

Elsa was wearing a pink confection, a crocheted merry-go-round, complete with little horses. It looked complex, weird, adorable.

Marc looked at Elsa's flushed, laughing face and thought he'd never seen anything more beautiful.

It must be the champagne, he thought. He imagined his friends, many of whom would be sipping their hugely expensive Christmas eggnogs in front of a roaring fire at the resort in St Moritz. They'd all be wearing après-ski wear, very chic.

Elsa was wearing a flouncy red skirt that looked as if it could well be homemade and a crisp, sleeveless blouse. She'd accessorised with a necklace of red tinsel and Santa Claus earrings. Plus her crazy hat. She'd braided her flaming curls and the two braids hung over her shoulders, tied at the ends with red and gold Christmas ribbon.

This was more Christmas cliché than he'd dreamed possible on one woman. Who knew it could look so great?

She was chuckling as she reached over and grabbed Wally's bon-bon. 'I can't believe you haven't pulled it yet!' Inside was a corny joke. She read it aloud to the table, and there was a roar of laughter.

'You guys take care of Marc,' she told everyone. 'He's had a very hard time so it's your responsibility to make him feel better.' And then she grinned. 'And don't be mean,' she added. 'Not one person is to mention hikers and satellite trackers and letting people know where you're going. Not one of you. It's Christmas. Cut the guy some slack.'

There was more laughter, all of it friendly, and Marc was seamlessly pulled into the general conversation.

Elsa hugged Wally and she moved on.

Marc wouldn't have minded a hug himself, he thought. He was her patient. The way he was feeling was totally inappropriate.

Maybe it *is* Stockholm Syndrome, he thought.

But he didn't feel like a victim.

It was time to turn his attention to eating, and the food was magnificent. The turkeys had arrived—somehow they'd been organised to be delivered on the evacuation flight. That must have been down to Elsa, he thought. How many medics had to juggle the needs of patients with the need for turkeys?

He watched Elsa and thought that this wasn't about her patients or, if it was, her patients were the whole island.

Between main course and pudding there was entertainment. Christmas carols were sung in three-part harmony, led by the local choir, with everyone joining in. A weathered fisherman with a hat and a rabbit made corny magician jokes. A group of elderly ladies in twenties gear danced the Charleston with gusto. At the end of the dance each of the ladies grabbed an unsuspecting diner and dragged them up to join them. Elsa was one of the first to be grabbed, and she Charlestoned with the best of them. Of course she would, he thought, dazed. She was magnificent.

And then there were the gifts. He watched Sandra Carter gasp and flush with pleasure as she removed his dodgy wrapping from around her geranium. He watched the hall roar with laughter as little May Trent opened her 'Beware, Vicious Dog' sign. May giggled and showed the sign to the little dog under her chair, and he thought her Christmas had been made. It seemed the same for every gift recipient.

Thanks to Elsa.

She had him enthralled. When the meal was done and

his footballer escorts decreed it was his turn to be wheeled back to the hospital, he looked for Elsa and saw she was already helping clear, chuckling with the locals as she worked. She looked busy and happy. And he thought that he really wanted to stay. Here. Now.

To do what? Help with the dishes? Ha.

He was a patient, an outsider, a visitor who'd already caused everyone massive inconvenience. He submitted meekly to being wheeled back to his ward, to his bed.

He'd missed a call from Kayla. It was early morning in St Moritz. He imagined how Christmas would play out over there—the magnificent, sophisticated Christmas he'd thought was perfect—and decided he hadn't missed it one bit.

'How's the leg?' Kayla's enquiry was perfunctory when he returned the call, and he wondered if she really cared. Was this just a duty phone call?

'It's set and healing. I should be back in Sydney in the next couple of days.'

'That's good,' she told him and then proceeded to outline all her very exciting plans for the holiday.

'Kayla…' he said as she finished.

'Yes?' And he heard the reservation. Did she think he was going to ask her to do something different, mess with her plans?

'Kayla, this isn't working,' he said gently. 'I just thought…while you're over there having fun…please don't think you need to be loyal to me. I think we both know that shouldn't happen.'

There was a silence. He could almost see her sharp mind processing, considering ramifications.

'I guess that's logical,' she said at last. 'You and I…we have had fun.'

'We have.'

'But it was never serious.'

'It never was.' It never had been, he thought. He didn't do relationships, or not the type of relationship he'd seen some of his colleagues fall into. The type where there was co-dependence.

And Kayla was the same. He heard a sigh and he thought he detected relief. The sound of moving on.

'I'll admit I might have more fun here if everyone stops treating me as poor Kayla who's pining for her boyfriend,' she admitted.

'I can't imagine you pining over anyone.'

'It's not my style,' she agreed, and chuckled. She really was a friend. Just a colleague.

No longer an occasional lover.

'Okay, then, I'm off to enjoy Christmas,' she told him. 'I hope someone gives you pudding, though I can't imagine it'll come anywhere near what they'll give us here. Poor you. But take care of yourself, Marcus. Bye-ee.'

And she was gone.

What was gone with her?

The knowledge that he wanted to be part of that set? He might well want to, he thought, as soon as he got back to Sydney. As soon as he brushed off the dust of this island.

As soon as he stopped thinking of one gorgeous doctor, dancing through Christmas.

And, as if on cue, there was a knock on his door and the doctor in question appeared.

She was still wearing her gorgeous red skirt and her crazy hat. She had a white coat over the top.

'Good evening, Doctor,' he said, and she grinned.

'Thank you,' she told him. 'A bit of professional respect, that's what I like. Every single patient on my list tonight has greeted me with caution, like I might prescribe enemas instead of antibiotics. Even though I swear the only alcohol I had was in the brandy sauce.' It was said with indignation, followed by a chuckle and if he'd been entranced before he was more so now.

Enthralled, even?

She took his chart from the end of the bed and read it while he watched her. Her chuckle had faded but there was still a trace of a smile on her face. Or maybe that dimple was a permanent feature.

This chameleon doctor, who trekked with her beagle, who'd abseiled down a hole to rescue him, who operated with competence, who'd made Christmas happy for so many...

'This is great,' she said as she hung the chart up again. 'And you're the end of the line. Not a single spike in temperature for the whole hospital, not even an unexpected tummy ache. Christmas has been a success.'

'It's been a success for reasons other than lack of medical repercussions,' he told her. 'You've done great.'

'We've done great,' she corrected him. 'The whole island. Even you with your wrapping.'

'*Even* me?' He managed to sound wounded.

'I mean especially you,' she said and grinned. 'Of course.'

Wow, she was gorgeous. Dammit, why was he in this bed?

'Elsa, when this is all over, if we can organise it, can I see you again?' he asked before he knew he was going to say it. Certainly before he'd thought it through.

It was dumb and she reacted accordingly. There was no hesitation in her response. 'There's no way that's likely to happen,' she told him bluntly. Was he imagining it, or did he hear a note of regret in her voice? 'In a couple of days you'll be out of here.'

'I could stay.' He still had two weeks' leave.

That brought a rueful smile. 'What, and hike on that leg? Not a hope. You'd be stuck in the local guesthouse, bored to snores.'

'But I could take you out to dinner.'

'Which would lead where?' She shrugged and he saw her dredge up a smile from somewhere. Trying to keep it light. 'Marc, you and I both know the rules. Doctors don't hit on patients. Patients don't hit on doctors. Especially when both of them are full of Christmas punch.'

'Asking you out to dinner isn't exactly hitting on you.' He felt like swearing. He was at such a disadvantage, sitting in bed in his borrowed pyjamas. Thankfully, they weren't Linus Larsen's purple ones, but persuading this woman to go out with him could well take more finesse than even the finest pyjamas conveyed. Someone had found him a shirt and loose trousers to wear to dinner but he'd put his pyjama boxers and T-shirt back on when he'd returned to bed. Now he wished he hadn't, but he also knew it wouldn't have made a blind bit of difference what he wore.

'Dating is encompassed in the same rules,' she said firmly. 'Thanks, Marc, but no. I don't do casual dating.'

'Does it have to be casual?' Again it was said before he thought it through, and he winced even as the words came out. Was he talking about being serious? *Now?* He saw her withdraw a little and any last vestige of her smile vanished.

'You have a girlfriend.'

'I don't.' He needed to clear this up. 'Things between Kayla and me were pretty much over even before this happened. This accident's just made our split formal.'

'What, she dumped you because you couldn't go to St Moritz?' She sounded incensed.

'No, it was a mutual dumping,' he told her, 'of a tepid

relationship. Maybe like the relationship the nurses tell me you have with Tony.'

She stared at him in astonishment. 'You've been gossiping.'

'I was encouraged to talk while my bed was made,' he said virtuously. 'And talking involves questions. The nurse was very pleased with my progress.'

That won a chuckle, but then her voice turned rueful. 'Well, I wish the dumping could be mutual. Tony's a local kelp farmer, dependable, stolid, and after one date he's utterly convinced that we can marry and raise a whole lot of little kelp farmers.' She sighed. 'But, moving on, your love life is nothing to do with me, and vice versa. Maybe if I'm over in Sydney on a case we can catch up, but you staying for two weeks just so we can date… It's not going to happen.'

'Why not?' He knew his approach was clumsy, but he was struggling here.

'Because at the end of the two weeks you'd go back to Sydney and I…' She hesitated and he saw a struggle to be honest. And honesty won. 'I could get even more unsettled than I am now.'

His gaze met hers and held it for a long moment. She tilted her chin and then dropped it.

'So tell me,' he said gently. 'Elsa, why are you unsettled?'

Maybe it was the brandy sauce. Or maybe it was because it was the end of a long day and she was still riding a wave of confidence.

Or maybe it was because it was Christmas and she was relaxed and he was just *there*.

Regardless, he saw her hesitate and then shrug and decide to go for it.

'Because this island has seven hundred residents and

it's too darned small,' she told him, and then she closed her eyes and shook her head. 'No. That's not fair. Gannet Island is what it is. It's always been remote, and I knew what I was in for when I came back here.'

'You came back for your grandpa?'

'I came back because this is my home. Because the islanders are my family. Because they've loved and supported me from the moment I arrived here aged all of seven, so how could I possibly leave them now? I can't, and mostly it's okay except when I think maybe I wouldn't mind dating and having fun and being taken out to a restaurant where the proprietor doesn't skip the bill as long as I give him a consult on the way out as to how to manage his hormonal teenage daughter, or what to do with his infected toe.'

'That happens?' he asked, stunned, and she managed a wry smile.

'Of course. If you stayed, and if we did go out to dinner, it's just as likely to end that way. With you patiently waiting while I head out to the kitchen to watch someone take off his boot.'

'Elsa...'

'It's fine,' she said, and there was another of her wry shrugs. 'I'm over it. Though sometimes I wonder if it'd be nice to be...just normal. But that's my problem, Dr Pierce, not yours.'

'But...'

'No buts.' She hesitated and then forged on again, totally honest. 'You know, I do think you're lovely,' she told him. 'That's a totally unprofessional thing to even think, much less say...'

'The feeling's mutual.'

'Thank you.' Another of her brisk nods. 'That does my ego a whole lot of good, and I'll take it as another

Christmas gift. But that's all. Your life's in Sydney and my life's here. There's not the faintest possibility, even if dating came to something...something more...that anything could come of it.'

'So you'll cut me off at the pass now?'

'I have no choice.' She met his gaze again, calm and direct. It was supposed to be a look of acceptance but behind that...he knew pain when he saw it. Almost involuntarily, he swung himself out of bed, steadying on his good leg.

'Elsa...'

'Don't you try and stand,' she said, alarmed. 'What if you fall? And I don't need this. Please. Back off, Marc.'

'Can you really say what you don't need? Or want?' He was balancing but only just. He took her hand and held on. One push and he'd be back on the bed.

But Elsa wasn't pushing. She stared down at their linked hands and he saw her lips quiver. There was an ache there, he thought. An ache that matched his?

'Don't,' she whispered.

'Do you really want me not to?'

'No. I mean...'

'Elsa, professional ethics or not, impossibility or not, I'd really like to kiss you.'

She closed her eyes for a moment and then looked up at him. Her gaze questioning. 'For Christmas?'

'If you need an excuse.'

'Marc, kissing you would be totally illogical.'

'Like any of the weird and wonderful gifts you've organised for everyone else this Christmas,' he told her. 'Where's your Christmas gift, Elsa?'

And that actually brought a smile. Her eyes suddenly danced with laughter. 'You're saying a kiss from you is equal to a black geranium?'

'Better.'

'Wow,' she said, and suddenly those dancing eyes met his and something changed.

'You'd have to prove it.' Her voice was suddenly decisive.

'Watch me try,' he told her and proceeded to do just that.

What she was doing broke every doctor-patient rule in the book.

Only it was Christmas and she didn't care. The moment his mouth touched hers she felt herself melting. She felt all sorts of things slipping away.

Mostly common sense.

She was standing in a patient's room. Her patient was in boxers and a T-shirt, balanced on one leg. He had a gammy shoulder. He should have his arm in a sling, but he had both hands on her waist. He'd tugged her close, so her breasts were moulding to his chest.

His mouth was on hers. Strong, warm, demanding. Totally, totally inappropriate.

Totally, totally delicious.

No.

It was more than delicious, she thought dazedly. It was wonderful. Magical.

She'd been kissed before—of course she had. Tony wasn't the only guy she'd dated.

It had never felt like this.

The way he held her…the strength of his hands on her waist…the way he'd hesitated as his mouth found hers, as if checking that this was indeed what she wanted…

How could he doubt it? Her lips opened under his and she felt as if she'd been catapulted into another world.

A world where heat met heat. Where desire met desire.

Oh, she wanted him. She ached for him. Her whole body felt as if it was surrendering.

She was surrendering.

She was being kissed and she was kissing. He didn't need to balance on his bad leg because she was holding him.

Maybe it could count as therapy, she thought, almost hysterically. Helping patient stand. Maybe this *was* a medical tool designed to make him feel better.

It was surely making *her* feel better. Every sense seemed to have come alive. Every nerve-ending was tingling.

More. Every single part of her was screaming that she wanted this man, she needed this man, that she wouldn't mind in the least if they fell back on the bed and...

Um, not in a million years. Not!

Because she didn't want it?

Because this was a hospital ward and any minute the door could open as a nurse arrived for routine obs. This was a patient and she was a doctor and...

Shut up, Elsa, she told her inner self fiercely. Just let this moment be.

So she did. Her mind shut down and she let herself just kiss. And be kissed.

The kiss was deep and long and magical, and as it finally ended—as all kisses surely must—it was as much as she could do not to weep. But Marc was still holding her. He had her at arm's length now, smiling into her eyes with such tenderness that...

No! She made a herculean effort to haul herself together. This was way past unprofessional. She could just about get herself struck off the medical register for this.

Right now she was having trouble thinking that it mattered, whether she was struck off or not. For Marc was smiling at her, and that seemed to be the only thing that mattered in the whole world.

But this was still well out of order. This man's life was

in Sydney. It could only ever be a casual fling with a guy who was bored.

Oh, but his smile…

'About that date…' he ventured, and she needed to shake her head but all she could do was look up into his dark eyes and sense went right out of the window.

But then reality suddenly slammed back with a vengeance. The hospital speaker system crackled into life and she heard Kim, one of the hospital's junior nurses. Even through the dodgy hospital intercom she heard the fear in Kim's tone. 'Code Blue. Nurses' station. Code Blue.'

Code Blue!

What was happening with Marc was pure fantasy. This was the reality of her life.

She was out of the door and she was gone.

CHAPTER NINE

WHAT WAS HE supposed to do—go back to bed?

Code Blue was hospital speak almost the world over for 'Get here fast because someone's dying'. Usually it meant cardiac infarct—heart failure.

He was a cardiologist. A heart surgeon.

He was a patient. He was wearing matching boxer and T-shirt pyjamas.

The wheelchair was still beside the bed, left there by the footballer who'd brought him back from lunch. 'No one seems to need this, mate. You might as well keep it; it'll let you get around a bit.' He glanced at it and discarded the idea almost instantly. It was too clumsy. It'd take too long.

He had no crutches but even if he did he'd be no use to anyone if his shoulder slipped out again. There were rails all along the corridor so ambulant patients could practise their walking. 'I'm ambulant,' he said out loud, and managed to hop to the door, grab the rail with his good hand and proceed to demonstrate just how ambulant he really was.

It wasn't hard to find the source of the Code Blue. Less than a minute's hobbling had him reaching a turn in the corridor to see a cluster of people outside the nurses' station.

He could see two nurses, one with a crash cart, another kneeling. Someone on the floor.

Elsa was also kneeling, her crimson skirt flared around her.

'Grandpa,' she breathed, and his world seemed to still.

He'd met Robert McCrae—of course he had. The elderly doctor had given him the anaesthetic while Elsa had set his leg, and he'd chatted to him a couple of times over the last couple of days. In his late seventies, he'd thought Robert looked a bit too thin, a bit too pale. Marc had had every intention of cornering him before he left and casually offering a full heart check. 'Just to reassure Elsa...' he'd planned to say.

It was too late now. Or was it? 'Grandpa...' Elsa murmured again, and there was a hoarse whisper in response.

'I'll be fine, girl. Don't fuss.'

Not dead. Marc had been present at so many cardiac deaths. Why did this seem so personal? Why was his relief so profound?

'You weren't breathing.' That was the nurse by the crash cart. She looked as if she was about to burst into tears.

'Let me up. Give me a hand, girl,' Robert attempted to snap at Elsa, but the snap was little more than a whisper and Elsa was having none of it. She had the portable defibrillator at hand, and before he could argue she'd ripped his shirt open.

The old guy could scarcely breathe but he was still indignation personified. 'This is my best shirt.'

'Ex shirt,' she told him. 'Kim doesn't make mistakes, and if she said you stopped breathing then you stopped breathing. And you were still unconscious when I got here.'

'I just got a bit dizzy, that's all.'

'I'm fitting the pads in case we need them,' she told

him. 'You know you'd do the same for any patient with collapse and a history of cardiac problems.' She looked up. 'Kim, contact Geoff and Ryan. Tell 'em we need to lift a prostrate patient...'

'Prostrate?' It must be hard to sound outraged when there was clear difficulty in breathing, but Robert managed it.

'And you'll stay prostrate until I say otherwise,' Elsa told him, bossiness underpinned with a definite shake in her voice. 'You taught me to be bossy in a crisis, Grandpa, so don't you fight me when I follow your orders.'

'It's not a crisis.' But he'd had enough. He'd been trying to lift his head. Now he slumped back and let his protests die to nothing.

'Elsa, would you let me help?'

She was fitting the pads of the defibrillator. Designed to jerk the heart back into motion when it stopped, it wasn't necessary now that Robert was conscious, but the elderly doctor had clearly lost consciousness, had clearly fallen. There was something else going on here. If there'd been a blockage then it could block again at any minute, and seconds would be precious.

She finished fitting the pads and then turned to Marc. 'Go back to bed,' she said quietly.

'Elsa, I have a broken leg, not the plague. You have a cardiologist on site, and I may well be what your grandfather needs right now. Make use of me.'

He saw her hesitate, torn. Every instinct would be to protect her patient—him. Every desire would be to do what was best for her grandfather.

'Please, then,' she said gruffly, and he could hear the emotion in the two words. Then she turned back to Robert. 'Grandpa, you remember Marc's here—Dr Pierce?

You know he's a cardiologist from Sydney? He's offered to ignore his broken leg and give his opinion.'

'What's he charging?' Robert demanded, and there was a hint of humour in his thready voice that further reassured Marc. He might have lost consciousness for a moment, but the blood supply hadn't been cut off for long enough to cause even minor mental impairment.

'Cut rate special,' he said as one of the nurses moved forward to help him hop from the support of the handrail to where Robert lay. 'You fixed my leg, so I'll have a shot at fixing your heart.'

'Might be a damned sight harder to fix,' Robert growled.

'It might,' Marc said quietly. Robert was still on the floor and he dropped to join him. It was hardly the usual medical scene—patient on floor, doctor dressed in pyjamas also on floor, his back slabbed leg stretched out before him.

He wedged himself around so he was side-on to Robert. Elsa was on the other side and a glance told him the strain she was under. Her face was almost as pale as her grandfather's.

And there was reason. Robert's breathing was fast, shallow, laboured. His skin was bluish, cool to the touch. Marc lifted his wrist and kept his face impassive as he noted the racing pulse. For all his fieriness, his attempt at humour, Robert was looking terrified.

'Pain?' Marc asked and watched him close his eyes for a moment and then decide to be honest.

'Bad,' he conceded. 'Chest. Shoulder. Another bloody heart attack. Must be a minor one this time, though. I'll be all right.'

'You'll have to go back to Sydney,' Elsa managed, and Marc could still hear the tremor. Finding her grandfather unconscious must have been horrific. 'We'll get you stabilised and call for evacuation.'

'Leave things for a moment,' Marc said softly. He was looking further, seeing things he didn't like.

The probability was that this was a heart attack, hopefully small, but there was no guarantee it wouldn't be a precursor to a bigger one. Yes, evacuation was called for, to a hospital with a state-of-the-art cardiac facility, with a team of trained medics on board the flight. But the look on Robert's face... And what was beneath...

He was seeing swollen, bulging neck veins and they were acting like flashing lights to Marc's trained eye. The heart was pumping blood out, but there was some impediment to its return.

'Can I have your stethoscope?' he asked Elsa, and she handed it wordlessly across. He listened to the muffled heart sounds, and his unease deepened.

'Blood pressure?' he asked, and the nurse fitted the cuff. Low.

'What are you thinking?' It was Robert himself who demanded to know. This was doctor to doctor. There'd be no sugar-coating what he was starting to suspect, and it'd be an insult to even try.

'I'm thinking we need to exclude cardiac tamponade,' he said briefly. 'Your veins are swollen. Low blood pressure. Muffled heart sounds. That's Beck's triad—the three symptoms that make me sound clever when I'm just fitting a pattern to what's happening.'

There was an expletive from Robert, and Marc gave him what he hoped was a reassuring grin.

'Exactly. No sweat though, Robert, because even if I'm right I've coped with cardiac tamponade before and I can cope with it now.'

He glanced up at Elsa then, and saw her face had bleached even whiter. She'd know the risks.

Cardiac tamponade was indeed frightening. Caused by

trauma, by cancer or sometimes by a heart attack, fluid or blood built up between the heart and the pericardium, the sac surrounding the heart. The pericardium consisted of two layers of tissue, with a small amount of fluid preventing friction between the layers. If this fluid built up, it put pressure on the heart, affecting its ability to pump blood around the body.

Robert might have just suffered a heart attack, or he might have suffered a minor attack weeks ago. The pressure might have built slowly, finally causing collapse. Or the leak could be recent, the pressure building fast.

Regardless, cardiac tamponade meant there was no time for evacuation. The pressure had to be removed now.

The two guys who worked as occasional orderlies, handymen or gardeners appeared and seamlessly went into action, helping Elsa transfer Robert to a stretcher and then lifting him onto a trolley. One of the nurses helped Marc to his feet. He was swearing inwardly. He wanted two good legs. He wanted to be dressed—at least in the soft shirt and loose gym pants he'd worn to lunch. He wanted to feel professional, fully functional—he *needed* to be at the top of his game. This was a situation he was trained for, and he wanted the capacity to move fast.

'Can you organise an echocardiograph and a chest X-ray?' he asked Elsa. Dammit, he felt helpless. 'And can someone help me get dressed?'

'Marc, you can't...' Elsa's voice trailed off. If the ECG and chest X-ray confirmed the diagnosis, there was no choice and she—and her grandfather—would know it.

'Robert,' Marc said, taking a moment to rest a hand on the shoulder of the elderly doctor, 'you know what's at stake here. If it is indeed tamponade then we need to get the pressure off fast. You'll need to go to the mainland to get any underlying problems with your heart sorted, but the tamponade has to be fixed now. I might be a cardiologist with a gammy leg and a sore shoulder, but that doesn't interfere with my skills. If the echocardiograph confirms my diagnosis you'll need percutaneous drainage and that's a skill I have. Will you let me and your granddaughter make you safe?'

And the old man's hand came up and gripped his, hard. Marc could feel the tremor. He could feel the fear.

'Do what you have to do, son,' Robert managed. 'You seem a damned idiot at bushwalking, but I assume you're not the same in an operating theatre.'

'I'm very good,' Marc told him. This was no time for false modesty. 'I'm who you need right now, gammy leg or not. Trust me.'

'I trust you,' Robert said and the grip on his hand tightened.

'Marc...' It was Elsa, and there was fear in her voice, too.

'And so must you, girl,' Robert said, forcefully now, as he directed his attention to his granddaughter. 'We're lucky to have a cardiologist to hand, even if you did have to crawl underground and sleep with him for a full night to get him here.'

The echocardiograph reinforced Marc's diagnosis. The chest X-ray and ultrasound confirmed it. Elsa stared at the image on the ultrasound screen and felt ill.

If she'd been on her own here she couldn't have coped. She'd have had to evacuate her grandfather, and with the pressure building in the hours it would have taken to get him to Sydney... The outcome didn't bear thinking of.

And doing such a procedure herself? She knew the principles, but to perform the drainage, especially on someone who was probably compromised with heart damage anyway… When that someone was her grandfather… To insert a needle into such a risky place, to do no damage…

She didn't need to. She had a cardiologist right here. The knowledge made her feel dizzy.

Marc was scrubbing. The nurses had found a stool with wheels and height adjustment. At full stretch it made him tall enough to use the sinks, to operate, to be fully functional.

He looked across at her as Maggie helped him on with theatre gear, and he must have seen the tension.

'It's okay,' he told her gently. 'We have this in hand. We'll try percutaneous drainage first. If that doesn't work then we'll move to the subxiphoid approach—taking away a slice of the pericardium. But I don't anticipate that. We'll give him the lightest possible general—I don't want any more risk to his breathing than he already has. While you monitor that, then I'll use the ultrasound to guide a nice fat needle into the cavity, set up a catheter and let it drain.'

Said like that it sounded simple. She knew it wasn't.

'Then we'll move him to Sydney and let the big boys deal with whatever the underlying cause is,' Marc told her, his voice calm, reassuring but firm. She wasn't the doctor here. She wasn't being asked to make decisions—she was being told the best course of action for her grandpa. 'Given his history, I'm almost sure this'll have been caused by another heart attack. Maybe a small one. There's no sign of neurological impairment. This seems straightforward. For me this is common or garden repair work, Dr McCrae, so you can take that fearful look off your face, accept that your grandpa's going to live and turn into the professional I know you are.'

His gaze was still on her face, his look steady, strong, sure. *You can do this*, his gaze said. And *I need a doctor, not a whimpering relative.*

Right. She could do this.
She must.

And half an hour later the thing was done. A light anaesthetic. An awful, breath-holding time while she watched as Marc used the ultrasound wand to guide the needle into position.

His approach was sure, unhesitating, skilled.

Using an eight-centimetre, eighteen-gauge angiocatheter—thank heaven for the comprehensive surgical kit the island possessed—watching the ultrasound every fraction of an inch of the way, he slowly, skilfully found what he was looking for. When the pericardial sac was entered there was a grunt of satisfaction as the ultrasound showed the needle where he needed it to be. Slowly he advanced the sheath and withdrew the needle. A guide wire was then advanced through the angiocatheter, followed by a dilator and a pigtail catheter.

'Yes!' he said with relief as the fluid started to flow, as the tamponade started to shrink, and that was the first time Elsa heard pressure in his voice. Even though he'd sounded sure, this was a procedure that took skill. Even now. Elsa was monitoring breathing, watching the heart monitor like a hawk, waiting for a reaction. Robert's heart was damaged. Any minute now...

'Not going to happen,' Marc said softly, glancing at the monitor and then her face. 'Fluid's coming off, and things are looking good.'

And so it was. Once the catheter was in place the pericardial fluid drained like a dream. The fluid would be submitted for culture and cytological analysis, checking for signs of something other than heart attack—trauma or cancer—but there seemed no sign of either.

She watched on, staring at the monitor as if she could will the heartbeat to strengthen. And it did.

'I'm only draining a thousand mil,' Marc told her. 'I don't want hypotensive shock. But I'm pretty sure it's enough to keep him safe.'

It maybe it was. Robert's heart had returned to a reassuringly normal rhythm. He was breathing on his own now, and when Elsa removed the oxygen his chest rose and fell normally. His colour was returning. He was safe.

For now. There was still the underlying cause to treat.

'I told one of the nurses to arrange evacuation,' Marc said briefly, once again watching her face. 'He'll need more aspirations, usually every four to six hours. We'll do another just as he leaves, and then the cardiac unit in Sydney can take over.' Robert was already stirring. The anaesthetic had been the lightest possible. 'Hey, Robert,' Marc said gently, and he took the old man's hand. 'All done. How do you feel?'

There was silence for a couple of moments while Robert got his bearings, while his world settled. They watched him take conscious breaths, watched him feel his chest expand, watched him realise the pressure was no longer there.

'Beautiful,' he murmured, and Elsa smiled and smiled and gripped Robert's hands and then decided she needed to wipe away a stupid tear that was tracking down her cheek. Only she couldn't because she was holding onto her grandpa.

And then Marc was leaning over the table and wiping it away for her, smiling at them both. 'Well done, Dr McCrae,' he told her.

'There was nothing well done about it,' she said gruffly. 'Marc operated, Grandpa, not me.'

'And your granddaughter held it together, acted professionally with a brilliant anaesthetic and didn't once behave like you'd scared her out of her wits,' Marc said, still smiling at her. 'But now she needs to act like a relative. Elsa, I want you to go pack for your grandpa and for yourself. Robert, we're evacuating you to Sydney. You know the underlying cause of the tamponade is most likely to have been another heart attack, or complications from the last one. There'll be an emergency physician on board the plane to keep you safe in transit. You'll be assessed fully in Sydney, so you need to be prepared to stay for a while. Hope for the best—maybe another stent—but prepare for a full bypass. That could mean a two-week stay before they let you fly home. Elsa, you know there's relative accommodation at the hospital. When we asked for the evac plane we asked for that to be organised as well.'

'But...' Elsa was staring at him in dismay '...I can't go. Two weeks...'

'You have no choice.'

'When Grandpa had his last attack and had the stent inserted, I was away for two days,' she told him, almost stammering. 'There was no one here to take over. We got away without a disaster that time, but for the island to have no doctor...'

'Elsa'll stay here,' Robert growled. 'There's no need to come with me. It's a fuss over nothing.'

But there was every need. Elsa stared down at her grandpa and saw it in his eyes.

This latest episode would have terrified him. Not being able to breathe... Feeling the pressure build... Oh, thank God for Marc, but the old man wasn't out of the woods yet, and she could see by his face that he knew it.

Yes, there'd be an emergency physician on the plane, but Grandpa needed family beside him. He needed her. She *had* to be with him, but she could see the warring needs on her grandfather's face. He would know the risks. And for there to be no doctor on the island at all...

'You have to stay,' Robert muttered grimly. 'Don't be a fool, girl. You think we can get a locum at this short notice, at this time of year? You know after Christmas half of Australia goes to sleep and the other half goes to the beach until mid-January. Or they come here and break their necks doing damned silly things. You have no choice. I'll be fine, girl.'

But still she saw the fear—and she glanced up at Marc and realised that he'd seen it too.

'There's no need for a locum,' he said gently. 'Aren't you lucky that you already have a resident doctor?'

They both stared at him, their expressions suggesting he'd suddenly grown two heads. 'You?' Elsa stammered, as if such a thing was tantamount to suggesting a five-year-old took over the medical needs of the island.

'Don't look at me as if I'm an idiot,' he told them. 'I know I'm a cardiologist, but I have basic skills as well. I'm sure I can remember the treatment for nice normal things like the common cold. Isn't it to give the patient honey and lemon drinks and it'll cure itself? I can probably cope with that.' He grinned, his smile encouraging them to override their fear.

'Seriously,' he continued, 'you have a great nursing staff. My shoulder's sore but it's firmly back in place and I won't be needing to lift any weights. I know a slightly battered doctor is less than ideal, but it seems a darned sight better than no doctor at all. I have a bung leg but I'll not be running any races. We can organise someone to drive me if I need to go off site. I have the next two weeks off. I know I should be in St Moritz but as far as prestige points go when I finally head back to work, two weeks on Gannet Island with a climbing injury cuts it almost as well.'

'A climbing injury? More like a falling down a hole injury,' Elsa said before she could help herself, and his grin widened.

'Are you intending to mess with my hero image, Dr McCrae?'

'Let him be heroic if that's what's needed for him to stay here,' Robert said gruffly, and reached out and took Marc's hand. 'I'll even sign something to say you fell down the hole saving…what, a kitten? Would that do?'

'A kitten?' Elsa said, astounded.

'He was saving Sherlock then,' Robert said, and the elderly doctor even managed a chuckle. 'Sherlock won't mind sacrificing his pride for the greater good.'

'I'll even take care of Sherlock while you're away,' Marc offered. 'Or Sherlock might take care of me.'

But Elsa wasn't smiling. 'Grandpa, you know I can't leave. We can't ask this of Marc.'

'Let's get this down to basics,' Marc demanded. 'Robert, do you want your granddaughter to come with you?' He fixed Robert with a look that demanded honesty. And the elderly doctor looked from him to Elsa and back again.

He'd know the odds. An underlying heart attack had probably caused the tamponade, and the damage wasn't yet diagnosed. He was still in peril and he knew it.

'I do,' he whispered, and Elsa's face twisted in fear and uncertainty.

'And Elsa, do you want your grandpa to go alone?'

'Of course not. But…'

'Then you have no choice,' Marc said gently.

'I know. But oh, Grandpa…'

'Now don't you make this into a big deal just because I said I need you,' Robert managed. He managed a smile, fighting to recover his pride. 'Love, you know I hate hospital coffee. I'll... I'll need someone to bring me a decent cup a couple of times a day.'

'So there you are,' Marc told her. 'You have two weeks of being personal barista for your grandfather, while a one-legged doctor takes over all your duties on the island. You might need to organise someone else to walk Sherlock, but for the rest... All sorted.'

'Marc...'

'Enough.' He put his hand out and cupped her chin, forcing her gaze to meet his, suddenly stern.

'As your grandpa says, don't make a fuss,' he said softly. 'Just do what you need to do. I suspect your grandpa's coffee needs won't be too extensive. You might even have time to see a bit of Sydney at the same time. You might even have time to have fun.'

Elsa disappeared to pack and probably to do a bit of panicking on the side.

Marc returned to his nice, quiet hospital bed and did a bit of panicking himself. What had he let himself in for? He'd offered to be the island doctor for up to two weeks. A family doctor.

He hadn't done any family medicine since a placement during internship. He remembered minor illnesses, minor injuries, stress, depression, teen pregnancies, the problems of the elderly with multiple health problems. He remembered being hit by an elderly patient because he couldn't justify signing a form saying the old guy could retain his car licence.

'You need to learn to care,' the family doctor he'd been working beside had told him. 'If you genuinely care for your patients, then everything else will follow. Empathy is everything—emotional connection.'

The experience had confirmed Marc's decision to specialise in heart surgery. He'd been raised to be emotionally distant. The idea of providing an emotional connection to his patients seemed impossible.

Elsa had the ability, he thought, remembering the faces of those who'd received her extraordinary gifts. She had it in spades. Which was why she was a family doctor and he wasn't.

Except now he was, for two weeks.

No one could expect emotional connection in two weeks, he told himself. He'd offered because it was the least he could do—after all, Elsa had saved his life. This would repay a debt. He could see patients in need and then walk away.

And then the door opened, tentatively. It was Maggie. Despite their initial conflict over the Dorothy the Dinosaur tablet, she'd helped care for him, she'd assisted in Robert's surgery with efficiency and he was aware that she was an excellent nurse.

'Are you ready to start work?' she asked.

'What, now?'

'Bradley Norfolk's just fallen off his Christmas trampoline,' she told him. 'It looks like a greenstick arm fracture. Are you up for it?' She eyed him, lying on his pillows, his bedding pulled up to his chin. 'You look like a new intern,' she said bluntly, and she grinned. 'Scared rigid.'

Maybe it was time to pull himself together. He pushed back his covers, sat up and swung his bad leg off the bed.

'We're setting you up with a permanent wheelchair,' she told him. 'With leg support so your leg's out straight.'

'I can manage without a wheelchair.'

'Elsa's orders. She says she doesn't want any more pressure on that arm, and if you're balancing then you're at risk.'

His first reaction was to reject the wheelchair out of

hand—he needed to act like a doctor, not a patient. But his shoulder was still painful. Elsa's suggestion was sensible.

He needed to be sensible.

'For today and maybe for tomorrow,' he told Maggie. 'By then I should be able to manage with sticks.' Even that revolted him.

'Very wise,' Maggie said, and her smile widened. 'You know, the islanders have learned it's much easier to do what Doc Elsa says. She's pretty much always right. If you're standing in for her you have pretty big shoes to fill.'

'Just lucky my foot's already swollen then,' he said grimly. 'Maggie, I'm going to need more clothes.'

'Elsa's already given orders,' she told him. 'We're on it.'

'Then Maggie…'

'Yes?'

'It's time for Elsa to stop giving the orders,' he told her. 'From now on, you're stuck with me.'

The evacuation crew oozed medical competence. The doctor in charge listened to Elsa's stuttered explanation, spoke briefly to Robert—and then did a hand-over with Marc.

Marc was in his wheelchair, but his medical competence matched the medic in charge. They exchanged notes, films, cardiographs. Elsa was on the sidelines, holding Robert's hand.

Robert was the patient. Elsa was family.

'Takes a bit of getting used to,' Robert growled. He was on the transfer trolley, waiting to be lifted into the plane.

'Yeah.'

'He'll do good by us. The island's in good hands.' He was trying to reassure her. For heaven's sake…

'I'm sure he will,' she managed, and as she listened to the clipped professional handover between the two men she knew she was right. 'Except…'

'Except Dotty Morrison might have to forgo her placebo pills for a while,' Robert said with a forced chuckle, and Elsa thought of the pills she'd been prescribing for the old lady affected by Alzheimer's for the last few months and grimaced.

'I haven't even told him about that.'

'Told me what?' Finishing his handover, Marc had wheeled himself across to join them.

'Dotty Morrison,' Elsa told him, thinking of all the other things she hadn't told him. 'She has Alzheimer's and high blood pressure. She's struggling to stay at home and her medication's the biggest hurdle—she takes it too often or not at all, but she hates the thought of not being in charge. So now I give her placebos, telling her to take one every morning, one every night. Her daughter comes around twice a day with her 'extra' pills—the real ones— which she tells her are multivitamins. Dotty takes them to humour her, but she knows the ones I prescribe and she gets from the pharmacist are the important ones. She takes them whenever she thinks it might be morning or night and everyone's happy.'

'And they're what? Sugar pills?'

'Sugar pills?' Elsa asked incredulously. 'No such thing. I give her a nice formal script that says "Disaccharide $C12H22O11$, twice daily".'

'Which is sugar.'

'If you're going to be pedantic, then yes,' she said with asperity, 'but don't you dare tell Dotty. I tell her it's to improve cerebral function—she likes that because she knows she forgets things. She takes her script along to the pharmacy, Doug puts her pills in a bottle with her name on and everyone's happy. Except she tends to go through her bottle about once a week and sometimes more, and she loses her repeat scripts so I expect you'll see her soon. Marc, there's so much I haven't told you.'

'He'll be all right, girl,' Robert said, gripping Marc's hand as the crew prepared to lift him into the plane. 'If he's got his cardiology ticket he must have the brains to prescribe sugar pills and he can always phone you. Thank you, son,' he said and then he was lifted up and away.

The medic crew boarded the plane, busying themselves, fitting Robert with the equipment, the oxygen, the stabilisers he'd need for the journey. Marc and Elsa were finally left alone.

'I don't... I can't think what to say,' Elsa told him.

'Don't say anything. You're not going out of contact. If someone presents at the surgery demanding medication for their leprosy or whatever, I have your number.'

'I can't thank you...'

'And I can't thank you. So let's not.'

'Marc...'

'Just relax. Robert's in good hands. He'll be fine. You might even have a chance of a holiday yourself.'

'If he doesn't need me, I can come home.'

'He will need you. Hospital's a lonely place with no family.' Before she could stop him he'd pushed himself to his feet. Instinctively she reached forward to steady him, but afterwards she couldn't remember whether he'd gripped her hands before she'd gripped his.

Regardless, she gripped and he held, or vice versa.

He was her patient. No, he wasn't her patient now. He was the doctor who'd saved her grandfather's life.

He was Marc.

The three images were blurring. Boundaries weren't being crossed, they were dissolving.

'Your grandpa will be fine,' he said, strongly now. 'I've phoned my boss—he's head of cardiology at Sydney Central. He's promised to take on Robert's care himself and there's no one better. This guy here...' he motioned into the plane, to the medic in charge '…he's the best as well. The only extra Robert needs is family, and in you he has gold. Take care of yourself, Elsa. Come back with a patched-up grandpa but come back rested yourself. I can't think of anyone who deserves a break more.'

'Marc…'

'Just go,' he said softly, but his grip on her hands tightened. 'But I'll be in touch and thinking of you every step of the way.'

She looked up at him, feeling dazed. Too much was happening, too fast.

He was holding her. For support, she told herself frantically but as her gaze met his she knew it was no such thing. His eyes were dark, fathomless, compelling. There was a faint smile, a question—an answer? She couldn't look away.

The question? It was being asked of her and all she had to do was respond. Which was what she did. Almost of their own volition her feet tilted so she was on tiptoe. So lips could meet.

And kiss.

Warmth, heat, strength.

Or maybe it was the opposite of strength. Maybe it was loss of control, for how could she be in control when she was being kissed like this?

Twice in one day. Twice! But this was different.

Behind them were Geoff and Ryan, the hospital orderlies who'd helped load Robert into the ambulance for transport to the runway and were now waiting to take Marc back to the hospital. There were a couple of airport workers round the plane—locals.

News of this kiss would be all over the island before the plane even took off.

But right now she couldn't care less. How could she

care? All that mattered was the feel of Marc holding her. He'd saved her grandpa. He was holding her steady. He was her rock.

Her rock with a broken leg. Her rock who was here for only two weeks. He was her rock who was supposed to be in St Moritz right now with his glamorous ex-girlfriend.

She had no right to kiss him, and he had no right to kiss her. But still she clung for one last, long sweet moment. It was a moment of madness, a moment that she knew must mean nothing, but she took it, she savoured it, she loved it.

And then there was an apologetic cough from behind Marc's shoulder.

'Sorry miss, but we need to get going,' one of the medics called to Elsa. 'You need to board. Don't worry, sir, we'll take good care of them and bring them home safe.'

Home safe... Two lovely words.

But the medic was looking at her with sympathy. He thought he was tearing her away from...her partner? Her lover?

No such thing. She didn't want sympathy, and she didn't...couldn't...want complications.

'I'm ready to go,' she managed, struggling to sound professional, as if she hadn't just been kissed so thoroughly she felt dizzy. 'Thank you for your help, Dr Pierce. I'll see you soon.'

'I hope so,' he said, and lifted the back of his hand to brush her cheek. It was a gesture of farewell, an acknowledgement of times shared, of forced intimacy that was now over, and there was no reason for it to make her feel even more disoriented than she already was.

But disoriented was too simple a word to describe what she was feeling. She needed to join her grandfather in the plane, but turning and walking away from Marc felt wrong.

CHAPTER TEN

'I'VE RUN OUT of pills.'

'Already?' It was just as well he'd been warned. This was the first clinic on Boxing Day—'for urgent cases only'—but Dotty Morrison had insisted she was tacked onto the end of his list.

'I think I might have doubled up,' the little lady said doubtfully. 'What with Christmas and all. But an extra pill or two won't hurt me, will it, Doctor?'

He checked. Elsa's notes were comprehensive and, worded in case Dotty caught sight of them, carefully benign.

'Dr McCrae wrote you a script with five repeats only last week,' he said cautiously. 'Have you used them all?'

'Oh, no, Doctor. It was much longer than a week ago. The chemist says I should leave the script at the pharmacy, but they keep muddling them. I do like to keep an eye on my own medications. It's my body, isn't that right, Doctor? I have a responsibility to care for what goes into it.'

'You certainly do,' Marc said, suppressing a grin as he replaced her script.

She accepted it with grace and checked it with care. 'Thank you, dear,' she told him. 'But you're not as neat as our Dr Elsa.'

'I'm afraid I'm not. I'm not as fast either.' Dottie had been kept waiting three-quarters of an hour for her appointment.

'Well, that's because you've broken your leg,' Dottie said reasonably.

It wasn't exactly that, he thought as he bade the elderly lady goodbye. It was because family medical practice required skills Marc had pretty much forgotten. He'd just had to cope with a teenager whose acne had flared up. She was hysterical because her family was heading to Sydney to meet friends—'and there's this boy…'

He'd had to excuse himself 'to take an urgent phone call' which involved hobbling out to Reception to check current meds for acne, correct dosages, contraindications.

There'd been many 'urgent phone calls' this morning. But finally he was done. He had house calls scheduled for later this afternoon—either Geoff or Ryan would drive him—but he had time to put his leg up for half an hour and field a call from Elsa.

'How's it going?' he asked.

Her voice sounded tense, distracted and he thought *uh-oh*.

'He's okay.'

Then he heard her pause and take a deep breath. 'No. More than okay. The tamponade's pretty much settled—they've stopped the draining.' That made sense. The pericardium had to retain a little fluid to protect the heart. 'But you were right. He's had another heart attack. When pressed, he admitted he'd had what he thought was an event during the night while I was on the mountain with you. It passed and he didn't want to worry me—he said he'd think about it after Christmas. Anyway, he's in the right hands now. He's scheduled for a quadruple bypass late this afternoon, but he's already worrying about the need to spend time here in cardio rehab. His biggest worry is me being here rather than back on the island.'

'And you? Are you worrying about being there rather than back on the island?'

'Of course,' she said simply. 'I can't help it. Have there been any problems?'

'No.'

'Not a one?'

'My biggest hurdle so far has been finding current treatment for teenage acne,' he admitted. 'I had Jess Lowan here, threatening suicide or worse. It seems she's in love with the son of family friends, and how can she face him with zits on her nose?'

'I hope you took it seriously,' she told him. 'Jess is… high strung to say the least.'

'I took it very seriously. The treatment's changed since I was in med school but, thanks to the internet, Jess has now been hit with a barrage of treatment that should effectively nuke every zit before it has a chance to interfere with the course of young love. I just hope he's worth it.'

'Oh, dear. You know she'll be in love with someone else next week.'

'Someone who prefers his women with zits? Then Houston, we have a problem. I see no chance of reversal.'

She chuckled but it sounded strained. 'Seriously though, Marc…'

'Seriously, I'm doing well.' He let himself sound serious too, still hearing the stress in her voice. 'There's been no pressure. I have two house calls to make this afternoon, then a simple ward round, and as long as everything stays quiet I'll be in bed with a book by eight-thirty.'

'When you should be drinking mulled wine with your mates in St Moritz.'

'I'm not missing it a bit.' And as he said it he realised

it was true. The situation here was challenging—and he didn't mind this phone call with Elsa. There'd be more of them, he knew. The thought of working as he was doing, of helping her out for two weeks…it wasn't a penance.

'You know things will hot up from today?' Elsa warned. 'The holiday crowds start streaming in on Boxing Day, and they do really dumb things.'

'Like falling down holes.'

'Like falling down holes,' she agreed. 'Though the guys have hiked back up to where you fell and fenced off that whole area, with huge warning signs saying death and destruction for all who enter here. It's a pity we can't do that for every peril on the island. Like the sun. What's the betting you'll have half a dozen cases of sunstroke by this time tomorrow? Our work practically quadruples in the holiday period.'

He thought about that. Today had been relatively quiet— no dramas, a simple clinic and stable inpatients. Still, by the end of the day he'd have worked reasonably hard.

If it quadrupled…

'How do you cope?'

'I have Grandpa.'

'You won't have your grandpa for a few weeks. He's going to need decent rehab. Seriously.'

'Which is why I'll rest up before I come home. I know I need to stay. If I leave Grandpa here he'll be on the next plane after me. But Marc, I'm worrying about you coping.'

'I'll read up on sunstroke before I go to bed tonight.'

'It won't just be sunstroke. You don't have… I don't know…a friend who could help? Maybe your Kayla? Is she another doctor?'

'She is,' he told her. 'But she's not my Kayla and there's not a snowball's chance in a bushfire she'll cut her holiday short to come here.'

'Another colleague then?' She was clutching at straws. 'If I stay here for two full weeks you will need help.'

'And you'll need help long-term,' he told her. 'At his age and after two heart attacks, it's time for Robert to think of retiring.'

'You think I don't know that?'

'So you need to think about hiring a full-time partner.'

'Like that's going to happen.'

'Why not?'

'Because it's not viable,' she said shortly. 'An island with a population of seven hundred provides a meagre income. The six islands have far too much medical need for me to handle alone, but they're too far apart to service. In an ideal world, with more doctors and a fast ferry service, we could set up a central medical centre on Gannet. But a ferry service requires money the islanders don't have and, even if there was one, no island doctor could make the kind of money I bet you're making in Sydney. Why would anyone come here by choice?'

She caught herself, and he heard her pause and regroup. 'Sorry. That was uncalled for. The money thing's minor but I am facing the problem that without Grandpa's help…' Her voice trailed off.

'Without his help maybe you need to leave the island?' he said gently. 'It seems harsh but someone else will take your place.'

'I couldn't think of leaving.'

'You need to think about it. With your grandpa's medical needs he'd be much safer on the mainland. And you… You've already said you feel constricted here.'

'But it's *my* island,' she said, suddenly angry. '*My* home. You don't get that?'

'There are lots of other places in the world.'

'Like St Moritz. No, that was mean. But where could I

work? In a city clinic so Grandpa could be within cooee of specialist help? We'd both hate that. Or a country practice where my problems would be the same—and I wouldn't be surrounded by family.'

'You'd have Robert.'

'He's only one small part of my family. My family's the whole island. It's home. You must see, Marc...' She broke off and sighed. 'Enough. My future's not your problem and you have your own problems. Acne to sort. A leg that needs resting.'

'The acne's sorted and my leg's resting as we speak.'

'Then rest some more,' she told him. 'I'll return as soon as possible.'

'As soon as the doctors say it's safe for your grandfather to be here?' He hesitated but it had to be said. 'Elsa, there'll always be underlying medical problems. It seems harsh to say it, but I won't be here to help next time.'

She faltered at that, but then gathered herself again. 'That has to be okay. We've managed to cope without you before. Go rest that leg, Marc. Goodbye.'

She abandoned her phone and walked out onto the balcony. The apartments designed for hospital relatives were spartan but the views were fantastic. At least they were fantastic if she stood at the very far end and leaned out. She could even see the Opera House and the harbour bridge, only her angle was a bit precarious.

She stopped leaning and stood and watched the traffic below. *So* much traffic. She could see the sea if she craned her neck, but she couldn't smell it. All she could smell was traffic fumes.

She was so homesick...

Oh, for heaven's sake, she liked visiting Sydney. She liked the shopping, the restaurants, the anonymity. It was only the fear of the last twenty-four hours that was making her feel bereft.

But it was also the thought of her conversation with Marc. The difficulties of continuing on the island as her grandpa grew older.

She thought of Robert's heart, the risks of returning long-term to the island, the difficulty of coping as the island's only doctor. Even if he wanted to, Robert could hardly continue—she knew that. She'd be on her own.

And with that came a wash of despair so profound that she found she was shaking.

'Oh, cut it out.' She said it out loud, scolding herself. 'You won't be on your own. You'll have all the islanders. And if things get really desperate you can always marry Tony and have a tribe of kids and never feel lonely again.'

Except...loneliness wasn't always about a lack of people. Loneliness was being without a person.

One special person.

Marc?

'Well, you can cut that out too,' she said, even louder. 'You've known the man for what, four days, and here you are fantasising about him...

'I kind of like fantasising about him.' She was arguing with herself now. 'If I moved to Sydney I might...we might...

'And ditto for that thought, too.' Her own two-way conversation was getting heated. 'He's a high-flying doctor with high-flying friends. If I moved to Sydney I'd be lucky to get a job in some outer suburban clinic, somewhere cheap enough for us to live, with an increasingly dependent grandpa. There's not the slightest chance there'd be anything between me and Marc.

'But he kissed me.' There it was, a solid fact. She tried to hug it to herself as a promise—and failed.

'So he's a good kisser,' her sane self argued. 'He only kissed me to make me feel better. It's probably quicker and easier for a guy like that to give a decent kiss than to say "I hope you feel better soon".'

Luckily her sense of humour stepped in there to make her grin at the suddenly ridiculous vision of Marc doing ward rounds, kissing everyone as he went.

Like he'd kissed her?

Her fingers moved almost involuntarily to her mouth, as if she could still feel the pressure of his lips. His warmth, his strength, his solid, comforting, sexy, amazing self.

Marc…

'You're behaving like a teenager with a crush,' she told herself harshly, and stared down at the traffic again. 'Me and Marc? You're dreaming. Like me and Grandpa moving to Sydney. No and no and no.'

The thought of Robert dragged her out of her pointless conversation with herself, back to reality. She needed to head back to Intensive Care to see him. He'd be nervous about the upcoming surgery—no, he'd be terrified. She'd need every resource she possessed to calm him.

'So stop thinking about Marc and think about Grandpa.'

'I am thinking about Grandpa,' she said out loud again. 'And I'm thinking about me and the island and a heart specialist with a broken leg who's so far out of my league that I need my head read to be thinking about him. I need to get Grandpa better and then go home. Maybe even to Tony.

'Are you out of your mind? Tony? No!

'Yeah, but five little Tonys might make you happy.

'Buy yourself five dogs,' she snapped to herself. 'Dogs are a much safer bet than people any day.'

CHAPTER ELEVEN

TWELVE DAYS LATER Elsa and Robert flew back to the island on the normal passenger flight. Elsa had told Marc they were coming. He'd had every intention of meeting the plane, but where medicine was concerned plans were made to be broken.

He'd been inundated with minor issues since Boxing Day—sunburn, sunstroke, lacerations, stomach upsets, a couple of kids with alcohol poisoning after drinking their father's high shelf spirits on New Year's Eve. The works.

When Elsa and Robert's plane touched down he was in Theatre, sewing up a lacerated thigh. Bob Cruikshank, the local realtor, had hired tradesmen to construct a cluster of holiday cottages, and progress was slow. In an attempt to hurry things up over the holiday period he'd bought himself a chainsaw to cut planking, with the aim of building the decks himself. It wasn't his brightest idea. That he hadn't bled to death was pure luck. A neighbour had heard his yell and knew enough to apply pressure while calling for help.

'I guess you need training to operate those things,' Bob had said feebly, as Macka's police van-cum-ambulance had brought him in.

'I imagine chainsaw operation doesn't get included in most realtor training manuals,' Marc agreed. The cut was deep and filthy. He was incredibly lucky he hadn't cut nerves.

Marc would have preferred to use local anaesthetic but Bob was deeply shocked and agitated. It had to be a general anaesthetic, using Maggie to monitor breathing.

It wasn't optimal but it was the only choice. Then, half-way through the procedure, Elsa walked in. 'Hi, guys,' she said as she stood in the doorway. 'Anything I can do to help?'

'Oh, thank heaven,' Maggie said vehemently.

Marc had his forceps on a sliver of wood that was dangerously close to the artery. He couldn't afford to look up. It didn't stop him reacting, though. Elsa was back. Maggie's 'thank heaven' didn't begin to describe the sensation he felt hearing her voice.

His reaction was disproportionate. Undeniable.

'Hooray, you're back,' Maggie was saying. 'Can you take over here? Doc Pierce has been talking me through it, but we're worried about his oxygen levels.' Then she amended the statement. 'No, *Dr Pierce* is worried about Bob's oxygen levels. My job's just to tell him what the monitors are saying and doing what he tells me.'

'They told me out front what's been happening,' Elsa said briefly. 'I've already scrubbed.'

'Then I'm back to being nurse assistant.' Maggie handed over to Elsa, and Marc's stress level dropped about ten-fold. He'd been operating at the same time as watching and instructing Maggie. Bob was a big man with back-ground health issues, and the anaesthetic was as fraught as the surgery itself.

The question slammed back, as it had hit him over and over for the past few days. How the hell could Elsa work here alone?

The splinter of wood finally came free. He gave a grunt of satisfaction and glanced up.

'Welcome back,' he said, and smiled. She looked strained, he thought, but she still looked great. Fantastic. Something deep in his gut seemed to clench. It was all he could do not to abandon Bob and go hug her.

'Thank you,' she said primly. 'How's the needlework?'

'Basic.' Somehow he made his voice prosaic. Professional. As if she was a colleague and nothing else. 'If I'd realised how grubby this injury was internally, I'd have had him evacuated. I'm just lucky we didn't try this under local.'

'Bob would never had cooperated under local,' she told him. 'He'd have been demanding to take pictures for his Facebook page and probably fainting in the process.' She hesitated. 'You know he has emphysema?'

'I read his file.' He was starting a final clear and swab before stitching. 'That's why we've gone for the lightest anaesthesia possible. How's your grandpa?'

'Okay. Resting.'

'He should have stayed another week.'

'You try telling him that. He's pig-stubborn.'

'Too pig-stubborn to accept he needs to back right off, workwise?'

'I guess...' She sighed. 'He accepts that.'

'Excellent.' And then he threw out the question which had become a constant drumming in his head as the load of tourist patients had escalated. 'Elsa, how the hell are you going to manage here on your own?'

There was a moment's silence. Too long a silence.

'I'll manage,' she said at last. 'Did I tell you I spent a year's surgery rotation before I came back to the island?' She sounded as if she was struggling for lightness.

'Yeah, but *I* didn't do a year's anaesthetic training.' That was Maggie, entering the conversation with force. She handed Marc a threaded needle and glanced at Elsa with concern. 'Marc's been great, talking me through anaesthetising while he worked, but it's given us both heebiejeebies. Is Robert going to be well enough to keep this up?'

'I guess. If…if that's all he does.'

'That's not viable and you know it,' Marc growled, thinking of the massive mix of human needs he'd been called on to fill over the past days. 'And you know I'm not just talking about this incident. Elsa, you need help.'

'No other doctor will want to work here with what we can offer.' She said it lightly, as if it didn't matter so much, but he knew it did. 'I need a full-time income, and there's not enough work during non-holiday periods to support two full-time doctors. Not unless we could somehow join the outer islands to form a bigger service, and where would we get the money to do that? We've approached the government before and it's not possible.'

'Then you need to leave,' he said bluntly. 'Maybe offer the job to a couple who might be happy to work here as one and a half doctors.'

'And where would that leave Grandpa and me?' She tilted her chin and met his look head-on. 'It's not your problem, Dr Pierce, so butt out. Right… Are you ready for reverse? You won't want to keep him under for any longer than you need to.'

'Go teach your grandmother to suck eggs,' Marc said, casting her a smile but seeing the strain behind her eyes.

'Sorry… Doctor,' she muttered.

'That's quite all right… Doctor,' he said and tried for another smile. 'And of course you're right to advise me. If you've done a year's surgery rotation and you know the patient you're equipped to give me advice.'

'I'm not sure what I'm equipped for any more,' she said heavily. 'But I suspect I'm about to find out.'

With surgery finished, and with Bob surfacing to hear his wife informing him she'd tossed his chainsaw off a cliff and if he ever lifted so much as a pair of scissors from now on she'd do the same with them, Marc was left with a gap until afternoon clinic. He escaped the escalating row in Bob's room—'Geez, Marjorie, do you know how much that chainsaw cost?'—and limped out to the hospital veranda. He needed to think.

The raised voices of the Cruikshanks followed him. There was little escape on this island, he thought, and then wondered how could Elsa stand it. But she'd been bred into it, he thought. She'd been inculcated with a sense of obligation to the islanders since she was seven. Plus she had her obligation to her grandfather.

But she loved her grandfather. Of course she did. He knew that, but he was on shaky ground here. There wasn't a lot of emotion in his background.

He didn't get the love thing, but somehow that was where his thoughts were heading. The sensation that had overwhelmed him when she'd walked into Theatre had almost blown him away. Was that love? It didn't make sense, and Marc Pierce was a man who liked to make sense of his world.

So make sense of the quandary Elsa has found herself in, he told himself. It was the least he could do.

The least he could do...

Elsa McCrae.

The two collections of words didn't seem to go together.

Elsa was a colleague. She'd saved his life. It made sense to feel gratitude, admiration, obligation. But none of those sentiments accounted for the wave of sensation he'd felt when she'd walked into the theatre just now, and that was troubling him. The way he'd felt then... The way he still felt...

'It's nonsense.' He said the words out loud and Ryan, who tended the hospital garden in between acting as an orderly, raised his head from where he'd been cutting back ferns and looked a query.

'What makes no sense, Doc?'

This dratted island! Was nowhere private? He hadn't realised Ryan was there. He'd been so caught up in his thoughts.

So say nothing, he told himself. This was his business, not the business of the whole island. Tell Ryan to mind his own.

What came out instead was, 'It makes no sense how two weeks can change your life.'

Ryan rose and scratched filthy fingers on his hat. 'Mate, you can drop dead in two weeks,' he said cheerfully. 'Hey, you might have starved to death in that cave and that wouldn't have even taken two weeks. That would have changed your life and then some.'

'I meant emotionally.' For heaven's sake, what was he doing? He was confessing all to a guy he hardly knew?

But Ryan seemed unperturbed—and also, to Marc's bewilderment, he seemed completely understanding. 'I'm guessing you've fallen for Doc Elsa,' he said simply, as though it was no big deal. 'Well, good luck with that, mate. Every young buck on the island seems to do it at some time. You'll get over it. They all do.'

'Thanks,' he managed weakly, and Ryan gave him a cheery wave and headed off to the compost bin with his wheelbarrow of fern clippings. Leaving his advice behind.

You'll get over it.

It was a sensible statement, the only problem being

that Marc didn't exactly know what *it* was. This thing he was feeling.

It was temporary, he told himself. It was the result of shock and relief and gratitude.

Be practical.

'What you need to do is help her see her way forward,' he said, only this time he said it under his breath because the walls had ears around here.

But that brought another thought. If she did leave the island, if she and Robert moved to Sydney… 'Then maybe we'd have time to…'

And that was where he stopped, because when it came to time to do *what*, he couldn't begin to imagine what that might be.

He should go find a cold shower, he told himself. He should at least talk sense into himself. Instead his thoughts kept drifting to a place that didn't seem at all sensible.

The way he felt about Elsa… The feeling in his gut as she'd walked into Theatre… It seemed a chasm he hadn't even noticed approaching.

So step back. Find solid ground. Accept the way you're feeling and work around it.

'Whatever happens, it'd have to be on my terms,' he said, and this time he said it out loud. He needed to reassure himself there was still room for him to be sensible.

He thought of his gorgeous harbourside house, inherited from his father, who'd died a few years ago. He thought of the space, the garden, the room for people to live pretty much separately.

'Even if we…' he started to say, but then he paused. He hadn't the least idea where his thoughts were headed.

Even as a child he'd known emotional ties were transitory and he'd never really considered the idea of a permanent relationship. When his friends fell in love he always felt as if he was looking at something totally foreign to him. But with Elsa suddenly his mind was going there whether he willed it or not.

'But my life wouldn't have to change all that much.'

Something at the back of his mind was suddenly flabbergasted. He almost felt dizzy.

'What the hell are you thinking?' he demanded, out loud again, and quickly looked around to make sure Ryan hadn't returned.

He hadn't. He was free to argue with himself.

'I have no idea,' he confessed to the sensible part of his brain, but sensible wasn't winning right now.

Nothing was winning. He kept sitting there. He needed to get his head clear. He needed a plan.

It didn't happen. The dizziness stayed.

Finally he shook his head and limped back into the hospital. He needed something to do. Something medical. Something that had nothing to do with the weird infighting that was going on in his head.

Elsa stayed busy for the rest of the day. Marc had insisted on continuing with the afternoon clinic so she wasn't needed there. She bossed her grandfather into settling down to rest, starting what she hoped would be the new norm. Then she did a round of the hospital patients. Maggie filled her in as she went.

'Marc's been pretty much over everything,' she told her. 'The islanders think he's great. Dotty Morrison has run out of scripts four times—I think she's fallen in love with him.'

'Who wouldn't?' Elsa said absently. She was reading a patient file as she spoke, and was aware of a sudden silence. She glanced up to see that Maggie was skewering her with a look.

'Yeah?' Maggie said softly. 'Really?'

'I just meant...' Elsa flushed. 'Oh, Maggie, cut it out. He's tall, dark and dishy, he saved Grandpa's life, he's taken over my workload and I'm incredibly grateful. What's not to like?'

'The word though,' Maggie said thoughtfully, 'was love.'

'As if that's going to happen.' She let the clip on the file she was reading close with a snap. 'I imagine he'll be leaving tomorrow now I'm back.'

'But you...'

'Oh, for heaven's sake, Maggie, please don't.' To her horror she found she was suddenly close to tears. She closed her eyes and her friend was right there, giving her a hug.

'Hey, Elsa, sweetheart...'

'It's okay.' She let herself savour her friend's hug for a moment and then pulled away, gathering herself together. 'This is just a reaction. From homecoming. From worry about Grandpa.'

'Nothing at all to do with Marc?'

'Maybe,' she admitted. 'But surely I'm allowed to have the same sort of crush that Dottie has? It's been a long couple of weeks and I'm overwrought. Marc's been great and I've let myself fantasise a little. There's nothing else to it.'

'No,' Maggie said thoughtfully. 'Of course there's nothing else. That'd require you putting yourself before the island, maybe even before your grandpa. As if that'd ever happen.'

'And it'd require interest on his part.' It was a snap, and she caught herself. She'd spent twelve stressful days in Sydney trying to figure out her future. What she didn't need now was her friend imagining a non-existent romantic interest to complicate things even further.

'You know, Tony's started to go out with Kylie from

the bakery,' Maggie told her, still thoughtful. 'He's obviously given up on you.'

'Bully for Tony.'

'So who else is in the offing?'

'There's no one,' she replied before she could help herself.

'Then why not do a little more than fantasising? Marc's here and he's lovely and he's not attached. He's just split up with his girlfriend and...'

'Have you been grilling him?'

'Of course,' Maggie said, grinning. 'Why not? So the field is clear. Why not go for it?'

'Because he's going back to Sydney and my life is here.'

'Your life might not be able to be here much longer. You need to face facts, love.'

'But not now,' Elsa said with a weary sigh. 'Leave it, Maggie. There are so many complications in my life anyway. Where would I find time for romance?'

'What's wrong with tonight? He's here. He's available. If I was twenty years younger I'd go for it.'

'Maggie!'

'Chicken.'

'I'd rather be a chicken than a dead hen.'

'And I'd rather have a wild fling with a gorgeous doctor than be a chicken,' Maggie said, and chuckled and headed back to the wards.

Elsa was left floundering. A wild fling? She'd never had such a thing. He'd be gone in the next couple of days. How could she possibly expose her heart like that?

She headed through to her house, adjoining the hospital. The locals had been in as soon as they'd learned she and Robert were home, and casseroles and cakes were lined up on the bench.

The islanders had helped her for ever, she thought as

she sorted them. They'd supported her grandpa in raising her. They'd helped cover the cost of her medical training.

A wild fling? She thought of Maggie's words and rejected them. A fling and then what? It'd leave her unhappy, unsettled, ungrateful for the life she needed to live.

'At least I'll never go hungry *if* I stay here,' she told Sherlock—who was already looking tubbier after two weeks of islander care—and heard the *if* that she'd just said.

Ouch.

Robert was asleep. She roused him. They ate one of the casseroles together but he was silent throughout, and then he headed straight back to bed. The last few days seemed to have aged him ten years or more.

She washed and wiped, then let Sherlock out. There was a brief bark and she thought there must be a possum on the veranda. She should chase it off to protect her grapevines and then she thought, *Who cares about grapevines?*

She felt totally, absolutely discombobulated. Then she walked outside, and if it was possible to feel even more discombobulated, she did.

Marc was sitting on the back step, under the outside light. Just sitting.

'Marc!'

'Hey,' he said, rising and backing away a little. 'It's only me. I know this looks like stalking, but I didn't want to interrupt you and your grandpa. We need to talk, so I thought—what would I do if I'd been off this island for twelve days? I'd want to soak it up, that's what. So I decided to come here and wait.'

She eyed him with suspicion that was definitely justified. 'So you just guessed where I might be?' she ventured. 'It wasn't Maggie who told you I mostly drink a glass of wine out on my back step after dinner?'

'Okay, it might have been,' he confessed, and he sent her a lopsided smile that did something to her heart that she somehow had to ignore. He motioned to a bottle and two glasses set out on the top step. 'I brought these. Just in case.'

She harrumphed her indignation at her scheming friend. 'I don't believe Maggie.'

'She's great.'

'She's incorrigible.'

'But she's still great.'

'Yeah,' she said, casting him another suspicious glare, but then she succumbed. This was her porch after all, and there was wine. She plonked herself down on the top step and filled a glass and then filled one for him. 'Everyone's great. I have seventeen casseroles jammed into the freezer, that's how great everyone is. I won't have to cook for a month.'

'Lucky you.' He sat down beside her. Not too close. Still giving her space. Sherlock, glorying in having his mistress back, but also extremely pleased to see his new friend, wriggled in between them.

Silence. The warmth of the night closed over them. The surf below the house provided the faint hush of waves. The moon had flung a ribbon of silver out over the water. A bush turkey was scratching somewhere in the bushes— she could hear its faint rustle.

This man had her so off-balance. The concerns that had been building over the last twelve days were still with her.

Marc's presence here tonight wasn't helping a bit.

It was Marc who finally broke the silence. 'Elsa, I've been thinking,' he told her. 'I came to tell you I can take another two weeks off before I need to return to Sydney. You don't need to jump back into work straight away. Give yourself some space. Your grandpa needs you.'

'Everyone needs me.' It was said flatly, an inescapable fact.

There was another moment's silence. And then, 'You know,' Marc said softly into the stillness, 'I could get to need you, too.'

And with that, all the complications of the islanders' needs, her grandfather's needs, fell away. There was so much in Marc's statement it took her breath away.

She sat with her wine glass in her hand, but she could well have dropped it. She was looking out to sea but seeing nothing. There was some sort of fog in her mind. Some dense mist that meant she couldn't make sense of what he'd just said.

She didn't want to make sense of it?

'I… That's not very helpful,' she said at last because, for some stupid reason, the first thing that came into her head wasn't rejection. It was simply impossibility.

In answer he lifted the glass from her suddenly limp hand and set it aside. Then he took her hand in his. He didn't tug her to face him, though. He simply intertwined their fingers and let the silence envelop them again.

His hand was strong. Warm. Compelling.

Impossible.

The word was slamming round and round her head, like a metal ball bashing against the sides as it bounced. It hurt.

'Elsa, you can't continue to do this alone,' he said softly at last. 'You know you can't. I've been talking to Maggie. She says you were barely managing before Robert had this attack. She said the walk you went on when you found me was the first time you'd taken time off for weeks.'

'What's that got to do…'

'With you and me? Nothing,' he told her. 'Except everything.'

'You're not offering to come here and help, are you?'

'I'd love to say I would, but no. I'm a cardiologist, not a family doctor. I need to go where my skills are most needed. In two weeks we have new interns starting rotation at the hospital, so I need to be back in Sydney.'

'Two weeks' medical help would be great,' she told him, struggling desperately to sound practical. 'But where does that fit with what you're saying about need?'

'I'm talking of possibilities in the future.' He spread his hands. 'Elsa, I come from a background that's emotionally barren, to say the least. My parents were rich and dysfunctional, and they used money as a substitute for affection. The way I feel about you has me confused. Blindsided, if you like. You and me…'

'There is no you and me.'

'There might be. I have no idea, but the way I'm feeling…isn't it worth exploring?'

She was well out of her comfort zone now, feeling as if she were swimming in uncharted waters, towards what seemed like a whirlpool.

'The way you're feeling?' She intended her voice to sound mocking, but she was mocking herself as well as him. There was no choice but to mock the impossibility of what he was saying. 'You've known me for what, four days?'

'We've talked every day while you were in Sydney.'

They had. Every night after Robert slept she'd rung him, ostensibly to check if there were any medical problems on the island. Which she knew there weren't. Or he'd rung to consult on something she knew he didn't really need to consult with her about. In the end they'd abandoned reasons and simply talked. She'd sat on her balcony in her anonymous hospital relatives' apartment and she'd talked to him as a friend.

Only now he felt like more than a friend.

When had that line been crossed?

It hadn't, she told herself frantically. It couldn't.

She needed to get a grip.

'Marc, what we're both feeling… It's just that we've both been thrown into fraught situations,' she managed. 'I've been frightened and stressed, and you've been a godsend. You came here for hours, with plans to head off for a glamorous holiday, with glamorous friends…a glamorous girlfriend.'

'And found a friend who's maybe not so glamorous,' he said seriously. 'But a friend who's beautiful. Who's caring, brave, funny, devoted…'

'To my island. To my people.'

'There's a complication.'

'You think?' She almost snapped it at him. 'If this really was…a thing…'

'It's interesting, this thing,' he said, and his eyes were smiling. Oh, that smile… 'We can't define it. To be honest, I'm all at sea with what I'm feeling, yet maybe I know what it might be.'

'Well, it can't be,' she said. 'And if it is…' She struggled to find a way to say what she had no words for. 'If this… thing…turns out to be, I don't know, more than just a passing thing, then where would we go from there?'

'Anywhere you like.'

'Like that's possible.' Anger came to her aid then, and it helped. 'You work in one of the most prestigious coronary care units in the world. I work on this island.'

'But you need to leave.' His words were gentle enough, but behind them she heard a note of implacability. 'Elsa, you know this island needs more than one doctor, and your grandpa can't keep working. I know the island will hardly support another doctor who needs a full wage, but there are medical couples who might well jump at the lifestyle.

Couples who'd like the opportunity for one to work part-time. For the island's sake, Elsa, you need to open up that opportunity.'

'By leaving?'

'By leaving.' It was said flatly. A truth that hurt.

'But how do I know any other doctor would give my islanders the care they deserve?' She'd thought this through—of course she had. She'd spent a long time in Sydney contemplating her future. 'What if some nine-to-fiver takes over? Where would my island be then? So what's the choice? If I leave here and make Grandpa safer, the islanders would be at risk and Grandpa would be deeply unhappy. If I stay here I need to accept that Grandpa will probably die earlier. But Grandpa and I have discussed it and it's no choice at all. He wants to stay.'

'So where does that leave you personally? Or...us?' His eyes were still on hers, serious, questioning. 'Maybe that's what we need to find out.'

'I don't understand.'

'I think you do. This thing we're feeling...'

'I don't want...' But her voice trailed off. She didn't want what? A nebulous something. A problem that had no solution?

This man?

All of him was compelling, she thought. He was drawing her into some sweet web she had no hope of escaping. But it was a web she had to escape, because her grandfather's happiness, the security of the islanders, depended on it.

'Marc...'

'You know, I don't understand it either,' he said, and there was a note of uncertainty in his voice that told her he was speaking the truth. 'Honestly, Elsa, I didn't expect to feel like this about someone so...'

'Unsuitable,' she finished for him, but he shook his head.

'You know that's not true. But different, yes. I've been brought up without family ties. My father was indifferent to his family, committed to his work. My mother was loyal in her own way—sort of—but her work and the mountains always came first. I was essentially raised by servants. But the way you feel about your grandpa…'

'It's normal.'

'It's great.'

'It's no big deal. It's just called love.'

'I get that. It's just… I didn't think I could feel…'

'Well, don't feel,' she said, breathless now but angry again. What was he doing, sitting on her back step looking like he was offering her the world when she knew very well that the world wasn't his to offer? Her tiny part of the world was prescribed, definite, and there was no escape clause.

'I don't think this thing is something that can be turned off at will,' he was saying.

'Then put a plug in it. Take your wine and go back to your side of the hospital.' While she was away he'd shifted out of his hospital bed and was staying in an apartment used for the occasional patient relative who needed to stay overnight.

'I will—in a moment. Elsa, I'm not threatening you.'

'But you are. My life can't change. I have no choice.'

'You have no choice but to change.'

'But not with you.'

'Elsa.' He reached out and caught both her hands, compelling now, assured. 'You sound terrified but there's no need. I'm not threatening,' he repeated.

'You are.'

'Is it me you're frightened of or the situation?'

There was no answer to that. She tried to sort it in her head, but her head was struggling to co-operate. Was she frightened of her situation? Being forced to leave the island to make her living somewhere else? Was she terrified of breaking her grandfather's heart by insisting he leave the island, too? Yes, she was.

Was she frightened of Marc? No, but she was frightened of the way she was feeling.

He was being practical whereas she...

She was totally, absolutely terrified, because falling for this man, exposing what she wanted most in all the world seemed unthinkable.

'Elsa, relax,' Marc said, gently now, as he watched her face. 'Stop it with the convolutions. Just feel.'

Just feel. So easy for him to say. But his hands were holding hers. His eyes were holding hers too, and what she saw there... She managed to fight back panic just for a moment, and in that moment something else surged in. Something sweet and sure and right. Something strong enough to drive everything else from her tired mind.

Love? Who knew? All she knew was that suddenly she was over trying to understand what she felt. He was sitting beside her in the moonlight, turned towards her. His eyes were gentle, kind and he was tugging her close.

She should protest. She should pull away. She should do a million things.

She didn't. The night seemed to dissolve. Everything melted away as his hands tugged her closer. As he released her for a nanosecond so that instead of holding her hands he was cupping her face. Tilting her chin. Looking into her eyes, searching for a truth she didn't understand.

The fight, the logic had simply disappeared.

Almost of their own volition, her arms moved to hold him, and with that hold came surety, strength, power. In the last few days her world had been tilting so much that at times she'd felt in danger of falling off.

This man was no long-term safe anchorage—she knew that—but for now he was here, he was Marc, and he was holding her.

He wanted her and she wanted him. Nothing more, nothing less.

He was holding her, but he'd paused, a fraction of a breath away from kissing her. This was no practised seduction. The final decision was being left to her.

And with that knowledge came a longing so strong, so fierce that any reservations disappeared into the night.

He was giving her space but she wanted no space.

'Yes,' she murmured. She hardly knew whether the word was said out loud or not, but there was room for no other.

His mouth claimed hers, and the way she was feeling there'd be no need for words for ever.

What was he doing?

He knew damned well what he was doing. He was kissing a woman he wanted in a way he'd never wanted a woman before.

To have and to hold… He'd heard those lines before, in the marriage ceremonies of countless friends, but until now they'd simply been a formality.

They weren't a formality. *To have and to hold*. That was what he wanted, what he was melting into—a sense of rightness…desire. Possession?

She was in his arms and she felt as if she belonged. She did belong there. This was his woman and as his mouth claimed her, so did his head.

Elsa. *His woman.*

She was letting him kiss her, and unbelievably she was kissing him back. The desire between them was white-hot, a fire that felt all-consuming.

The porch light was on. They could probably be seen by half the island—and indeed Sherlock had backed away and was watching them, his head cocked to one side as if this was a moment he should take note of. It was merely a kiss, but it felt like much, much more.

It felt like a joining. A claiming. It was a sensation of being where he belonged. Home? Who knew what such a word meant, but it suddenly seemed like a siren song.

And when they finally pulled apart, as pull apart they were forced to do because Sherlock finally decided what they were doing seemed interesting and he might just join in, Marc knew his world had changed.

'Elsa...' The word was a caress. She was looking at him in confusion. Her hands were cupping her cheeks and a blush of rose had spread across her face.

'I don't...'

'Don't understand? Neither do I.' He went to take her hands again, but she pulled back. As he watched he saw her confusion turning to fear.

'Marc, don't.'

'You don't want this?'

'Yes. No! I can't.'

'Why not, my love?' Was this the first time he'd ever used such an endearment? No matter, it felt right.

But the look of fear was still there. 'Marc, I can't afford to fall in love with you.'

'Hey, I'm cheap to run,' he told her, trying to take the fear from her face. Trying to make light of what seemed so important. 'In fact, I might even run in the black rather than the red. I make a decent income as a cardiologist, you know, and I'm wealthy in my own right.'

She tried to laugh but it didn't happen. It turned into a choke that seemed perilously close to a sob.

'As if that matters. Marc, this can't happen. It's far too soon.'

'Well, *too soon* is something we can do something about,' he told her. 'We have all the time in the world to sort out *too soon*.'

'You're going back to Sydney.'

'Which is where I think you should go, too. I have friends, influence… Love, there'll be a score of jobs for a doctor with your skills. You'll find work in a minute. My house is huge and you're welcome to stay there, but if it's indeed *too soon* then we can find you and Robert a decent apartment while we figure how long is soon enough.' Then he glanced at Sherlock who was looking at him in confusion. 'Or,' he added practically, 'a house with a backyard.'

'So Sherlock can stay in the backyard all day and Grandpa can stay in the house?'

'Your grandpa will die if he stays on the island,' he said bluntly. 'You've seen the cardiology reports and the reports from the renal physician. He needs constant monitoring. That heart of his is no longer strong enough to cope with anything worse than a bad cold.'

'You don't know that.'

'I can guess it, and so can you.'

'Then it's Grandpa's choice.' Her hands were still holding her cheeks. She looked stressed, frightened—but also angry. 'Marc, why are you saying this? It has to be our decision, mine and Grandpa's, where we live, and our choice is here.'

'Then we'll never see how our relationship might work.'

'That's blackmail!'

'It's only blackmail if you want what I think we both want. To see if you and I…'

'There is no you and I.' The anger was still there. 'There can't be a *you and I* unless you decide that being an islander is part of your life plan. But people don't come here to live. They're born here, and some of them stay and some of them don't. Apart from half a dozen hippies who live at the far end of the island where the surf's best, no one's migrated here for decades.'

'I know that, which is why…'

'Which is why I have to leave if I want a life with anyone other than another islander. But that's okay because my other islander is my grandpa.'

'He won't live for ever.'

'So you're threatening me as well as blackmailing me?'

'Elsa…'

'Leave it.' She closed her eyes for a moment and when she opened them again he saw a wash of weariness so deep it was all he could do not to reach out and support her. But she was holding out her hands in a gesture that said she was warding him off, not wanting him to come closer.

He'd stuffed it.

He'd totally, absolutely stuffed it.

He'd only spoken the truth.

But it hadn't worked. She was tipping the untouched wine from her glass onto the garden. She was done.

'Go back to your quarters, Marc,' she said quietly. 'I have enough to think about tonight without a proposal that has so many impossible conditions that it makes me feel ill.'

'It wasn't a proposal,' he denied automatically.

Or was it? The way he'd framed it…

'Then I'm glad,' she said, and sighed and clicked her fingers. Sherlock sidled to her side, cocking his head to one side as if he was trying to figure what was wrong. Then he nuzzled next to her leg and pressed his body against her knee. It was an unmistakable gesture of comfort, and

Marc looked down at the dog and thought that Sherlock had got it right.

And he'd got it impossibly wrong.

'I'll still stay for two weeks anyway,' he told her, searching for anything to allay the pain he could feel washing over her in waves. 'That should take care of the worst of the tourist season.'

'Thank you,' she said simply. 'We'll pay you full time clinician rates.'

'There's no need...'

'There's every need,' she said, suddenly angry again. 'From now on... Well, we'll start as we mean to go on, Dr Pierce. As medical colleagues and nothing more.'

CHAPTER TWELVE

MARC HAD TWO weeks to repair the mistakes of that night. He had two weeks to find a way to undo the damage.

In two weeks he found not a single solution.

She was pig stubborn, he told himself as it neared the time he had to leave. She had to face a future off the island.

And yet, as he saw Robert gradually regain health, as he watched the elderly doctor sitting on the veranda with Sherlock at his feet, with his islander mates sitting beside him, as he saw Robert's devotion to the islanders and the islanders' devotion to Robert, he had to concede that it'd be extremely hard to drag him to a new life in Sydney.

Yet it meant that Elsa could have no new life. Until...

Yeah, that was a good thing to think—not. Wait until her grandfather died to move away? How bleak was that? But meanwhile, for Elsa to work herself into the ground holding this practice together while she waited for her grandfather's health to fail, as it surely must without specialist care...

It made him feel ill to imagine it, but there was nothing he could do.

He worked beside her, taking clinics while she did house calls and took care of the patients in the hospital. That had been pretty much the set-up before Robert fell ill, and it worked. The island could function on one and a half doctors, but that doctor couldn't be Robert.

Nor could it be Marc. He'd thought of staying on the island—of course he had—but he wasn't so deeply thrown by these new emotions that he failed to see the impossibility of such a plan. He was a cardiologist and there was little here for him to do. He'd worked hard to achieve his skill set. Managing the occasional imperative heart problem on Gannet with no support staff... No.

But the more he saw of Elsa, the more he knew how much he wanted her. He also knew how badly he'd messed up his proposal. Blackmail and threats? It honestly hadn't seemed like that to him—surely he'd only been laying out the truth—but he knew he'd hurt her.

And that hurt him. As he saw her flinch whenever she caught sight of him in the distance, as he saw each flash of pain in her eyes, as he watched her quickly turn away, he knew his clumsy attempts to get her to accept a future off the island had done nothing but cause her distress. He felt gutted.

So what to do?

There was little he could do. He worked on. Elsa paid him and he couldn't refuse—she said she'd lock the clinic doors on him if he didn't accept it. He funnelled the payments via Maggie into funds for a new incubator, something the hospital desperately needed.

'I'll tell Elsa it's from an anonymous donor,' Maggie said when he proposed it. 'She might suspect it's from you, but she doesn't need to know for sure. If she did... well, she's already grateful to you for the lift chairs and this might stress her more.'

'Because?'

'You know very well why,' she said, irritated. But then she softened. 'I know it's an impossible situation and I'm desperately sorry that the pair of you can't take this further, but this is our Elsa we're talking about. Ours.'

Ours. The island's.

That line wormed its way back into his head. *To have and to hold.*

The island had staked its claim and it was holding on. Elsa was staying, and the bottom line was that he had to leave.

So he worked on, but as he did he racked his brain as to how he could help her. Half a doctor—that was what she needed. That was what Gannet Island needed. It couldn't be him, not long-term, but she had to have help.

None of his colleagues would be even vaguely interested. They were all high-flying achievers.

So where to find half a doctor?

And then, a week before he was due to leave, he found himself thinking of his mother, mixing medicine with mountain climbing.

Half a doctor...

He started making phone calls. Half a doctor couldn't be him, but at least this could help Elsa.

It wasn't nearly enough, he thought as his departure date loomed closer, but at least it was something.

It seemed *something* was all he had left to offer.

Saturday. The day of his flight home. He'd asked Elsa to have dinner with him on Friday night and she'd agreed— 'But at our kitchen table with Grandpa. We still have a mountain of casseroles.'

What followed was a stilted dinner where he and Robert talked medicine and island history, and Elsa said little at all. She saw him to the door afterwards and he wanted to kiss her—no, he was desperate to kiss her—but she backed away. The closed look on her face said there was no compromise. Ryan drove him to the airport the next morning, and that was that.

But then, just as the incoming plane landed, he saw Elsa's car pull into the car park. He watched and waited, saw her hesitate as if she was regretting coming and wasn't too sure she was doing the right thing, but then she came right in.

This was a tiny airport. There weren't such things as separate arrival and departure lounges. She walked through the swing doors and saw him straight away.

'Hey,' he said as she reached him. Her eyes were troubled. Sad. He desperately wanted to hug her, but somehow he stopped himself and managed to smile. 'Going somewhere?'

She tried to smile back. 'You must know that I wish I could.'

He did know that. It was breaking something inside him, but he understood.

'I just... I couldn't let you go before I thanked you again,' she told him. 'Last night was too formal. Too... unhappy. I didn't say it, just how grateful Grandpa and I are for all you've done.'

'You don't need to say it,' he told her. 'The thanks on both sides just about balance themselves out. And I've brought you trouble. I'm so sorry, Elsa, that I've made you feel...'

'Trapped?' she told him and managed a smile. 'That's not your call. I felt trapped long before you arrived.'

'But you still won't come to Sydney.'

'Don't go there again, Marc. You know it's impossible. I'd still be trapped in Sydney, only it'd be worse. I'd have an unhappy Grandpa and I'd have the islanders on my mind for the rest of my life.'

You'd have me. He wanted to say it, but he couldn't. The time for that was over.

'So I just need to say goodbye,' she told him, and she reached out and took his hands. Around them a small group of his fellow travellers were doing much the same, hugging goodbye, shaking hands, shedding tears.

That was how he felt. Like shedding tears. How could he feel like this about a woman he'd known for such a short time?

How could he feel like this about any woman?

No woman but Elsa.

'Goodbye, Marc,' she told him and the tug on his hands was suddenly urgent. She pulled him close and then reached up and kissed him.

It was a light kiss, a feather touch. A friends' farewell. Good friends. Friends who could never be more.

His instinct was to kiss her back, tug her arms around him… *To have and to hold.*

He couldn't. He didn't. She stepped back and he let her go.

'Marc!' It was a booming yell from the far side of the lounge, where a cluster of incoming passengers were collecting their baggage.

He turned and saw a woman, middle-aged, small and dumpy, dressed for what looked like a two-week hike. She'd just gathered a gigantic pack from the pile of baggage and was hitching it onto her back as she yelled.

'Stella,' he said and then grinned. Of course it was Stella. He'd thought she wouldn't get here for days, yet here she was.

She was stumping her way towards him. With the pack she was carrying she was almost as wide as she was high.

'I'll go,' Elsa said quickly but he caught her hand.

'No. I'm glad this has happened. This is someone I'd like you to meet.'

'Marc,' the woman said again as she reached them and she gripped his hand with a ferocity that made him wince. 'Excellent,' she boomed. 'A handover. How long do we have before the plane leaves?'

'Only minutes,' he told her, 'but Elsa can fill you in.' He turned to Elsa, who was looking faintly stunned. 'Elsa, this is Stella Harbour—Dr Harbour. Stella, this is Dr McCrae. Elsa, Stella's a hiking friend of my mother's. She retired from family medicine a couple of years ago and has been hiking the world since.'

'And starting to get bored doing it,' Stella said bluntly. 'Not that I haven't seen some amazing places, but Marc's call seemed a godsend. I'm missing my medicine. Not that it's a sure thing,' she said hastily, seeing Elsa's look of incomprehension. 'I'm here to hike all over this island, and while I'm doing it I'll be seeing if there might be a place here for me. A work place, I mean.'

'What...?' Elsa managed.

'He didn't tell you? No, he said he'd leave it up to me to explain. Now, you don't have to have me if you don't want me. Marc was clear on that. He said there might be the possibility of work that'd fluctuate according to need. Not much in the quiet times, but full-on in the peak of the tourist season. Which pretty much suits me beautifully. I don't depend on work to provide an income. I love this island—Marc's mum and I hiked here together a couple of times. Peak tourist times are the times when I hate being on the trails anyway and I'd far rather be sewing up cuts and being busy. Anyway, no decision needed yet, my dear. Marc just put it forward as an option, so I thought I'd come over, do a couple of hikes and maybe see if you could make use of me.'

Elsa stared at her as if she couldn't believe what she was seeing—and then she turned to Marc. 'How...?'

'I thought laterally,' he said, smiling at the confusion—and hope—he saw on her face. 'I remembered the host of lady bushwalkers my mother collected around her, thought of their demographic—pretty much all nearing retiring age—so I rang Mum's best friend.'

'And Lucy rang round all of us with a medical background—there were a few because you know Marc's mum was a medical researcher? And when Lucy rang me... Well, it sounds perfect. To live and work here...'

'I need to go now,' Marc said apologetically. The boarding call for his flight was getting insistent. 'Elsa, Stella knows this is an idea only. If you don't like it then...'

'Then I get a walking holiday here, and no one's the worse off,' Stella added cheerfully. 'Of you go, dear,' she told Marc and gave him a gentle push. 'Back to your cardiology and leave the nuts and bolts of general medicine to us. Byee.'

'Marc...' Elsa said helplessly.

'Do what's best for you,' Marc told her. He hoisted his bag over his shoulder, found his balance on his still-plastered leg and looked at her for one last time. 'Goodbye, Elsa.'

'Marc,' she said again, and then, before he could anticipate what she intended, she reached up and cupped his face and tugged it down to hers.

And kissed him. Fiercely. Possessively.

And then she let him go with a gasp that turned into something that was suspiciously like a sob.

But it was cut off. She put a hand to her face as if to hide her emotions, and when her hand dropped again she had herself under control.

'Goodbye, Marc,' she said and somehow she managed it without so much as a tremor. 'Thank you and farewell.'

He sat on the plane, looking out on the island receding in the distance below and felt blank. Empty. Done.

His leg ached. Everything ached.

Work was piling up in Sydney. He had interns starting on Monday. He had a paper to present at a conference in New York at the beginning of next month. He had a meeting this week with researchers investigating a new drug that promised to reduce blood pressure without the current side-effects.

His diary also showed a party next Saturday that sounded amazing—Grant Thurgood's fortieth would surely be the social event of the season. Grant was a cardiologist at the top of his game, his wife was a socialite extraordinaire and the money and effort they'd thrown at this event would take their guests' collective breath away.

He tried to imagine Elsa throwing such a party, and couldn't. He tried to imagine Elsa living in that milieu, and couldn't.

Unbidden, his hands moved to his face. To his mouth. As if he could still taste her.

Elsa.

He glanced down at the island beneath him. Somewhere down there Elsa would be talking to Stella, planning a future. Without him.

That was okay. It had to be. Solitude had been pretty much drilled into him from childhood, and it was the easy retreat now.

Life would move on, he told himself. No matter what Elsa decided, it was hardly his business now. He'd thought of marriage when he'd suggested she move to Sydney, but honestly…would he be any good at it?

Elsa would be good at it, he thought. Loving was her specialty, but she surely deserved better than him.

But the pressure from that kiss was still with him and it wouldn't leave. Maybe solitude wasn't so appealing.

But maybe... nothing. Was he still thinking about marriage? If she couldn't leave the island it was impossible to go down that road unless he joined her, abandoned his career, became a part-time generalist.

But that thought was rejected almost before it was formed. He didn't have the empathy, the skills, to be a really good family doctor. A month of such medicine had left him in awe of what Elsa did, but he'd also accepted she had a skill set that was just as important as any cardiology techniques he'd learned. He'd go crazy, watching Elsa seamlessly do what he couldn't. He had to have a challenge.

A challenge... The word seemed to hang.

From up here he could see all the islands, the six that made up the Birding group. He'd seen patients from the outer isles while he'd been at Gannet. He'd even visited a couple, with their remote medical clinics run by capable nurses.

Six islands.

They were Elsa's responsibility. Not his.

Why did it seem as if they were his?

He'd booked a double seat so he could stretch his leg. That meant he was undisturbed, so now he sat back and closed his eyes. Forcing his mind to go blank was a technique he used when he was struggling to find a solution to a fraught medical dilemma—clear all preconceived ideas and start from scratch.

This was surely a dilemma. He needed his technique now.

And suddenly it worked. His mind switched into overdrive and fragments were shooting at him like brightly lit arrows from all sides.

Six islands.

A career that was challenging.

Stella and her mountain climbing and part-time medicine.

Part-time doctors.

A jigsaw that could be put together?

Maybe.

The jumble was coalescing into a whole that was making him feel dizzy.

'It'll never work,' he said out loud, and the flight attendant was suddenly at his side, looking concerned. She was being super helpful to someone she obviously saw as disabled.

'Sir? Is there something wrong?'

She was middle-aged, friendly, reminding him of Maggie. She smiled encouragingly, and amazingly he found himself talking.

'Just a problem I'm trying to solve.'

'Is there anything I can do to help?' The plane was half empty. Clearly she had time to chat.

'I don't think anything's wrong,' he said slowly. 'Except... I might just need to toss my job.'

'Oh, but surely your leg will get better.' She still sounded worried. 'This is the only plane that services Gannet so we know all about you. You were trapped underground. That must have been an awful experience, but surely your life can get back to normal now.'

'But maybe it wasn't being trapped that stopped me feeling normal.' He was feeling as confused as she was looking. 'Maybe it was being rescued.'

'I gather it was Dr McCrae who found you,' the woman said, and smiled encouragingly. 'She has quite a reputation among the islanders. She'd have kept you safe if anyone could. The islanders think she's wonderful.'

'She is indeed,' Marc said softly.

'Well, take care of yourself, sir.' Duty done, she left to check on the other passengers and Marc was left with his circling thoughts. Which centred now around Elsa.

He let his mind drift back to that time of being trapped with Elsa. Her warmth. Her humour. The feeling that he was safe with her.

And then later… The way she'd melted into him as he'd kissed her. The feeling that he'd found his way home.

Home?

Home was Sydney. Home was a demanding clinical life, his research, cutting-edge medicine, friends who felt the same as he did.

As a lone kid of wealthy but dysfunctional parents, his studies and his career had become his refuge. They were still his pole stars. His career and his research were the most important thing, and everything else fitted around the edges.

What if home was the pole star?

'You need two pole stars,' he said out loud. He'd read that in an astronomy encyclopaedia his father had given him when he was seven.

Earth's pole stars are Polaris, a magnitude two star aligned approximately with its northern axis, and Polaris Australis, a much dimmer star…

The book had been a birthday gift when he was seven. His parents had been shouting at each other before he'd even unwrapped it, and afterwards they'd been rigidly formal, bidding him goodnight with their anger still obvious.

He'd buried himself in the pole stars. Two pole stars used for navigation for thousands of years.

Pole stars guiding him home. There was that word again.

Home.

Elsa.

He was thinking laterally now. His father's gift of the astronomy book made him think of Elsa's gifts. Her carefully nurtured geraniums. Gifts given with love.

And now he was remembering again the line that had come into his head as he'd held her and kissed her.

To have and to hold.

He couldn't hold her. What sort of arrogance had made him demand that? He wanted to hold Elsa, but she wouldn't be held just because that was what he wanted.

He wanted to have, but Elsa needed to have as well. She wanted her island. She needed her island.

And there suddenly was his idea, his light bulb moment. His astounding plan.

He thought of his salary. His inherited wealth. His skills, his contacts, his resources. If he couldn't do it, no one could.

It might be impossible, but his light bulb plan was coalescing by the second.

'I won't know unless I try,' he said out loud. He saw the passenger across the aisle eye him with caution, and he grinned. Maybe the guy thought he was nuts and maybe he was. What he was hoping for probably made no sense at all.

'It's politics and funding and feet on the ground,' he muttered. 'And realistically… It'll take at least a year to organise, if it's even possible.'

A year without Elsa? He wanted to turn the plane around now, share his idea with her, tug her into his arms.

To have and to hold? No. Because if it failed, or if he failed... It wasn't fair to either of them.

'A year,' he told himself. A year to change. A whole dammed year.

'You can contact her. Phone her. Go visit her. Be a friend.'

A friend. Friend with benefits?

'As if that's likely to happen. What if she meets someone else? What if she hooks up with that Tony guy?

'It's a risk.' He struggled with the thought, but common sense had to prevail. 'If this is real, if she feels like I do...' He sighed. 'Back off, Pierce, and get your ducks in order first. She's worth fighting for. She's worth risking all. Prove to yourself that you love her enough to wait.'

Love... There was the biggie. Could he really love?

'If you love her then you'll do what it takes,' he told himself. 'Fight for what *she* wants, not for what *you* want. Starting now.'

But still he hesitated, staring out of the window as if he could still see the islands. The urge to turn around and head back to her was overwhelming. Maybe he could do this from Gannet?

He knew he couldn't. He needed to be in Sydney. He needed to be networking, politicking, fighting for something more important than both of them.

'And if I tell her my plan and it fails, then I'll break her heart,' he said out loud. 'But by next Christmas...'

Eleven months. Was it possible?

He turned from the window and flicked open the memo function on his phone to write the first hopeful outline. He was suddenly a man with a purpose. A man with a woman worth fighting for.

'If Elsa can produce a black geranium then surely I can produce a dream,' he vowed. 'But dreams aren't real...

'And neither's Santa Claus,' he told himself. 'But by next Christmas… It's the season of miracles after all, so at least I can try.'

CHAPTER THIRTEEN

Christmas Day, eleven months later:

MARC STARED DOWN at the mountainous Birding Isles, set in a ring against the sparkling sapphire sea, and felt an overwhelming sense of peace.

Last time he'd come here he'd brought a simple day pack. Today he had three bags of gear in the cargo hold. Most of it was medical equipment which would stay here regardless of today's outcome. Some of it was personal.

Some of it was the baggage of a man who hoped he was coming home.

Nothing was settled. He should be apprehensive and part of him was, but there was also a core within him that felt complete.

These last eleven months had been long and fraught. He'd worked desperately hard to achieve what he'd be presenting to the islanders today. It had been an enormous challenge, and there were challenges yet to come.

But underneath... As the months had worn on, as the 'friendship' calls to Elsa had grown longer, as he'd had to summon an almost superhuman effort to hold his emotions in check during her one visit to Sydney in July... As he'd fought with his desire to drop everything he was working for and go to her, any doubt of how he felt had fallen away.

He loved this woman with all his heart, and he'd do whatever it took to win her. He hoped today that he was providing enough, but if it didn't succeed...

'Then I'll figure some other way to be with her,' he said to himself. 'On her terms. I'll do whatever it takes.'

They were circling now, coming in to land. The landing gear settled into place with a gentle thump. The runway loomed ahead, and then they were down.

He was back on Gannet Island.

And the last barriers to his carefully guarded heart seemed to fall away right there and then. Years of solitude, of isolation, of carefully constructed independence faded to nothing.

His heart was in the hands of one slip of a red-haired doctor.

It had to be right.

He was home.

It was a great Christmas Day—as far as Christmas Days went. There'd been no emergencies, no unexpected illnesses. The hospital was quiet. Grandpa was looking good. Elsa had planned her Christmas gifts with love and care. The island's cooks had cooked up a storm. The hall was looked great, the decorations superb. It was crowded, full of laughter, friendship and Christmas cheer.

Then why was she so flat?

So sad.

It was Ghosts of Christmas Past, she told herself, and struggled to act happy, even if something inside her felt like lead. She watched Eileen O'Hara unwrap dozens of balls of leftover wool collected from knitters all around the island during the year, squirreled away for just this moment. Eileen's crocheted rugs were legendary but she struggled to afford wool. As her parcel opened she burst into tears and then beamed her happiness. Around her the islanders whooped at her delight and Elsa thought that this was the most important thing in the world. Community.

Not self.

Not Elsa, who still felt as if a gaping hole had been ripped open inside her and would never be filled.

Except by Marc. And that could never happen.

She'd been in contact with him during the year. He'd phoned, often, but only as a friend.

In July, Robert had needed a check-up and Elsa had gone with him to the mainland. To Sydney Central. They'd stayed for only one night, but Robert had gone to sleep early and Elsa had had dinner with Marc.

She'd felt almost light-headed, jubilant with the all-clear her grandfather's check-up had produced, but totally thrown by the Marc who'd picked her up at their hotel and taken her to a gorgeous restaurant overlooking Sydney Harbour.

It had been a different Marc. This was where he was meant to be, she'd thought. He'd looked a million dollars, a surgeon at the top of his game.

And he was her friend. He was only her friend.

'How's it going, working with Stella?' he'd asked.

'It's so good, Marc,' she'd told him. 'I still don't know how you conjured her up, but we work brilliantly together. Plus she plays chess with Grandpa almost every night and sometimes she even beats him. We're so happy, thanks to you.'

'But you? Are you happy?'

'I have everything I want,' she'd said, a little too firmly. 'A healthy Grandpa. A colleague I adore. A fantastic medical set-up for the island. I can't ask for more. Now, tell me about you. I read one of your research papers in *Cutting-Edge Medical* last month. Wow...'

And that was as personal as she'd got. She'd shaken hands formally at the end of the evening and that was it.

Back to the occasional phone call. Back to being friends.

Back to the rest of her life.

They were almost at the end of their gift list now. There was a bundle of new fishing sinkers for Tom Hammond, a dozen assorted envelopes of different poppy seeds for Chrissie Harding and they'd be done.

And then there was a stir at the doorway. She looked up to see a group of strangers gathered at the glass doors. A mix of maybe twenty people? It included young couples, a few older folk, a smattering of kids. A woman holding a baby.

They were all dressed in Santa hats, even the baby.

This must be the group who'd booked out Bob Cruikshank's cottages, she thought. The cottages had only been three-quarters done when, in September, a team of builders had arrived from the mainland and completed the job in weeks. Bob had been going around looking like the cat that got the cream ever since, but he wouldn't say where the money had come from to bring in the builders, nor would he say who the first occupants would be.

A family group? Who?

It was Maggie who opened the door, but she put her body in the way of anyone entering. 'I'm sorry,' she said, kindly but firmly. 'This is a private function.'

And then there was a stir in the group. It parted and someone from the back made their way through.

A man. Tall, dark, lean. Wearing a Santa hat.

Marc.

Elsa had been standing by the Christmas tree, handing presents to Bob Cruikshank, who'd been playing Father Christmas. Bob, the realtor whose thigh had healed beautifully after his argument with the chainsaw, held out his arms in welcome.

'Ho-ho-ho!' he boomed. 'These people are welcome, Maggie. These people are a gift to all the island.'

She couldn't make any sense of what Bob was saying but it didn't seem to matter anyway.

Marc was here.

Maggie stood aside, stunned, and they trooped in, a weird assorted bunch. Robert rose stiffly from his seat, beamed and shook Marc's hand. As if he'd expected him? Then Marc led them up to the front of the hall, leaping lightly up onto the stage to where Elsa stood beside the Christmas tree.

He smiled at her, a huge enveloping smile that made her heart turn over. He took her hands and for a moment she thought he meant to kiss her.

He didn't. His gaze was a kiss all on its own, but they were in front of a hall full of people. She was totally confused, and maybe he sensed that a kiss would send her right over the edge.

'Happy Christmas, love,' he said gently, and she felt as if she was over the edge already.

But then he released one of her hands and tugged her around so they were both facing the audience. Who'd fallen silent, stunned. Expectant?

Bob Cruikshank was still beaming and so was her grandfather. What the…?

'We have a gift for you all,' Marc said, his words falling into a void of hushed bewilderment. 'And that gift might be us. If you want us.' And then he smiled and motioned to the two gifts left under the tree. 'But we've interrupted. Can Santa give these out first?'

'No!' It was a roar of dissent from the confused guests, but when it finished there were two faces reflecting dismay.

Tom and Chrissie.

'Yes,' Elsa managed, and Tom received his sinkers and Chrissie beamed over her poppies, and then everyone looked at Marc as if he was a genie about to produce... who knew? Nobody knew.

'Can I introduce the new residents of Bob Cruikshank's cottages,' Marc told the gathered audience, and proceeded to do just that.

'This couple are Ellen and Graham Parkes,' he told everyone. 'Ellen's an obstetrician, Graham's a renal physician, and these are their three kids, Hamish, Archie and Kim. Next is Angus Knox, a family doctor, and his little son Noah. Then we have Arthur and Lois Campbell. Lois is a gerontologist, Arthur's a general surgeon. David Wyndham behind them is an orthopaedic surgeon. Next is Cathy Graham, a theatre nurse. Then Nic Scott, a paediatrician...'

A host of supremely qualified medics. Here on holiday? Apparently not.

'We're here to see if we can make Gannet Island the centre of the best regional health service in the world,' Marc said, and Elsa thought her legs might give way.

'No pressure,' Marc continued, still speaking to the stunned and silent islanders. 'This is a try-it-and-see. Some are here for quick visit, to see if they like it. Some are here on a month's vacation, hoping to talk to you all, plus the residents on the outlying islands. We're all specialists, and all of us would like to back off from our city practices. Our thought is to build up a medical base on Gannet that's second to none and, in doing so, provide a comprehensive medical service to the outer islands.'

She stared. She tried to think of something to say.

She couldn't.

'We have tentative plans—and funds—to build a helicopter pad and purchase a decent chopper,' Marc continued, smiling at her before he turned back to the audience. 'Plus we can afford a decent fast boat, capable of transfers between the islands. We'll need to extend your hospital. That'll need your cooperation—everything will need your cooperation—but our approach to the government for funding has already met with unqualified approval. Your Dr McCrae—Robert—has been assisting us from this end. The government funds your health care, either here or in Sydney. It'll cost the government a whole lot less if every major case doesn't need to be evacuated.'

What…? How…? Her jaw had dropped to her ankles.

'This is impossible,' she breathed, staring from Marc out to the group of newcomers—who were all smiling and laughing—and looking really, really hopeful. 'How can it possibly work?'

'Your grandfather thinks it can work,' Marc told her, and Elsa turned to look at Robert. He was grinning as if all his Christmases had come at once.

'These people might just have consulted me,' he told her happily. 'I am, after all, Gannet Island's senior doctor. I had the first call last February, and we've been working on the plans ever since.'

'Hey, does this mean I won't have to go to Sydney for my hip replacement?' someone at the back of the hall called, and Marc nodded.

'If you can wait a couple of months, mate. It'll take time to get things in place but surgery such as hip replacements will be our bread and butter. Also obstetrics. Mums shouldn't have to fly to Sydney to have their babies. If everyone supports us there'll be far fewer evacuations. But, as I said, there's no pressure. We're all here for a try-it-and-see vacation, with no compulsion to commit on either side.'

There was another moment's silence while everyone in the hall took this on board. And then another.

And finally it was the redoubtable Maggie who broke it. She lifted her amazing crocheted hat off her head and walked forward and stuck it on Marc's head, replacing his Santa hat. And then, as of one accord, there was a rush as every islander tried to put their island caps on the newcomers. The silence was more than broken—the noise in the hall was unbelievable as the incoming medics were welcomed into the celebration with jubilant enthusiasm.

Elsa stood on the stage and stared out at the melee and thought the ground beneath her was giving way.

Before a hand took hers and drew her away. Out through a side door, out behind the hall. Out to stand underneath the giant eucalypt, with its towering canopy laced with glorious crimson mistletoe.

Out to where she could be thoroughly, ruthlessly kissed.

She was being kissed by a guy in a crocheted elf hat with a tail and a pompom. She was being kissed by someone who'd just offered her the world.

She didn't believe it.

But she didn't struggle. She couldn't. This was Christmas Day, the time of miracles, and why not let herself believe for this short, sweet time? Why not let herself be kissed and kiss back as if miracles truly could happen? As if she had any choice?

And he felt so good. So right.

His elf hat was drooping forward. The pompom had swung round and was hitting her nose.

There was nothing like a drooping pompom to mess with the Christmas spirit, she thought dazedly, deciding— deep into a magnificently prolonged kiss—that sense had to surface soon. But not yet.

Just another few minutes. Minutes of holding him

close, feeling herself surrender to his touch, wanting, aching to believe...

And in the end it was Marc who pulled away, who held her at arm's length and smiled and smiled.

And said, 'You don't believe me, do you?'

'I don't have a clue what's going on,' she managed, and her voice sounded...bruised? She felt bruised...or was it winded? She didn't have a clue. 'Is it...? It has to be some kind of a joke?'

'No joke, my love,' he told her and pulled her in to hug her against him again to kiss the top of her hair. 'I'm hoping to put everything I own and then some into this venture, so it'd better not be a joke.'

She let herself sink against him while she tried to make sense of his words. Finally she tugged away. He tried to catch her hands but she was having none of it. She held her hands up as if to ward him off and he accepted it.

Inside there was the sound of celebration, of shouts of laughter, of welcome. Someone had put the carols back on the sound system. *We wish you a merry Christmas, We wish you a merry Christmas...*

A sudden soft wind sent a shower of mistletoe flowers floating to the ground.

Her head was spinning.

'You know I'm wealthy,' Marc told her.

'Medical specialists are always wealthy,' she managed. 'You gave us two great lift chairs. Plus the incubator. I know that was you.'

'But didn't I tell you my parents were independently wealthy? Very wealthy. I've often thought I ought to do something with the family trust rather than keep it mouldering, ready to pass to the next generation, but indecision has left it in the too hard basket. This Christmas...thinking of the impossibility of black geraniums…and thinking of you… I decided why not?'

'The black geranium isn't doing so well now,' she told him, searching for something solid to hold onto. 'We think it's the sea air… Sandra's had to put it in a hot house and hope for the best.'

'I guess there's a bit of hoping for the best in what I plan to do too,' he told her. 'So many things are yet to be decided. But I put feelers out for medics who weren't focused on income, who put working on an island like this right on top of their list of priorities. Amazingly, one column in the *Gazette* had them coming out of my ears. These medics aren't in it for the money. Yes, we have a restricted patient base, but every one of these people value the lifestyle these islands can offer as much as the medicine they can provide.'

'I still can't believe it,' she stammered.

'Then watch this space,' he told her, and he reached out and cupped her face with his lovely hands. 'This is your own Christmas gift, Elsa. Your generosity to me and to this island has made it possible. Happy Christmas, love.'

She stared up at him, speechless, and his gaze met hers. There was no smile. His look was deep and sure and steady. His gaze said that he meant every word.

'And I have another gift for you,' he told her. 'Or maybe not. Maybe it's a gift on hold.'

Releasing her for a moment, he fished in his pocket, then brought out a tiny box, flicking it open to reveal a ring so exquisite she could only gasp. It was a twisted plait of ancient gold with tiny rubies set into each twist, rounding to one magnificent diamond front and centre. It glittered in the sunlight, a siren song, a temptation so great…

'But not for now,' Marc said softly, and her gaze flew up to his. He was smiling with understanding—and with love? 'I know that, sweetheart. I love you with all my heart and I believe, I hope, that you love me right back. But your deep loves—your island, your grandpa—they need to come first. If I love you—and I do—then I need to respect that.'

'I...' She was struggling to get her voice to work. 'Marc...'

'Yes, love?' The words were a caress all on their own.

'You blackmailed me,' she managed, breathless, trying so hard to get the words out. Trying to force herself to sound sensible. 'Then you... you threatened me. Now you're trying to bribe me?'

'I am,' he conceded and—reluctantly, it seemed—he closed the box. 'But know, my love, that this project doesn't hang on you agreeing to marry me. I won't be taking my bat and ball and going home if you reject me. For me this will be a challenge, and I hope I'm up to it. But Elsa, with all my heart I want you beside me as I work on this.'

'I can't...'

'Hear me out.' He put a finger on her lips and brushed another kiss onto her hair. 'Elsa, when I left last year I wasn't really sure what love was. I was fumbling with emotions I'd never felt before, but if there's one thing the enforced wait of this planning has taught me it's that those emotions are true. Elsa, I love you and want you for ever. No matter what else, that's the bottom line. I want to work on this project, but you take precedence. If these plans succeed then I can see work for me here as a cardiologist, but I'll learn to prescribe sugar pills and cope with teenage acne if I must. I'll even give up medicine and learn to fish if that's what it takes. Because, Elsa, my love is yours and, no matter what you want to do with it, I'll love you for ever.'

'Oh, Marc...' She stared up into his eyes, and what she read there... He was speaking the truth. He loved her.

Her Marc.

She was trying so hard to be sensible—and suddenly she knew what sensible was.

'Then you'd better give me that ring right now,' she managed, her voice a wobbly whisper. She reached for the box and struggled through tears to undo the clasp. 'I love you so much. I know you won't be happy fishing...'

'Hey, I like fish and chips,' he told her, his eyes smiling down into her teary ones. 'That has to be a start.'

'It's a great start,' she managed. 'But Marc, the way I feel about you, the way I've been feeling all this year... The way I've been missing you... Even if this medical scenario turns out to be too good to be true, whatever happens, I know that I want you as my husband for the rest of my life.'

There was a long silence at that. A silence where everything changed. Where everything settled.

Where the pole stars became truly aligned and would stay that way for ever.

'Then I guess that's pretty much perfect,' he said huskily, and somehow the box was unfastened again and the ring was slipped onto her finger. It was a trace too big, but there was all the time in the world for them to set that right. 'So this means that you and me...'

'Us,' she whispered. 'Us.'

'Definitely us,' he agreed—and then there was no space for words for a very long time.

How did Christmas come around so fast?

How could so much be achieved in so little time?

Another twelve months, a score of enthusiastic medics, a government badgered by Marc, whose extended circle knew people who knew people who knew people, islanders who were prepared to throw everything they had to give the island group a medical service second to none... Twelve months had achieved a miracle.

The extension to Gannet Hospital had opened in October but even before that the medics had been working in what had essentially been a field hospital. Most had come for that initial month and simply refused to go home. Bob Cruikshank's holiday cottages had been full to bursting, and there were now a dozen permanent homes either planned or partly built across the island chain.

There were enlarged clinics now too, on the outlying islands. A dedicated boat. Marc's chopper plus a pilot who'd also had paramedic training.

A miracle indeed.

Bob Cruikshank was playing Santa this year at the island's Christmas dinner. He'd pleaded for the job and Elsa had gracefully conceded.

In truth she hadn't felt at all confident she'd be able to carry it off. For the last week her tummy was letting her down at odd intervals.

Hmm.

But she wasn't thinking of her tummy now. She was watching Marc play Santa's helper. He was giving a pair of elbow-length leather gardening gloves to the very elderly Rina Ablett who loved her roses above all else but struggled with thorns against her paper-thin skin.

Rina opened her parcel and beamed, and Marc swept her up into a bear hug before setting her down again and heading back to get the next gift from Santa.

But not before glancing towards Elsa and smiling that smile that warmed her heart, that said no matter how much he was starting to love the islanders, his heart was all hers.

As hers was his. Her Marc. Her husband.

Their wedding had been one special day in November,

a ceremony on the bluff overlooking the sea, a celebration that couldn't be held in the island church because every islander and then some had to be present. Every islander had contributed to the celebration in some way. Every islander had been part of it.

It had been a day she'd remember all her life.

Robert had given her away, with pride and with love. Maggie had played matron of honour. Sherlock had been ring-bearer—sort of. He'd been roped pretty firmly to Maggie. There was no way they wanted their ring-bearer scenting a rabbit halfway through the ceremony.

Not that it would have mattered, Elsa thought mistily, fingering the slim band of gold that sat against her gorgeous engagement ring. Not that any of it mattered, the ceremony, the words, the festivities. Not even the glorious honeymoon they'd just spent in St Moritz. She'd felt snow for the first time and it had been magical.

She'd felt married from this day last Christmas when Marc had proposed.

Her Marc.

Home.

'That's the end of them.' The last present distributed, Marc headed back to his seat beside her and kissed her. 'All done. No more presents until next year.'

'There's just one more,' she said serenely.

'Yeah?' They'd exchanged gifts this morning, small, funny things because so much had been given to them this year they could hardly think of anything more they could want.

'I have one more gift for you,' she told him and she took his hand. In private, underneath the loaded table, her hand pressed his downward onto the flat of her belly. Or not quite flat.

His gaze flew to hers, questioning, but as his hand

felt what she wanted him to feel she saw his eyes widen with shock.

And then blaze with joy.

'Elsa! Oh, love…'

'Happy Christmas,' she breathed, and it was too much. Surrounded by a sea of islanders and medics, by a Christmas celebration to end all Christmas celebrations, this took it to a new level.

He stood and swept her up into his arms, whirling her around in joy. His was a shout of gladness, of wonder, of the promise of things to come.

And then, as he lowered her so he could kiss her, as he gathered her into his arms, as he held the woman he loved with all his heart, the hall erupted into cheers around them.

They weren't too sure what was happening, but they knew one thing.

Their island doctors were where they belonged.

With each other.

They were home.

* * * * *

MILLS & BOON

Coming next month

HIS BLIND DATE BRIDE
Scarlet Wilson

Ivy took another bite of her cake. It was going down well. 'What do you think would have happened if we'd actually gone on that blind date?'

She could have kept things simple and stuck to chat about work. But she didn't want to. If she wanted to work easily with Travis, they had to deal with this.

There was no one else around so they wouldn't be disturbed. It was just her and him in her cabin. It was now or never.

Travis made a little choking noise as his cake obviously stuck at the back of his throat and Ivy burst out laughing, 'Sorry, did I make that go down the wrong way?'

He laughed too and shook his head, leaning back in her chair. 'You just like to keep me on my toes, don't you?'

There it was. That teasing tone. The one that had completely drawn her in, whether it was spoken or in texts. The thing that had made Travis King something more than a potential blind date. Even if that had never been her intention.

She gave an easy shrug. 'Why not?' She held up her hands. 'It's not like there's much else to do around here.'

She was joking, and he'd know she was joking. But shipboard life was so different from being back at home where bars, cinemas, open air and long walks could easily fill her life.

Travis sat his tea on her desk and folded his arms. 'I think,' he started as he raised his eyebrows, 'if we'd gone on a blind date before meeting here, it would have been an absolute disaster.'

Really? What was it with this guy? Had none of his sisters taught him the art of talking to a woman? The words were like being hit with a tidal wave of icy water.

'Okay, then,' she said shortly, feeling like a fool, because in her head their blind date would never have been a disaster.

He held up one hand. 'No, wait, you didn't let me finish. Let me tell you why it would have been a disaster.'

She swung her legs off the bed. 'I don't need microscopic data on why we're a never-happened,' she said, pushing her 'not good enough' feelings away again.

He reached over and put his hand on her knee. His voice was low and throaty. 'Our date would have been a disaster, Ivy Ross, because one meeting would have had me hooked. Who knows what might have happened? It keeps me awake enough at night just thinking about it.'

Continue reading
HIS BLIND DATE BRIDE
Scarlet Wilson

Available next month
www.millsandboon.co.uk

Copyright © 2020 Scarlet Wilson

COMING SOON!

We really hope you enjoyed reading this book.
If you're looking for more romance, be sure to
head to the shops when new books are
available on

Thursday 24th
December

To see which titles are coming soon, please visit
millsandboon.co.uk/nextmonth

MILLS & BOON

WE'RE LOOKING FOR NEW AUTHORS FOR THE MILLS & BOON MEDICAL SERIES!

Whether you're a published author or an aspiring one, our editors would love to read your story.

You can submit the synopsis and first three chapters of your novel online, and find out more about the series, at **harlequin.submittable.com/submit**

We read all submissions and you do not need to have an agent to submit.

IF YOU'RE INTERESTED, WHY NOT HAVE A GO?

Submit your story at:
harlequin.submittable.com/submit

MILLS & BOON

LET'S TALK

Romance

For exclusive extracts, competitions
and special offers, find us online:

[f] facebook.com/millsandboon

[y] @MillsandBoon

[o] @MillsandBoonUK

Get in touch on 01413 063232

For all the latest titles coming soon, visit
millsandboon.co.uk/nextmonth